Kate Dunn was born in Ely in 1958. She was educated in Kent and Essex before gaining an Honours Degree in English and Drama at the University of Manchester. Following in the footsteps of her uncle, actor and author Simon Williams, she worked as an actress, touring Britain and the Middle East, and appearing in television series such as *Casualty* and *The Bill*. She now lives in Stratford upon Avon with her son Jack.

Rebecca's Children

Kate Dunn

KNIGHT

Copyright © 1990 Kate Dunn

The right of Kate Dunn to be identified as the Author
of the Work has been asserted by her in accordance with the
Copyright, Designs and Patents Act 1988.

First published in 1990
by Barrie & Jenkins Ltd

First published in paperback in 1991
by HEADLINE BOOK PUBLISHING PLC

This edition published 1998 by Knight
an imprint of Brockhampton Press

10 9 8 7 6 5 4 3 2 1

Although portions of this novel are derived from
real events, each character in it is fictional, a composite
drawn from several individuals and from imagination.
No reference to any living person is intended
or should be inferred.

ISBN 1 86019 6640

Typeset by Medcalf Type Ltd, Bicester, Oxon

Printed and bound in Great Britain by
Mackays of Chatham PLC, Chatham, Kent

Brockhampton Press
20 Bloomsbury Street
London WC1B 3QA

For my parents

Acknowledgements

I am greatly indebted to Pat Molloy's book *And They Blessed Rebecca*, published by the Gomer Press in 1983, for detailed facts about the people involved in the Rebecca Riots and the events which took place. I also found David Williams' *The Rebecca Riots*, which is published by the University of Wales Press, an extremely useful source of information.

May I express my gratitude to Xandra Hardie for all her encouragement, and thank Sarah Molloy and Manon Eames for their help.

Author's Note

Since my childhood I had been told of a shady ancestor who was known in the family as 'Hugh Williams of the Hundred Bastards'. He was my great-great-grandfather and is the Hugh Williams of this story. He was married twice, first to a woman some twenty-five years older than he, then subsequently to my great-great-grandmother, who was thirty-nine years his junior. Of his many liaisons there is documentary proof of only one: a girl called Mary Jenkins bore him a daughter, Eleanor, in 1847. Hugh was known to have a friend and follower called William Jenkins, and for the sake of my narrative I have made them into brother and sister.

In telling the tale of the Rebecca Riots I have tried to stick as closely as possible to what actually happened, but I have taken one or two liberties: as far as I know Jac Tŷ Isha and Mary Jenkins never met and their relationship as I have described it here is entirely fictitious. To avoid confusing the reader too much I have reduced the number of figures in authority, so that Timothy Powell, Captain Davies and the Mayor are representative of several more members of the establishment; likewise on occasion I have felt it necessary to hone down the number of rioters who appear. A few characters such as Isaac and Meredith Hughes are imaginary, and there are other minor inventions which experts in the subject will be aware of, but by and large I have done my best to convey Rebecca's children and their exploits as accurately as I could, and in a spirit which I hope my great-great-grandfather would find acceptable.

Kate Dunn, 1990

Prologue
August 1861

Anne took a long time to die. Twenty-five years too long, if the truth were told. In his chair at the end of her bed where the light from the oil lamp couldn't reach him, Hugh Williams sat, chafing his hands. It was gone two o'clock at night and the cold was intense. Surely she would go before morning? But he had thought that every night for the last ten days, and still she lingered. Bloody obstinate woman. She had been obstinate when they first married, twenty-five years ago, or was it thirty now? He was surprised that he couldn't remember. Not that it mattered. But this wasn't obstinacy any longer, this was vindictiveness. This was pure malice. There was a time when he had hated her, but he had given even that up now. All he wanted was to see her die. There would be a small satisfaction in that. Not that it would make up for everything, but it would give him a little pleasure, and little pleasures were hard to come by these days. Why wouldn't she go? She was ninety, for God's sake! Why didn't she just give in gracefully and go? Not her. Not if she could possibly help it.

The great black bed creaked as she half turned over, but her weight and bulk were such that she couldn't complete the movement. Instead she gave a sticky sigh and her tongue was slack and noisy in her mouth. Medicine had formed a white crust on her lips and there was sleep in the corner of her eyes. Her face was bloated and the proportions were all wrong; she appalled him. His wife.

He shifted his weight slightly; now that he was old himself his feet were always going to sleep on him. There was tingling in his upper arms as well. He chafed his hands again, as if it were a means of igniting his resentment. Still. He could be terribly patient, he had waited all this time: ten, twenty, thirty years of waiting. What could one more night matter to him now? As long as he saw her go, that was the main thing. The oil lamp needed trimming. He thought of getting up to tend it. The minutes ticked by and the shadows began to gutter and dance along the wall above Anne's head. He sat patiently with his hands folded, waiting. The light spluttered and went out, but Anne's determination kept her breathing. In the darkness of the bedroom only Hugh's eyes shone. They shone relentlessly, as the hours elided into one another.

At last, at five to five, Anne twisted her neck round, said, 'Is the doctor coming?' and died. Hugh hardly heard her. He had given up listening to her years ago. He knew that she was gone, but he wasn't going to let that interrupt his calculations. His life with Anne had been a series of calculations which had gone awry. A seris of misjudgements, of errors, of false hope. She had money. His wife, his dead wife, had had money. To Hugh, the son of a tin miner, full of hunger and calculation, her wealth had seemed unlimited. She owned land; the Gardde estate with its hundreds and hundreds of acres. She was a woman of property, and this property, to Hugh, meant access, access to power, access to Parliament. To stand for a seat in the House of Commons a man had to have land. Anne owned Gardde. It was as simple as that.

It was she who pointed this out to him. She was sixty-four then, and he was thirty-nine. She must have felt the sap rising within her as she said it.

'Don't you think that it might suit us both? I want companionship. You want –' her bulky fingers spread cajolingly – 'you want a chance in life. You deserve one. We can help each other. It makes sense, doesn't it? My time is running out. I want to feel that I've done something . . .'

It was that which bit into Hugh most of all. *My time is running out.* Those were the words which had mocked him now for nearly thirty years. My time is running out. If she had had the decency to die at eighty, or even eighty-five, things might have been so – things might have been . . .

He didn't listen as she twisted her neck round, and spoke to him, and died.

When the dawn broke he walked around the house and opened all the windows. He wanted to be rid of her. He wanted the smell of Anne, the thought of Anne, the old stale breath of Anne blown out of every corner. Then, for as long as he could bear it, he stood naked in front of the basin, sponging his neck and shoulders with icy water until his skin felt razored by it. If the sterilising coldness of the water could wash away those lost and wasted years . . .

When he felt clean again he made himself some breakfast. Eggs, bacon, a tomato, some tea. He ate it slowly, with the beginnings of a feeling of relief. The doctor came and went. Thomas Lewis from Carmarthen.

'Please –' With a movement of his hand Hugh put a stop to the condolences.

The two men went into the study and Hugh watched closely as the doctor wrote out the certificate. Heart failure. It seemed unlikely. Hugh doubted that she'd ever had a heart at all. He took the paper silently, folded it, then locked it in the safe.

'If there's anything else that I can do . . .' but Hugh showed the doctor quickly to the door.

The undertakers would come that afternoon, which left him with three, perhaps four hours. He went back to the study. My time is running out . . . The words apply to me now.

He would marry again. There was no question about that. He'd chosen the girl some months ago. Little Elizabeth Anthony. He'd spoken to her father, who didn't seem to mind. Hugh smiled stiffly to himself. All of Anne's money was gone now, but he still had his reputation. He was of sufficient standing in the neighbourhood for allowances to be made, for little Elizabeth to be persuaded she was lucky. She was only twenty-six, he was sixty-five. People would say it was obscene, but never mind. It was an obscenity he wanted to taste in his mouth, on his tongue. He wanted to reek all over with the

4

indecency of it. He'd earned it, he'd paid his dues, and sowing and reaping with Elizabeth was his prize.

He had no qualms about the future. It was spoken for, it was taken care of. No. The hours before the undertakers came must be put to different uses. He had an account to settle with the past and as long as Anne had been alive any reckoning was impossible. He had to wait until she died. That was why he spent those long nights watching.

Hugh sat for a long time with a blank sheet of paper on the desk in front of him. One letter, one brief note was all that it would take, but it meant peeling back so many years, all the discarded pain of a different time. The pen sat vacantly between his fingers. It was a difficult indulgence for him, this going back. Back to the days of Rebecca, before then, even. Fifteen years ago . . . It was fifteen years since Mary Jenkins had stood on the far side of his office in Carmarthen, distant even then, and said that she was going away to Cardiff and it was best that they should never meet again. Mary Jenkins. She was his real prize. Lost. Not won. He had been tied to his bloated wife and she made all of that impossible. Mary Jenkins . . .

She had gone to Cardiff, gone on some trumped-up excuse. And she had stayed away for nearly three years. Then people started saying they had seen her, that she was back, that she was teaching at the little school again, that she had a daughter . . . Hugh had made inquiries; the talk was of a husband who died of consumption. There was certainly a little girl, aged three or thereabouts. People were rather vague, but he wanted to be sure. The child would have made sense of Mary's sudden going. He had to know. She had never contacted him, she had asked for nothing. All these years of wondering, of waiting for the right moment. He picked up the pen again and began: *Mary Jenkins, Dolwilym Farm*. Did he dare to bridge the gap which had lain between them all these years? He wasn't sure. He only knew that it was now or never, and that the letter would be difficult to write.

Even now a letter was an alarming breach of privacy at Dolwilym, although the seclusion of the valley had been broken open years ago and the narrow fields and hillsides divided up for other men to cultivate. Behind its knuckled flint walls in the wildest part of the valley, Dolwilym still belonged to Mary. She and her brother William had lived in the L-shaped stone embrace of the farm since they were born, and their father before them, and his father before that. The family was part of the landscape. It had always been there, stitched into place as jealously as the clustering woods and the scrubby fields, and any intrusion, on the whole, was unwelcome; but this letter most of all.

William's routine was inflexible and he depended on it absolutely. He knew about the letter but said nothing. Instead he watched as Mary packed him up his bread and cheese; he would be out in the fields all day today. He could see the shape of the folded paper in her apron pocket, and wondered if she had read it yet. She wasn't saying much this morning, although it was like her to be quiet. She helped him with the tapes that tied his withered arm into place, so that it formed a useful ledge around his middle. Otherwise there was a danger of it getting in the way, getting hurt. That had happened quite a lot at first, all those years ago. He was used to it now though, hardly thought of it at all. As long as nothing happened to disturb his routine.

'Eleanor awake yet?'

'No. I'll give her twenty minutes more.'

'All right then. See you later.' He kissed his sister and stamped out into the sunshine.

Mary leaned in the doorway and watched him go. His grizzled figure clumped its way across the yard, past the water pump and along the path which led down to the hayfield. Soon he was out of sight but she kept watching, looking at the air where he had been.

He was like an old man now, grey way before his time, his face lined and his movements slow and awkward. That was what made him look old: the stooped and laborious way he moved. And his arm. Poor William. He was miserable at harvest time, he always was; there was too much work to do, and she knew that he felt out of step with the fullness of the summer. He was only thirty-nine but he was old beyond his years. Well, that was what the past did to you. It made you old and set you in your ways, and then when you least expected it, it jumped out at you with its jaws red and snapping.

Mary closed the kitchen door, cleared away their breakfast bowls and laid a fresh place for her daughter, then she glanced up at the clock: a quarter past seven and not a sound from Eleanor. That gave

7

her fifteen minutes at least, fifteen long and dreadful minutes on her own. She stood irresolutely for a moment, then sighed. She didn't want to read the letter, she didn't want to know. She crouched down by the grate and stoked the fire, leaning over to put another log on, then with one slow careful finger she brushed the little tails of lichen from her hands. A blue flame burned round the new wood without seeming to touch it, and all that Mary wanted to do was to tuck the letter into that hot clear space between the flame and the bark and watch it burn, and then forget about it.

Instead, almost in one breath so that she had no time to think about it, she sat in her chair, took the letter from her pocket, opened it and read it. There. It was done. The note was very short. Fifteen years of silence and then a few brief lines.

She smoothed the page and read again.

Dear Mrs Jenkins [*Mrs* – was that cruelty or politeness?],

You may remember that years ago I acted as solicitor for your family and it is in that capacity that I am writing to you now. I am happy to inform you that your daughter – [he doesn't even know her name] *– is in receipt of a legacy. I would be delighted to furnish her with the details of it if she would be kind enough to attend my office in Carmarthen at her convenience. Hoping this finds you in good health,*

Yours sincerely,
Hugh Williams

Hoping this finds you . . . Mary was staring at the fire. *Hoping this finds you* . . . What was Hugh doing? What did he want from her, from Eleanor? To let all this time go by . . . There was a gentle bump on the ceiling; it was Eleanor getting out of bed. Mary looked at the letter one more time and wished with all her might that Hugh had never sent it. She wanted to put it out of sight, but she didn't quite dare to put it on the fire. In the end she folded it up and then went upstairs to the landing and put it right at the bottom of her mother's black oak chest.

'Will you be long, poppet?' She hardly knew the voice as hers.

'Five minutes, Mam. That's all. Just doing my hair.' Mary went back to the kitchen and made her daughter warm bread and milk with honey on top. Over breakfast she hardly said a word.

That evening, when the last check on the animals was finished, the dishes had been done, and Eleanor was in bed and safely out of earshot, brother and sister sat by the kitchen fire as they had done each night for twenty years or more. Mary had her mending on her knee – socks to darn and trousers to be patched for William and the letting-out and lengthening of dresses for her daughter. The girl was fourteen now and it was impossible to make her clothes last from one season to another, she grew so fast. William was biding his time, pretending to be busy with the paper. Occasionally he read out snippets he thought Mary would find interesting. They both knew what he was waiting for.

At last she spoke. 'I had a letter today.'

'Oh yes?' William's grey head stayed bent over the

paper. Mary went on sewing for a moment. I'll have to get some spectacles one of these days; if only they weren't so expensive. She was thinking irrelevantly, putting off the moment, and she knew it.

'It was from Hugh.'

William's face jerked up at her. 'Hugh? What does he want?'

Mary drew her needle through the cloth. 'He wants to see Eleanor. That's the only thing I can think of. He said something about a legacy . . .'

'A legacy?' William's astonishment was as clear as her own had been.

'Yes, I know. It's not very likely, is it? All day I've been racking my brains and I can't think of anyone who might leave Eleanor some money – there just isn't anybody. I've ended up not knowing what to think. I just don't know what's going on.'

'But Hugh doesn't know – '

'Exactly. That's what makes me wonder if it might be genuine after all. I would hate Eleanor to miss anything. But on the other hand – people talk, they imply things – maybe somebody has said something and he has put two and two together and now he wants to see her. I don't know.'

William said nothing and Mary watched as a washed-out greyness seeped round his mouth and under his eyes. It was fear making itself at home in his face. He shook his head, as if to himself.

'I wish he hadn't done it. Whatever his reasons, I wish he hadn't done it.'

'I know. So do I. But that doesn't really help things.'

'What are you going to do?'

10

'Tell her, I suppose. There seems to be an awful inevitability about the whole thing. I've always known that this might happen, and now it has. It's funny, years ago I was prepared for it, even waiting for it, and we heard nothing. And now, now that I'm unprepared and I've stopped expecting it, here it is. And I don't know what to think or what to do. Don't you think that's silly?'

William couldn't match the wanness of her smile. Instead he looked at the ashes in the grate and said nothing.

'I'm trying to be fatalistic about it and accept that what will be, will be. But in my heart I think the past is better left buried. And now suddenly it's all out of our hands.'

'Have you thought what you will say?' William watched his sister as she stitched her way through a long, isolating silence. Finally she cleared her throat, interrupting the quietness. 'Only what the letter says. I won't say anything else.'

'Shouldn't you prepare her just in case?'

'William, none of this is of my choosing. Telling her, opening up all those old wounds and splashing about in them is something I never want to do. It's better that she doesn't know. It's past and over, dead, gone, forgotten, finished. Hugh must see that too. I'm sure he does. He probably wants to do his best to help. That must be what it is. He wants to see her and see if he can help. It will be all right, I'm sure.' Mary stood up abruptly and put her mending away in its basket, wishing from the bottom of her heart that she could believe what she had said. 'Let's talk about it tomorrow. I'm tired. I want to go to bed. You're not to worry now.' She kissed her brother absently. 'Don't read too late,' although she knew he wouldn't read at all. 'Turn the lamp out when you come upstairs.'

Eleanor was beside herself with excitement. She simply didn't know how to contain herself or how to sit still for a second and she seemed to fill the kitchen to the rafters.

'A legacy? For me? Why? I mean, why me? Who is it from? How do you know about it? Oh Mam, I can't believe it's true. You're having me on, aren't you? It's all a joke.'

Mary only wished that it was.

'Don't get all worked up about it, poppet, it might be nothing at all. It's probably just a little memento from another part of the family. Distant cousins, something like that. It won't be anything exciting.'

'Does it make me an heiress, though?'

Mary smiled. 'I suppose it does. A very pretty heiress too, but not, I think, a very rich one.'

'Maybe.'

'There's nobody in our family with two pennies to rub together, so don't set your hopes too high. Just look on it as a nice day out in Carmarthen.'

'What shall I wear, Mam?'

'You'll wear your Sunday best.'

'Can't I wear –'

'No.'

The little face drooped.

'I'll put your hair in rags the night before if you like.'

'And a ribbon on the day?'

'All right. And a ribbon on the day. There now.'

'Oh Mam, I'm so excited I could burst.'

'Well, kindly don't burst all over the kitchen when I'm cooking.'

'When? When can I go? Does the letter say when?'

'Uncle William has said he will take you in next Wednesday.'

'Will you come too?'

'I've got work to do.'

'Oh please, Mam. A day out in Carmarthen. It will be such a treat. You must come as well.'

Mary was stolidly rolling out pastry.

'It's not a family outing, poppet. It's just sorting out a little bit of business. Tying up a few loose ends. You don't need me as well. Where are you going?' Eleanor was heading for the door. She filched a Welsh cake from the cooling rack. 'You'll spoil your tea if you do that.'

'I'm just going down the valley to tell Honor. I won't be long, Mam, I promise.' And in a flurry of knees and skirts she was gone; the kitchen returned to its normal size without her. Mary felt stiff from standing so long and she stopped work for a moment, straightening up and rubbing at the small of her back. There now, that was better. It didn't stop the ache inside her though; aching with worry over Eleanor, over what had already happened and what might happen next, and aching a little on her own account as well.

'Just give me two more minutes to finish this and then you can show her in.'

Hugh's heart was pounding in his throat. Old Mr

13

Ashe, the clerk, gave an unpleasant, allusive smile as he closed the door.

'Very good, Mr Williams.'

Hugh reached for his spectacles and put them on. He looked anxiously round the office, paused with an expression of dread on his face, then took them off again and ran his fingers through his hair. He rose to his feet, thinking it would appear less formal if he stood by the window and that also he would have the light behind him. He stood on the faded rug and swallowed hard. The moment was unbearable for him. Two little, long minutes.

Should he have written at all? Was it the right thing to do? And was it Mary who had come?

'A Miss Jenkins to see you, sir,' was all that old Ashe had said. Malice. The clerk was eaten through with malice now that he was old. He knew the truth. Would it be Mary standing there? He had no picture of her, nothing to remind him. Fifteen years . . . She must be in her forties now.

'Mary Jenkins.' He said her name aloud, as if testing it out. Mary? His necktie felt tight round his throat and he put his hand up to the knot to loosen it. He was arrested by the gesture; it reminded him of her, the way she spoke when she was nervous. He closed his eyes and tried to find her face: her brown hair, plaited and worn up, her leafy eyes, her white skin with its half-hearted freckles, her nose, her neck, that mouth . . .

There was a knock at the door. His time was up.

'Miss Jenkins, sir.'

At the last moment Hugh sat down at his desk again and rested his chin against his hands. He did

14

that because his head was shaking slightly and he didn't want her to see. She came into the room. It wasn't Mary.

Her hairline was exactly like his own. That was the first thing that he noticed. Afterwards, he thought that rather strange. He didn't see her eyes or her smile; all he saw was the high forehead and the black hair swept back from it. It gave her a look of surprise; it had always made him look bullish. She had his high, flat cheekbones, his careful mouth, and the blackness of her eyes was his as well.

'You're very like your mother,' he said out loud, searching her face again for a sign that she was Mary's child in any way. That she was his was all that he could see. His child. His unsuspected self. She smiled at him. His daughter.

'Some people say I look like Uncle William. Although, of course, he's fair.'

'Won't you sit down?'

'Thank you.'

She had the same lavender smell as her mother. She sat across the desk from him and he could not take his eyes off her. She crossed and uncrossed her hands in her lap and then decided to take her gloves off. Her cheeks were pink. She's nervous too. Like me. I wonder if she knows.

'How was your journey?'

'Oh it was very good, thank you.' She wetted her lips. My habit, Hugh thought. That's mine, that's what I do.

'It's a long time since I've been to Dolwilym.'

'Oh? Do you know the farm?'

'I went there once or twice. It used to be the devil

of a job to get a carriage down that road. All those twists and turns.'

'Still is. Silas hates it. He's our horse,' she added as an afterthought. It made Hugh want to cry to see her. The feeling shocked him. *How much does she know?*

'How is your mother?'

Her innocence was undisturbed. 'She's very well. And if she wasn't, she would never say. You know what she's like.'

Yes.

'And your uncle? How is he?'

'He's all right. Still gets bothered by his arm, sometimes. You know about his arm . . . ?' She ended uncertainly.

She doesn't know where to place me, she doesn't know where I fit in, Hugh thought.

'Yes, I knew him when it happened.'

'Oh really?' The first real light of interest in her face. 'He doesn't talk about it any more. My mother says he's very different now.'

There was a silence. She glanced round the office. Hugh cleared his throat.

'Well, Miss Jenkins, there is the matter of this legacy.' In his drawer was sixty pounds. Suddenly he wanted to give her everything he had, all that was left, everything. But he was going to be married again. It was impossible. Sixty pounds would have to do. Before she came into his room it had seemed a reasonable amount, but now that she was here, only an arm's length away . . .

'Yes, sir.' Her cheeks were even pinker. She fiddled with a glove.

16

'It's a very simple matter really – ' This was the moment he had been dreading. He had been frantic to think up a story she would believe, that Mary would accept as well. He spoke very quickly, in a rush of panic, and wondered if he sounded idiotic.

'My wife Anne died some weeks ago. She knew your mother once. She thought this would be a way of being remembered to her. She had this idea that Mary would be pleased if it were left to you. Small sum. Only sixty pounds.' He began to fumble at the drawer. 'All I need is your signature in receipt. And then the business is finished with.'

It was awful. He could feel the sweat in the small of his back and behind his knees. He pushed the envelope across the desk towards her. He wanted her to go. It was too much. He was an old man now.

'Sixty pounds, sir?' Those beautiful round black eyes. 'Your poor wife. I'm very sorry.'

'Don't be. You, of all people. She was ninety. It was high time she went.'

Some of the shine went out of her face for a moment.

'Where shall I sign?'

Hugh picked up a piece of paper. 'Here. Anywhere. On there.'

She wrote her name slowly. She wasn't as skilful as her mother.

'Is that it, then? Is that all I have to do?'

'Yes, that's it.' Now that she was ready to leave he didn't want her to go. Not now. Not yet. Must make her stay somehow.

'My wife was very fond of your mother.' It was a

17

lie. Anne had disliked everyone on principle, and Mary in particular. 'She worked for me for a time.'

'Really? As a teacher?' The girl seemed confused. Her politeness was impeccable. Did she care?

'She did teach too. At the little school in St Clears. But she used to help out in my office. This office. Here.'

'Oh.'

'And sometimes she would sit with my wife, who was an invalid for many years. Mary was a sort of companion.'

'Oh, I see. She only ever talked about teaching.'

'Oh.'

That hurt him. He bit his lip. He felt eaten up, strung taut. He had to know. He had to know the limits of his daughter's knowledge, how much she had been told.

'Only the teaching? Nothing else?'

The child looked puzzled. 'Well, the farm, and when she was little, and what it was like in Cardiff when I was born. You know, the usual things.'

'Didn't she ever talk about Rebecca?' He regretted it immediately, but all the same he couldn't stop himself.

'Rebecca?' The child seemed to be considering. 'No, I don't think so. I don't think she ever mentioned – Rebecca who?'

'Nothing. It doesn't matter. Long time ago. It's easy to forget.'

His daughter smiled obligingly.

'I won't keep you any longer.' He was curt once more. The whole idea had been wrong.

Eleanor rose to her feet and stood awkwardly for

a moment. 'I am most dreadfully sorry about your poor wife. She must have been a very kind lady.'

'She wasn't kind at all. It was only because your mother –' He took the slim hand that she offered him. Flesh of my flesh. He wished that he could hold her close. 'Give her my regards. And your uncle. I'm glad to have met you.'

'Thank you, sir. Well.' There was an uncomfortable pause. Strangers parting. 'Goodbye then.'

'Goodbye, Miss Jenkins.'

She was gone. Hugh sat at his desk. He picked up the paper she had signed. Eleanor Jenkins. His unknown daughter. He folded it and put it in his breast pocket.

In the outer office Mr Ashe watched the young girl go. He stood by the door so he could see her walk right down the street and round the corner. Well, well, well. What a turn-up. He brushed at the shoulders of his jacket, and then a noise caught his attention and made him cock his head to listen. It was the sound of Mr Williams weeping.

'Save it till we get home to your mother,' said William, as Eleanor settled into the cart beside him and opened her mouth to speak.

'But Uncle Wil –'

'It'll keep till then. Otherwise it won't be fair on her.' He had his eyes on Silas' ears, staring between them at the road ahead. He didn't want to be unkind, but when all was said and done, he didn't want to hear much either. Best to leave the past alone. That way it was easier, it was better. He chirruped at the horse to fill the silence. They rumbled their way down Water Street in the little open cart, past the spot where the toll house used to stand. The mean brown face of Henry Thomas flashed into his mind. It always did when he drove past there. Ah well.

'Hope the rain holds off.' He screwed his eyes up at the sky. Eleanor didn't answer, and when he glanced in her direction she looked away, secluded and crestfallen. She was clutching her bag close to her chest. Whatever Hugh had given her must be in there. That was the only moment of curiosity William felt. Mostly he was wondering: what has Hugh gone and told her? What has he stirred up now? It was all he could do to stop Rebecca's fist tightening round his heart. He didn't try to talk again until they reached Dolwilym, and the child seemed willing to let the silence go. He told her off once for biting at her nails. That was all.

Mary had run out into the yard to greet the cart at least four times before it actually arrived. The last time her hands were wet from the washing and she stood on the edge of the grass drying them on her apron and straining to see her daughter's face. Difficult to tell. Eleanor could be very close at times, she hid her feelings well. Her mother's trick. William looked stony-faced.

'I can manage,' he grunted, when she moved to help him with the unhitching of the cart. Every action for him was a proof of independence.

'I'll do this. You take Eleanor into the house. I'll be in directly.' The air was tense between them. He did not come inside to join them. It was gone ten o'clock and dark when he came home. Off somewhere on his own again. Poor William.

'Now. Tell me all about it. Have you eaten?' She poured Eleanor some cold mint tea and fetched her some bread and cheese. The food went untouched.

'He gave me this.' Wide-eyed, the child took the packet from her bag and handed it to her mother. 'I had to sign a piece of paper and then he gave me this.'

With an overwhelming sense of sadness and foreboding Mary took the packet and looked inside. The grief from fifteen years ago was fresh in the back of her throat, behind her eyes, and in the reluctant moving of her fingers.

'There's sixty pounds there,' she said stupidly.

'I know.' Eleanor nodded. 'Sixty whole pounds. I can't believe it, Mam. Sixty pounds. I had to keep pinching myself all the way home to make sure it was true.'

'Did you see Mr Williams?' There was something, a raw nerve or a heart string, that jangled so much inside Mary that she hardly dared to ask. Not because of Hugh himself, but because of all that he brought back with him. 'Did you speak to him?'

'Well, not for very long. Not really. What a strange old man, Mam.'

Yes . . . He must be old now, in his sixties. He looked so young, there in his daughter's face, that Mary found it hard to imagine that he had grown old, that he would seem old even to her.

'Who is the money from?'

'His wife. She died. He said she wanted to be remembered to you.'

Anne dead? He always said there would be money when she went. Poor Hugh. She certainly made him wait for it.

'I didn't know you used to work for them. He said that was why. Because you looked after his wife and she wanted to be remembered to you, but she thought you would rather the money came to me. Something like that. So it was nothing to do with a cousin at all.'

'No.'

He must have found out somehow. Mary shook her head. Had she been naïve to think that he never would? It had been so difficult to work things out then. Had he known for long? Had he been waiting all this time for Anne to die so that he could settle his debts? Not that he owed her anything, not at all. He had given her Eleanor, so how could there be debts between them? Mary sighed and waited for the blow to fall.

It didn't come that night. Eleanor started on the bread and cheese and talked a bit about how they should spend the money – maybe they could buy out the lease on Dolwilym, or go to Bristol for a holiday? Wouldn't that be wonderful? There were so many possibilities. She smiled and talked and ate her sandwich, but Mary found her rather solemn and restrained, considering. When she dared to probe a little about what else Hugh had discussed, his daughter said blandly that the solicitor had sent his best regards.

'I'm a bit tired, Mam. I think I'll go upstairs and read a while. I'll do the dishes first, don't worry.' She picked up the packet with the money in it. 'Will you look after this for me?'

'I'll put it in the Bible. It'll be safe there. I'll tidy away, you go up.'

Eleanor stood in the doorway briefly and then came over to her mother and hugged her.

'I love you, Mam.' A kiss on the cheek. 'Good night.'

Mary watched her go. My private, secret child. She stood deep in thought for some moments, and then began the chores that she always did, and after that she sat up in her chair to wait for William to come home. Her head was supported in her hands, and she couldn't stop thinking . . .

Three days later Eleanor asked her who Rebecca was.

1

Life was easy at Dolwilym in the early days. Mary could remember evenings in those dusty summers, sitting on her father's shoulders while he did the last round of the day, checking on the animals. He used to walk from the Afon Tâf up along the shoulder of the valley to Castell Garw. That had been the boundary of the farm then, before it was divided up into tidy, manicured fields for strangers to tend. Funny to think of it now. In those days Mary could look out of her bedroom window and not see where the farm ended. Not like today. Her father only took her with him when the weather was fine, and she used to ride on his bony shoulders as if he were some tall-masted ship with the falling darkness lapping at his prow. If she really tried hard she could remember the feel of the collar of his smock, her hands holding on tight . . .

One summer her mother had swelled up and then William had come to live with them. The walks went on, but now William was carried in the rigging: Mary's moorings were loosened and she used to trail behind the two of them, in their gritty wake, until her legs were tired. Her mother swelled up again, and there was a dead baby in the house, and then her mother died as well. After that the summers were no longer fine, and the walking stopped. At the time Mary thought that the weather was wet and grey and unrelenting only because of her mother's death, that those summers seemed dreary because the happiness had been taken out of them. But they really were liquid and dismal, and that was where the family's troubles started. The black circles round her father's eyes never went away again. She remembered the sound of him crying on his own down in the kitchen at night, and then the nights when he went out and came home drunk. Because the harvests were bad. Because August was now as pinched and hungry as December. There was no let-up for any of them.

At first Morgan thought he could get by, that the children could be taught to do the simple jobs so that he need take on fewer hands to help out. They managed for a year like this until another harvest failed. It was about this time that Thomas Bullin moved into the district. The Whitland Turnpike Trust hired him as their manager; they said it was his brief to make a profit from the toll roads. We need to have more money, they explained, to carry out some necessary repairs. Not a single hole in any road was filled, but the tolls rose steeply. Farmers like Morgan scrabbled together a small load of produce to sell at the markets in the town, only to find that they paid more in tolls than the whole load was worth. It cost ten pence to drive a score of sheep to market at a time when you would be lucky to clear one shilling and six for a whole week's wages. It didn't make sense to him.

Evening after evening he sat with his head in his hands at the kitchen table and thought that he must be stupid. No matter how he tried he couldn't find a way to cope. He juggled the figures this way, and then he juggled them that way, and then he gave up juggling them altogether and simply felt inadequate. The drink quickly turned this into anger and then into a pent-up, immobile bitterness. At times it was difficult to feed the children, the obligation to sell the produce was so strong and there was little left over. Night after night Mary boiled up a pan of potatoes in some buttermilk – she was old enough to do the cooking now – and night after night the three of them sat down to this dispiriting dinner, which they finished unappeased, with empty plates and even emptier stomachs.

In the inn one evening over at Efail-wen with Tom Rees, Morgan had one of his ideas. They were sitting at a table. A good talker, Tom Rees was. Not like Ivor Eames who was there as well. Ivor was their nearest neighbour, had the farm at Llwynhugh. Not a talker, Ivor, but a man of understanding all the same. You felt he knew what you were getting at, and he was partial to his pint and Morgan liked that in a man. Ivor had five sons, lucky sod, so shortage of labour was never a problem for him.

That's what the three of them were talking about, that was all they ever talked about really – how to keep the kids' bellies full and how to make them pay their way. Oh, and sometimes they talked about the latest rise in tolls, but this only made Tom angry, and that meant trouble.

'You ought to put your Mary out to work for you.

Time she was pulling her weight more. I won't deny a woman is useful on a farm, but we all know there are certain things they just can't do.' Tom Rees pulled at his pipe. 'That's what I would do if I were in your shoes, mate. Put her out to work.'

'As what, though?' Morgan wrinkled up his nose and shook his head. 'Certainly she's a nice little cook, and she keeps the place in order, but that's what men like you and me have wives for. You don't expect to pay good money to have someone come in and do that kind of thing for you.'

'Put her into service. Find her a place somewhere.'

'What, away from Dolwilym? I don't know about that.' Morgan took a swig from his mug.

'Speak to the minister,' Ivor suggested, trying to be helpful.

'Ivor's right,' said Tom. 'You talk to Mr Morris. He knows all the nobs round here. He'll know if anyone is looking for somebody to do for them.'

'Hmm. Well. We'll see.' Morgan shifted in his seat. 'I suppose it's my round now?'

When he finally weaved his way home later that night the idea had firmly taken hold. The very next Sunday he spoke to the minister after Chapel; took him on one side and asked him straight.

'I'm looking for a place for my girl. In service, like. You don't happen to know if there's anything going? It's not that I want to see the back of her or anything.' He scratched his head and felt embarrassed. 'It's just that, well, you know how things are. Times are hard, see.'

Caleb Morris ducked and nodded, his spectacles winking gravely in the sunshine. The whole valley knew that times were indeed hard for the Jenkins family now. He wondered how the poor man coped. No wife to help him, a big place like Dolwilym to look after, those two children . . .

'I'll ask around if you like. See what I can do, anyway. It would be good for young Mary to strike out on her own a bit. She's a bright girl. I'll see what I can manage.'

What Caleb Morris came up with was not exactly what Morgan had had in mind, but after a few drinks with the lads and a lengthy discussion of the pros and cons of the proposition he began to warm to the idea. By the time he got round to telling Mary, it was as if the notion had been his all along.

'You're to go and work for the minister. Keep house for him, like. Help out. It's all right, you'll still be living at home, see; there isn't room for you to stay at his place, and anyway people might not think that it is right, you being a young girl, and so on. Now he won't be paying that much money at first, but that's a private matter between him and me; you don't have to worry yourself with that. What he will be doing is teaching you book-learning.'

Mary was staring at him and nodding. You couldn't take his girl by surprise no matter what you said.

'Yes, Dada.'

'You do see, don't you? You do see what a great, great favour the minister is doing you? He says that once you've learned the reading and the writing and the sums and so forth, you'll be able to help out in the Chapel School, and then you really will be paid.' Morgan nodded eagerly. 'And he thinks that when you're a bit more grown up you might be able to get work as a teacher or governess. Think of that, Mary.'

Mary thought. She was torn by a feeling of dubiousness and a desire to please. 'Yes, Dada,' she nodded.

'Book-learning's a wonderful thing, my girl. Keep that thought fixed firmly in your head. You start on Monday.' He clapped her on the back. There was an anxious, hoping look in his reddened eyes.

'Yes, Dada,' said Mary.

Mary applied herself to her new work obediently and diligently and, as her grasp and understanding grew, her father's slackened off. There was another bad harvest that year and he used to come back from market each week with his pockets lighter and lighter. If he came back via the inn in Efail-wen, often there was nothing in his pockets at all.

'There's not enough money anyway, so what's the point of even trying to make it last? May as well enjoy ourselves while we can. It isn't going to get any better, is it?' His voice was shrill and defensive when he spoke like that. William always left the room when Morgan started shouting; he couldn't stand the rows. Let Mary cope with it – she seemed to know how to handle their Dada. She let him have his say, and when he was calm again, then she would answer him. It just upset William. Let Mary cope, she knew best.

Thomas Bullin went on charging more and more for use of the turnpike roads, and the crops continued to fail, and then the tithes went up by seven per cent. Morgan Jenkins got blind drunk when he found that out, and he never came home that night. He missed the milking the following morning and when he finally tottered into the kitchen his face was green and liverish under its stubble. Before Mary could ask him where he had been, he put up his hand with faded authority.

'I've had an idea. I've been, er, discussing it with some colleagues. I think I've found the answer.' His jacket was rumpled and there was gravy on his smock. Mary looked at him with resignation.

'What's that, Dada?'

'Heat me some water, will you? I think I shall take a bath.'

It was then that Mary knew there was something afoot. Her father only took a bath about twice a year; normally he was content to sluice himself down under the pump in the yard. He said he disliked washing in hot, stagnant water, that all it did was redistribute the dirt. But that morning he had a bath and put on his Sunday clothes. In retrospect, Mary thought she should have known there was trouble on its way.

'I've got business in Carmarthen,' was all he said. 'I should be back by dinner time.'

In the event he didn't return until long after William was in bed. Mary was sitting at the kitchen table with her books spread out in front of her, trying to finish the work the minister had set for her. The light from the rush candle was skimpy and once or twice she almost singed her hair, she was sitting so close to it. She was printing laboriously, copying out verses from the Bible.

'Take note of what it is you're writing, Mary,' Mr Morris had said. 'Don't just copy it out blind. Read

31

and understand. That's what matters. These passages that you do for me are important.'

And so, at the end of another weary, aching day of caring for two households, Mary sat with her books and wrote, mouthing each syllable as she did so.

And they blessed Rebecca, and said unto her, Thou art our sister, be thou the mother of thousands of millions, and let thy seed possess the gates of those which hate them. And Rebecca arose –

She put her pen down. There was a whistling in the yard. Dada. She hurried to put his soup to heat over the fire. The door swung open and he stood there, beaming and hiccoughing. She had never realised that he was so small.

'I've done it, Mary.' He patted his jacket pocket. 'I've fixed it for all of us. There won't be troubles any more.' He sat heavily in his chair and tossed a thick packet of papers onto the table. 'That's it. The answer to our prayers. I've got a mortgage on the farm.'

Mary was tidying away her books but she turned, as if to hear more clearly, as if she must have been mistaken.

'You've done what, Dada?'

'I've got a mortgage on the farm. Put my mark on it this afternoon. The lads in Efail-wen suggested it. They said everyone's doing it these days and, once I'd thought it over for a bit, I could see what a good idea it was. They put me on to Mr Evelyn in Carmarthen. He's well up in this kind of thing. Nice man. We've done a good deal, I think.'

Mary picked up the packet and weighed it in her hand. It felt heavy with conditions and demands and promises which would be difficult to honour.

'How much?' she said.

'What?' Her Dada looked bleary and untriumphant all of a sudden.

'How much did you get?'

'Enough.'

'What's that supposed to mean?' She began to peel the papers open.

'Here. You give that over here.'

'But, Dada –'

'It's my farm. It's my business. You're lucky to have had a good home here for so long. Now, give it here.'

Mary put the packet on the table. She said nothing.

'I'm sorry.' Morgan gave an irritated sigh. 'I don't mean to snap. I'm sorry. Look, it's been a long day, don't think it's been easy.' He didn't look at her. 'Is there anything to drink?'

'There's some soup.'

'Don't want soup.'

Mary shrugged, angry in surrender.

'Look, girl, I know what I'm doing. I've taken good advice, and Mr Evelyn is an honest man. It'll be all right. Now, off you go to bed. This isn't your concern.'

But it was Mary's concern, and it became even more so as the months went by. Morgan was often absent, and when she asked where he was going he said, 'Politics,' and banged the door behind him. She didn't know what he was talking about, only that he was out a lot and that it meant more work for William and for her. The minister kept her busy enough as it was, without that too.

Morgan was out the night the barn burned down. It was 12th April 1839. The first of so many black days to remember. He elbowed his way into his jacket, took all the loose change from the tin on the dresser and said he was going to a meeting. Mary knew now what that entailed.

'Don't look at me like that, my girl. A man's time is his own. I've done a good day's work today. Cleared the ditches up near Maes y Felen, branded them new lambs, and I burned all the rubbish too. So don't you go saying a word.'

He slammed out of the house. Mary didn't give a second thought to what he said, except that she felt cross again. She wiped her arm across her forehead, sat in her chair for five minutes and did absolutely nothing.

She was fast asleep in her bed when William ran into her room, shouting. She rolled over sleepily and had almost incorporated him into her dream when he began to shake her wildly.

'Mary! Mary! It's the barn. Mary, you've got to wake up!'

She half sat up, still lolling and disorientated with sleep.

'What? What did you say?'

William was into his clothes already, tucking and buttoning with shaking fingers, hopping about on one booted foot.

'Get up. The barn's burning. Quick.'

'Where's Dada?'

'Not back yet. Come on.' He was halfway down the corridor as he spoke. 'Hurry!'

Mary sat frozen for a moment. *'I've branded the lambs and I've burned all the rubbish.'* Oh my God. She pulled a skirt on over her nightdress. She didn't bother with her boots, there wasn't time. Glimpsed through her window, flames from the barn were fingering the sky. The fire had got a hold and was ravenous. It would be too late. Oh, Dada, what have you gone and done?

William had emptied the horse trough a bucket at a time when she came panting into the yard. He was running towards the barn slopping water everywhere. His face was already black and his fair hair was like the lightest edge of a flame against the darkness. Mary ran after him, not knowing what to do.

'No. You start pumping. We need as much water as we can. I'm going to try and bring the rain barrel over.'

She pumped savagely until her hands were raw, each lunge wrenching at her back and shoulders and soaking her skirt right through. If she craned her head around she could see all the food for the animals, all the food for themselves, everything they had left, being burnt to a cinder. After a while she could not bear to look.

'We haven't got a chance. If only there were more of us . . .' William's voice was hoarse with the smoke.

'Shall I run over to Llwynhugh −?'

'No. Keep pumping. Whatever you do, keep pumping.'

It was almost light when the king-post went. The

timber creaked and then stretched as if it were tired and had had enough. With a sound which would have cut the night in two, it snapped – a sudden failure of the heart – and went jouncing to the ground, bringing the roof down with it. After that the fire became conspiratorial: it turned in on itself, whispering around the burning wood. The flames were less rangy now, they folded themselves like sleepy wings around the body of the building and slowly burned themselves away. Mary stood stock-still and watched it for a while; there was nothing more that they could do. She was beyond weeping, and the dawn was cold. There was no sympathy in the day which broke. William came and stood beside her. He looked as if his body didn't fit him any more. He looked frightened and tired to death. She reached up and picked ash off his cheek.

'We did everything we could, didn't we?' His voice had been scorched and sanded by the fire. 'We couldn't – well, there was nothing . . .' He tailed off, and Mary didn't answer. She was thinking at that moment it would be easy to walk out of her valley and not come back. Leave the hissing cinders, leave their gutted hopes, just go away and forget it all. If her Dada had taken his mortage money and set fire to it, note by note, he could not have destroyed them all more effectively. What now? What next? She felt only disbelief.

'I don't understand what started it.' William shook his head.

'Dada lit a bonfire today. To burn the rubbish,' Mary said dully. 'It must have been a spark from that.' She walked to the side of the barn. 'There. Too close. What a stupid thing to do.' The ground was scarred with a round black blister where Morgan had made his fire. 'What was he thinking of?'

Neither of them spoke for a moment. Mary watched as the wind tickled a smut along the ground.

'That's it then, isn't it?' William's voice was as dead as her own.

'I don't know, William. I don't know where we even start.' She slipped her arm through his, and they stood, linked together, lost in thought.

'Breakfast maybe.' His smile was forced.

'Yes. Breakfast. And a wash, and then lots of time to think things out.'

'Come on then.' He turned stiffly towards the house. 'Are you coming?' He put his arm around her and they left the smoky yard without turning to look back.

In the days following the fire Morgan kept going back to the barn. His wispy, rickety figure could be seen foraging amongst the charred bones of the building, hunting, searching . . .

'There's nothing there, Dada. There's nothing left. It's all gone. You're wasting your time.' But Mary could tell he wasn't listening. He would sniff, wipe his face on his sleeve and then tramp back to what he was doing. There was nothing he could say, but he was dogged in his scrabbling about. He dragged out timbers which he thought they could use again and lined them up in the yard, and sifted through the debris for six − seven − eight roof tiles which had survived uncracked. Then he found some glass jars which Mrs Jenkins had used to keep preserves in and he piled them up forlornly in a space amongst the wreckage. A few hedging hooks with their handles burned away, and there was no more salvaging he could do. After that his energy deserted him. He would pace about amongst the things which he had rescued, looking at them, at the ground, anywhere but at his children, but the little pile of flotsam was too small to redeem him.

When there was no longer any reason for him to hang about the yard, Morgan used to trail around behind William, watching him work. Mary he avoided all together. The two men took their old path along the valley to Castell Garw, William emptying the traps he had set, and Morgan remaining tentatively a few paces behind him. In one of the traps a hare was arched back stiffly with its muzzle wide open, as if it were the act of screaming for life which had killed it, and not the snap of metal on its spine . . . The jaws of the trap were slippery with blood and although William wiped them carefully he found it difficult to get a grip.

'Here, Dada, catch hold of this, will you? If you pull on that one, I'll pull the other and we can lift the hare clean out.'

Morgan stuck his hands quickly into his pockets as if someone had accused him of stealing.

'Dada – ' William tried to check his impatience, but Morgan shook his head vigorously.

'No. Don't ask me. I'm just bad luck. Probably take your hand off. You mustn't ask anything of me. I'm no use to you any more.'

So William freed the animal himself and shoved it into the sack along with three pigeons and a mole.

He wasn't quite sure what they could do with the mole; he supposed that Mary would think of something.

'Come on, Dada,' he said curtly, hoisting the bag onto his back and setting off up the slope. He gritted his teeth as he heard his father give an anxious and unhappy little sigh.

Walking along the crest of the hill they could see Dolwilym, smoke-black and convalescent at the far end of the valley. William remembered all those other walks they had taken, so many years before. He wondered if he had been such a responsibility to his father then as his father was becoming to him now. Riding on Morgan's back, the unimaginable distance from there to the ground, the fear of falling and the knowledge that you wouldn't, that Dada would stop you . . . He glanced behind him. Morgan's gaze slid guiltily away. There was nobody to stop your Dada falling though, that was the trouble . . .

William shifted the sack onto his other shoulder. His shirt was soaked through with different kinds of blood.

'Come on, Dada,' he said, 'or Mary will be wondering where we've got to.'

After that evening Morgan detached himself from William too, as if he were scared the boy would start to demand more things of him. He didn't want his children's patience, their irritation, their sense of obligation to him. He wanted to be left alone. When Mary wasn't looking he took a few pence from the tin on the dresser, put them in his boot so they wouldn't chink, and pulled his jacket close about him

– he felt the cold more now, even though it was, what? May already?

'Going to Chapel. Need to think.'

Mary didn't answer, but she watched him tramp up the flinty road at the front of the house with her heart in her mouth.

Morgan did stop off at the Chapel. He spent some time on his knees with his forehead resting on the pew in front and his mind a blank. Then he stood under the gallery examining the rafters, and went upstairs and hung over the rail to see them from above. After that he went to Efail-wen and when he came back to the farm he was swathed in the smell of spirits.

The next day was the same. He spent a long time alone in his room and when Mary had returned from the minister's, he passed her in the kitchen and said, 'I'm going to Chapel. There's not much I can do around here.'

'Dada, don't, please,' Mary said, with all the gentleness she could find. He shrugged her off. She never saw the hank of rope slung round his body under his coat.

That night Mary went up to turn her father's bed down, just in case he did come home. Laid out on the counterpane were all the mortgage papers, a Bible, her mother's wedding ring threaded through with a plaited lock of hair. She gathered them together with a kind of end-of-the-day tenderness, as if she were gathering a child's toys, and put them where he would find them easily. She folded back the sheet, smoothed away the wrinkles on the bolster, closed the curtains and then shut the door behind her.

They cut him down at four o'clock the following afternoon. Mrs Pritchard went to do the tidying in the Chapel, ready for Sunday service, and found him strung up from the rafters under the gallery. He must have stood on the font to tie the rope, and then jumped . . . Half the valley said privately that this was sacrilege, while the other half said openly how sorry they felt for the poor family he left behind and whatever would become of them? Mrs Pritchard fetched Thomas Lewis, the doctor from Llanboidy, and it was he who cut the body down and took it home to Mary.

He'd been her childhood sweetheart, this man who brought her Dada home to her, with the bruise from the rope burned into his neck.

'I'm sorry, Mary. I had no idea that things had got this bad . . . I'm so sorry.'

Blankly she cleared the kitchen table to receive her Dada's body. Blankly she let Thomas Lewis do all the things that were necessary to prepare her Dada's body for the ground. Under his crinkled ginger hair the doctor's forehead shone; he was busy being impersonal and the effort made him sweat.

'I should have come round more often. I'm sorry, Mary. I had no idea.'

Seeing his daughter married well had been one of the plans that Morgan had never quite attended to. Thomas Lewis had always been the obvious choice: he lived close by, he was a bright lad, and the neighbours said that if he went in for that doctoring he was bound to make a tidy living for himself. Morgan sent old Mother Lewis a chicken every Christmas and encouraged friendship between the two families. It was made perfectly clear to Mary that Thomas would one day be her husband. Whether this fact was equally clear to Thomas, Morgan could never be quite sure. At any rate, when the lad went off to do his studies in Carmarthen, he came round less and less, and eventually Morgan took his daughter to one side and explained that things didn't always turn out as you expected them to.

Mary thought it fitting that her father be brought home to her in the arms of Thomas Lewis. It was as if the past were coming home to roost – only things don't always turn out as you expect them to. Thomas wouldn't stay for tea when his work was done, although Mary asked him to. He couldn't look her in the ey, couldn't stop jangling the coins in his pocket, couldn't get out of the kitchen quick enough.

'I'm sorry, Mary. I'll try and call round more often, it's just that . . .'

So many disappointments her Dada had to bear.

William dug a grave for him near the burial mound at Gwal y Filiast. It was the nearest they could get to doing the right thing by him. They put him not too far from the path so that he wouldn't feel he was all alone. Ivor Eames came over, and Tom Rees too. Caleb Morris sent his best regards, but said that in the circumstances it was impossible for him to attend. And throughout all this, Mary felt as if she'd been axed in half.

After they had buried him and the visitors had finished their tea and gone, she and William said prayers for their father on their knees on the kitchen floor. Mary read from the prayer book and hoped the

Lord would pardon them, for she had a feeling they were doing wrong. Together they sang a hymn.

> 'Did ever mourner plead with Thee,
> And Thou refuse that mourner's plea?
> Does not the Word still fix'd remain
> That none shall seek Thy face in vain?'

But it seemed to her that the ears of the Lord were pretty deaf that evening. She said goodnight to William, formal in her grief, then shut herself in her own room and found that she couldn't weep. How can you begin to mourn when you can't accept the thing has happened? She lay on her bed looking out at the night and hoping that her father's soul was out there somewhere. Keep an eye out for us, Dada. It's going to be very hard. She hardly slept at all.

Their Dada must have been looking in a different direction altogether. That was all Mary could think as she stood at the kitchen sink with the muslin for making cheese sticky in her fingers. A black, boxed-in carriage was battling its way down the flintstone track which led from the main road to Dolwilym. The driver was clearly a city man, not used to country lanes. He'd never make that bend if he went at it like that. She watched him back the horses up and try again. He was swearing, she could see that from the angry jags his lips made. The coach was tight and neat and shiny. Mary scraped the curds from her hands so there should not be any waste, then wiped her fingers clean. The carriage stopped in the yard. Angrily, the driver mopped his face with his sleeve, shoved the whip back in the clip which held it, then jumped down to help the passenger alight.

It was Mr Evelyn. Although she had never seen him, Mary had no doubt about that. He stood in her yard and shivered sleekly. He was as tight and neat and shiny as his carriage. He shot his cuffs and straightened the jet pin he wore in his cravat, all the while staring at her home with narrow eyes. She could see him taking in the grey stone, the pretty gothic windows, the lawn at the front, the yard around him, the stables. Oh yes, Mr Evelyn, Dolwilym's a peach. Hadn't you realised? Over his shoulder he gave an exclamation of petulance, anger almost. The driver glanced up. Evelyn was peering at the haggard blackness where the barn had been, the irritation fussy in his face. She saw him shrug his shoulders, move as if to flick a smut from his glove, then walk briskly towards the front door. There was a sense of acquisition in every stride he took.

'Miss Jenkins?'

There on her threshold was his yellow smile. He cleared his throat with just the right degree of delicacy. He was dressed in suitable black. Everything he did – the way he stepped into the kitchen, accepted the chair she offered, removed his hat – was appallingly appropriate, it was nicely judged. It was nice.

'I'd like to offer you my sincere condolences.' His feeling of anticipation was delicious. The girl dropped her head. He could see her swallowing hard. There was a slight flush to her neck, her throat to be exact, although her face was white. Pretty little thing, this one.

Cornered, Mary looked around the room for something to offer him.

'Can I get you some barley water?' was all she said in reply.

'How kind.' He gave her time to pour the drink. 'I was a business associate of your father's,' he said smoothly, taking the glass from her shaking hand. 'To be more specific, your father was one of my clients.' To Mary everything about him was unnecessary. 'My name is Evelyn. I have an office in Carmarthen.'

'Aah.' She nodded, waiting, waiting.

'Did Mr Jenkins talk about . . . ?'

'I think he mentioned you once.'

Evelyn regarded her again. Defensive, this one. Well, best to get to the point. Time was money, after all.

'Your father and I concluded a business deal shortly before he, er, passed away. Put at its simplest, in exchange for a sum of money, he assigned the freehold of the property to me on the understanding that he would own the lease for the term of his natural life — '

Mary sat down abuptly. Oh dear God, what now? The mortgage, the wretched mortgage. Underneath the table her hands clenched and unclenched a fold of her skirt.

'Of course, if I had known the way his thoughts were tending, I would never . . .' Mr Evelyn tailed off, with what he thought was decent vagueness.

Mary put her hand up to her neck. She felt as if she couldn't breathe.

'Please, just tell me what it's all about.'

Slickly he began his speech. 'I'm so sorry, my dear. You've no idea how disagreeable this is to me. That's why I came myself to tell you. The fact of the matter is that, as of now, I am the unhappy owner of Dolwilym.' There was a shining in the corner of the girl's eyes. He hoped that she wouldn't start to cry. 'What I've come to discuss is how to make things easy for you, my dear.' It was always the worst part of the job, this.

'What do you suggest?'

At least her voice was steady. Mr Evelyn was a great believer in keeping up appearances.

'Well, I tried to work out something on my way over here, something that I hope will be acceptable.'

'I hope so too.'

There was a cool edge in her voice that made him look at her more closely. He couldn't have known that she was drowning inside.

'Good. Well.' He coughed. 'What I propose is this.' From a pocket book he drew a sheet of paper. Mary glanced at his writing; it was small and meticulous. 'As a mark of my sympathy for your situation I would like to give you two options. Firstly, I would be only too happy to return possession of the farm, lock, stock and barrel, for a consideration of, say, two hundred pounds.'

Mary never took her eyes off him. You paid my father eighty pounds for the same thing only two months ago. It gave her a grim pleasure that he was unable to look her in the eye.

'On the other hand, I have a mind to divide the property into lots. It must be such a burden for one

46

family to manage – one only has to look at your poor father to see that.'

Mary felt sick inside.

'Better to spread the load, don't you think? No reason why four or five tenant farmers shouldn't co-exist in a valley the size of this.'

No reason at all. Except that it had been her home all of her life. But why should that be an objection? Mr Evelyn clearly saw no problem there.

'You would, of course, retain the main farm building and I would include, say, four acres of land in the lease. The two fields nearest the house should be enough to support your needs – keep on a few of your animals, plant some vegetables. You see, my dear – '

Mary pushed her body back against her chair as he leaned forward.

'You see, it's really a question of re-adjustment, of changing your perceptions . . . Before very long you and your brother might be prosperous small-holders. You don't want the bother of this great farm.'

'How much do you want?'

Evelyn paused before he answered.

'I'll sell you a lease for the term of your life for eighty pounds. In addition there will be an annual ground rent of five guineas and you retain the right to buy me out for the sum I originally mentioned.'

'That's very thoughtful, Mr Evelyn. I'm glad we still have that right, anyway.'

He gave an uncertain laugh.

'As a matter of fact, I've taken the liberty of drawing up an agreement. You only have to put your cross at the bottom.'

'I'll sign it when my solicitor has seen it.' Mary was surprised by how level she sounded; inside she felt wild, clutching at straws.

'I don't think you'll find that necessary. I believe it's all in order.'

'All the same.'

'I have to say I think you're wasting your time, not to mention your money, you know. It's all perfectly legal.'

Mary remembered the meanness of his handwriting.

'I'm sure it is,' she said. 'Nevertheless, you said that I have two options. I would just like to be sure of my position, then I can make a proper decision.'

'Miss Jenkins, I don't really think – '

'If I might just have a copy of your agreement.' Mary stood up and went to the door, waiting. 'Then I needn't keep you any longer.' Her hand was shaking on the door latch. Had Mr Evelyn noticed it he might have felt easier in his mind. As it was, he felt put out. It wasn't for the girl to baulk like this, she should sign and be grateful. He didn't like her imputations, he didn't like them at all.

'If you really think it is necessary – ' he broke off halfway through. He was beginning to feel angry, and it wouldn't look right if he were to lose his temper now. There would be plenty of time later. ' – of course,' he finished with self-restraint.

'Thank you.' Mary took the document he offered. The paper was apt and yellow like his smile.

'We are agreed, aren't we, that it is in both our interests to settle this as soon as possible?'

Mary said nothing; she only wanted him to go.

Mr Evelyn was gathering his things together. 'I look forward to hearing from you then.' He oiled his way past her and into the yard. She saw him snap at the coach driver and then climb into the carriage out of sight. She had to put her hand over her mouth. She wanted to spit on his shadow.

At his desk by the window the clerk was cleaning his nails, using the corner of a writ that he had folded over for the purpose. Mr Ashe, Mr Aske, something like that, Mary wasn't sure. He had greeted her and William with all the burdened doubt of a bureaucrat.

'No appointment? Oh dear . . .' He leafed his way unnecessarily through a large diary. Mary knew he wouldn't oblige them unless he absolutely had to. 'Mr Williams is a very busy man . . .'

'I appreciate that. That's why we are here. When I asked around the town, people said that he was the best for, well, for people like us.' In fact, the people Mary had asked had said – go to Mr Williams, he's the only one who will give the poor a second look, otherwise the fees, dear, you'll never be able to afford the fees . . .

'Hmmm.' Mr Ashe rolled the grime on the writ into a tiny pellet. He knew what the girl was saying: she had no money. Here we go again. He shook his head. 'Mr Williams takes on too much as it is.'

'Five minutes would be enough.'

Five minutes is all you are likely to get, my girl, thought Mr Ashe.

'You'll have to wait. I can't promise I'll be able to fit you in.'

'We don't mind waiting, do we, William?'

William shook his head, and then regretted it. She had made him wear a collar that morning and his neck was rubbed raw. He didn't see why his sister had wanted him to come at all, but she had. She had come over all stubborn. 'I can't do it all on my own. Anyway, it concerns you as much as me.' He couldn't argue with that, and now he was sitting beside her in this cramped little office feeling like a chicken dressed for Christmas.

The door to Mr Williams' room opened and a family filed out: father, mother and four children in descending order of size. The two oldest children had their feet bound in rags, the little ones were better clothed, in cast-offs. They looked as thin as paper. Mary stared at the floor. That could be William and me, we could be like that soon. They filed past her and the baby began to whimper. When she looked up she saw the lawyer standing in his doorway, watching them go, his mouth bunched to one side as if he were thinking. He gave a sigh that was almost a whistle and turned back into his room, catching her eye as he did so.

Mary went bright pink and didn't know why.

With a pen, Mr Ashe was picking the dirt out of the cracks in the wood of his desk. He glanced at Mary as the colour died from her face.

'He's his own worst enemy,' he said. Mary wasn't sure if he were speaking to her or not; there was something unseemly in the confidence. 'Although it's no good my telling him. Take that lot, for instance.' He jerked his head after the departing group. His fingers ceased their picking and he leaned forward on the desk. The sleeves of his jacket were too short

for his arms. 'Take that lot. If we have one family
like that in here a week, we have half a dozen. But
Mr Williams just won't be told. Got a bee in his
bonnet about The Working Man. Says he must be
helped to better himself, given the opportunity . . .
But you can't help people like that. I mean, they just
can't be helped. There's the workhouse for them,
and that's all there is to it. But Mr Williams doesn't
see it like that. He'll give you an earful about
practical application of political beliefs and then rip
their bill in two. Next thing, an election comes round
and he's bellyaching about not having the funds to
fight a campaign properly. The man just won't be
told, though. You're in next,' he finished tartly, as
Mr Williams put his head around the door.

Mary rose and waited for William to get to his feet.

'The way I see it,' concluded Mr Ashe, 'is that
we're all working men in any case. I don't see why
he has to have such scruples.'

'Come in,' said a voice as Mary knocked on the
open door. Her hand groped for William behind her
as she walked into the solicitor's office.

He was seated at a table before the window and
Mary had to duck her head to see him better against
the light. He had a used face, with black and white
badger hair swept back from it. He was in his mid-
forties, confident, with a kind of blackened brilliance
about him, in his smile, in the squandered elegance
of his movement. There was experience of loss,
acknowledged waste, and resentful, continued hope
in the look that he gave her. He was rubbing his palm
along his jaw when they came in.

'Won't you sit down?' he said softly.

51

Mary sat, pulling William down with her and wondering what it was about authority that made one automatically feel guilty. Guilty before being charged.

Hugh watched the girl as she spread some papers on his desk. One glance at the handwriting and he knew what she had come about: another of Mr Evelyn's minnows, harpooned, caught, unhelpable. He watched the curving retraction of her body as she moved to point something out to him. Her features were as fresh as if the wind had only just blown them into place. Life with his elderly wife made the insides of his veins feel dry, in need of wetting, and here was this girl looking as if she had been newly picked in the garden that morning, with the moisture still on her. Hugh sat back in his chair, watching rather than listening as she talked. He noticed that the boy said nothing whatsoever.

When she had finished, he leaned forward in his chair.

'I'm afraid I've seen several cases like this in recent years. People are terribly fallible and your Mr Evelyn is a crook. Perfectly decent and above-board, but a crook all the same. He's got you in a corner and the law is quite content to let you stay there.' He leaned forward and his face loomed out of the light at them. Mary was rigid and inarticulate. William fumbled for her hand.

'What is your financial position? Can you afford his terms? I hate to be brutal, but they are probably the best that you will get.'

Brother and sister exchanged a look that was resigned and bleak, then Mary went rustling in her bag and pulled out a packet with some money in it.

'There's a little bit over fifty pounds here. It's what's left from the money Mr Evelyn originally gave our father. We have to pay to have the barn rebuilt. It won't leave much for buying up the lease.'

'Ah.' All the time that she was speaking, Hugh had been searching for a means of seeing her again, although he knew there was little he could do to help. Now he saw the glimmering of an opening. 'Ah . . . I might be of some use to you there.' Out of the light his smile flashed for a moment. 'Technically, as landlord, Mr Evelyn should be responsible for repairs. I see no reason why you should foot the bill for that. I can certainly look into it for you. That's not difficult at all.'

'Will it, er, will it be terribly expensive?' Mary hesitated, feeling her colour rise again.

'I shouldn't think so. Not in this case. I shouldn't think there would be a charge at all.'

Around the town it was murmured that Hugh Williams set himself up as a champion of the underdog because he was a vain man with a craving for people's admiration. It wouldn't help him to get a seat in Parliament, if that was what he was thinking, because it wasn't the poor who could vote him in. Politically his altruism was superfluous to requirements, so the Carmarthen gentry viewed it with suspicion. It never crossed their minds to take his philanthropy at face value, as an inclination that he simply couldn't help. He was known to be a Radical, a supporter of the Chartists. He believed that every man should have the right to vote – even the beaten poor! The Tories in Carmarthen shuddered at the thought of this and put it firmly from their minds. He would be better off cultivating his own kind. Why didn't he curry favour with his rich wife's friends, in spite of the fact that they were in trade? The Carmarthen gentry sneered at Mr Williams' conscience, and then took their custom to other, less contentious lawyers.

Hugh himself believed he had a burning sense of what was right, and that what was right was change of all kinds, but political change most of all. To effect this change it was necessary to win a seat in Parliament, and to do this he was expected to abandon those whose lot had inspired him in the first place in order to appease the people in the town who held wealth and influence. This conflict, and the evidence of his own eyes, made him bitter, and that, in turn, bred a defiant kindness in him: he never turned a case away, and he certainly never turned a pretty woman from his door.

'Where is the farm?' He fiddled with a pencil, wanting to make the girl talk. Beside her, her brother was looking at his boots.

'Near Efail-wen. It's called Dolwilym.'

'Efail-wen? Oh, really?' Hugh dropped his pencil and hunched forward with an interest which now went beyond the girl herself. 'Then you must have heard about the riot?'

'I'm sorry.' Mary shook her head and the boy looked up.

'Two nights ago. It must have been just near you.'

'We haven't heard anything at all. We're rather tucked away at home.' Mary looked at her brother for corroboration.

'Well, well, well. All hell is going to be let loose. Chap called Tom Rees, some sort of prize fighter, definitely a person to be reckoned with.'

'I know. He was a good friend of our father's.'

Hugh's interest in the Jenkins was increasing.

'Well. Your father's friend got himself all dressed up as a woman. Bit pointless really as it seems his ugly face is known in all the valleys round there. Anyway, in the name of Rebecca he smashed down the toll gate at Efail-wen. He had a bit of help, of course. They say two hundred men went along to lend a hand as well.'

Mary fought the sinking feeling in her stomach as she remembered her father stamping out of the house. *'Where are you going, Dada?' 'Politics.'* Maybe it was better that he wasn't here now. Would he have been one of those two hundred men? She didn't dare to think.

'Why do they bother to dress up? Who's "Rebecca"?' It was the first time William had spoken, although he had been studying Hugh's face intently for some moments.

'Well, practically speaking, it's a useful form of disguise against those who aren't in the know. And as for Rebecca, she's the Biblical justification for the operation. Proof that God is on their side. Something like that. There's a passage in Genesis about Rebecca's children breaking down the gates of their oppressors. Or so I believe. I haven't looked it up myself.'

Mary felt as if her stomach were falling away from her now. I must be very slow on the uptake, she thought. The verses from the Bible I wrote out for

Caleb Morris. Is he involved as well? The minister and her Dada? Was nothing safe? She gave a shiver and drew a breath with as much finality as she could muster. 'Would you see about the barn for us?'

'Of course.' Hugh knew that he would have to let them go. 'Have you thought how you will raise the other thirty pounds?'

Mary shook her head. 'I'll work. I'll think of something. Maybe he will let us pay in instalments. I don't know.'

'I'll see what I can do for you. I'm sorry – '

The girl was standing now. He shook her hand. Tiny wrists. Thin like a violin. He shook her brother's hand as well, and showed them to the door. He watched them go with the same bunched, thoughtful face that Mary had first seen. He was wondering how to get her back again; not just for his own sake, it might prove a kindness to her as well . . .

Hugh wrote a letter quicker than he had intended and quicker than Mary had expected. In it he said that Mr Evelyn would accept a down payment of fifty pounds with quarterly instalments of ten pounds each to make up the balance, including ground rent and interest. In the last paragraph he said he knew how difficult her situation must be, and that if she were interested in a position as companion to his wife, who was elderly and an invalid, would she care to be in touch?

Mary accepted his offer.

2

Mary put her signature to the document and William followed suit. They paid back to Mr Evelyn the money which, only months before, he had given to their father as part of the price of his land. Within days of the agreement being sealed, Evelyn's labourers appeared in the valley. They were all of them men whom Morgan had known once, some of them he had employed himself or at least shared a drink with, and Evelyn bought them for a couple of pence a day to do his dirty work for him. Soon, drystone walls, pale and new, lay like sloughed skin at the edges of Dolwilym, and viewed from her bedroom window it seemed to Mary that they were closing in around the house. The new tenants would not be far behind: five families, all of them strangers, making free with her valley. There was a tightness in Mary's stomach that would not go away.

As soon as the new walls were in place, the problem of what to do with all their livestock became pressing. She walked round the farm on her own for the whole of one afternoon, trying to decide who should go and who they could afford to keep with them. It was betraying old friends, and that night, when all the other work was done, she sat at the kitchen table and with callous pen and paper drew up a notice of sale: all the cows save two (the best milkers), all the sheep except the youngest eight, but the hens, which had always been her special concern, she could not bear to touch. Phoebe the mare would have to go, which would only leave them with the ageing gelding Jonah, because he was more used to pulling the cart. The plough could go as well: they were only allowed one field for cultivating. That, and the hayfield which fanned out at the end of the track along the valley floor. It was as if Mr Evelyn had tossed them a few bits of change that were not worthy of his attention, and for Mary and William it felt as if nothing was left for them at all.

Mary arranged her first visit to Mrs Williams so that it coincided with market day. She couldn't bear to sit at home and wait for William to come back and tell her who had been sold and for how much, or even that there was an old sheep or one of the goats that nobody could be bothered with. She wouldn't be able to bear that. And so she arranged her introduction to the solicitor's wife for the first Friday of the month, in the hope that it would make her forget that their livelihood, their dignity, almost everything that remained to them, was up for sale that day.

At the promise of a few pints when the job was done, Mike Bowen came over to help William drive the animals across the hills to Carmarthen. Mary surprised herself: she felt pleased to see him. Normally his big body and his huge smile filled any room to bursting point. He never stopped talking –

chat, gossip, tips for the dogfight, it all streamed out
of him without a pause for breath, and he was
incapable of sitting still. He would pick things up,
look at the bottom of them, see how they worked,
taste them if they were edible, weigh them in his
hand, fiddle. It drove Mary mad. Nothing was ever
in its proper place after he had come to call. But that
morning, watching his curly head bent over a second
breakfast which was quickly disappearing, Mary was
glad that he was there. He was kind, he knew the
trouble they were in, he knew what it meant. Before
he and William set off, he nipped out into the yard
and returned with a little curl of wool cut from one
of the Jacob sheep. He pressed it into her hand.

'There. Something to remember them by.'

It was a strange, sentimental gesture from a lad
who could be so brash. Mary put it carefully in her
pocket and then bundled the two of them out of the
kitchen so that they would not see the wretchedness
that she was feeling.

'Get along, the pair of you. Be careful of the money
when you get it – I don't want you stopping off on
the way home and spending it all. Have you got
enough for the tolls on the way there?'

But they were already gone, lost in a welter of
gentle protest from the animals, the crunching of
hooves on flint, and whistles and calls to one
another. The newest calf was the last to straggle its
way round the curve of the hill, and when it was out
of sight the valley seemed deadened, empty, utterly
finite. Mary couldn't wait to get out of it herself. She
saddled Jonah and as she rode up the twisting track
the air was full of the echoes of all the animals which

had once belonged to her. The arch which marked the entrance to Dolwilym seemed plundered, shrunken, and Mary felt its shame herself as she rode underneath it.

It was early summer and the lanes looked as if they had been ransacked; the hedgerows trailed their leaves and splashy flowers like underclothes and lace, and as Jonah trotted by them, the breeze continued to rummage amongst the greenery. By the time she reached Kidwelly, Mary was starting to feel nervous. The town was sandy-coloured and full of dust, beached around the castle in the middle. She had to stop and ask the way twice, because she wasn't really concentrating on the answer the first time. She was twenty minutes late when she dismounted outside a low, dark building tucked away in a side road off the main street. She saw that the old horse's legs were trembling and she rubbed her hands along his tired and hanging neck, buying time for herself as well.

When she knocked at the door it was answered by a local girl, plump and shiny, her delinquent flesh reined in under a white apron. She looked at Mary, her eyebrows raised and waiting.

'Yes, Miss?'

'My name's Mary Jenkins. I think Mrs Williams is expecting me. I've got an appointment with her.'

The maid held her ground and looked Mary over. 'She's waiting for you. She's in the parlour. You'd better follow me.'

'What shall I do about . . . ?' Mary still had Jonah's reins looped between her fingers.

'There's a ring at the far end of the wall.' The maid

stood with her hands on her hips and waited while Mary looked. 'Over there. By the gate.' She sighed as if Mary had done her some personal injury. 'All right?'

Indoors, the ceilings were low and the white-washed walls were peppered with must and faded prints. The maid took her to the end of the hall, announced her as if she were an oversight she had forgotten earlier, and then left her standing in the doorway. Mary peered uncertainly into the room. It was the parlour. The walls were tall and conifer green, and she felt as if she were stepping into the corner of a darkened box. All the furniture had clearly been designed for a larger space – a tallboy jockeyed for position with a violet Knowle sofa and the whole place was littered with tables and footstools and scuttles and screens. The curtains were fringed and festooned and dusty arrangements of dried grasses, fanning out of huge Chinese vases, formed part of the undergrowth. Amongst all of this, an oil lamp burned continuously and in the thick, yellow light that it shed Mary caught her first sight of Anne Williams.

She was a large, reddened woman packed into a wing chair which sprawled under her weight. Her hair was scanty and scraped into a bun which did not cover her scalp. It matched the iron grey of her spectacles, which in turn framed the iron grey of her eyes. Her face rolled over several chins into her ample body, which was splayed out beneath black silk. She was old, blowsy, and defeated by successive self-induced and unspecific illnesses.

She stared at Mary for several seconds and then nodded slowly.

'I see,' was all she said at first, and then at length, 'sit down.' She indicated the huge sofa and Mary lost herself in a corner of it. 'You're late, you know.'

'Yes. I'm most terribly sorry. I got rather lost.' The old woman's hostility put Mary on edge.

'Did you have far to come?' Anne had a strange, smacking way of talking, as though her tongue were cumbersome inside her mouth.

'No. Not very far.'

There was a silence. Mrs Williams picked at the shawl which was stretched tightly round her shoulders. Mary felt a kind of desperate anxiety.

'Not that it matters to me if you are late or not. To be honest with you, this idea has nothing to do with me. It was my husband's.' Her meaningful look was lost on Mary. 'I'm quite happy to manage as we are. Bethan, our maid, can cope with all that we need. But Hugh was insistent, and it is he who makes the decisions in this house.'

'Perhaps he thought you needed cheering up?'

Anne gave her a mirthless stare. 'Is that what you think?'

'I really have no idea.' Mary could not understand why the old lady was so intent on attacking her. She felt like some inept pawn that husband and wife were playing with, but the game was way above her head.

'And how do you propose to go about "cheering me up", as you call it?'

'It depends on what you're interested in. I thought that maybe we could sew together, or perhaps that I could read to you. Or maybe we could just talk. It's really up to you. The only reason that I'm here is to do what you want.'

The same cheerless stare was directed at her. 'What a green girl you are.' She fiddled with her shawl some more. 'You're not the first, you know. Don't think that. Hugh's done this many times to me before. I suppose I should expect it – he's so much younger than me, you see. There's more than twenty years between us. Does that shock you?'

Mary shook her head. She was beyond shock now.

'I know I should be grateful. I'm lucky to have a husband at all. No. I'll correct that. I'm lucky to have money. Because that is why I have a husband. The two are not unconnected.'

Mary would have given anything to stop these unwanted confidences. 'I thought it would make your position that much easier. Your knowing that I know, if you see what I mean,' Anne went on.

'Mrs Williams, I'm afraid there must be some dreadful misunderstanding. I've only met your husband once.'

Anne moved her gums against her lips and fiddled with a ring. Her fat, immobile face looked lost and sad for a moment. 'Oh, I understand perfectly,' she said softly. 'I wonder if you do.'

The door opened and Bethan bustled in. 'Tea, madam. Where shall I put the tray?'

'Leave it there.' Anne nodded at a table. Bethan gave a tight-lipped glance at Mary as she bustled out again.

'Will you pour? You'd better earn your money somehow.'

Mary poured two cups and longed for an escape.

'Do you play cards?' The words might have been slapped down in front of her.

'I used to play cribbage with Da — with my father.'

'Awful game. But I suppose it will have to do. I'm under strict instructions not to let you go until Hugh has spoken to you.'

Mary panicked even further. The price, whatever it turned out to be, was much too high. Obeying instructions, she found the cards and dealt them out. They played in silence for twenty minutes and Mary felt as if she were being watched the whole time.

The tea was cold and the bread and butter curling at the edges when Hugh came home. They could hear his voice in the hall, talking to Bethan and, by the time he walked into the parlour, Mary felt hot from her neck, down her spine, to the backs of her knees. She stood up when Hugh entered, but his smile was preoccupied as he motioned her to sit and went over to his wife and kissed her. He leaned over to look into the teapot, flicked out the tails of his coat and sat down between the two women. He looked at his watch.

'It's not really worth asking Bethan for more tea, is it?' he said.

Anne struggled to reach the bell rope. 'If that's what you want, I'll get her.'

'No, no, don't worry. It can wait.' There was a silence.

'Busy day,' Hugh said conversationally, crossing one leg over the other.

'It might have been for you,' said his wife.

Mary said nothing, but kept twisting at a fold of

her dress, down in the depths of the cushions where they wouldn't be able to see.

'Have you two been getting along well, then?' Judiciously, he addressed them both. Anne seemed to be torn between being sullen and trying to please.

'We played at cards,' was all that she could manage.

For a beat in time Mary felt sorry for her.

There was another silence.

'I think I will have some tea, if it's all the same to you,' said Hugh.

Bethan came and went, the swish of her apron and the distant ticking of a clock were the loudest noises in the room. Hugh looked from his wife to Mary. The violet colour of the sofa made the young girl seem soft and translucent in the darkness of the room. The yellow light from the lamp revealed Anne as plainly as if she were stuck on a pin beneath it, but Mary reflected back its glow and kept her secrets. He had a momentary desire to walk out of the room and leave them both together in its gluey quietness. Instead, he stood, picked up his cup and leaned against the mantelpiece. In spite of the suffocation of the heat from the fire he felt better standing up.

'I think there will be more trouble from our friend Rebecca,' he remarked.

'Whose friend?' Anne's head swung round accusingly.

'Miss Jenkins tells me that she lives near Efail-wen. There was a riot there a little while ago. Led by a – person,' he lingered on the word, 'who calls herself Rebecca. She and her gang took down the toll gate there.'

Anne grunted, reluctant to be mollified.

'You think there will be more trouble there, sir?'
It was the first time Mary had spoken. Hugh's dark,
supposing eyes rested on her as he answered.

'Almost certainly. Thomas Bullin has had a new
one put up in its place. He does that every time a
gate is wrecked. I think the Whitland Turnpike Trust
is asking for it.'

'I see.' Mary's fingers stopped working the material
of her dress. 'Oh dear,' she said.

'You and your brother will be all right. You must
be well out of harm's way on your farm.'

Mary dropped her head and longed once more to
get away, back home to her valley, back to Dolwilym.
Hugh must have read her mind.

'In fact, isn't it time you were setting off? With all
these brigands on the roads, it won't do for you to
be out too late.'

Mary looked at him gratefully.

'Oh don't worry, I can take care of myself.' She
glanced at Anne's pouting, waiting face. 'Mrs
Williams, is it all right if . . . ?'

'Go, go. Do what you want. It's nothing to do with
me.'

Mary looked uncertainly at Hugh and he nodded
towards the door.

'I'll see you out, Miss Jenkins.' He moved to his
wife's chair and tucked her rug around her knees.
'I won't be long, and then I'll ask Bethan to bring
you in your medicine.'

There was hunger in the look the old woman gave
him. Mary felt the same flash of sorrow for her again.
'Goodbye, then. See you soon, I hope,' she said
politely.

Hugh followed her into the hall and ran his fingers through his hair. 'Phew, it's hot in there,' he said.

Mary nodded without speaking. Hugh was watching her profile.

'Did she give you a hard time? I thought she might. She's very lonely here; she doesn't get about much. She feels her age so much these days.'

Mary was looking anywhere but at his eyes.

'I think it's her means of drawing attention to herself. She can be very demanding in that way. I expect she told you I have a string of women and that I neglect her dreadfully.'

Mary looked at the flagstones along the corridor and wondered how much work it took to keep them buffed so clean.

'Not true, of course.' Hugh turned some change over in his pocket. 'Not strictly true.' He looked at the captured strands of hair around her neck. 'Can you read and write?' he asked, as if a decision had been made. 'Stupid of me. Of course you can. A girl like you.'

Mary met his gaze cautiously. 'Yes, sir.'

'We're very busy at the office just now. We can always use some extra help there. General stuff – filing, writing letters, accounting. I'm busy on a case over at Llanidloes at the moment, and the work piles up when I'm away. If you find my wife a little overbearing, perhaps you might consider – of course, it's up to you . . .'

Mary looked at him more fully, a feeling of mistrust keen inside her, and then she remembered the bunched-up sadness in his face as he watched the pauper family leave his room in Carmarthen. She found him difficult to make out.

'I'd – I'd have to talk it over with my brother,' she began.

'Certainly. I only thought I'd mention it. It might cause a bit of a rumpus on account of your being a woman, but don't you find the idea of equality rather attractive?' His movements, as he spoke, were loose. His eyes suggested that it wasn't the aspect of equality about the suggestion which appealed to him. 'Maybe you could visit Anne once a week, and help me out at other times? It's up to you entirely.'

Mary felt a tiny glow of warmth light up her smile. New beginnings . . . She hadn't felt any warmth at all since the day that Morgan died, but still the caution was obstinate inside her.

'Well, it might be a help to us at the moment,' she hesitated.

Hugh's hand was on the door. 'Drop in on Monday if you like and we'll see what we can sort out. You can always change your mind if it doesn't suit.'

He ushered her out into the dusty evening, stayed while she mounted her horse and then watched as she rode off down the street. Closing the door behind him, he turned straight into the button-brightness of the maid's watchful gaze.

'Thank you, Bethan,' he said. 'My wife will be waiting for her medicine.'

Bethan brushed a speck of dust from her apron.

'Very good, sir,' she said with lowered eyes. Her skin was shiny in the half-light of the hall. 'I'll see to it directly. Will there be anything else, sir?'

Hugh shook his head and the hem of her skirt brushed his shoes as she walked past.

Mike Bowen and William were in high spirits as they clattered their way down Water Street and out of Carmarthen. Their pockets were stuffed full with money from the sale, comforting noisy coins, and that in itself was a pleasant feeling. The two of them were straddling Mike's fat white pony – Phoebe the mare had been sold that afternoon – and William was convulsed with laughter as he bounced around; only his arms round Mike's waist were keeping him from being thrown onto the cobbles. He was laughing from relief and because he couldn't help it, and the sound streamed out behind him so that people turned, raised their eyebrows and shook their heads as they went past.

Mike reined in the horse as they drew near the toll house; William was still panting slightly. Nobody appeared. They waited and the pony pulled peevishly against his bit. He wanted the journey to be over.

'Oy!' Mike cupped his hand round his mouth. 'Oy! Anybody home?'

There was a pause, and then the front door of the cramped house creaked open, and stringy Henry Thomas idled his way onto the street. His eyes and skin and clothes were all as brown as dirt.

'You lot must be running scared then,' said Mike with considerable bravado. William nudged him from behind.

'And what would you be meaning by that?' drawled Henry Thomas, with a malicious, smiling stare.

'Oh, I dunno.' Mike smoothed his pony's mane. 'People are saying that gate-keeping has become dangerous work these days.'

'Well, that just proves you didn't ought to go believing everything you hear, doesn't it?' Henry Thomas held out a grubby hand for the money.

'How much?' Mike knew full well how much it cost.

'Penny ha'penny. Come on, lad, don't mess me about.' The hand was thrust closer so that the grime rolled into the lines on his palm was clearly visible. Mike tossed the coins at him and one of them clinked onto the road.

Henry Thomas swore. 'You'll do that horse of yours serious damage riding it like that, you will. Two of you up on it at once.'

'Open the gate, will you? We haven't got all day.'

William tugged at Mike's jacket. 'Steady on,' he whispered.

With a malevolent slowness Henry Thomas ambled to open the gate. As they rode through Mike muttered something about the money-grubbers who worked for Thomas Bullin in a tone intended for all to hear. The gate slammed shut behind them making William jump, and looking back over his shoulder he saw the man's arm curve through the air in an arc of focused anger, and a nervous tug in his innards told him that the blow would find its target and be felt again in the time to come. It gave him a coldness round his shoulders that he couldn't shake off.

When Mary reached home that evening the light was dusting the hills and making them greener, and the farm seemed luminous in its valley. She unsaddled Jonah in the yard at the side of the house and they walked together down to the little hayfield at the end of the track. The old pony's muzzle was wet and careful at the back of her neck, and as he nudged her gently along the path she felt a quick beat of love for him because, with everything else that had gone, he was still hers. She led him into the field, closed the gate and leant on it for a while, watching as he flicked his tail, shifted his weight and waited for her to go with tolerant politeness. She strolled back through the dusk where the flowers were closed and pinkish in the fading light, and loved again the slate grey and silver of night time at Dolwilym.

William was back already, which surprised her, for she had expected him to take advantage of being in Carmarthen with money in his pocket. Mike Bowen had come back too, which would mean another mouth to feed . . . The two of them had a furtive air which she noticed as soon as she walked into the kitchen. The sale must have gone badly – she waited to be told.

'Thirty-odd pounds. Not bad, eh?' William handed her the money wrapped in smudged receipts. It felt very heavy in her hand. Abstractedly she thanked them both and went to the far end of the room to work out the accounts in peace.

'We won't be disturbing you here, will we?' Mike called over, but he didn't really wait for her reply.

William was right. The sale had realised almost forty pounds, a figure which Mary calculated would give them security for the next couple of years, if nothing else went wrong.

It would cover the shortfall on the lease, pay for the ground rent and leave them a few pounds to put by for an emergency. Meanwhile they would have to feed themselves with whatever they managed to raise on the farm, and eke this out with what she could earn helping out for Hugh Williams. Mary rested her cheek against her hand and wondered what her Dada would think. Would he mind her working in an office in the town, working for a man? Would he think it proper? Might he be pleased, even? She would never know. Maybe it was just as well.

And then there was the minister . . . She had all but given up her lessons with him. He said he had taught her all that he could, but she still went over from time to time to visit him, take him a hare and onion pie, make sure he was up to date with the dusting. Just for old times' sake, and to honour her Dada's arrangement with him. When Morgan died, the minister had promised to see about getting her work at the Chapel School. That had also been part of the original understanding. Sometimes she wondered how she was going to fit everything in . . . She gave a small and private sigh. If she went to work for Hugh Williams, and to sit with his wife, and to teach Sundays at the school, William would have to manage the farm all on his own.

She looked across the kitchen at him, chattering in whispers with Mike Bowen. There was something so tentative, so vulnerable about her brother that she felt raw inside herself. She hurt on his behalf, hurt for no good reason, simply in anticipation. His fair-haired, eager face looked anxious, bent in close to Mike's. You couldn't long to please that much and not be hurt . . . She watched them quietly for a little while, her pen held in her hand as if she were busy still with the accounts. The boys were lost to her, absorbed in their conversation, and after a time the sense of her being excluded grew quite strong.

She cleared her throat. They didn't notice. She shuffled the receipts into a tidy pile, but they remained oblivious. She coughed again and put her pen down with a snap on the table. Nothing. They kept on talking. It wasn't like William to shut her out so utterly. Everything he did was with reference to her – the clothes he chose to wear, the walks he took, most of the thoughts inside his head, the food he ate, everything. Yet here he was, hunched on his stool, turned away from her, apparently choosing to leave her out. She strained to hear what they were saying.

Mike was speaking in an animated whisper. 'I know you're tucked away here, but you can't be as clueless as all that. You must have heard of the Ceffyl Pren. Now that is a brilliant night out. All you need is for somebody to step out of line a bit, you know.' Mike sniggered and then whispered more quietly, 'Adulterers, informers, cheats, almost anything will do, then sometimes a whole village will turn out. I've only been on one, a few months back. A fellow was caught with his trousers down when they shouldn't have been and the woman's husband set the whole thing up. We all get togged up – girls' petticoats, the odd turban or bonnet, whatever comes to hand. Blacken our faces, then about midnight we all go round to this bloke's house, about forty or fifty of us, bang on the door, chap comes out and we bundle him onto this wooden horse cum hurdle. That's the Ceffyl Pren, you see. We make sure he's tied on good and proper, then he's carried through the streets to the Market Cross. There's nothing to beat it. It's absolute magic. The blokes at the back all firing guns, the horses scared and jumpy, but not half as scared as the man himself. We get to the Market Cross and he's propped up against it, completely helpless, then the woman's husband and some of the others put him through a sort of trial. That's punishment enough in itself. It was such a laugh. Bloke didn't know what had hit him. Then when all the fun is over, it's home the way we came and we pop him back into bed as if nothing had happened. Well, he's not going to say anything, is he?'

Mike looked round and Mary glanced down rapidly at her work, then up again equally as rapidly as he continued. 'There was another one a few weeks back. Man caught cheating and out comes the Ceffyl Pren. Only that time they didn't try him, they sold him at auction. Can't imagine he went for a very good price. I didn't hear about it till afterwards. Wish I'd been there. Worth travelling a few miles for, they are.'

'What's that got to do with Rebecca?' William's question came out almost as a breath.

'Well, it's the same kind of caper. Only they don't take the Ceffyl Pren out and it's the gate which is on trial, rather than a person, if you see what I mean. Same kind of do, though. All the lads get into petticoats, faces all blacked up, and one of them is chosen to be Rebecca for the night. Boy, now that is something to work towards. Off you all trot, get the business over with, and then vanish into the night. Nobody's any the wiser in the morning, so there's bugger all the magistrates can do about it.'

This was quite enough. Mary pursed her lips and then scraped her chair back loudly.

'Well, that's all sorted out. I expect you boys will be wanting some supper.' She moved in on them fast, determined to put a stop to the conversation. Mike Bowen was all very well and he had been kind to them that day, but she didn't want him exerting any dubious influence over William; innocent, easily-led William. Anything that would endanger William would endanger everything they had left. With a slight nod of his head, Mike changed the subject.

The three of them celebrated that night. William had brought back some mutton from the market which they set about roasting and Mary uncorked one of the few bottles of elderflower wine that her father had left untouched, to mark the occasion. As they chattered and drank she was aware that what they were toasting was the selling of their roots and their inheritance, but with an effort she pushed the thought from her mind. It became less of an effort as the night wore on; she sat back in her chair and let the warmth of the evening soften and relax her. For the first time since her father's death she felt at peace. She had done all that she could, she had traded and sacrificed and fought where possible, and now that it was over she had a sense of well-being. She looked up at her little brother, laughing at Mike and swinging back on his chair, and for the first time felt a tentative confidence that the old cycle of death and loss and fear was beginning to give way, and that maybe there was room for hope.

'Over my dead body,' said Mr Ashe, his shiny white hands tightening into fists against the seams of his trousers.

Unperturbed, Hugh continued writing up a court report.

'I'm sure it isn't my place to say so, Mr Williams, but it's against my conscience not to. You simply cannot have a woman working in an office. It's unheard of. It's indecent. You'll lose custom, you mark my words. You'll lose clients if you go ahead with this. I don't like to think what people will say around the town. Even your Chartist friends won't approve of this step.'

Hugh laid his pen down neatly, reached for his blotter, and without looking up he said, 'I don't believe I'm doing it to gain approval.'

'Just as well,' spurted Mr Ashe under his breath. He gave a pursed little sniff. 'As to how it will affect my position here . . .' he said in martyred tones.

'It will affect your position here as much or as little as you let it. I am engaging Miss Jenkins for several reasons. Firstly, if we can keep even one family out of the workhouse then we are doing society a service, although society may not see it that way. Secondly, you may have noticed that many of our clients are often in an extremely distressed condition and a sympathetic female touch might be an immense asset in such situations. And lastly, I don't see why a woman shouldn't do the work if she is capable.' For the first time Hugh looked his clerk in the eye. 'And I have no doubt that Miss Jenkins is perfectly capable. I'm sure she'll do the job just as well as you.'

'I can only say, sir,' Mr Ashe was finding that he could, indeed, only just say it, 'that I hope you won't start complaining when what is left of your business disappears elsewhere. Your charity cases cause enough trouble as it is.'

'My dear Ashe, if we lose custom over a little thing like this, then I feel certain that it is custom we are better off without. Will that be all?'

Mary looked on anxiously as Ashe, the balding clerk at Mr Williams' office, making his disapproval extremely plain, moved a pile of files off a table, clearing a small space for her to work in. It was a niggardly gesture – better not to have done it at all, she thought – but he returned to his place at the window with the air of having done his bit and therefore being obliged to do nothing further. By and large this was a stance he maintained all the time that Mary worked there, unbending occasionally to emit a small 'tut tut' about something which particularly rankled. Otherwise he took care to make it amply clear that he knew his place, and that whether she knew hers was none of his concern.

The office had a maroon frontage with gold lettering stencilled on the door. Mary was intimidated by the sight of it, and so the realisation of how dilapidated the rooms inside were came as a relief. The leather seats of the chairs were cracked and split, and the polish on the floors was thinning to sandy blond in places. There were files everywhere: paper files, cardboard files, dusty files, files which were bulging to the point of animation. They were stacked on the floor, on seats, on the tops of the glass-fronted bookshelves, and you couldn't hope to move without dislodging something. Gingerly Hugh showed her around, and everywhere he turned there was a constant reminder of work to be done. He perched at her table, working his way through the day's mail. Letter after letter was opened and thrown to one side, then filed away and lost for weeks at a time in a tray marked 'Pending'.

'It's all to do with the Llanidloes case. That's why it's so bad at the moment. It's not normally like this,' Hugh said in a tone which suggested that it was precisely like this all the time.

'What's the Llanidloes case?' Mary felt she should show an interest. And anyway, she was more comfortable when he was busy talking, it was easier to ignore the studied fluidity of his movement, and the unfamiliar edge that he had. She was acutely aware that he was watching her, and that Mr Ashe, the clerk, was watching Hugh watching her, looking for the situation's secret, looking for the key to its significance.

'It's all to do with the magistrates – it always is. If they went out searching for trouble they could not be more effective. There's been a lot of tension in Llanidloes, as there is everywhere these days, so what do they go and do? Instead of keeping a low profile and showing a bit of sense, they go and swear in a mass of Special Constables. It's madness: a stupid thing to do. So several Chartist activists within the town arm themselves and storm the Trewython Arms

Hotel where the constables are billeted. They sack the place, loot it, and throw the new policemen out. What's more, they managed to hold their position there for a week, and even declared the town a Chartist stronghold. You've got to hand it to them . . . But I suppose it couldn't last. The Government put Lord Clive onto it and his troops overpowered the rebels and threw forty of them into prison. These are the men I am hoping to defend. It's not an easy job.'

'I see.' Mary nodded.

'I have a lot of sympathy with the Chartist cause, so this case is particularly important to me.'

Mary didn't really know what he was talking about although she knew his reputation as a Radical. Best not to get involved in all of that. Politics. She could feel herself tightening up inside.

'What is it you would like me to do then?'

'Sorry? Oh. Well, you could start by sorting through this lot — ' he gestured at the letters. 'Put them into their appropriate folders. They might take some finding, I'm afraid. Then we've got a man coming in at eleven who had a scrap with Henry Thomas, refused to pay the toll at the Water Street gate. We need to take a statement from him. Perhaps you could make some preliminary notes? If you run into any difficulties, don't be afraid to ask.'

He stood up as he spoke, collected a sheaf of papers from Ashe's desk and went back to his own room. Mary smiled as he passed her with the same anxious pliancy that she had so often noticed in her brother, and feeling rather as if she were on the run, she sat down in the scrimpy clearing that Mr

Ashe had made for her and began her first day's work for Hugh.

Back in the inner office Hugh came to a decision. He sat with his eyes closed listening to the hum of Mary's voice as she and Ashe were talking. There was no edge to it at all, only sweetness, so it carried badly. He had to close his eyes and concentrate to hear it at all. In front of him on his desk was a book. His own book. A collection of verses called 'National Songs and Poetical Pieces'. One of the men arrested at Llanidloes had been taken into custody solely because a copy of a poem by Hugh had been found in his pocket. *The Horn of Liberty*. That in itself was enough to make him a subversive. Hugh smiled at the thought and opened his eyes. He flipped through the offending poem.

''Tis time that the victims of Labour and care
Should reap for reward what is labour's fair share;
'Tis time that their voices in council be heard
The rather than pay for the law of the sword.'

It seemed harmless enough to him; he couldn't see what all the fuss was about himself, although he was flattered nonetheless. That wasn't the point though. The point was, he was going to seek out Mary's brother and lend the book to him. He closed the pages softly, feeling cynical about himself. Would he be accused of using the boy? And was it misuse, when shy, reserved William was plainly ripe for the picking? Is it wrong to take from people what they are keen to offer anyway? Hugh had a sneaking suspicion that in some cases it was, but he pushed the thought away. He looked back at the only time they'd met. At how, when the subject of Rebecca came up, he'd been aware of the lad's eyes watching him, studying him, hanging on his words. He had the leafy, tentative eyes of his sister . . .

Hugh put the book of poems in his pocket and fell to justifying himself once more. It wasn't only because William had her air about him, her caution, the same light swinging of his elbows as he walked; it wasn't just that. The lad had the makings of a political animal as well, he looked suggestible, and that could be very useful. Hugh was going to give him the anthology because it provided an opportunity to sound him out, to ask him more about Rebecca, find out how much he really knew. He wanted to be involved, Hugh was sure of that, and if he wasn't already it was only a matter of time . . . Soon there wouldn't be a young man in the county who hadn't climbed into a stolen petticoat and gone out gate-breaking, even if it were only once. He couldn't believe that William would prove an exception to that rule.

Hugh chewed at the skin on the inside of his lip. All that he wanted was a bridge, a link; he wanted to scatter his ideas amongst Rebecca's sons and daughters so that when they ceased to be her children any longer and had gained political maturity, he would be there to garner, to welcome, to employ . . . But to do that he needed to establish contact with them from the first, and he intended to make William his key. He had no qualms about that — opportunism was a part of politics, that wasn't where his guilt lay. It lay in the fact that he

planned to encourage the boy's political interest as
a means of gaining further access to his sister. There
was something unacceptable in that. He shook his
head bitterly. But there was also something
unacceptable, unbearable even, in the way he was
beginning to burn for Mary. He was fearful that the
quiet, determined flame which fed him now would
one day come to scorch him.

It was ten o'clock at night. In the centre of the
kitchen table William's bundle stood ready. William
himself was jumpy, unable to sit for more than five
minutes at a time. The creak of a door in the yard,
the crack of a flexing branch, the soft flick of a moth
against the window, anything, and he would be up,
out of the house, scanning the rim of the valley. The
flooding rate of his pulse made the blood drain from
his head, leaving him giddy. Everything depended
on Mary coming home late. His luck had held this far
but each long minute made his chances slimmer. And
then he heard, thought he heard, yes, heard, the
seductive crunch of hoof on gravel. He grabbed the
clothes from the table and raced out into the yard.
What if it were his sister? Quick with the bundle into
the bushes. Crouching low he could hear his breath,
furtive and echoey, filling the hollow between his
knees. A short whistle slit the silence. He waited for
a second one. There it was. Out of the bushes,
running close to the ground, along the fringes of the
lawn and to the track beyond. Horse and rider eerie
and luminous in the half-light, a flickering projection
amongst the trees.

'Here, give us your clothes.'

The small bundle was handed up and hooked to the front of the saddle.

'There was a meeting at Glynsaithmaen. They said you can come, but you must keep your mouth shut.'

Mike's tone was abrupt and he spoke with the false superiority of an inexperienced 'old hand'.

'You can sling your clothes on when we meet the others. Best not to be ready too early, just in case.' He looked at William more closely. 'Idiot. You haven't done your face.' William's cheeks shone as palely as the tremulous moon. Mike rubbed his hands against his own and smeared the younger boy's face with transferred soot.

'Get up behind me.' He wheeled the horse around as William jumped and scrambled to get on.

'We'd better go the back way. Mary could be home at any minute.'

And the horse dissolved slowly into the darkened woods.

A quarter of an hour later Mary slipped like a stone from Jonah's back. The slow rhythm of the ride had had a lulling effect, gently rocking the day's stress from her, leaving her with nothing but dead tiredness. Hugh pressed her to come home for supper with him and Anne, and, longing for her own kitchen, Mary had been unable to refuse. He was her employer; to her the invitation sounded like an instruction.

It was not an easy evening. Anne pointedly refused to join them at the dining table but ate her meal from a tray on her lap. Bethan the maid was tart with the visitor and showed a new solicitousness to her mistress, deftly realigning her position as she saw fit. As the evening wore on, small drifts of silence began to build up, insulating thought, and at length even Hugh seemed to tire. Mary left shortly after nine and rode home with a heavy feeling of peacefulness. She lingered on the little track that wound down to Dolwilym and loved the shadowy lack of sound in the yard at night. It meant home and bed to her. She was stiff from the ride and took slow pleasure in stabling Jonah and giving him his feed, knowing that the same ease was waiting for her in the house. She paused for a while, where the moist warmth of his box mixed with the night air in an eddy of different smells – his sweat, her own, and the scent of the wood in the darkness. She liked the feel of the rust and the dust and the grime of the stable door beneath her hands, and she let the weight of her chin rest on them as she watched the horse. A moment taken and enjoyed.

Turning at last, she noticed that the kitchen door was open and the room unlit. Inside, she knocked a cup over trying to light a candle. William had left restlessness and disorder behind him – a meal not cleared away, a chair thrust back from the table. There was a feeling of abruptness in the room which was unfamiliar. Although she knew he could not be in the house, she called up anyway, mostly out of irritation. There was no reply and she set about trying to tidy things away.

The clock on the church tower had said a quarter to eleven. Even as she wondered where he could possibly be at such a late hour, she guessed the answer and felt piqued. Out with Mike Bowen, drinking maybe, not caring to stay at home to listen to the news about her first day. Sometimes she felt he wronged her. Her mouth was small with worry as she banged out of the house and into the yard in order to draw water to wash and clear up his mess. Tight-lipped, she pumped the handle and the water leapt into the pail, splashing, like her anger, round the dark outbuildings.

Mary sat in her chair for hours, a sense of injury and principle keeping her awake. For a while she worked on the mending, continuing the wistful process of sorting through clothes which had belonged to her father to see if they could be altered to fit his son. It was an economy which saddened her, dulling the edge of feeling. After a while the candle began to gutter and she sat quite still, her hands at rest in her lap, watching the shadows convulse along the plastered wall. Her head started to swivel on her shoulders as she drifted in and out of sleep. The noise of hooves in her dreams became the noise of voices in the darkness outside. The chord of a laugh was stifled, the kitchen door swung open and Mary lurched awake.

William stood uncertainly on the threshold. As they looked at one another, the beating sound of a departing horse marked out the silence between them. She could see that he was drunk, he had the look of their Dada about him; he was sweating slightly and the soot was damp and uneasy on his flushed cheeks. An old petticoat of hers that she had put aside for mending swung brassily from his hips, his jerkin had spilled open, and in the midst of all her rage she saw his pulse hammering apology at the base of his throat. He took a swaying step towards her, with the smile of a man who knows he has been caught out.

'Sit down,' said Mary icily.

His mouth working, William floundered in the petticoat like a drowning man, his boots trampling on the lapping edges of the lace. He fumbled with the drawstring and at length the skirt slithered to the ground and he dropped back into a chair, defeated.

'Now.' Mary felt that to keep control of herself was as much as she could hope for. Tolerance, understanding, humour – they were all out of the question. Her brother was no better than a felon. 'Now. Perhaps you can explain yourself.'

''S late,' said William, his eyes sliding hopefully towards the door.

'I'm well aware of that. I've been sitting up waiting for you. Worrying. Wondering what on earth could have happened to you. You don't have to tell me how late it is.'

'Sorry.' William made as if to move, but his wrist skidded against the chair arm, causing him to slump again.

'And you needn't think you can disappear off to bed just like that. Not before you've given me a proper explanation. And not before you've apologised.'

'Keep your hair on, Mary.' Before he'd got the words out, he saw that making light of the business wasn't going to work. 'I've just been out with the lads, that's all. Out with Mike Bowen. No harm in that, is there? Just having a bit of fun, that's all.'

Stingingly Mary scooped her petticoat from under his boots.

'Yes?' she snapped, waiting.

'Oh. That. Well . . .' She saw him glance uncomfortably at the door once again. 'That was only a bit of a lark. Nothing . . .'

'You've been out with Rebecca, haven't you?' Somewhere underneath the exhaustion and the anger there was a sad note in Mary's voice.

'Yes, well . . . There you are.' He shrugged and ran his hand through his hair, streaking the soot on his forehead.

Mary sat in her chair nursing the rolled-up petticoat to her chest.

'What have you done?' she whispered.

'It was nothing, Mary, honest. We just had a go at some gate or other, just took a few swipes at it. That's all.' For a moment he felt bile rise in his throat, and thought he might be sick. He hiccoughed with alarm, and then relief. His sister was shaking her head.

'I thought better of you. Really, I did.'

'Oh come off it, Mary. You've grumbled about the tolls as much as the next person.' He felt burned by her contempt as she turned to face him.

'Grumbling is one thing. It's all right to make a complaint in a proper, decent manner. Going out rioting at night is something different altogether. That's law-breaking. Only ruffians behave like that. I thought better of you. I really did.'

'They're not ruffians. They're just ordinary people like me and Mike Bowen –'

'Yes, and Tom Rees, and the minister too, I

wouldn't be surprised. Fine example he'd be setting.'

'All we did was sing a few songs, have a few drinks and take the gate down. Then it's tidy home to bed and nobody that matters is any the wiser. Where's the harm in that? Don't see what the fuss is about.'

'You'll see,' said Mary bitterly. 'You'll see. One day.'

This time William managed to stand. Unsteadily he felt his way round the table to touch his sister's shoulder.

'It's in the Bible, Mary. Like that solicitor said. You can't get more just than that, now can you? The dressing-up is only to make it a bit special. We're not ruffians, Mary. Honest, we're not. You've got to fight for what you want these days, that's all. Nothing comes easy – we both know that.'

'Yes.' Her voice was bruised with disillusion. 'We both know that.' She stood up and, with a kind of profligate defiance, dropped the petticoat into the dying fire so that lace and flame billowed up together in the grate. William stared at her, appalled by her lack of thrift.

'Don't ever do it again, will you?' Mary said quietly. 'Ever.'

The door closed behind her, leaving a gulf between them which had never been so wide.

3

After that July night when Tom Rees had led the burning of the gate at Efail-wen, and William and Mike Bowen had followed in his wake, Rebecca disappeared into the valleys with the same speed and secrecy that she had ridden out of them. The lady was silent for nearly three years, and during this time the gates she had demolished were repaired or replaced. Between brother and sister nothing more was said, and Mary chose to assume that William had ceased his night-time activity on her account. She did not know that the loyalty which Rebecca demanded was absolute and that William did not repeat his venture simply because he had not been requested to do so. The gate at Efail-wen had been destroyed three times in all, and one at Maes-gwyn nearby had been burnt to the ground as well. The threat had been made, and for the time being no further action was required, so the night-riders hung up their petticoats for two and a half years.

Mary had been lucky when she was small. Trying to teach a child the reading and the writing was no easy matter as the poorest families were obliged to keep their children at work in the fields or down the mines, which didn't leave much time for going to class. Some had a few hurried lessons at Madam Bevan's charity school when it stopped off in the neighbourhood, but it never stayed long enough to do any real good. After a short period of pointless cramming, it moved off to the next dark and smoky hut in a parish at the other end of Carmarthenshire, leaving, only half-interested and half-taught, the scanty number of children who had appeared. There was always the Sunday School, where you turned up smudged and shiny from the weekly bath, with a warning glare from your Dada to behave, or else. The brighter children, or the show-offs, were able haltingly to read aloud some verses from the Bible; the rest had to learn them by rote. Of a class of sometimes eighty children, up to half of them could write their names, the A B C, the days of the week, and usually an impressively large number of rude words.

But Mary had been lucky; she had been keen to read, she liked the stories that she heard in class, the Old Testament in particular, and besides, the Bible was the only book her Dada had at home. She used to stay behind on Sundays for help with words that she found hard, words she had underlined in pencil so as not to spoil the book, and Caleb Morris had been pleased to help her: it was a change to see a child who was not rushing around to the back of Chapel for an illicit game of jacks . . . He had been pleased to help her then, and happy to teach her properly when Morgan came to him with his plan. And the same soft spot he had for Mary, together with the duty he felt towards her poor dead father, meant that he put himself out to secure her a place as assistant mistress at the Chapel School when she had been fully taught herself.

So at the same time that she was struggling to find her feet as a helper at Hugh's office, under the watchful, annotative stare of Mr Ashe, she spent Sundays teaching the under-sevens in St Clears all about Moses and Elijah and how to write their names in capital letters. And amongst all this, when she had time to stop and think, she found the path her life was taking unexpected and incongruous, as if it were out of her hands.

The master of the little school was Mr Phillips. He frightened Mary to death because he'd been to university and therefore must know everything there was to know about anything. She could see that the job bored him, all the same. What he was really waiting for was a curate's appointment. He told her this the first morning she arrived, anxious to make his place in the scheme of things quite clear to her. Loftily he scooped up the juniors and moved to the end of the room which had both the stove and the only window in it, leaving Mary to manage the infants in a tight ring of semi-darkness. She began uncertainly, telling the children all the stories she had loved when she was little, about David and Jonathan, Abraham and Isaac, and Ruth standing amongst the corn. All the time she could hear Mr Phillips rattling through his lessons at a speed which left her breathless. Her own class hardly made a sound at all.

Except one.

Harry Howell. He was trouble from the start, like

the rest of his family. Both his big brothers had wrought havoc in the Chapel School in their day.

One Sunday late in October 1842, Harry Howell was being particularly trying. As soon as he sauntered into the room, Mary could see that he was looking for trouble. She was trying to teach her children the names of the Apostles, but Harry was having none of it. He started in on her straight away. 'Miss, Miss, just a minute, please, Miss.'

'Matthew, Mark, Luke and John,' chanted the other children. She could hear the bravado in Harry's voice; he must be on a dare, she thought.

'What is it, Harry Howell?' Mary could be sparing with her attention.

'Miss, me brother Thomas says I'm to ask you a question.' The little black bullet of a head was bobbing and cocky.

'If you'll stand up properly when you're talking to me, I'll do my best to answer you.'

Harry got to his feet and stood with his legs apart, looking seventeen instead of seven. He gave a glance towards the back of the class where his real audience were, and then he began. 'Well. The other night Thomas was having a scrap with me Mam, see, about the new gate that's been put up at the Mermaid. He said that we should put our faith in God and in Rebecca and then we should see justice done, and me Mam shouted back that the only justice Rebecca would give him would be to see him hanged for his trouble.' Harry was warming to his tale. 'And then she said that he and me other brother David were never to mention that name in her house again, especially not in front of us little ones.' A shuffle of delight ran round the classroom; Harry's diversion was going better than they had hoped.

'When things had calmed down a bit I asked Thomas who the Rebecca lady was, and he said that she was doing God's work helping out the poor, and that any honest churchman in Carmarthen would say that she was right. So I said, "Would our Sunday School teacher say so?" And he said, "You ask her and see," and so I'm asking.'

Mary's heart was beating with an anger that stretched back over the three years Rebecca had lain low. She was aware of every separate eye upon her.

'Now you listen to me, Harry, and all you others. Your Mam was right. Rebecca is not a name which anyone would want to hear spoken in their home, and certainly not in the house of the Lord. What she stands for is wrong: men taking the law into their own hands and showing no respect for people or property. God teaches us that we must love each other, and to strike out violently, like Rebecca does, is no way to show that love.' She looked intently at Harry and hoped she had taken the wind out of his sails.

'I wouldn't want to be associated with Rebecca because the people who involve themselves with her are evil and thoughtless. You should all of you feel the same. I don't want to hear the subject talked about again.'

Mary shook with indignation for minutes after she had finished, but when she thought about it later on she felt glad that she had spoken. It had been a shock to hear Rebecca's name because she thought that the issue was dead and buried, but if children at the school were talking about it, then the Lord only knew what their families were saying, or what they were plotting now. During the next few days she watched her brother carefully, but he never gave a sign.

Her work at the Chapel School stopped being an anxiety to her when she got used to it, and soon it became a pleasure instead, but it was her involvement with Hugh Williams and his wife which preoccupied her time and thoughts. Anne was slow in showing even a basic civility towards her. She remained on the defensive for months, guarding the empty fortress of her husband's affection and exploiting the peculiar liberty which her bulk and her immobility gave her. She behaved like a woman who had nothing to lose.

Hugh, on the other hand, made it clear that he had all the time in the world for Mary. There was never a moment when he wasn't busy, especially when the Llanidloes case was on, but she used to look forward to the afternoons when Mr Ashe would fidget his way out of the office and leave the two of them alone. Hugh would put aside what he was working on in order to explain things to her, to show the responsibility of the lawyer's position in a system where a prisoner was not allowed to be heard in his own defence. He took her through the ins and outs of the Turnpike Laws, as more and more of their work consisted of representing defaulters who could or would not pay the tolls they were asked for.

Mary was flattered by his attention, but when he used the examination of a file or the looking up of a reference as an excuse to stand too close she turned away, embarrassed. It amused Hugh to play a waiting game. He liked the *frisson* that her pretty presence gave him, welcomed the suggestiveness that the situation sometimes permitted, and enjoyed the lovely curve of her neck where it entered her blouse. She was an adornment in his life, the taste of pleasure in a working day, but he had other things to think of, although sometimes he had to remind himself of this.

William took to collecting Mary from work whenever he was able, and seemed keen to hang about waiting in Hugh's office and she felt guilty that she was unable to take this new solicitousness at face value. Hugh was happy to encourage William's presence. Occasionally she felt like a jealous wife as she studied her brother when he was unaware of her. She could not stop suspecting his allegiance to Rebecca, nor could she understand why it threatened her so. It must be fear of loss – of losing out, of losing him. And so she watched and waited; but nevertheless she was completely unprepared for the news which a twitching Mr Ashe brought into the office one morning.

'Mercy on us, it's started again.' He took his coat off and hung it behind the door, adjusting the folds and smoothing the line of it in a way that had come to drive Mary mad.

'What's the matter, Mr Ashe?' she asked, not knowing whether to expect a minor domestic drama or a renewal of the wars with France, and, if she were honest, not caring to hear the answer.

'The burning of the gates. Didn't you know? I would have thought that everybody knew by now.

The new gate at the Mermaid came down last night. It had only been in place five weeks. If it's not one thing it's another, these days.'

Her thoughts staccato, Mary went through the events of the previous evening in her mind. William had been at home the whole time. Indeed, he had been demonstrably useful, fixing the back of a broken chair, and he had been specially affectionate when he came to say goodnight to her. Nor had anything been untoward when she had woken him in time for the milking that morning.

She felt too puzzled to be relieved. When she asked Hugh if he had heard the news, he looked at her, and with a slight, ambiguous movement of his head, said nothing. Later, with William, it was the same; he even met her gaze as he shrugged his shoulders and said that he had heard a few mutterings but had written it off as just talk.

It made her feel disorientated to have apparently got things so wrong. She was further baffled when Mr Ashe, who rather surprisingly seemed to have his ear to the ground in this matter, said that two further gates had gone down at Trevaughan and Pwll Trap. There was something in her gut telling her not to trust the situation, yet William's behaviour continued to be flawless and sunny, so that her suspicions were complicated by a sense of guilt. She could not dispel either of these feelings, but dared not talk to her brother. Her watching continued.

'I'll pick you up this evening if you like.' William pushed his chair back from the kitchen table to tie up a boot-lace. His head was bent and his fair hair flopped over his face. He often didn't look at her these days.

'There's no need.' In spite of herself Mary felt the muscles at the back of her neck go tense and alert. She cleared the breakfast bowls away.

'No, I will. I'd like to. I've got to come into Carmarthen anyway, so I might as well.'

'What for? What have you got to come into Carmarthen for?'

'Oh, odds and ends. I said I'd drop in some material for Hugh. He has this idea of designing a flag.'

'Oh, Hugh, is it now? You're very friendly all of a sudden.' The words came almost unbidden.

'Not really.' William was patient. 'It's just that I've been to a couple of his meetings, he's lent me some books . . .' All the same he couldn't look his sister in the eye.

'What meetings?'

'For the Chartists. That's what the flag is for. He thinks it might help to have a rallying point for the groups, a kind of symbol, or something.'

Mary walked deliberately round the end of the table and stood where William couldn't avoid her face.

'What's going on? I think I have a right to know.'

'Nothing. Nothing's going on.'

'Then why can't I trust you any more?'

'I don't know. You tell me.' William never got angry, he only ever became sullen.

'You're always off somewhere, out with Mike Bowen, out at meetings. You're so secretive. You never tell me anything.'

'Mary, it's because there is nothing to tell. Yes, I

see Mike sometimes, and yes, I go to meetings. They interest me. I like Hugh. He's a man with good ideas.'

'I hadn't realised you were so close, that's all.'

'We're not so close. I see him when I come in to visit you. It's nothing more than that.'

'Is that why you come in to see me?'

'Don't, Mary, please . . .'

'I suppose it's politics, is it?' Mary just couldn't let go. 'You, Dada maybe as well, everybody. You're all the same.'

'Well, it's not always politics, actually.'

'What then?' Mary knew she was being unreasonable, and the knowledge drove her on.

'I'm just living my own life. Is that all right with you?' He was standing straight now, grey eyes glaring into hers. 'Now, do you want me to call for you tonight or not?'

'Don't bother.' Mary stalked angrily out of the kitchen. 'I don't want to interfere with your precious life, after all.' The words made her feel miserable all day.

However William did appear at the office in the late afternoon. He carried three large parcels which he propped on Mr Ashe's desk while he asked if Hugh was busy. When he walked past Mary and in to the inner room he hardly gave her a nod.

She found the first excuse that she could to go in after him. The two men had their heads bent over a diagram. Hugh looked up and smiled, but everything was unacceptable to her that day.

'Your brother is very kindly helping me with a little extra-curricular activity.'

'Yes. I see.' She was polite and measured.

'I want to design a flag for some of the Working Men's Associations round here, to see if I can't get them interested in the People's Charter. What do you think of green, white and blue? Do you think they go well together? I thought green for the earth, blue for the sky —'

'Could you sign these for me?' Mary placed some sheets of paper on his desk.

'Look, William,' Hugh's eyes were on the boy's sister as he spoke. He could see that something was wrong. 'Look, can I leave the cutting to you? I've written down the dimensions there, and I've co-opted some of the wives to tackle the sewing at the weekend. I would help you myself, only I have things to attend to . . .'

'Is Friday night still on?' Reluctantly William was gathering his things together. He was aware that it was his sister who was really driving him from the room.

'Friday? I don't see why not. It rather depends if Mary can bear to sit with my wife.' Hugh turned to her appealingly, 'There's a meeting at Pontypool . . .'

'I expect so. I'll have to see.' It was the most that she could muster.

'All right, then. I'll see you there. I'll try and have the cutting finished.' William slid the heavy parcels off the desk. He did not say goodbye to Mary.

Hugh signed the letters as if he were unaware of the atmosphere.

'He's a good lad, your brother. He's done a lot of things for me lately.'

There was no reply. Mary felt she couldn't speak. She felt cold, clamped up, excluded. 'What are the meetings about?' she said at last. 'The ones that you and my brother go to. Are they to do with Rebecca?'

'Rebecca? No, no. Well, only in so far as everybody seems to be talking about the gates these days. Why? Do you think William – ?'

There was a long silence. Mary felt culpability settling about her. 'Sometimes he worries me. I don't know what to think . . .' This wasn't strictly true. She occupied herself with pushing back the skin around her nails, waiting for Hugh's response. There was so much she felt she needed to know.

'I wouldn't worry about William. He can take care of himself.' The boy's cautious, diffident face flashed across Hugh's mind, making him wonder for a moment how true that glib statement was. 'It's time he was his own man, you see. Maybe you should give him a bit more rope to play with. If he chooses to go and hang himself at the end of it, well . . .'

'That's easy to say.'

'I know. I'm sorry. I wouldn't go having sleepless nights about him, though. If he is caught up with the Rebecca lot he won't come to any harm. A few thrills and spills might do him some good. They're terribly secretive. There's no chance of any of them getting caught . . .'

'You sound as if you think it's a good idea.' Mary looked at Hugh without comprehension.

'Well, in some ways I do.'

'But they're breaking the law.'

'Yes,' his face had that bunched-up, thoughtful look that it often wore.

'I give up, I really do. You of all people. If you condone actions like Rebecca's – the gate-breaking, the rioting – then we will soon be living in a world that is only governed by violence. I don't like the conditions we have to live in any more than the next person, but I'm not stupid. Even I can see that there must be better ways of changing things than by taking the law into your own hands. I'm sorry –' she broke off. 'It's because I'm angry with William, and frightened for him too. I shouldn't talk to you like this.'

For once Hugh kept his distance. 'How would you change things, then?'

'Oh, don't ask me. I don't know. I'm just –'

Hugh gave her a slow, logical smile. 'The People's Charter. That's how to change things. That's what the meetings are about.' He pulled a chair up for her. 'You see, the only way to change things is to change the law. I know you'll think I'm bound to say that because I work with the law, but it's true. And to change the law you must first change the law-makers. It's as simple as that. Change Parliament, or, if you can't do that, at least change the way that men are voted into it.'

Mary looked extremely doubtful. If William was interested in this then she really didn't know him at all. 'Is that what your Charter is about?'

'Exactly.' Now he leaned forward. Mary could smell the oil that he used in his hair. 'Six main points really: every adult man should have the vote; all the electoral districts should be the same size; we should have voting by ballot so that a man is free from pressure; annual Parliaments . . . It's all common sense. If we got rid of the MP's property qualification and paid them a proper wage it would mean we would have poor men as well as rich in the House. It's bound to make it more representative like that.'

Mary's face was a blank, she was thinking of her brother.

'There's nothing so terrible in what I've said, is there? Nothing so awfully subversive?' Hugh lifted his shoulders lightly. 'I quite agree with you. Violence isn't the answer and I hope I would never do anything which would suggest I support it as a means to an end. But within that context I will do all I can to be of service to Rebecca. Apart from anything else, her strength is useful. She is the most potent means of awakening some kind of political awareness in the ordinary people round here, and although I wouldn't go so far as to ride with Rebecca-ites out of their valleys at night, I hope that I might be one of the people they turn to when they have lost their direction. So in that case I suppose we are all in it together. I wouldn't have it any other way.'

Mary sat still for a moment, before she stood up and pushed her chair back. She felt out of her depth and a little raw. She wished she had never brought the subject up. Better to have said nothing, to have backed off and left well alone. She felt as if her brother were lost to her, in some other life, taken up by interests in which she had no part – taken up by Hugh. As she picked up the papers from his desk, Hugh touched her wrist. It felt sensible and restrained under her woollen sleeve. His touch was swift; her moving away was quicker.

'Are you all right, Mary? You are upset, aren't you?'

'It's nothing.' She straightened the papers in her

hand. 'I will do Friday for you, with your wife.' A too-bright smile and she was gone. Hugh frowned and toyed with his pen for a while, and then returned to work. He wanted to write a speech to give at the Working Men's Association when he presented them with their flag. 'A banner with colours as predominant as Equal Rights are universal . . .'

Mary rode back to Dolwilym that evening in a glum and solitary mood. It wasn't just because of the rift with William, she knew she was upset because she fell so far short of her own expectations, and the act of falling hurt her badly. She felt as if she were floundering in a world which didn't make her welcome, and was overcome by the need to struggle back to where the limitations were known and familiar. But she had lost the old world on her way, and now it seemed they wouldn't let her back inside. That was the trouble, really.

There was a certain mulishness in Mary's decision to go to the fair at Narberth on her own. The message from William was quite clear: he wanted liberty from her, so she did not even ask him if he wanted to come. Instead, crisply crucifying her feelings of loneliness, she rode Jonah off into the silvery December afternoon. A huddle of tents and booths lay like pleated cloth round the edge of the little town. Some of them were full of cold, angular men and women looking for work as the new season began, but most of them were given over to the sports and competitions and curios which still gave Mary the same thrill that used to attach her to her father's smock as if she were a fifth limb, as he towed her from sight to smell to sound when she was a small child.

She had the same feeling now, as, grown and alone, she went from tent to tent. The first flap of dark blue canvas which she lifted revealed twenty or thirty straining male faces, shaky in the light cast by half a dozen rusty hurricane lamps; it was the boxing. In the tiny central area two men sparred with one another. Their skin was greased and unfamiliar to Mary, who had only ever seen strange glimpses of her father or William naked, preparing to wash. The first blow which found its mark made her want to bolt outside at once, but she was held in the crude doorway for a second longer than she knew was proper. It was the rhythm of gasped breaths and thudding bone which caught her pulse into its own and kept her there, watching.

A man with a black and red face and an accent she didn't know called to her across the group, 'Come on, lass, make yer mind up. Are yer stopping or not? If ye are, it'll cost yer tuppence, if yer not it's us'll lose. Either way will yer stop letting the cold air in?'

Mary needed no further urging. With a start of embarrassment she let the tent flap fall behind her. Back in the night she hunted for the warmth and light of a brazier, and for a farthing she bought a buff bag of chestnuts and a place by the fire while she ate them. The nuts inside were soft and yellow like a mouse's brain between her blue fingers. The thought made her lose her taste for them, so she gave the rest to one of the children who were always drawn to the fair, belonging nowhere and to nobody. At the far end of the enclosure two men were putting the finishing touches to a makeshift stage. They swung a few planks between barrels of beer which were greenish and empty, held in the loose embrace of the iron hoops around them. Disenchanted and damp with winter effort, one of the men climbed up, tested their stability and, with a godforsaken look at his assistant, began his patter.

'Roll up, roll up, ladies and gentlemen. What 'ave you come to – er – come to . . . ? Oy, Wilfred –'

Wilfred obliged: 'Narberth.'

'What 'ave you come to Narberth to see? Is it the boxing? Most certainly not. Or the waxworks? I doubt it. Or the cock-fight? No. What you have come to Narberth to see is something you won't find in yer local, you won't find it down the High Street, you won't see it any old day of the week. Because what you 'ave come to Narberth to see could well be described as one of the wonders of the modern world –'

The pitch of the man's voice rose with anxiety as the size of the crowd that he was drawing made it clear that the good people of Narberth had indeed turned out to see the boxing, the waxworks and the cock-fight.

'I am asking you now, what 'ave you come to Narberth to see? Is it a man? Is it a woman? Nah, it's both! In a matter of minutes, and for the price of a mere –' he broke off. Wilfred had been assessing their chances and whispered up accordingly.

' – ha'penny, you can see one of the strangest sights that nature has to offer. Never before in Wales will you 'ave 'ad the hopportunity to see –' a big, dramatic pause ensued. People talked through it.

'*A lady wiv a beard!*'

The bearded lady was a regular figure of the Narberth fair. She was a devalued, dumpy woman with crêpe hair stuck messily to overcrowded cheeks and was usually drunk by the time she came to do her act. During the maudlin song with which she began, men made bets as to whether she would avoid falling off the stage in the shuffling dance which followed. Once she had a dog which sat up and begged, holding a cap for coppers between his teeth. Now even he had gone on to better things.

Mary turned away; she wanted something to show for her visit, a proof of her independence to take home to William, and she had given away her chestnuts. She wandered over to the coconut shy and in return for the remainder of her small change secured a pile of rough wooden balls to throw. Her first three shots were loose and the balls fell short, rolling along the muddy grass for the last few inches. The men watching made mocking noises with their tongues against their teeth. The fourth one hit the post and was then deflected to the canvas at the back. The fifth one she threw with more force than thought and it ended its flight with a sharp rap on the coconut itself but the prize refused to fall.

A man's voice close behind her whispered, 'Most of them are nailed in place anyway. Have a go at the one on the end. I've already given it a good loosening myself.'

In her concentration Mary did not turn but hurled the ball as directed. The shot went wide and she looked round.

'Bad luck,' the man said, with a minimal smile. He

had a serious face, thin and pointed, its angles barely smoothed over by pale white skin. His eyes were brown and sombre, with brows to match. It was a sad, fine face that Mary saw. She smiled encouragingly. 'Never mind, eh?'

'If it's a prize you're after, then you can have this. It's no use to me.' Looking away, he pushed something small and spiky towards her and she began to back away uncertainly.

'I don't mean anything by it. I won it for my girl, but it seems we're not talking now . . .' He held it towards her again. It looked like a pin cushion.

'It's no use to me. You might as well have it. I'd rather it went to you than her. She's got her hands plenty full enough tonight. Go on, take it, it won't bite you.'

Mary's smile returned, with more warmth than before. She held out her hand and took the little scrap of a heart, made of red corduroy with pins stuck furiously into it.

'It says "True Love". That's what those pins say. It makes me sick.' He turned, glad to be shot of the thing.

'Don't take on so,' Mary began, but he moved further away. 'It's a nice pin cushion. It's very kind of you.' He looked at her again, half-staying, half-going. 'You really don't want it? I'm sure you'll make it up with your girl, then you'll be sorry not to have it to give to her.'

'I doubt it. Not this time.' His tone was bitter. 'That doesn't matter anyway. I'd still rather you had it – I'm sorry, I don't know your name.'

'Mary, Mary Jenkins.'

'Mary, then. I'd rather you had it, Mary.'

She smiled and ducked her head in embarrassment.

'Thank you – '

'Jac. Jac Tŷ Isha.'

'Jac.' He smiled and then she did.

'Jac.'

They were silent for a moment. Mary tucked the prickly heart into the pocket of her skirt.

'I must be getting home now. It's dark, it's late. I've got quite a way to go,' she said.

'How are you travelling?'

'My horse is over there.' She indicated Jonah, who was guzzling his way around the sapling that he was tied to.

'I'll walk you over.' He loosened the tether and helped Mary into the saddle.

'Thank you, Jac. I hope you get things sorted out between you now.'

He shrugged, looked over his shoulder and then back at her. 'Which way are you riding?'

'Out beyond Efail-wen.' The vagueness, the instinct for privacy, made no sense to her.

'You take care now. There are some nasty characters around these days.'

'Oh, I'll take care. Goodbye, now.'

Jonah ambled off, glad to be going home at last. As they rounded the corner Mary looked over her shoulder. Jac Tŷ Isha was half turned away from her and she followed his stricken gaze to the far end of the fair. The bearded lady was heaving herself into motion and in the little knot of people in front of her one couple stood out particularly; the dark girl on tiptoe, whispering, the staunch boy bemused. This little portrait of betrayal made Mary feel oddly upset herself; in her pocket the spurned present of the spurned lover pinked against her leg, the rebuff lodged finally with her.

It was not fear but a wish for company which made her trail loosely in the wake of a family returning from the fair. Including the baby there were seven of them piled into the ramshackle cart, the father and the eldest son up front driving, the other five whining, writhing and chattering in the back. They made so much noise that Mary did not notice the first round of gunfire which rattled through the thicket to the left of the road ahead; if Jonah heard it he did not seem to mind. In the cart the children continued to scream, the mother vainly trying to entertain them with a song.

At first the plume of smoke ahead was no bigger than the trailing wisp from a cottage fire, but as they drew nearer it thickened and filled out beneath the blanket of cloud which flattened the sky above. It had the acrid, sterile smell of fire which burns to destroy, and not to warm. Mary drew level with the family and as they rounded a crook in the road all of them had their first sight of the flames themselves; forty yards ahead of them the toll gate was burning like a child's farmyard toy. On the far side in a swirl of falling ash and cinders and smoke, Mary could just make out half a dozen riders galloping in the direction of Carmarthen like some grim carousel out of control. As many men remained on the near side of the gate.

Mary felt as if all her blood were draining through her neck and into her stomach. She felt sick and swallowed convulsively, the rough, searing air hurting her throat. Next to her, various members of the family set up a wail which the biblical Rebecca herself might have heard. The mother was hauling children onto her massive lap, while the father, in a hail of oaths punctuated with orders to remain calm, began the complicated manoeuvre of trying to make the frightened pony turn the trap around. Thus they were in a clumsy broadside in the road when the Rebecca-ites first noticed them. The night riders stopped slashing at what was left of the gate and with their blood chasing the scent of the quarry, thundered towards the little group.

They brought the heat of the fire with them; it rose like steam out of the petticoats which billowed along the horses' backs, and ran in sweat down their riders' blackened faces. Most of all it burned with unleashed whiteness in their eyes. Mary was paralysed, her thoughts racing in a frenzy which made movement impossible. One of the horsemen swerved towards her and seized Jonah by the bridle, and it was then that she began to scream. The man swung her half out of the saddle as he slammed a hand across her mouth and then shook her long and violently as if she too were a piece of wooden gate which could be burned or smashed. There was blood in her mouth, and some distant, other Mary wondered if the man was going to break her neck. She could not tug any breath at all into her body, so intent did her attacker seem to be on pushing her face into some dark central part of her skull.

She felt broken open by his brutality, and the

detached other self heard a distant voice saying, 'Hey, give over, she's only a little thing.'

'I can see that. But she's making more noise than the rest of that lot put together.'

'Look you now, we've been told not to hurt anybody, least of all a woman. Will you leave her be?'

'If you want every Special Constable from here to the coast raised, then that's your business, Ewan Jones.'

'Quiet there,' a third voice intervened. 'There's to be no mentioning of names. Let the girl go.'

Mary was slung back into the saddle and slumped over Jonah's indignant neck. Blood was collecting in the back of her throat, making her retch. She was shaking all over.

The third voice was still speaking. 'Our quarrel is not with any of you. In fact, it is on your behalf that we have taken up this fight. By the end of the evening every Whitland gate round St Clears and between here and Carmarthen will be down. In return for our services, all that we ask is for you to donate what you would normally pay in tolls to cover our costs in this expedition.'

The man allocated to Mary yanked at Jonah's bridle, startling the old horse and forcing Mary to draw herself weakly upright.

'Once this is done we will detain you no longer.' There was menace now in the third man's voice.

'That'll be a penny ha'penny from you, missie.'

Mary flinched as her man spoke, and replied in a voice which was thick with fear and blood, 'I have no money. I spent it all at the fair.' She was appalled as the man put his own hands into her pockets to test her word. He brought out the pin cushion heart, looked at it, laughed, and then flipped it into the mud where it lay, its rejection complete.

'Well, what will you be offering us instead, missie?'

The driver of the trap piped up, his voice conciliatory and tremulous. 'I've only got a sixpenny piece. You keep the change. It will pay for the girl as well.'

Mary caught her first ordinary breath. The exchange was completed and as the Rebecca-ites rode after their fellows, two men on the fringes of the group fired their guns into the air in salutation. Mary's man blew a kiss in her direction and she burst into tears.

The driver and his wife assisted her, still crying, down from her horse. As the man went to hitch Jonah to the back of the cart, his wife helped her up amongst the children, who were all crying as helplessly as she was. The woman was shaken herself, but was kindly to Mary.

'There we are, *'nghariad i*, it's all over. It wasn't so bad, anyway.' She scrutinised her carefully. 'Come along now, it wasn't as bad as that.'

Mary and all the children disagreed.

'What's it cost us? A sixpenny piece and a cut lip. That's not so much to pay now, is it?' The woman became more businesslike, for her own sake as much as for the others'. 'Now, *merch i*. Will you look after the little one for me?' A tiny, sobbing boy was deposited in Mary's lap. 'We'll be taking you home, of course. You are in no fit state to travel on your own, tonight.' Mary held the child as if it were her

112

own and as the great orchestration of sobs subsided the cart creaked slowly on its way through the night to Dolwilym.

'Have I to come in with you now, and see you safely into your own bed?' Mrs Pryce offered as the cart covered the last few yards down to the farm. The light from a candle burned, smugly, snugly in the kitchen.

'It's very kind of you, but my brother is home. He'll be able to help me with what I need. I don't want to trouble you any further.'

'Well, I'll just be putting your horse into the stable and then we'll be on our way.' Mr Pryce jumped to the ground.

Mary did not know how to thank them enough, and leaned weakly against the jamb of the door while the rickety cart with its rickety bundles on board negotiated the yard and laboured up the hill and out of sight. With a final wave she went indoors and straight to her room. She wanted to wipe the crusting blood and spit from round her mouth, to purge away the taste of her assault. She sat on the edge of her bed, her shoulders bowed with tiredness. She unpeeled her shawl. There was blood round the neck of it. She dropped it on the floor with vague distaste and, in an unfocused state, undid some of the buttons on her dress.

William. She needed him now more than she could ever remember needing him. She called his name, but there was no reply. With uncertain steps she went to his end of the landing and repeated her call. Again there was no reply. She scratched on his door and pushed it open. She could see his body making

113

its habitual ridge down the centre of the bed. The room was half-full of moonlight and Mary was unsure whether to wake him. She touched his shoulder indecisively with her hand and it gave way completely beneath her. Pulling back the patchwork cover Mary was jeered at by the bolster underneath. The bed was empty; William was out riding the night with her attackers.

Four silent, bruised days passed as quietly as if nothing had happened. Skimming through the *Carmarthen Journal*, Mary saw an article which made the newspaper scorch between her fingers.

'. . . The leaders of the mob were disfigured by painting their faces in various colours, wearing horsehair beards and women's clothes. We understand that these depredators had patrols in every direction, preventing all travellers from proceeding on their journeys during the time that the demolition was going on . . .

'On this day the Narberth fair was also held, and the mob stopped all drovers coming in the direction of Carmarthen and levied a contribution from them, stating that they had destroyed all the toll gates and that therefore they had no tolls to pay.'

She sat very still, a tide of evocation sweeping through her thoughts, and though memory was sharper than print could ever be, she tore out the clipping and buried it far out of sight in her mother's black oak chest. It was a testament to her ordeal and she had continually to resist the urge to take it out, re-read it and re-live it, and to absorb it whole. It bore witness to the fear which surged at her out of the quiet moments of each day. Every man she saw – running through the cold with rag-bound feet, pushing against the hot body of a girl in a hard and public embrace, haggling . . . drinking . . . spitting – she put on trial inside her head, but nowhere could she find the burning eyes, the guilty voice and the big black hands which had held her.

Mary did not tell William what had happened to her, or how much she knew. She was tired of confrontation; she did not want even that intimacy between them any more. Although it had bled a lot, the cut on her mouth was not large and quickly hardened into a crumpled bluish badge upon her lip. This she wore with the same unreckoning dignity with which hundreds of Welsh women bore the scars that Welsh men inflicted upon them in their anger. People did not refer to such things.

Only Hugh noticed it; Mary white and hollow in his office, Mary with the injury to her spirit painted across her whiteness with the same gaudy colour that her split lip was splashed across her pretty face. The desire and the tenderness which he had felt the first day he saw her, which she had diffused with the sexless friendship that she offered him, and which daily contact had made commonplace anyway, suddenly flared inside him and stormed back. He could not bear to see her, her leafy bloom lost, so pinched and jumpy and so hurt. He wanted to put his lips to her wound, to know what rough arms had so abused her, and to hold her in more gentle ones. Instead, he remained on the far side of his desk, writing, working, seemingly unnoticing, lost in thoughts of gentle quiet Mary

115

being brutalised by a lover that he didn't know about.

Mr Ashe came in twittering, busy with news, and shattered the peace.

'What a to-do there is in the town today; quite a little crowd outside the Blue Boar. That's where they'll be staying, you see. I expect they will have their headquarters there too. Well, it would make sense, wouldn't it?' Once again he had a monopoly on the news.

'Haven't you heard?' he asked their blank faces, sure in the knowledge that they had not. 'The Home Office has sent a police inspector and two constables down from Bow Street in London, on account of the troubles. Well, after all the business at Narberth, and then the Mermaid gate going down again two nights ago, the magistrate here has been in a state of unholy panic – messages, reports, pleas for help flying off in all directions. And at last he's got what he wanted: a few professionals on the job.'

The dark flicker in the back of Mary's eyes at this announcement would have given Hugh the clue that he was looking for, but he was busy working out the consequences of the news for his own interests.

Inside, Mary felt only despair. She knew that she should feel comforted. The authorities were beginning to take the situation seriously, something might actually be done to contain Rebecca's vileness, and yet the arrival of the opposition made the continuation of the conflict inevitable. She sighed from the bottom of her heart. It was as if the lines of battle were only just being drawn up.

4

Timothy Powell was giddy with relief. He had been chosen as magistrate because of his social accomplishments rather than any legal or administrative ability, and had been quite content to potter his way through stray bits of parish business, swear in a special constable or two, examine a few accounts and turn up at the odd poacher's trial. Moreover his work was extremely lucrative, particularly in connection with the Turnpike Trust, of which he was both trustee and accountant, and he was able to demand high fees elsewhere.

No fee, however fat, would ever give him the same gratification that he felt at the arrival of George Martin and his men. The worry and irritation that had kept him awake at nights since the rioting began evaporated at a stroke. After all, he had done his duty, assessed the situation locally and responded as he thought fit: by smartly passing the responsibility on to somebody else. Not just any old person, mind, but men from the new police force, trained as professionals in keeping law and order. Relief sparked an unusual flurry of activity in Timothy

Powell, so that with petulance and stronger pressures he bullied his way around the county, until he had rustled up fifty-four men to act as special constables under the London policemen. Now he had the situation well in hand, Rebecca would not dare even to squeak in the face of such strength and efficiency from the authorities.

Mary was right. Those sad Christmas days in 1842 saw the tension, tight as a cheesewire, humming in the air as the two sides flexed their muscles and made their different preparations. Christmas Day was as sparse as she could remember, both in terms of food and festivity but, more importantly, in the affection and warmth between her and her brother. It was as if the love between them had dribbled away. Their walk to the Chapel was silent and bitter, and instead of the customary hugs and kisses amongst them and their friends after the service, William and five or six other men stood darkly in the doorway, talking, talking. The rift between them, so public now, embarrassed Mary, for she felt strangely jilted. Yet looking around the fragmented congregation she thought that some of the women's faces bore the same marks as her own; these wives, mothers, and sometimes sisters, were all washed up on the tide of men's passion, which ebbed away to some other shore, leaving them bleached and dry at the high-water mark, always wanting.

Mary welcomed the New Year with apprehension; each year that passed seemed to take so much comfort, affection and hope away and she did not want to let another one slip too easily through her fingers, for fear that all which was left would go with it. For years now she had felt as if she had been flying in the face of threat: emotional, economic, and now with the outbreak of the rioting the threat was physical as well. She wondered how close she could get to having nothing in her life before she ceased to have a life at all. Thank God for Hugh; he helped her when he could, sometimes without realising that he was helping at all, even if it was only that to him she was not simply provider or preventer, that for him she was more than the creature of subsistence that she sometimes felt herself to be. He liked her to be in the office, she knew that; he preferred it to the artificial intimacy of those occasional, difficult evenings when she had been looking after Anne and he came home to find them both together. What confounded her were those silent, unacknowledged moments when she felt his breath on her neck or her cheek, the intimacy of his eyes. She hated that. It wasn't right: he was married, and she was embarrassed, and that was all there was to be said.

That New Year's Eve, Thomas Lewis paid his usual call. Looking at his round and gingered face, Mary found herself thinking of him more in terms of the family doctor than as the family friend he once had been. He had come over very little since the day that Morgan died, but before that, when he was living up the road with his mother at Llanboidy and working at his studies, he had been round all the time. Morgan had liked to think he showed a special interest in Mary and had been confident that, one day, Thomas would be his son-in-law, certain that he followed her round the kitchen with his eyes – a doctor was a useful man to have in a family. You couldn't argue with that. But he was qualified now, his sandy hair was thinner than it used to be, and his visits were less frequent. He brought her a pair of gloves from Cardiff; thick, sensible brown leather gloves. He had never given her anything before and, as he watched her pull them from their wrapping, he rather wished he hadn't now. But what was a man to do? Nothing had been said between them, ever, but recently he had spent long hours worrying over what might have been thought and what had certainly been the hope of Morgan's heart.

He cleared his throat. 'They're a kind of parting present, I suppose. I think that's what you give. Gloves. Isn't it?'

Mary nodded and hoped that he would leave it at that. He was rubbing one palm against the other, anxious to do the right thing. Or just anxious.

'I think it is, Thomas. Yes,' she said quietly.

'You see, I won't be able to come like this again. I'm getting married.' She watched him rubbing the moisture from his palms, sorry for his discomfiture. 'I'll be leaving mother in Llanboidy, and setting up with Katherine in Carmarthen. I hope to be able to work there. Of course, we'd like to stay in touch, but you know how these things are.' He ceased his rubbing and dared a bland, uneasy smile. 'No hard feelings, eh, Mary?'

'No, Thomas, no hard feelings.' Mary turned the gloves over and then laid one upon the other, thinking: I don't know how these things are; how could I? 'I hope you'll both be very happy,' she said.

At that moment William came bursting into the kitchen. He must have known that Thomas would be coming, because it was long-established habit, and yet, after giving him a nod of minimal politeness, he said bluntly to his sister, 'You shouldn't have cooked for me as well. I'm going out.'

Thomas started rattling change in his pocket, his unease deepening. Mary looked at the table, all brightly laid, with holly in the middle.

'But it's New Year's Eve and Thomas has come over specially.'

'Well, I can't help that. I'm sorry, Thomas, I've got some business to attend to and it won't keep.'

Thomas nodded and laughed, the coins in his pocket clinking uncomfortably.

'William, please – ' Mary began, but already he was turning to go.

'Happy New Year, then, William.' Thomas's forlorn round face had a pinkness that was not festive. William closed the door on them both without returning the good wish.

She gestured to Thomas to sit. 'I'm so sorry. He's going through rather a bad patch at the moment . . .'

'Oh, I know old William. He doesn't mean any harm.' His bluffness lacked conviction. 'Well, what about you, Mary? You've heard my news, now what about you? What kind of a patch are you going through?'

'Oh, Thomas, the same as ever, really. You know me, nothing ever changes.' Especially loss. Loss is the most constant thing of all, loss of face, even this new loss of an old suitor. 'The farm, well, Dolwilym, has got so small now I find I have time on my hands. I'm keeping quite busy with Mr Williams though.'

'I'm not sure it's a good idea for a woman to be

working in an office, Mary. I don't think I would be wanting any wife of mine – ' he broke off, appalled. 'I'm sorry. You must do what you think best. It's not my business.'

'It's all right, Thomas. You know how it is. We have to live as best we can.'

The evening was hardly a success; a straggle of merrymakers passed through the darkness along the rim of the valley and strains of their songs filtered through the shutters making the room melancholy. For the first time ever, Thomas left well before midnight.

'I hope this year is a happy one for you, Mary. You look as if you need it.'

He kissed her hand, a new formality which Mary found oddly touching, and was gone.

She did not see William until the following evening. He had been busy, and bent on his defiance all day. Eventually she could not help herself, could not bite back the words.

'You didn't have to be rude last night on top of everything else. Poor Thomas. How could you do that to him? I don't know what has got into you. No. That's not true. I do know. I do know exactly what has got into you – '

William flashed round at her and she saw the sadness in his face. 'I don't like the situation between us any more than you do. But it's not just of my making, you know. Haven't you heard of the word principle, Mary? Don't you even know what it means? It means making a stand for something you believe in. You're so wrapped up in your own self-righteous, private little world that you don't see past the end of your own nose. I'm not particularly brave and I'm not bright, and I'm not strong. But open your eyes for once, Mary, and watch me. I'm going out of that door now, to fight in the only way that I can, for the only thing that I really believe in. And you can just watch me go, Mary, and think what you like.' He wiped his sleeve across his face, fettered with frustration.

Mary began, very tentatively, 'William, you don't understand –' but his look stopped her.

'No, I don't understand. I probably don't. But it's not just me, is it? There's not a lot of understanding goes on round here.' And with that he went out, bitterly, into the night.

She expected to hear the stable door being flung open and the patient, logical whinnying of Jonah's protest, but no sound came and the night was quieter than ever. She peered through the window. The yard was milky and cold, skimmed with frost. William stood at the pump, his head bowed under an icy stream of water which trailed fine streaks of silver across the opening of his smock. Mary could feel the coldness on her own skin as she watched, knowing that it was her he was washing away.

'Just watch me, Mary . . .' and she was watching . . . At last William shook the water from him, scrubbing his face dry on a petticoat that she recognised as hers, that was snatched from a bundle on the grass. She looked away wearily, she had seen enough; but as she looked away she almost jumped out of her skin, for she found herself staring straight into the eyes of a second watcher; a man on a horse, which was grey and skittish, half-hidden in the dark folds of the trees and the lane. She strained to remember the thin pale-boned face but instead saw only the gun slung across his saddle.

'Is it you, William Jenkins?' The whisper was lighter than air. William's head snapped up in acknowledgement.

'I must saddle my horse. I didn't realise the time.'

'We're late already. You had best get up behind me.'

She could see that William wanted to argue, preferring to be his own pilot in the matter, but the man made a sharp gesture of dismissal and held out his hand to hoist the boy up behind him. The agitation of the horse and the independent spirit of William's voluminous bundle made the operation unnecessarily complicated. The animal was outraged by its added load and gave Mary some satisfaction to think that at least the wrong-doers would have a difficult and uncomfortable ride that night.

Mary turned into the room with an almost physical distaste for herself. She felt restless with fractured anger, the kitchen was too small to contain her and all the feeling that was inside her. She wanted to kick the furniture, her mother's furniture, to crack and break and scar . . . *'Watch me, Mary, just watch me . . .'* She could still hear the irregular clatter of the horse's hooves outside; they crunched in her head with William's words, *'Open your eyes for once, and watch me, Mary . . .'* until she could not stand still any longer. She wrenched the door open and ran across the yard; Jonah looked at her in disbelief, but she saddled him up with a speed which was startling, pausing only to hunt out a jerkin for herself, for it was very cold.

Within minutes they were off. The same compulsion which drove Mary to open the black oak chest, smooth out the rumpled piece of newspaper which told of the Narberth attack and read it through and through, now drove her into the night in pursuit of Rebecca. It was a kind of pornography to her, irresistible, furtive, wrong. By keeping the two in front within earshot she could manage to gauge where they were going. She dreaded catching up with them and was careful to hold Jonah back, something he was deeply grateful for as he laboured through the blackness.

The two men were headed for St Clears and as they drew nearer to the town the trees receded from the road, leaving only a few matted hedges for Mary's protection. It was a clear night, the sky was jostling with stars and Mary felt as if the moon were shining only on her, it shed such brightness.

It was an almost impossible equation, to keep the springy horse in sight without giving away her own presence. Once she lost them completely, for they left the lane altogether and several minutes passed before she saw the dark figure of the horse and its riders pressed against the hillside like a Bronze Age silhouette which the night had brought to life. She reined Jonah in for a moment. They probably were not going to St Clears after all; if they were cutting across the fields like that they were probably headed for Pwll Trap. She thought quickly. If she was to follow their path exactly she risked them becoming aware that she was shadowing them, and yet she was not sure if she could trust her assumption and race on to Pwll Trap in the hope of rediscovering them there. She scanned the hillside again: the horse was barely discernible now, picking its way along the hedge at the far side. Yet if she and Jonah were to follow them there, his huge lumbering greyness would light up the escarpment like a flare torch. Better to take a chance, act on her intuition and go the long way round. They would have to be quick though.

Mary gave him a sharp kick; she wanted a speedy canter over the remaining mile to the village. Jonah had more of an evening stroll in mind and eventually they compromised on a rolling, rumbling trot. She kept looking behind her, to where their paths had diverged, but the other horse had disappeared from sight. Suddenly Jonah stiffened, his loose joints locking as first one bundle then another sailed over the hedge to their right and landed on the road in front of them. He shied violently and then with a snort recovered his dignity as two figures pushed and scraped and scratched their way through the clutching twigs.

One of them made as if to quieten Jonah, while the other hissed, 'Didn't you hear? We're on foot tonight. Don't want to draw attention to ourselves –'

But the one who was closest to her silenced him with a clip across the shoulder, saying in tones layered with meaning, 'Evening, missie. You're out late tonight.'

Mary shook slightly with remembered fear but kept her voice as even as she could. 'I've been visiting my auntie – she was taken ill. You know how one thing leads to another; I couldn't get away. I'm that tired now, I'm just wanting to get home to my bed.'

They were as anxious to get rid of her as she was of them.

'You shouldn't be hanging around here at this time of night, lady. You don't know what you might get mixed up in. I should get along now if I were you, and mind you keep your eyes on the road.'

Was it a veiled threat? She did not wish to find out, but spurred Jonah on, the men engaged in heated argument behind her, punctuated by two soft thuds as their bundles were lobbed into the field on the other side. She was soon beyond their reach, moving as fast as she dared until the first straggling houses of Pwll Trap came into view. She made straight for the inn at the centre of the village, thinking she could leave poor Jonah tethered in the yard at the back without attracting too much notice. The usually silent streets were thronged with knots of people; she must have passed six or seven huddled groups. As she rode up, expectant faces turned towards her, only to be quickly hidden as she passed by. People were talking amongst themselves, occasionally splintering away from group to group, and Mary wondered how long it would be before they all conspired to head her off. She disappeared into the inn yard before this could be deemed necessary. There was stabling of a kind at the back: three loose boxes and in the corner a general dumping area where a dog cart was stored amongst odd pieces of flotsam and jetsam – a broken wheel, a chimney pot, some firewood. Mary looped Jonah's reins through a ring in the stable wall, hoping to goodness that he would stay quietly. She stood uncertainly by him for a moment, his head was heavy and wet with saliva against her shoulder. She stroked and patted him, and asked him to be as quiet as he could, all the time wondering desperately why she had ever thought of coming, trying to fend off the feeling of regret.

The cottages on each side of the inn had little ragged gardens which petered off into the fields beyond. Much safer to chance her luck down here than to risk the main road. She felt there was no turning back now; this time she would surely be stopped and, even as she had the thought, she felt again the rough hands across her mouth and the sweet blood at the back of her throat . . .

The toll gate was at the top of the village. She gave Jonah a final hug and began to clamber over the loose rubble and rubbish at the corner of the yard. Part of the wall had given way and the stones were furred with moss where they had fallen, making them awkward and slippery to climb. She kept walking up the hem of her skirt and for a moment she envied William his physical freedom as well as everything else. At last she was over. Her hands had a mosaic of pieces of rust and grit pressed into them and she stopped to rub them clean. The silence seemed to swell around her, as if about to burst; she knew there must be at least fifty or sixty people not a hundred yards away from her, yet not one of them made a single sound – the village might have died.

What were they waiting for? What were they going to do? She had to know. To her left the cottages were blank, their curtains drawn and shutters closed in a self-inflicted blindness. With a decisive sweep the valley had turned its back on the village and saw nothing. Mary crept along beside the crumbling wall, pounced upon from time to time by the hedge springing through. There were only three cottages now between her and the road. Hardly breathing, she rounded the corner. Only a few feet and some undernourished bushes separated her from a crowd so still and silent they might have been made of stone. In the shadow of the straggly hedge was a ditch; Mary thought this was the safest place to be and inch by careful, painful inch she edged her way towards it. Her skirt caught on a briar and the tearing noise seemed to shred the air, but nobody except she noticed. At last she slipped down the little incline and into the soft wet mud at the bottom. She sat unmoving for a moment, to be sure that she really was safe, and then slowly, tentatively, she parted the stems of hawthorn and hazel until she could see clearly what lay beyond.

The crowd was about thirty yards from the gate. The men looked like refugees, their blackened faces gaunt and unfed in the moonlight, trailing clothes that were not their own, ill-fitting, torn and grimy. Some wore petticoats, some nightgowns, a few were even draped in sheets; anything was suitable, anything that came into those blackened desperate hands. All of them carried weapons: scythes, hedging hooks and axes glinted in the thin night light like stolen money.

From a group of five or six at the front a figure detached itself, a reedy old woman, bent low in a white nightdress, tapping her way forward with a shiny blackthorn stick. She wore a mob-cap and from underneath this fell thin wisps of what Mary took to be horsehair, which caught in the silvery stubble on her cheeks. The old lady tottered past Mary, who could see that she was wearing sturdy, villainous boots beneath her costume. She drew level with the gate; the crowd followed at a respectful distance.

Frail beyond belief, the small figure tapped at the gate with her stick. The rabble behind her held their breath. 'Children,' she said, 'there is something put up here. I cannot go on.'

'What is it, Mother?' her daughters called in unison. 'Nothing should stop your way.'

Rebecca, peering through her unaccustomed fringe, answered, 'I do not know, children. I am old and cannot see well.'

Anticipation began to creep into the voices of her children. 'Shall we come on, Mother, and move it out of your way?'

The wizened figure at the front grew taller for a moment and Mary was spellbound.

'Stop!' said Rebecca. 'Let me see.' And once again she tapped at the gate with her stick. 'It seems like a great gate put across the road to stop your old mother.' She was whining now, and plaintive. How could her daughters be deaf to these tones?

'We will break it, Mother. Nothing shall hinder you on your journey.'

'No.' Rebecca was persistent. 'Let us see. Perhaps it will open.' Her stout labourer's hand felt along the wooden bars to the lock. 'No, children, it is bolted and locked and I cannot go on. What is to be done?'

Her children were moving closer now. There must

have been about eighty of them, their knives raised, hemmed in closely to the gate.

'It must be taken down, Mother, because you and your children must pass.'

Gone were the cracked tones of the crone. With a savage shout Rebecca's voice echoed down the village street. 'Off with it then, my dear children. It has no business here.'

Iron and steel were raised in the darkness and the blows fell in such a storm that Mary turned her head away, afraid that the men would end by dismembering one another. She buried her face in her woollen skirt and felt cold and miserable in the mud. Blade after blade bit into the wood, sending chips flying in all directions. One landed on her shawl as lightly as a benediction, but the spell was broken, she had seen enough.

There were voices everywhere now, voices and laughter. Only the standing posts of the gates remained and they were soon reduced to stumps. The blows slackened off, to be replaced by great whoops and shouts. At the edge of the crowd somebody fired a gun, and then another, and a shower of sparks lit the scene for a moment, so that what Mary saw was stamped on her mind with a dusting of fire. Any one of the men could have been William, capering and caterwauling in a celebration of destruction. Like splinters of light from a Catherine wheel, men at the edges of the group were beginning to splutter off into the blackness, and she huddled close to the earth in case any of them should chance upon her as they left.

There was no apparent signal to make the great

tide of voice and movement begin to ebb. Like a scarlet flash of desire it consumed itself, and Mary had to strain to see lumpy figures running along the boundaries of the fields, only a gleam of white here, and an uncontainable cry over there, to suggest that they were anything other than small, transient creatures of the night scurrying about their business. Soon just a handful of men were left in the lane; they were deflated and still, grey embers of a fire that had raged and then passed on its way. They talked briefly to one another and then sealed the night off with a quick salute.

Mary wondered what decisions had been made in that desultory moment of parting. The last of them trudged out of sight, like disconsolate and unsatisfied lovers, and Mary sat for a long time in the sticky cold, the mud liquid around her thin boots, and damp seeping into her skirt, drawing her down into the ground. At last, when she was sure that she was quite safe, she pulled herself out of the clogged ditch and pushed her way through the hedge and into the lane. She walked stiffly down the centre of the street, dissociating herself from the furtiveness of earlier on, and thought she saw a curtain twitch in one of the cottages as she passed.

Jonah was asleep on his feet and, as she untied him and climbed heavily into the saddle, she wondered how they had hidden the springy young horse. William must be home by now, warming himself by the fire. As she rode, Mary thought back over all that she had seen; not a single flame had been lit and yet the scene burned with a fire as real as the one in the kitchen grate at home. What she remembered was

132

the delight and passion of a carnival; there was a strange festivity in the hands which pulled the knives. Her own fingers on the reins were numb with cold and yet she still denied the heat and attraction of the riot which she had spied upon.

When she walked into the kitchen, William was sitting with his back to her and she looked straight over his head into the eyes of the man with the pale face who had been watching earlier. Memory registered in both their eyes at the same time. She spoke tentatively.

'Hello, Jac Tŷ Isha.' And her words elided into his.

'Hello, Mary Jenkins.'

William's face creased in astonishment. His sister appeared to have left her careful compactness, her neatness and her self-containment behind in some hedge. Her boots oozed water onto the stone floor and her stained skirt hung wetly round her legs. She looked frozen and her skin had a blue, transparent bloom. There was something wild about her although she stood completely still.

'Do you two know each other?' He glanced incredulously at Jac for he had looked enough at Mary. The current in the air crackled and Jac felt that he had to speak, that somehow it fell to him to ease the situation.

'We met briefly at Narberth on the night of the fair. Your sister was kind enough to listen to a stranger who needed to grizzle.'

'I didn't know you had been to Narberth –' William's words were quicker than his thoughts. 'Oh . . .' The note of realisation was long and drawn out and low.

'Won't you sit by the fire?' Jac was doing his best, but felt that he was swimming against the tide. 'It's a very cold night, isn't – ?'

'Mary, what are you up to?' When William spoke it was like the slow unsheathing of a blade. She turned to him, animated at last, her chin jutting in a way that he remembered from childhood.

'No questions asked, and no explanations. Isn't that the rule?' Her tone was acid and she could not stop herself. There was both innocence and defiance in the look that she gave them and then she marched to the door.

'Just a minute, Mary.' William was there before her, but the threat emptied itself and he dropped back and let her pass. On the flagstones where she had stood her ground there was a sprinkling of water, each drop lightly clouded with particles of mud.

'Oh no! Now what? What do we do now?' William dumped himself in a chair.

'Will she talk? How much do you think she saw?' Jac's face looked even thinner with anxiety although he had regained some of his composure since Mary left the room.

'Oh she's very thorough, my sister. She'll have seen all that she wanted to. I don't know about her talking. There aren't that many people that she talks to. I suppose she might say something at the school. And she's very thick with Hugh.'

'Hugh Williams?'

'Mmm, you know, the lawyer. I can't quite make him out. He's a great one for revolution and social change, but he's sharp. You can bet your life that he won't be caught on the wrong side of the law if he can help it. But he'd jump at the chance to take up the fruits of other people's labours. I suppose even if Mary did speak to him, we're still quite safe.'

Jac nodded slowly, looking beyond William into the darkness at the edge of the kitchen. He said nothing.

'I'll tell you what bothers me, Jac. I don't know what she's up to. I don't know why she's doing it. Not that you can ever tell with her. She's the most private person I know. But she has been harassing me ever since Rebecca first got going. She's got a bee in her bonnet about it. I don't know why she won't let the whole thing drop. She can go her way; I just wish she'd let me go mine in peace.'

It was William's turn to stare in agitation at the shadows of the room.

'So what are we going to do?' Jac stood and rested his arm along the beam above the fireplace. A great trail of early-morning smoke was lost in the folds of his shirt.

'I don't know. You can't really threaten your own sister –'

Jac looked thinly into the curly flames of the fire. 'You'd be surprised what goes on.' The words poached upon the silence.

'Oh, Jac, come on, I couldn't.'

The angular figure by the fire turned back into the room.

'Don't be stupid. I'm not saying that you should. But people do. Some of the men have gone one step beyond desperation.'

William felt uneasy. The whole business with Mary was wretched. The question now lay with him.

'So what are we going to do?'

'I'll go up and speak to her. We got on rather well when we met before.'

'Yes. You kept quiet about that.'

'So did she, it would seem. We might be safe after all.'

Jac went cautiously up the stairs, a stub of candle in his hand; the light that it threw over his pointed face made him look like one of the martyrs, lost somewhere in the Middle Ages. He tapped on Mary's door.

'Go away.'

'Mary Jenkins, won't you let me in to talk?' His tones fell softly on the oak door. After a minute the latch lifted and her head appeared in the gap, the chin still very much in evidence. He raised his eyebrows with a smile and she inched the door further open, using it as a shield against her body. He eased himself into the room. There was a little light and he could see that she was in her nightdress. One side of her hair was plaited, the other fell about her shoulders. She was wrapped like a doll in a blanket quickly snatched from her bed. As he entered, she backed right into the corner of the room.

'Yes?' The little face in front of him was tight, and hurt like a child's. 'Yes?'

Jac was stooping slightly. The room was tiny, the roof was low and he was aware of how out of place he was. Mary was bunched into the corner, almost under the eaves, and as Jac glanced at her he thought how many faces of hers he had already seen: this little puckered daisy of a face, crumpled and on edge; the white cold face sketched by anger on the glass of the kitchen window earlier that night; the sweet, intent face of the girl at the fair.

'Were you hurt that night at Narberth?' She unfolded a bit at this question and stood straight and still, her gaze intent upon the floor.

'Is that what you came up here to ask me?'

He paused and in that brief silence he could feel the strain in her. 'No. I came up here because you seemed upset and I felt that, well, that I owed you a kindness.'

'I lost your pincushion.'

He smiled, and for a second she glanced up at him. 'Probably just as well. It didn't seem to bring much luck.'

'How's your girl?'

Now the silence was his. He looked at his hands, cracked and still sooty from earlier. 'Mary Jenkins, don't ask me that,' he said softly. 'She has the most beautiful and blackest heart I know and nothing I can do will change it. I can't try any more.' He rolled the flake of a cinder down the centre of his palm.

'Since you ask, I *was* hurt that night. Not very badly. Frightened more than hurt. You see, I had the honour of a meeting with Rebecca. Rebecca, who helps the poor, and the needy and the weak. Well, she wasn't giving much help that night.'

'What happened?'

'I don't want to talk about it. Anyway, you're one of them. You should know what goes on. You and my brother.'

'There are different groups across the county. Nobody knows what goes on in other people's patches. But we're never supposed to turn to violence; at least, only against the gates and the people who defend them. And none of us would ever hurt a woman . . .'

'You ought to be sure of your facts, Jac Tỹ Isha.'

'I'm sorry. Whatever happened to you, I'm sorry for it. I know that doesn't help, but –'

'There's no need for you to apologise.'

'Why did you come out tonight, if you were hurt before?'

'I don't think I can answer that, not properly. I suppose I thought that William was taunting me, urging me on. So partly because of that. But mostly because I just wanted to see . . .' she trailed off in confusion at herself.

With a deep breath Jac asked the question that had brought him up the stairs and into this delicate, cautious interview. 'Will you report us?'

'Good Lord, no. The thought had never crossed my mind. Not for a moment, no.' She looked at him earnestly and took a step forward into the room. 'I seem to have a peculiar need to object, make a protest; it's not a need that I like or understand but it appears to be there, somewhere inside me. However, that doesn't mean I'm going to go racing around blurting it out to some policeman from London who shouldn't be here in the first place. If that is what you think, then you have got me completely wrong.'

'No, of course I don't think that.' Jac was relieved all the same. 'I only said it really for your own protection. You see, the single most sacred thing about Rebecca is that the secrecy regarding her is absolute. That is something which must be made clear to you. Turn informer and you will be in trouble, and there will be nothing that William or I will be able to do to help you.' He turned away from the hurt freshly scoured across her face. 'Oh Mary, it's not a threat. I'm not threatening you, I never would, but others might. That's the way things are, and you must know that.'

She turned back into the eaves and rested her forehead against one of the arthritic beams which shored up the gloom at the edge of the room.

'In the end you're all the same. You and William, and all the others. All that matters to you is your precious Rebecca and the rest of us can go hang . . . William had the goodness to explain to me the nature of Principles earlier tonight. Maybe you can tell me, as you are so keen to put me in the picture, what is the point of your worthy Principles if you haven't a single decent human feeling to back them up with? All that any of you seem to understand are hatred and violence and revenge. Well, they are Principles that I can do without.' She followed the line of a spidery crack in the floorboard, her eyes narrow and her focus quite specific. 'I'm sorry. My quarrel is not with you, and I know you meant well.' Slowly, tiredly she sat on the bed, bringing the talk to an end. 'You needn't worry, I won't breathe a word. Not because I support you and not because of all the threats in the world. It's not in my nature, that's all. Goodnight, Jac Tŷ Isha.' She looked at him one last time. 'And thank you for your trouble.'

He shrugged briefly and moved to go. 'That's nothing, I wanted to talk to you.' He turned back. 'And, Mary, my friends all call me Jac.'

The closing of the bedroom door brought William to the foot of the stairs in an instant. 'What did she say? What's she going to do? You don't think she'll tell anyone, do you?'

Jac crossed to the window and looked out; it must be nearly three and he was beginning to feel deeply, wretchedly tired. He felt wooden in the unfamiliar kitchen and wondered why he had ever allowed himself to be dragged into a family squabble. This was not the kind of allegiance that Rebecca demanded. This was all waste, worth nothing; it was not for him.

'Don't ask me, William. She's your sister. I don't think she'll talk, if that's what you want to hear. You're right about one thing though, she is private. All locked up inside, Maybe that's the problem. But what she's up to, I can't say. I'm really not the person to ask. I haven't got the hang of women at all; I just know that they always seem to be trouble.' He stretched and reached for his tangled things, which were looped over the back of a chair. 'Anyway, it's late. I should be off.'

'Thanks, Jac, thank you. I'm – I'm just sorry about it all.'

'Right. I'll be in touch. Or somebody will.'

'It was a good night otherwise, wasn't it?'

'It was a bloody marvellous night. God bless, now.'

Timothy Powell was comfortably immersed in his copy of *The Times*. It was a luxury he allowed himself only occasionally, for, after all, he was a busy and a most important man. He looked up from his article. Outside the tall, fine, sash window the grass billowed away from the house, anchored by a small fringe of trees at the bottom of the slope. The thing about being at Penycoed was that it gave him a bit of peace. Good to get away from the scrum of Carmarthen; nobody to badger you down here. Looked like a cold day. He sniffed and his gaze dropped to the massive dining room table. There was something about a stout breakfast that set you up like nothing else could. He was extremely partial to a bit of kidney. Mrs – whatever-her-name-was, his unsightly cook-housekeeper, didn't look too good close up, but by God, she knew what was what when it came to kidneys. Her cured ham was quite a treat as well, and what she didn't know about breakfast eggs just wasn't worth the knowing. Certainly made up for her other shortcomings. He lifted the heavy lid of the salver nearest him and peeped inside. Four or five perfect little kidneys, lightly glazed with hardening fat. He tested the temperature. Bit cold now. He looked at the clock on the mantelpiece. Ten to one. Wretched woman was probably up to her eyes in luncheon already. He replaced the lid and rattled his paper, disgruntled now. What was a chap to do, after all? He felt for his pipe in his dressing-gown pocket and began to suck on that instead.

He was just settling down to a good read when, blast it, if the door didn't open and the ghastly woman herself appear.

He glared at her unforgivingly. 'More kidneys?' he said.

The low, fat figure in the doorway quivered and pursed its lips. 'If you wish, sir. Luncheon won't be long though, sir. That wasn't what I came about actually, sir. Sorry to disturb you, I know it's your quiet time, but there's a gentleman called. He's ridden all the way from Carmarthen and is most insistent that he see you. He's an Inspector Martin. Have I to show him into the drawing room, sir?'

'Blast his eyes, the man's got no sense of timing. I suppose in London it's all right to call on people in their private homes at any hour of the day. Bring him in here. I'm not having a bloody policeman in my drawing room before one o'clock and that's for sure.'

Seconds later, the flushed face of the London policeman lit up the dining room of Timothy Powell, Esquire, JP. He stood in the doorway and watched with faint longing as the massive shape of the housekeeper disappeared down the passage. He jumped as the landowner barked from the other side of the room.

'What's brought you, then? You haven't come all this distance just to stand in my doorway. Come on man, Martin, whatever. Over here. No. Closer. I want to have a good look at what I'm paying for. That's better.'

By now George Martin had made his way down the endless breakfast table, holding onto the carved backs of the chairs for good measure.

'Good God, man, you stink of drink. What have you got to say for yourself? What's your business?'

'Mind if I sit down, sir? I've come rather a long way, bit of a bad head, and, well, the news isn't that good, I'm afraid.'

'You'll sit down when I say. Right. Out with it.'

'Well, it's been pretty quiet since Narberth, as I expect you've noticed. People showing a proper respect now that the Law is fully represented down here. However, I have to report that there was a little incident last night. Just the one gate, sir. Very regrettable. Of course we got there as soon as we heard. Pwll Trap it was, sir. Birds had flown though. Usual thing.' He scratched his head and pulled at his moustache. A copy of *The Times* went spinning down the considerable length of the table, coming to rest near some scrambled egg that the Justice had not quite got round to.

'Do you know what it costs for the privilege of having you and your two constables down here to work for me? Five pounds nineteen and sixpence per week.' He repeated the figure with a sense of injury that made the policeman flinch. 'It seems to me that this princely sum is poured by the glassful straight down your ignorant throat.' Timothy Powell began to stride about the room, working himself into a fever in order to prise away the fingers of panic that were clutching at him. This was the worst possible news. He cleared his throat and his voice shot several notes up the octave. 'I've done my best for the poor people in this district; the people who depend on me for help. I went straight to the top, got them the best protection that money could buy. Trained policemen in Carmarthen. Nobody ever thought that they would see the day. But look at you. Drunk at breakfast time.'

'It is past one o'clock, sir. And me and the men have had a very hard time of it — '

'Hard time, my arse! I could have done the job better myself. Well, there is only one thing to be done and let it be said that your conduct has driven me to it. I'm going to send you to Pembroke. You are to report to the Commanding Officer there and ask him to send me as many of his men as he can spare. You're to report this afternoon and for God's sake, man, make sure you're sober.'

The Inspector slumped. Pembroke was miles away. He wouldn't even get a spot of lunch and by the time he had sent one of the men . . . He looked wistfully at a splendid joint of ham on the sideboard.

'You're under orders, d'ya hear. Don't dillydally. I'm going to get this bitch Rebecca licked if it's the last thing I do.'

So it was that a few days later, when Mary was stitching quietly in the parlour with Anne Williams, whiling away a chilly afternoon, that a company of thirty Marines marched into the village.

Their crisp, unfamiliar procession took them along the main road past the little lane in which the Williamses lived, and Anne wheezed herself half out of her chair to catch a better sight of them. Mary's heart sank. This could only mean more danger, more trouble. Within minutes the men reappeared, marching with the same perfect precision but this time in the opposite direction. The two women exchanged glances of bewilderment, Mary hoping against hope that it was simply a false alarm.

Bethan brought in the tea at four o'clock. Even though it was more than two years that Mary had been popping in and out, the maid was still reserved with her, and with a great show of propriety and making a suitable fuss, she addressed all her remarks to the old lady. Today she was bristling with the gossip of the village.

'Not wishing to disturb you in any way, ma'am, but there's that much talk going on, and I thought you might like to hear the news, eh?' Her round dark face was plump with self-importance.

'It seems the Marines have come, ma'am. They've come all the way from Pembroke and they're going to be stationed here. It's all on account of Rebecca.' This last was delivered in a stage whisper, as she straightened out the tea things.

'Bronwen from next-door-but-one saw it all happen. No sooner had the Marines reached the Town Hall, like, when somebody gives them a note from Rebecca herself. Whoever heard of such cheek eh? And the note said, according to Bronwen, that is, that Rebecca was planning to attack the gate at Trevaughan. So all those poor brave men had to turn round in their tracks, like, and march right back the way they just come. It'll take them an hour and a half at least.'

'Thank you, Bethan. Miss Mary will pour the tea now. You may go.'

That was where the real affront to Bethan lay. She never sat down of an afternoon and had tea like a real lady, whereas this jumped-up Jenkins girl thought she owned the place.

Mary sat for what seemed like hours, while Anne, comfortably settled on all her chins, droned on about Rebecca; her impudence, her brazenness, how all those involved deserved a good hiding. How she suspected that deep down Hugh was on their side; how glad she was that the magistrates were taking a firm line. Mary sipped her tea and wondered if William was, even now, face to face with a Marine across the gate at Trevaughan. The soldiers were carrying bayonets; it was barely dark. She shuddered, and tried not to imagine all the trouble, the arrests, the carnage there might be.

In her anxiety, Mary did not wait for Hugh's return but made her excuses and went home to Dolwilym early. William greeted her at the door, a broad, pleased grin on his face.

'Here I am, Mary. Safe at home like a good brother should be.'

She smiled wanly. 'I can't think why, William. There must have been plenty of work for you to do today.'

'Not called upon. Rejected. They didn't want me.' He sat on the kitchen table, swinging his legs. 'Sounds like I missed a good one though,' he said ruefully.

Mary smiled in spite of herself. 'Well, I must say, I'm glad to hear it.'

'They've brought in the Marines now. The Marines! Can you imagine it? They marched all the way to St Clears, then off on a wild-goose chase to Trevaughan, but the gate was already burned to the ground when they got there. So it was about-turn and back to St Clears, only to find the gates at Pentre and Maes Oland both down on the way home. You've got to admit, that's classic.'

'William, don't you ever stop to think? You can't go tweaking the soldiers' noses like that and expect them to take it lying down. Don't you ever consider what reprisals there might be, the recriminations, the consequences of what you do?'

146

'That's where you're wrong. There won't be any reprisals. They wouldn't know where to start, how to go about it, who to look for. I'll bet you Mary, listen, I'll bet you this. Those Marines will be out of the district within the month.'

And William was right.

Lewis Griffiths stuck his legs out in front of him, flung back his head and roared and rolled about his chair with laughter till he was helpless with it. The tears coursed down his cheeks and clung with marmalade stickiness in his beard. He wiped his eyes, rocked and laughed again. The men around him, penned into the small inn room, exchanged glances. He'd had a good day at the fair in Whitland and since then, with his money fatly stuffed in his pocket, he had lurched from inn to inn on his way home to Pantyparc. Another raucous, belching laugh bounced around the room. David Howell caught his brother's eye and shook his head with distaste.

'Come on, Griffiths, pack it in. There's some of us in here trying to have a decent conversation.'

Griffiths twisted his bulk around in his chair and blinked a few times, trying to make his swivelling eyes seek out the face of the man who had spoken to him. It was not an easy task, so he gave up, hawked noisily and spat over his shoulder in the general direction of the voice. The phlegm looped clumsily through the air and hit the leg of a chair, where it hung stickily before beginning its oozing, snail-like descent to the floor.

David Howell gritted his teeth, but his brother

Thomas touched his sleeve and for a moment the room was quiet.

'Such a delight to have a bit of decent conversation these days, wouldn't you say?' The sarcasm rumbled thickly round the room.

David thumped the bar. 'Griffiths, I've told you once.'

Immediately hands were raised to pacify. There was tension enough that night, a sense that people were straining to hear other sounds beyond the ruddy circle of the room. The three or four men nearest Griffiths shifted their weight uneasily on their stools, guilty by association, anxious for a chance to get away. The pig dealer talked on, his stomach packed uncomfortably on his knees.

'You'll like this one. I'll make you a present of this. There were these two women standing at a graveside . . .' and so it went on. Once, he staggered to his feet, a song burbling like wind from his slack, wet mouth, but in his great rendition he toppled too far over backwards into a corner by the fire. He was still for a moment, his veined cheek lying on the quarried floor; spit was running down his neck and his shoulder felt awkward under his ear. He giggled hopelessly.

'You can't keep a good man down, eh?' He was floundering, clutching, half-upright, but he could get no further. Sitting amongst all his flesh he looked like one of his own pigs.

'Give us a hand, then.'

His small eyes, in the brief moments that he could focus them, looked impatiently for his mug. Two men hoisted him to his feet and, as soon as he was able, he drained the beer noisily.

'Another one of these and I'll be out for the count.' He wiped his mouth on the collar of his smock and looked hopefully round the room. His group of drinkers were now lost in other knots of conversation.

'Is that a promise?' David Howell carried a pint across and put it down maliciously in front of him. By now, Griffiths was too unsure of his balance to contemplate a response, but guzzled privately into his mug. As long as the stuff kept coming . . . Twenty minutes later his sticky head lay unconscious on the table, his arms either side in a gesture of surrender amongst the stale, discarded pots. The inn door was open and the room was emptying out through it, men moving swiftly and silently, their belongings left where they had first been dropped that night. As he went, one of the pig dealer's companions from earlier in the evening gave him a shove and poured some flat beer over him for good measure.

'Becca is come,' he hissed into his ear, and vanished after the others.

Parting the thick curtains of a dream, Griffiths spluttered and sucked his teeth. The edge of the table dug into the soft underside of his jaw and he could not get comfortable. He half sat up.

'What? Eh? What d'ya say?'

He swung his head round. The room was empty. The buggers had gone home and left him.

'Any chance of a drink round here?' He heaved himself to the door and looked out. Where the hell was he anyway and in God's name what was all the noise? His head felt too big and painful and heavy for his body. Experimentally he put a foot outside the door, and then another. Seemed to work all right. Christ, he'd a thirst on him though. Trusting his feet to their own devices, he looked about him quizzically . . . Ah hah! So he was at Trevaughan; well, that made sense. On his way back from Whitland. That was right. Funny though. He looked around him again. Not like Trevaughan to be so busy at this time of night. Place was full of old ladies . . . Then he remembered, 'Becca is come,' and lurched forward, hallooing above the heads of the crowd, 'Me too, me too, I want to –'

In the peculiar blur of frocks and knives he saw several faces from the inn, and others that he did not know at all. There was a lot of splintering and smashing. He held his head in his hands; it felt as if the bones inside it were being torn apart. He couldn't stand the breaking noise; he put his head between his knees to blot it out. Then he was sick. It burst violently out of him with a life all of its own and splashed over the dresses which were whirling round.

'For God's sake, not Griffiths again.' It was a voice that Lewis knew. Somewhere deep down inside him he knew he knew that voice . . . Now whose was it . . . ?

'The Marines might have gone from Carmarthen, but they've got troops there now instead, and we're going to have the whole lot of them down on us if somebody doesn't shut that bastard up.'

It was one of the Howell boys. That's who it was. Again the vomit ricocheted from his mouth and shone in the road under the yellow moon. Somebody kicked him hard from behind. The fall went on and on . . . it seemed to last forever . . . Somebody would pay . . .

'. . . And I'm prepared to stand up in any court in the land and swear that what I've told you is the truth. Plain and simple. Exactly like I saw it.' There. It was done.

Lewis Griffiths' head hurt him hugely. He needed a drink like nothing else on earth. George Martin paced up and down the room in the Blue Boar at Carmarthen, hardly able to believe his ears or his luck.

'You say you were at Trevaughan; you saw the crowd breaking down the gate and you are certain that amongst them were David and Thomas Howell?'

'As I said. Now, where's me money?'

'Ah. Unfortunately I'm not in a position to deal with the matter of the reward. That's up to the magistrate. It will, of course, be necessary for you to come with me to see Mr Powell and tell him what you have just told me.'

'That's all right with me, but let's not hang around, shall we, mate? I expect we could both do with a drink.'

Within days Thomas and David Howell found themselves in prison. They were told that they were to be tried at the Pembroke Assizes in March and that they had only themselves to blame. George Martin's sense of victory was absolute.

Rebecca was distressed and outraged at the loss of two of her beloved children. The old lady and her daughters did not sit idly in grief and anger for long. Lewis Griffiths received so many threats against his life that the authorities, after due consideration, placed him in the same gaol for his own safety. It was the only way they could guarantee his protection. It was at about that time that a series of unexplained fires broke out on the Penycoed estate of Mr Timothy Powell, JP.

5

'Gwynne Roberts?'

'Yes, Miss.'

'John Matthews?'

'Yes, Miss.'

'Aled Rhys?'

'Yes, Miss.'

'Harry Howell?'

Silence.

'Harry Howell? Cat got your tongue, Harry?' That's not like you.' The silence continued until a dark girl at the edge of the group wriggled to her feet, picking at the worn threads in her pinafore as she spoke.

'Please, Miss. Harry lives in the same street as me. He used to, that is. But not any more. Not since that trouble at Trevaughan.' She looked nervously over her shoulder and sidled closer to Mary. 'The family can't manage any more. Not since David and Thomas got taken to the gaol. They just can't get by without them extra pairs of hands. Their mam and Harry and the others all drove off in a cart at the beginning of the week; had all their things piled in it too, they did. Mrs Owen who runs the bakery told my mother that they'd gone to the Workhouse. I don't expect

Harry will be coming to Sunday School no more.'

There was a twitter amongst the children, oohs and aaahs of surprise growing in volume.

'Quiet, please. Thank you, Ellen, you may sit down. Now. Myfanwy Thomas?'

'Yes, Miss.'

'Michael Thomas?'

'Yes, Miss.'

It was April and the hedges were singing and green, bright fresh colours soaring from hue to hue, and spring's pulse busy across the landscape. In spite of this, walking home from the Chapel School Mary was subdued, crestfallen. As she wound her way down the steep slopes to Dolwilym she thought of Harry Howell; he was like a bullet shot from a gun, small, black and fierce, and she wondered how the Guardians at the Workhouse would manage to contain his spirit, knowing in her heart that he would be starved until it was broken. Waste. Everywhere you looked there was poverty and waste. She had seen Mrs Howell at Chapel a few times, a desiccated woman, overrun with children. The husband was a labourer, and his eldest sons, too. Not much money in the winter months at the best of times, never mind now. Even so, Mary had never dreamed they were so close to the edge.

As she rounded the final corner, two of the newest lambs left their post by the kitchen door and wobbled to meet her. Their mother was one of the elderly ewes, too old to carry twins easily and she had suffered a rupture at the birth. They had not been able to stop the bleeding. William had sat up with her all night and then watched her die as morning came. Another link with the past went with her. Between them they had hand-reared the babies and Mary smiled to think that even now they could not get it into their heads that their place was in the field with the others, not curled up by the kitchen range. Laughing, she shooed them out of the yard and watched their indignant dance down to the fold.

She called William up to the house. Because of the death they had been eating better lately and he was filling out; his new solidity made him adult and unfamiliar. Over dinner she told him about the Howells.

'There's nothing new about that, Mary. It happens all the time. Ever since the Parish stopped giving outdoor relief people have had no choice. It's either starve or go to the Workhouse. Most often they starve in there as well. It was almost bound to happen to the Howells once the two boys were arrested.'

The steam from a dish of mutton filled the room with forgotten luxury. Mary felt her appetite slipping away as, with every mouthful, a raddled picture of the Howell family rose before her eyes.

'I wish there was something we could do. It just seems so unfair. Why didn't Harry say that things were hard?'

'Because they're hard for everybody. There are hundreds of families in South Wales like the Howells. They can't all go round bleating that life is hard.'

'But what else can they do?'

William raised his eyebrow and Mary looked at him bullishly. 'I know, I know. You don't even have to say the name.' She sat in silence for a while, angry. 'I'd like to think that there was some way I could help. I don't want that poor woman to feel that she's been swallowed up by that place and then forgotten.'

'Why don't you go and visit her then if you feel that strongly? They might let you in if you say that you were Harry's teacher at the Chapel. Worth a try.'

'At least I could take them something to eat then. It's not much, I know, but she might think it's better than nothing. Don't you think, William?'

On her next visit to Carmarthen Mary took with her a cloth-wrapped packet of cold meat and cheese. The woman who answered the door of the Workhouse looked like a species of insect. She had untended corkscrew hair which seemed to be about to crawl off the side of her head and the whites of her eyes were veined and watery. Her comfortable belly, which no apron could disguise, belied the skinniness of the rest of her body.

'Yes, Miss?'

'I'd like to see Mrs Howell, please. I believe she was admitted here last week.'

The woman sucked her teeth, shaking her head doubtfully. 'It's not the most convenient time to call, Miss. You'd be best advised to come back in the evening when my husband can make the necessary arrangements.'

'I'm afraid that, for me, it is the most convenient time to call.' As she spoke, Mary's determination grew; she was not going to be put to one side by this midge of a woman. 'I'm from the Chapel School at St Clears and I'm afraid that the members of the Board will be most disappointed to hear that I have made this journey on their behalf,' she barely hesitated, 'only to be denied admission by you, Mrs – ?'

'Ah, never mind that.' The woman was a martyr to irritation. 'Mrs Howell, of whom you speak, is working at the moment, same as all the adults, and she won't thank you for disturbing her. She finds it hard enough to keep up with her quota as it is – '

'Then I'd like to see Harry, please.'

'He's in the schoolroom.'

'I don't mind waiting till there's a convenient gap in the class.' Mary gritted her teeth and remembered that attack was the best means of defence. 'And in the meantime, perhaps you'll let me see the rest of your facilities, then I can make a full report to the board when I get home.'

The woman moved back sullenly and let Mary into the building.

'You can see the Women's Ward, if you must. At least they keep themselves a bit more decent than the men.'

'Don't you keep the families together then?'

'We're not running an hotel here, Miss. These people are living on charity. They should thank the Good Lord on their knees for what they get.'

What they got seemed desolate to Mary. The woman's ward was giant-sized, with a pointed roof and meagre windows built so high in the wall that one could not look out of them. Stone met white-washed plaster in a mean and angular equation. The beds looked pinched and grey; there were about fifty of them lined up against the edges of the room like grubs under a stone. Blazoned across the far wall was the insistence that 'God is Love'; Mary thought it was a bold claim to make in such a place.

They kept her waiting a long time before she was allowed to meet Harry. When he came he looked surprised to see her.

'They haven't got you in here as well, have they, Miss?'

'No, Harry, they have not. But I heard at school about your poor parents and you and as I was passing I thought I'd call to see that you were managing.' What began with a laugh at Harry's shocked face ended lamely, for the look in both their eyes said, 'How could we possibly manage in this place?'

'Is there anywhere that we can go outside? I think it's warmer out there than it is in here.' She spoke quickly and took him by the hand; her comfort embarrassed him.

'I could take you out into the yard, Miss.' He seemed a bit doubtful and had already reclaimed his hand.

'Let's do that then.' Mary was slightly flustered, wondering if her visit had been ill-judged. The yard was narrow and dim and was overshadowed by the Workhouse so that more than half of it never saw the sun. Running along one side was a long low building that looked like a stables. The sound of the smashing of bricks came from it.

'Me mam works indoors, she's quite lucky really. But me Da works in one of them sheds. He's the third one from the left.'

Mary nodded slowly, deadened by all that she had seen. 'What does your Da do in there?'

The child became quite proprietorial, pushing stubby little fingers into the pockets of his smock.

'Well, Miss, he breaks up stones. See that grating by the door to his shed?' The small hand gestured authoritatively. 'When he's broken up them big stones into little bits he pushes them through the grating and someone comes and takes them away, and that's what he keeps doing until his shed's empty and then they let him out, except that sometimes that's quite late because me Da's a bit slow really. They told him off on Monday. Said he'd have to go before the Magistrate.'

Mary looked at the ground but out of the corner of her eye she saw a handful of children too young for lessons staring at her gravely. A woman leaned against the doorpost. She looked ashen and reedy. From time to time her bony hand pulled at her apron, wiped her neck and cheek and then dangled again by her side.

Harry was whispering something.

'And that woman,' he had a knowing look, too old for his young face, 'that woman is Mrs Parry, except that she isn't a missis at all. Simon Davies in my class, he's been here for ages and ages and he told me –'

'Harry, you're like an old gossip.' The woman's hand was busy again, mopping, wiping, dropping to her side.

'No, listen, Miss. It's true. She came here a few months ago, thrown out of her house because she was . . . you know . . . going to have a baby.'

'You shouldn't tittletattle. It's not right.'

'It's a really sad story, Miss. You'll be sorry if you don't hear the end of it.'

'You're being very rude, Harry. She must know we're talking about her.'

'Oh she don't know nothing, Miss. She's in a dream world half the time. Anyway –' Harry raced along, anxious to tell his story before he could be stopped again. 'Anyway, she had the baby a few weeks ago and it died, like, and she hasn't been the same since. She's been very poorly and me Mam says she'll turn soon, no doubt about it. She was sick again today, that's why she's not at work.'

'Harry!'

'No, no, no. It means she won't get it all done on time and that means –' the child was all puffed up, the end of his tale in sight, 'that means she won't get her supper – tonight.'

Mary fingered the parcel she had brought. In the face of so much hardship it meant nothing. She turned her back on the doorway. The children were having an argument.

'It can't be Siân because Siân doesn't look a bit like the lady on the money.'

'How do you know, Tom Pryce? You haven't got any money anyway.'

'I have so.'

'Liar.' Mary and Harry faced one another, their worlds only just touching.

'Is the food all right, then?' she said, hoping to redirect the conversation.

'Ugh. It's disgusting, Miss. Me Da wouldn't have given it to the pig, when we still had it. Monday: black barley bread, potatoes and soup. Tuesday: black barley bread, potatoes and soup. Wednesday –'

'All right, all right, I see what you mean.'

But Harry was unstoppable. 'Mondays and Thursdays we get an ounce and a half of cheese,

Sundays and Wednesdays we get three and a half ounces of meat and on Fridays we have fish dinner.'

'You're very precise, Harry.'

'Well you would be too, Miss. It means a lot. Tuesdays is a bit grim though, and if you put a foot out of line they take your food away altogether.'

'Isn't it lucky that I brought you this, then? I should think your foot is permanently where it shouldn't be.'

Harry had the packet open in a trice. 'Eh, Miss! This is real brammer!' and there was a proper warmth in his smile for the first time that afternoon.

'Harry, I want you to do something for me though.'

'Ooh. I'll do anything, Miss.'

'Will you make sure that Mrs Parry gets some of this as well? I'd give it to her myself, but she might take it wrong. Promise?'

He looked a bit muted at this, but promised all the same. Mary could not help being sceptical about whether he would keep his word.

'Come along now. You've had your little visit.' The strident voice of the Warden cut across the yard. Mary whipped around, caught in complicity. 'I'd invite you to stay longer but unfortunately I've other business to attend to. Now, Howell, thank the lady for coming to see you.'

'Thank you, Miss Jenkins,' and in a whisper, 'will you come again, Miss? And, Miss – thank you.'

Mary looked at him. The little packet was nowhere in sight. She smiled. 'Bye Harry. You be good now,' and the Warden led her tartly from the yard.

The smell of the Workhouse stayed with Mary for a long time; it was cold and permanent in the air.

She thought of Harry's father, locked up, breaking his stones. She'd heard somewhere that they had to break up a ton and a half a day; all that just to be fed on what was it? Black barley bread, potatoes and soup . . . Mind you, sometimes that was all they had at home, but they weren't locked away in sheds like animals. Down the mines was one thing, but they got a wage at the end of the week there. But these poor people . . . she tried to shut Mrs Parry's broken gesture from her mind.

At work in Carmarthen, Mr Ashe continued to be an inexplicable and over-excited source of news about Rebecca. Hardly a day went by but he would bustle into the office, carefully hang his coat behind the door, smooth its folds, then clap his hands together and deliver another morsel about the rioters. Did they know that Rebecca was almost certainly a gentleman? – the gatekeeper at Robertson Wathen had said she would stake her life on that. Some even said that they could put a name to him, that he was Owen Tucker Edwards, no less, son of William Edwards over at Sealyham. And while he was on the subject of the gate at Robertson Wathen, had they heard what happened? The old lady reported that once the gate was down Rebecca had stood up in her stirrups and issued a warning on behalf of Thomas and David Howell, right at the top of her voice, mind.

'Should any harm now happen to the two men at Haverford West gaol for trial on suspicion of having been concerned in these riots, I shall show no mercy to anyone, but harry the whole country.'

Fancy that! Mr Ashe kept a careful tally of all the

gates which went down. Mary saw him one day making a fresh entry in a list that he kept in a notebook hidden at the back of his drawer. He came in one morning shaking his head. 'Dearie me. Pwll Trap down again. That'll be, let me see, the fourth time.' Mary's body tightened at this, and she wondered where he got his information from. After all, her own brother and his cronies were probably there, and yet they told her nothing.

The old curiosity, which she could never suppress, made Mary anxious to attend the trial of the Howell brothers because, with Hugh defending, it promised to be quite an event. When the time came she could not slip away and sat working in the office, yearning for news. Of course, Mr Ashe went; fastidious, superior Mr Ashe. Mary had to sit down hard on her feelings of resentment. When he returned he was disturbed, a man divided in himself; he had all the delightful satisfaction of having predicted the result exactly, but it was spoilt for him by his lawyer's suspicion that justice had not been done.

'They got off, didn't they?' he shook his head.

Mary nodded keenly, wanting to hear it all.

'Go on then, Mr Ashe.'

'Well, no jury were going to stick their necks out and find those two guilty, were they? Not with all that talk going round. They said that Lewis Griffiths' evidence should be discredited on two counts: firstly that he was drunk, and secondly that he was an accomplice himself. I shouldn't think that there will be much tale-telling about Rebecca after this!'

In the inner office Hugh paced the length of the rug and reflected on a job well done. Getting Thomas and David off scot-free meant that the whole family might be released from the Workhouse, so that they could pick up the threads of life as it used to be before Rebecca crossed their paths. There was gratification in that. There was gratification in having been instrumental in securing their freedom, although he couldn't deny that Rebecca's threats had played the greater part in this. There was no sign of gratification in Hugh's face, however – he wasn't smiling and, as he paced, he sometimes kicked out angrily at the tassels on the rug. Mr Ashe had accompanied him to court; it was only right and proper that he should. Even Hugh wouldn't dream of being so publicly assisted by a woman. Yet when they returned to the office, Mary had dismissed him with her brief, uncomfortable smile, then looked to Mr Ashe for news. A simple turning of her head like that, the unintentional unkindness of it, gave Hugh a racing sickness in his stomach. He paced and kicked out at the rug.

William had sneaked into the court. Hugh spotted his slight figure on the fringes of a burly group of farmers: Rebecca's Children making their presence felt. His wooing of the lad had been successful; he had last seen him at the meeting of the Working Men's Association in Pontypool. Seventy men crowded into the village hall, some of them standing because there weren't enough benches to go round. Hugh presented the meeting with the Chartist flag he'd had made, then gave a speech garnering support for when the next election came around, promising change, promising them all the right to vote, just promising lavishly . . . as he spoke he was aware of

164

familiar, leafy eyes upon him, but eyes that belonged to William, not his sister. When the speech was over and the men stood up to clap, Hugh wished that it was Mary who was crushed in the enthusiasm of the people at the front, that it was Mary who was waving her hands and applauding so wildly, and not her brother.

He stood still in the middle of the rug, wrenching his fingers through his hair. Daily he had to remind himself that the time would come eventually, it always did, that if he waited long enough he'd have her. And daily he found it hard to be that certain.

As for Mary, she was the moth to his candle, unaware of the orbit she travelled. How could Hugh know that she was beginning to collect up her blushes, her private smiles and imaginings, and save them all for Jac Tŷ Isha, and that when she closed her eyes at night, it was a thin, pale-boned face that she found inside her head.

Henry Thomas was a changed man. Gone was the insolence, gone was the painful slowness with which he would open his front door, sniff the air, look up Water Street in one direction, then down it in another, scratch himself, spit, and then amble up to the waiting farmer and accept his proffered toll contemptuously. Then with movements so slow that they were barely discernible, he would open the gate just wide enough to let the traveller through, bang it so as to startle the horse, then pin his eyes uncomfortably to the traveller's back until he had rounded the bend at the top of the road. Water Street was busy, it was the main route out of Carmarthen to the northern hills and villages and was always pattering with people in and out of the town on business. Some irate farmers even told of how they were kept waiting in their carts, or maybe with a flock of sheep while Henry Thomas finished his dinner, wiped his mouth and then began the looking, scratching and spitting routine.

Since the outbreak of the rioting all this had utterly changed. Meals in the Thomas household were a rushed affair and, after dark, the slightest exhalation of breath would make all three members of the little family jump out of their skins. Mrs Thomas twittered compulsively about the riots. With her chattering child clamped to her stringy hip, she would wail:

'Henry *bach*, have you heard the news? The Master of the Workhouse in Newcastle Emlyn had a letter written in blood. What a terrible, dreadful thing to be sure, Henry. And the poor man only trying to do his job, just like you and me. What will happen to us when our turn comes?'

And again:

'Henry *bach*, have you heard the news? They sent a letter to the High Sheriff. Said he and all the other landlords like him were doing wrong by their tenants and they had better mend their ways. Oh, Henry *bach*, what will we do when our turn comes?'

Poor beleaguered Henry *bach* shuddered to think what they would do when their turn came. All he could hope was that his wife would keep her head.

'Now don't take on so, *'nghariad i*. Threats is one thing, but not even Rebecca would come into the centre of a big town like this and do any mischief. Think about it, love. Especially not now we've got

166

all those policemen not five hundred yards away. Don't fret, my pet. No. If we're polite and do our job in a civil manner,' he gave a nervous cough, '. . . then I'm sure that we can sleep easy in our beds.'

And his leathery figure, newly spry, would nip out of the front door and have the gate wide open at the distant hint of a horse or cart approaching. He was determined to earn the right to sleep in peace at night. Occasionally a difficult customer would refuse to pay and Henry Thomas would bow and ingratiate himself and then bow some more. 'I do understand, sir, that for you this is a matter of conscience, and who am I to stand between a man and his conscience?'

And then he would be off around the corner to the magistrate to file his report without wasting any time. If the law chose to take the matter further, as it frequently did, then it was no concern of his. This was how he managed to shore up his life against the fears and threats which at times were only a hoofbeat away.

'Henry *bach*, Minty wants you to come upstairs and kiss her goodnight now. You really should be turning in yourself. It's market day tomorrow and that means we'll be rushed off our feet from first light.'

There was a long pause while Henry yawned, stretched and scratched at his back. He checked the shutters and then went to the door and looked out. Not a whisper. Ten o'clock and all was well.

'Henry *bach*, are you coming up now?' His wife appeared at the top of the stairs, filmy in her petticoat and shawl, her hair haphazard over her shoulders.

'Yes, pet, I'm coming up.' But he waited a little longer and pictured her sitting on the edge of their bed, frightened to get under the sheets until he was safely in the room. He went upstairs and closed the door behind him. Her face turned towards him, smiling with relief. The long shadows of the candle warmed her skin and he thought that it must taste like honey. She was lovely in this light, the secret, bedroom light which hid her lines and angles from him. And the light also fell on his sleeping child. He grunted and started to undress. Not the best arrangement this, but since the riots had begun the missis had insisted . . .

The three of them lay in a row in the narrow bed. Henry pinched the candle out and fell to wondering if there would be boxing in the town after the market. Sometimes some of the drovers had a bout or two at the end of the day, informal, like, a few coppers in a hat, that sort of thing. Mrs Thomas held her child to her and thought how sweet the infant embrace was compared with the sinewy advances of her husband, and little Minty Thomas dreamed on . . .

Mrs Thomas woke to a splintering noise; the sound was so close, so brittle, it was as if her own spine was being split in two. She sat upright in the bed, rigid, and pulled the drowsy child closer in her arms.

'Henry. Henry, you're to go and see –'

Her husband was already halfway to the door when it was flung back on its hinges. In that strange, elasticated moment she thought how frail, how stupid, how typically Henry he looked in his vest and leggings.

'Aaaah. Becca has come,' he gulped, glancing back at her as if for confirmation. She hugged the baby closer to her, pulling her shawl around them both and sat hunched and frozen, speechless, staring into the face of her own particular nightmare.

Two figures stood in the doorway. To her they might have been seven foot tall, faces as black as night, turbans on their heads, and long golden curls which were as dangerous as the swords they were carrying. Henry's spindly body looked like bait in front of them. He turned to her again, shaking, his mouth working, swallowing air, and she shook her head unable to speak. His mind raced and he swallowed again; we must come out of this with our skins at least, that's not too much to ask. The two swords made a thin cathedral arch of gold before him. He cleared his throat.

'Please . . . go on with your work . . . you are . . . quite welcome.'

Minty's shrieks now filled the bedroom. The two figures exchanged glances and one of them stepped into the room lowering his sword.

'Do not be alarmed, we will do no injury whatever to you.'

A silent scream rose up inside Mrs Thomas. Please God, why be so formal? Why not get on with the butchery and have done with it? This was the worst, this was the most unkind – why didn't they get it over with?

Henry was stuttering now, wringing his hands.

'Please sir, kind sir, my wife . . . my child . . . we've done our best . . . nothing wrong . . . we have to earn a living same as you do . . . Have pity please.'

Rebecca moved to the window and opened it wide. Jigging at her elbow, it seemed to Henry that the whole of Water Street was blistered with men in white robes, most of them on horses, all of them armed. Torches flared, inflaming the picture. There must be three hundred people out there. Sweat ran down the back of Henry's thighs.

As Rebecca appeared at the window the crowd erupted into whoops and cries.

'Now, my beloved children, listen to your mother, and listen closely. What is it we are fighting against?'

Like a great roar came the reply: 'We are fighting against the toll gates, Mother.'

'And what is our cause?'

'Our cause is Justice, Mother.'

'Then in the name of Justice let us confine our fight to the gate and the toll-house –'

In the roar that followed the second figure whispered in Rebecca's ear.

'Peace, my children. In this, as in all things, I am guided by my dear sister Charlotte –' Here the crowd cheered and whistled for dear sister Charlotte. '. . . and she implores you to touch only the roof of the house, to leave the walls and ceilings standing as protection for the family inside.'

There were a few cat-calls at this, but they faded as Rebecca raised her hand.

'And now, my children, you may set about your task with your old mother's blessing.'

Rebecca's daughters were industrious on her behalf. No sooner had she turned back into the room than their work began. It sounded as if the whole street were being dismantled stone by stone. Wood

and mortar came crashing down to screams of
delight. The four horsemen of the Apocalypse could
not have been more thorough.

'You.' Rebecca poked Henry in the ribs. 'Back into
bed with you. Right. Now listen, all three of you.
You're to sit tight there and not move. You've seen
nothing and you've heard nothing. Is that quite
clear?'

Henry skipped back into bed without a backward
look, and lay shaking under the sheets. Rebecca
curtsied deeply and her sister Charlotte followed
suit.

'And now may I wish you a peaceful and a pleasant
night. It has been a privilege to do business with you.'
And with that they closed the door behind them and
tiptoed quietly down the stairs.

'I done it. I done it at last and it was bloody brilliant.'
Mike Bowen threw back his head and flung out his
arms in an embrace that took in the whole of the
kitchen. He pulled his wig off and sent it sailing
through the air till it landed like an angry cat on the
dresser in the corner. Then he seized William by the
waist and danced him round the table, singing at the
top of his voice, 'Oh, Rebeccas may come and
Rebeccas may pass; That's all very plain to see, but
no one will be such a comely fair lass, As Mike Bowen
Esquire, as me!' He crowed irrepressibly and swung
William down to the far end of the kitchen.

'Be quiet, you'll wake your sister.' Jac Tŷ Isha was
peeling off his petticoat by the fire. He rolled it
neatly into a ball as the two men fell apart in a spiral
of grubby lace.

'Don't be a wet blanket now, Jac. We've done a gate in the centre of Carmarthen, not five hundred yards from the police headquarters, and we got clean away. The police! Well, you got to laugh, haven't you? A little peppering of shot and you've got five grown men running for their lives away from trouble. I should like to be a fly on the wall when Chief Constable John Pugh makes his report in the morning. ''Please your Honour, it was like this, see. Me and the men just got a tiny bit scared. In fact we shit ourselves and we thought it was more dignified in the circumstances to run for cover, begging your pardon, your Honour, sir.'' I'd bust me sides out laughing. God in heaven! Tonight was the best it's ever been, and all because of me!' And off he went trumpeting down the length of the room.

William sat on the floor, his legs stuck out in front of. 'I wish I could be Rebecca one day. Oh God, I wish I could.'

Mike Bowen was dancing round and round on his own now. 'No reason why not,' he said carelessly over his shoulder, 'specially if you copy my magic, brilliant example.'

William picked at his clothes. 'Oh no. Not me. I never could. I'm not the type. I'm the kind of man that follows, not the kind that leads.' He sighed and for him, in that moment, the joy went out of the evening.

Jac was in his usual position, staring hard into the fire, lost somewhere on his own. 'I'm going to be Rebecca and I don't care if I die in the attempt. I'm going to do it. One night, one black and fighting night, I'm going to do it.'

Mike was off again. 'Oh, Rebecca and her daughters sweet destroyed the gate in Water Street.'

Jac turned on him. 'Give over, will you. You treat it all as if it were just some stupid lark.'

'Well, that's what it is, isn't it? It's a bloody hoot. It's the most fantastic game there is and we played it and we won it and it's all because of me.'

'For heaven's sake shut up, will you –' and then all three of them held their breath. The floor above them creaked, giving away its secret.

'Come on, you two, the work's not over yet.' As he spoke, Jac sat at the table and took some paper from his pocket.

'What do you mean? There's nothing more to do, is there?' William flopped into a chair beside him.

'Mike, are you coming?' Jac looked to the other end of the room. Mike was sitting in a tousled sulk. He had his wig in his lap now, and was curling the golden horsehair round his fingers.

'If it's serious business I'd better leave it to you. Bit above my level, I expect. Thanks all the same.' He swung one leg over the side of his chair. At the table Jac talked earnestly.

'I just think we must take every chance to push the message home. I should think old Henry Thomas has got the general gist of things by now,' he smiled thinly as he spoke, 'but we must make absolutely certain that the people he deals with know that we are deadly serious.'

In his corner Mike Bowen began to whistle a hymn.

'So I think if we wrote some kind of a note to that effect – have you got a pen?'

William looked uncertainly round the room.

173

'Oh yes, there's the one that Mary does the accounts with.' He fetched it, hoping to goodness that his sister would never find out what it had been used for.

'Now. Something to the point, that will leave no doubt in people's minds. How about: This is to give notice . . . ah, but this is to give notice what? . . . Mmmm . . . This is to give notice that the goods of all persons who will henceforth pay at Water Street gate will be burned . . . Is that all right? . . . will be burned . . . and their lives will be taken from them at a time they will not think . . . Oh, most important: Becca . . . There.'

William felt uneasy. 'Jac, isn't that a bit strong, that bit about their lives being taken? I know this isn't a game, but equally we're not in it for murder. I mean, that's another matter altogether.'

'You know that and I know that. But it's just as well that the rest of them are kept guessing. This should focus their minds wonderfully well.' He blew the ink dry and folded the paper carefully. 'I'll put this in some prominent place in the next couple of days. I think that's all. I'm home to bed now. Mike, are you staying or going?'

Mike heaved himself out of the chair, muttering and mumbling that if you hadn't got a sense of humour what else mattered in life? William stood at the door and waved them off. And all the while Mary lay in her bed straining to hear, listening as if her soul would burst.

6

'Henry *bach*, what are we going to do, how will we ever put things right?'

Again and again the words jangled in Henry Thomas's ears until he thought he would commit murder. The nerve endings seemed to unravel inside his head; he felt burnt and angry, but most of all he felt unforgiving. The toll-house, its roof torn off, was bruised and disfigured, covered in plaster dust as a widow covers her head in ashes. At the height of the attack one of the rioters had put his foot through the bedroom ceiling and now each night as they tried to sleep the rain poured through like grief.

No amount of rain could put out the fire which burned inside Henry Thomas. He'd fawned and toadied to those farmers, licked their arses for them every time they went through his gate, and this was how they him paid back. How dare they? How bloody dare they? So. This was serious. This was war. Round one to Rebecca, but the game was only just beginning. He'd get them, show them what a real fight was like. And how better to do it, how better to rout bastards who took the law into their own vicious, conniving hands, than with the weight of the

175

law itself? That was it. That was the way. He'd got right on his side after all. Just let one person try to sneak by without paying and he would be out and on to them before they knew what had hit them.

Within a few days there was a smile on the face of Henry Thomas. Three trips to the Magistrate's office was all that it took. John Harries, I've nailed you, and you, Thomas Thomas, and Samuel Brown. All of you. He stood in his doorway reciting their names like a litany – it gave him physical pleasure to get his tongue round the syllables. It gave him even greater pleasure when he heard that all three of them had been convicted and fined. Two pounds eight and six each. More than a year's pay for a no-good like John Harries. Serve him right. Serve 'em all right. Rebecca could go to hell now for all he cared.

'Blast and damnation, how dare they! Jumped-up little ploughboys.' Timothy Powell laboured across the room, spit flying from his jowls as he spoke. 'Right. That's fine by me. If that's how they want to play it. All right. I'm issuing distress warrants for the seizure of the goods belonging to John Harries, miller, Thomas Thomas, shopkeeper, and Samuel Brown, all resident at Talog. And if they breathe a word of protest, perhaps you would be good enough to point out to them that refusal to pay a fine is a criminal offence. God's teeth! I will not be put upon. I won't be held in such contempt and I'm going to make that quite plain to those half-wits. Don't hang about, man. Get on with it.'

The Inspector scuttled out of the room. When Mr

Powell was having one of his bad days didn't they all know about it? Ah well. This warrant business was a bit of a brute. Talog was not exactly round the corner, and what with all that bluster he felt he had earned himself a nice snug, sustaining drink somewhere. Could send one of the lads. But then which one? Much better if some of the locals handled it. Been a lot of hostility against the London policeman. Couldn't think why . . .

The four Special Constables crept back into Carmarthen with their tails between their legs. They had not even managed to reach Talog, never mind issue the wretched warrant. Somebody must have tipped Rebecca off. How else could she have known? There she was, she and her daughters larger than life, barring their way at Blaencoed. The constables had had no choice. What else could they have done? She instructed them to go straight back to Carmarthen and back to Carmarthen they had come.

'I want George Martin in my office and I want him there now! Do you hear me?' Timothy Powell's assistant quivered, thinking that in all likelihood Robert Peel would have heard him as far away as London.

'I believe Mr Martin is on his way, sir. He was most anxious to obtain a full report from the Special Constables involved in the operation, sir, but we are, um, well, we're expecting him very shortly.'

George Martin's feet dragged him reluctantly into the Magistrate's office. As his hand sweated on the doorknob he doubted if even the brandy would get him through this in one piece. Timothy Powell's massive shape was silhouetted against the window and throughout the interview his creased, plump fingers played with a ruler on his desk.

'Ah, Mr Martin, how kind. How very good of you to see me. I'm well aware what a busy man you are and, believe me, I appreciate you giving up your time like this. After all, I'm only the magistrate. I manage to keep myself fairly busy though. Not like you, of course, but I've had quite a morning of it all the same.'

George Martin watched the movement of the paper knife with a sick and bleary feeling.

'Shall I tell you what I've been doing?' The Justice's tones were razor-sweet. 'I've been having a cosy chat with Captain Davies. He's a magistrate too. Perhaps you know him?'

With a mouth as dry as India, George Martin replied, 'Ah yes, sir. I believe I have had the pleasure of his acquaintance.'

'You've had the pleasure of his acquaintance, have you? What a shame. I wish I'd known. Then I could have asked you to explain how it was that the Special Constables failed to execute the warrant that he had so obligingly countersigned for me. I could have got you to explain how they failed to arrest Rebecca. And while you were about it, you could have apologised to him. For poor Captain Davies, with whom you are so pleasurably acquainted, had his boundary wall burned down by this same Rebecca as soon as she had sent your Specials packing. She said it was some kind of warning. You could look on this in the same way. I want those three men. Now get out.'

* * *

David Evans was chosen to mastermind the operation. He was a road surveyor, and having a vested interest in the well-being of the Turnpike Trust was happy to do his bit on their behalf. He glanced at his pocket watch. Ten more minutes and they should be off. Inspector Martin weaved towards him, a pleased expression on his puffy face. 'Think I've done all right by you, Mr Evans. Got you a fine collection of men. Pick of the county, I'm told. Wish I could be with you myself, but the powers that be thought it might be a touch provocative, given the circumstances.'

Neat as a row of bright red berries, twenty-eight army pensioners were grouped in pairs, their whiskered, bilberry faces turned into the wind. Rickety chests were pushed out as much as rheumatism would allow and the faint drumbeats of earlier battles hung in the air around them. Shame they could not be trusted with proper weapons though. One of the old boys had nearly shot his foot off in the practice drill and it had made the others jittery. They seemed relieved when their pistols were removed and they were given batons instead. The rest of the men had guns aplenty. Ten Special Constables and four serving police officers, all armed to the teeth. It didn't matter that the Specials looked dubious and the four constables plain scared. They were a splendid force, certain to give Rebecca a good dressing-down. If they could not bring the three men in from Talog then nobody could. David Evans took up his place at the head of his patrol and was about to give the order to set off when he heard a faint click of heels behind him and a knotted hand wavered in the air.

'I think we should do this properly, sir, if we're going to do it at all.' All the veterans strained to hear the thin, polite voice, tremulous with a century of use.

'May I propose three cheers on behalf of Her Majesty? God Bless the Queen. Hip, hip, hooray!'

David Evans raised his eyes heavenwards as twenty-eight squeaky different notes scratched at the air round the Town Hall. Lord preserve us all, he thought, as he gave the order, 'Forward march.'

The odds in Rebecca's favour were roughly ten to one and she and her daughters surrounded the shuddering patrol with ease. As they were herded into a group, David Evans looked long and hard at the leader, a loose-limbed figure, with innocent freckled arms and a face as black as a Bible. Scowling, Evans dropped his head. He could fight as well as the next man but he was not going to be made a fool of, and today Becca's children did not seem to have fighting on their minds. He glanced sideways at his own men; twenty-eight parchment profiles united in one; their opaque, unseeing eyes watery, remembering the smoky plains of Waterloo. The eyes of the Specials, on the other hand, were infinitely mobile, trying to dodge the caustic, black-rimmed stare of neighbours, who were mounted, armed and accusing.

Rebecca, riding a massive cob, circled the group, trailing the coarse calico hem of her robe against the cheek of the scrawniest Special.

'The flower of Welsh manhood, eh? Pride of the Valleys? Look at you, boy. Egg yolk on your smock and your face not washed this morning. Here you are, standing in line with the cream of Her Majesty's Army and you turn out like this. Your mother would be ashamed of you.''

'Reckon his mother has her mind on other things, from what I've heard.' There was laughter in the crowd and the Special shrank into his offending smock. Rebecca bent her face very close to his. 'I don't think you're showing proper respect for my daughters, boy.' She turned and gestured to one of her children.

'Line them up. We'll have a proper military inspection. It's the least we can do to make the veterans feel at home.'

Disorientated, the old men stared mistily through her as she paraded by. The great horse stopped and Rebecca's black face, unsmiling, looked down at one of the diminished figures in front of her. His head shook with palsy and the gleaming medals on his chest trembled to the same rhythm. His breathing could be heard in every corner of the clearing. When Rebecca spoke, it was in the quietest tone. 'Old man, you have no business here. You should act as a father to my children and not be ranged against them. But you have served your country as you saw most fit, and for that I must commend you. Also, you came here today unarmed and for that I must commend you too. But, father, do not come this way again. It will go badly with you if you do.'

The old man's frame grieved and creaked and his breathing slowed its pace, but his unwavering eyes were fixed on the horizon as though through the sights of a gun. Rebecca's soft-skinned hand sketched a salute and she passed on to the last of the veterans.

'My inspection finishes here. The men beyond this point are worth – ' The quiet conspiracy of leaves and the breath of men and horses were suspended for a moment. One of the rioters forced his way to the front of the crowd and spat with all his strength into the face of the nearest Special. David Evans could feel the hot breath of the rebels all around him. One of them placed the flat blade of an axe against the small of his back and held it there. He could not see the man's face. The menace was excruciating.

At a sign from their mother, Becca's children lined the patrol into pairs and made them march. The policemen marched with resignation, the Specials with panic in their hearts and the old army pensioners with a desolate automation. They marched through villages to the sound of doors and shutters closing in a beat which echoed their own feet. Faces were averted, heads turned away and people washed their hands of the whole affair.

The salty pleasant smell of wood-smoke brought the convoy to a halt. On the brow of the hill to their right stood the home of Captain Davies, Justice of the Peace. The house was closed and silent. Around it the boundary wall was broken, partly burned by rioters only a few nights ago, giving it a kind of shattered modesty.

Rebecca wheeled her heavy horse around.

'I'm an old woman and I look upon my daughters as the comfort of my age.' There were whistles and cheers and clapping from the crowd. A few of the farmers tore their bonnets off and threw them in the air, blowing noisy kisses at their mother. Rebecca

continued, 'My girls are good to their old mother;
loyal, hardworking, but they cannot bear to see a
task that's incomplete. So it's on their account that
you have kindly come today. Now, my children, I've
brought you – 'swiftly she counted up the Specials
and the police, 'fifteen willing pairs of hands to help
you in your work.' As she spoke, the volunteers were
pushed and kicked out of the line.

David Evans, the four policemen and the ten
Specials were made to scramble to the top of the field
and Becca's children watched as, brick by brick, they
took down what was left of Captain Davies' wall.
Below them, impossibly distant, the army pensioners
stood in the road like twenty-eight patient drops of
blood. One by one Rebecca shook them by the hand.

'Go to your homes,' the gentle mother said, 'and
you will not be molested.' She watched the simple,
empty men turn as one and trickle down the road
towards Carmarthen.

Edward Crompton Lloyd Hall, a lawyer with publicly
avowed liberal sympathies, leaned in the doorway
of Emlyn Cottage and looked long and pensively at
the retreating backs of the two farmers. He pushed
a wisp of hair back off his forehead. He had the clear
white skin of someone who does not often see the
light of day and his pale eyes felt uncomfortable in
the sunshine. He turned on his heel at last and went
indoors, and for a long time he sat picking at his nails,
thinking.

The men had arrived at his cottage as if straight
from the Middle Ages. He shook his head. They
plainly had no concept of the machinery of modern

living. He stood up and began pacing the room; their whole outlook was barbaric, medieval, but they had an awareness of their own power that he found disconcerting. He wondered how they could be persuaded to use this undeniable force which they had in a constitutional manner, when they clearly had no understanding of what that meant. Above all he wondered what he was to do about it. He sat again and looked at the neat line of quills in front of him. Why the blazes hadn't they taken this to Hugh Williams? He would have been a much more suitable choice. He was a practical man, after all; he got things done. Edward began pushing back his cuticles with the end of a pen. What was he to do with this dangerous confidence that the men had rested with him? Asking for his help in putting Rebecca's case to the authorities. Really. It made his position ambiguous, to say the least. Of course, any shred of liberalism dictated that he should do his best for them and indeed he would. But where did that leave him in the eyes of the Law? Siding with the rebels against the Queen's Government? Impossible. And what about this meeting with the Mayor? They said they were expecting up to ten thousand men. The whole scene was bound to conflagrate – and where would that leave him? No. It would not do. It really wouldn't. Carefully he wiped the tiny flakes of dead skin from the end of his pen and dipped it in the ink, and began his letter. 'To Sir James Graham, The Secretary of State for the Home Office . . .'

The click of the door closing woke her. Meredith Hughes reached out sleepy arms for her Isaac; the sheets where he had lain were lightly crumpled under her fingers. She blinked her eyes open and rolled over onto her stomach so as to have a better view through the narrow window. The first faint light of day was warming the barley field opposite. Piqued, she rolled back under the blankets; a tiny sleepy bubble lingered at the corner of her lip. She hadn't married Isaac never to see him again. He'd been glued to her side all the time they were courting, but since the wedding day . . . well! Comings and goings, late nights and early mornings and her mouth not kissed for five days at least. She curled a piece of her hair round her finger and inspected the ends carefully. If this was married life, you could keep it. She pouted hard. If she had stayed at home, her mam would have the breakfast on the table by now; as it was, she would have to get her own. She slithered out of bed and pulled on her clothes, tying her hair carelessly round her head. What was the point of taking any trouble when Isaac was not even here to notice?

She padded down the stairs and into the empty kitchen. The sun was strong now, and cast unpeopled shadows in the angles of the room. From a cupboard she pulled out a black loaf of bread which her mother had sent round the week before. Already the edges were grey and crumbly and she looked at it uncertainly. Now her mam would dice it up and pop it in a pan of milk to warm over the fire . . . but there was an unpromising blanket of ashes across the hearth. Isaac had not even thought to fetch in some logs when he came back late last night. Meredith banged the bread petulantly into the back of the cupboard. That meant she would have to go to the woodshed herself, and she'd told Isaac a hundred times that she was frightened of the bats; their soft squashy bodies ready to drop on you at any moment. She bit her lip fretfully. Best get some kindling together, she could do that at least. Outside, in the little garden at the back, the early morning sounds were sharp and clear; the first scrapings of insects around the flowers, Mrs-Pugh-Next-Door's baby screaming for its feed and the laconic rumbling of the cows across the way. These were the small sounds that hemmed Meredith into her cottage every day. She picked her way along the hedgerow at the bottom, filling the scoop in her skirt with twigs and leaves, gingerly scrutinising each little splinter for the grubs and woodlice which made her skin prickle and crawl. She was just turning back to the house when something caught her eye: fresh crisp white paper screwed up and thrown under the struts of the garden gate. She dropped it into her lap with the rest of her findings and padded back into the kitchen to see what she could make of the fire.

The bits of wood were smoking rather than burning, but Meredith did not want to give up the starchy paper until she had worked out exactly what it said. It was definitely Isaac's name at the top; the words were written in brownish red ink and lurched across the page in a way that she found completely confusing. As the twigs in the hearth sputtered and died out, she smoothed out the creases and searched for letters that were easy and familiar, for small words that she knew. For ten minutes she tried to spell out the alien syllables until she felt as crotchety

as the baby that grumbled and screamed next door.
Next door! Of course! Mrs Pugh would surely know.
With fresh determination Meredith padded round to
her neighbour's, the unhelpful page clutched in her
hand.

Mrs Pugh was like a woman on the run, she was
moving around her kitchen so fast, and five of her
eight children were on the move too, ducking and
weaving to clear her a path and to avoid colliding
with one another as well.

'No, dearie, I'm no good at the reading and writing
myself. Couldn't really see the use of it, if you know
what I mean – Owen, will you stop that right now.
If I've told you once this morning – and besides, I
never had the time really – I'm watching you, Owen
– I tell you what though, my love. Frances, my
eldest, has been going to that Sunday School in St
Clears just lately and she's had a little try at the
reading, Bible stories mostly, but she might be able
to help you out. You should learn yourself: all that
time on your hands and no babies to drive you mad.
Samuel, will you go and fetch our Frances back from
the fields. Don't you argue with me, young man. No,
I don't care who fetched the milk this morning.
You're to do as you're told.'

Whining and protesting, young Samuel dawdled off
down the back lane. Meredith eyed the breakfast
which was rapidly disappearing into his brothers and
sisters with envy. When Frances arrived she was
already tousled and grimy from her work in the fields
and the hands which spread out the paper had the
shiny, used look of those of a woman of thirty.

'I can't make out them big words at the beginning

. . . Something . . . something . . . will bring . . . looks like "vengeance" . . . on your head.' At this, the eating stopped and the smaller children cluttered round her, their eyes opened wide with excitement. '. . . And most likely you will be landed into eternity without the least warning . . .' Frances looked up, pleased with herself. 'This bit's easy, just like Bible classes. Now it goes on: If you . . . something . . . yourself in the People's Cause, all well and good. If not, Monday will decide your fate.'

Meredith's face was now as white as the paper itself.

'Is it signed, Frances? Who's it from? Who could have sent such a thing to my poor Isaac?'

Mrs Pugh looked at Meredith with pity for the girl's ignorance, as her daughter replied, 'Oh yes, Mrs Hughes, it's signed all right.' The young girl, bursting with her own skill, leaned importantly over the table. 'You see them letters at the bottom there? Well, that's a B and that one there's an E, then those two together are both—'

Straddled by two children, Mrs Pugh intervened. 'Thank you, Frances my pet, Mrs Hughes has all the information that she needs to know.'

Meredith looked stricken; it was as if all the terrible stories she had heard about Rebecca were printed on her pretty face. 'Oh my goodness. What's my Isaac thinking of? How's he got himself mixed up in all of that?' She spoke almost in a whisper, 'What's me mam going to say? She'll be that cross if she ever gets to hear. Isaac's bound to land himself up in trouble somewhere.' She clenched her little hands together. 'Ooh, this is just like him. This is so typical—'

'I shouldn't trouble yourself too much if I were you, dearie.' Mrs Pugh spoke mildly. 'My Mr Pugh's been at it all summer. At first I was hopping mad when I found out – gave him a piece of my mind, I can tell you. But you know, when all's said and done, it has its advantages as well. Keeps him out from under my feet, makes him feel he's a bit important, keeps him off the beer . . .'

By now Meredith was on a different tack.

'How could those wicked people do such a terrible thing to him? I mean there's threats in there; you heard them. Frances, read that bit again, ". . . you will be landed into eternity without the least warning . . ." That's a dreadful thing to say. My poor Isaac's gone off today in fear and trembling, I shouldn't wonder. I expect he's frightened for his life. Oh, Mrs Pugh, what am I going to do?'

Mrs Pugh rocked her babies peaceably. 'Why don't you stop and have a spot of breakfast here, dearie? You can sit tight with us until the men get home.'

By ten o'clock there were close on six thousand people outside The Plough and Harrow, and amongst them not a bonnet or a petticoat in sight. For the men that streamed grimly down the valleys, out of the woods and through the fields, the festival days were over, and now they wore the browns and blacks and greys of the peasant farmer. Today the myth was out of place and they stood together, six, seven, and now eight thousand of them, men without margin, for whom there was no leeway left. True, the Rees brothers rode at the head of the march decked out as Rebecca and her sister Charlotte, but most of the men who walked behind them felt that the time for pantomime was past. Today they were going to speak as honest men with one voice. For them, it was now or never.

William ducked sharply as a man with a familiar back turned round to reveal a stranger's face. Again and again this happened as he searched through the crowd for Jac. He could not contain the excitement by himself, he needed a friend to march with. Near the front of the mass, three men carrying long hunting horns struck up a chord and the talking and the fidgeting stopped. Men looked at one another. Was someone going to address them? Was this the signal to be off?

In that short expectant silence, from the centre of the crowd, right from its very guts, a single voice began to sing. The clear Welsh tones soared and rippled like a red banner on the wind above the marchers. 'Abide with me,' it sang, and soon the words were bursting out of the thick necks of working lads and from the chicken throats of their grandfathers who felt that the ties of blood were as nothing to the indissoluble brotherhood of song. With her fist clenched above her head, Rebecca moved off towards Carmarthen, and the body of the march uncoiled and elongated behind her, while the hymn still swelled above the brim of the valley.

As they moved away from the inn, William spotted Jac's face, pale as a penitent's, at the edge of the crowd. He was carrying a placard which fought against the breeze. William strained to read the lettering. '*Cyfiawnder a Charwyr Cyfiawnder Ydym ni oll*' – Justice, and Lovers of Justice are We All.

How typical of Jac. William smiled a great smile of affection for his friend and jumped up and down until he caught his eye. Jac called to him across the bobbing heads of the crowd. 'Will you come and help me with this blasted thing? I haven't got the struts across the back right. Nobody's going to be able to read what it says.'

The hymn was changing now, and to the strains of 'Fight the Good Fight' the farmers marched from their valleys along the lanes towards Carmarthen.

Major Parlby twisted in his saddle, gave an order and his troop of the Fourth Light Dragoons lumbered to a halt. For the tenth time that morning he cursed the inability of the Welsh to do anything as simple as stick a signpost in the ground so that it pointed clearly and unambiguously in the direction in which one wanted to go. At a bark from him, one of the officers behind rode forward with the maps and as he turned to look at them, he saw the soldiers at the back of the rank smirking and exchanging glances.

'Sampler,' he said to the officer holding the maps.

'Yessir.'

'I want that soldier's name. He's to report to me as soon as we reach our billet. We are on active service and insolence will not be tolerated.'

'Of course, Major Parlby, sir,' but the young officer could not help smiling himself as yet again the major scanned the map, turned it round, looked at the horizon and looked at the map again before exclaiming, 'Well I'm darned if I know where the hell we are. Map must be twenty years out of date. How can the Home Secretary expect us to deliver the goods when he sends us out into the field with third-rate equipment?'

Even as he spoke, the Major regretted ordering full battle-dress for the morning's ride. Already the noonday sun was bouncing off the baked earth roads, searing the braid on his uniform and embossing his ribs with molten gold. He flicked at his boot with his riding crop, sunk in gloom.

'Might I suggest, sir,' Sampler's cautious voice roused the Major from his thoughts, 'might I suggest that we ask the way at one of the cottages over there?'

Parlby followed the young man's pointing hand. Two red brick cottages were toasting themselves in the sunshine and burning gold of the barley field opposite. The Major sighed. 'If we must, we must. Myself, I prefer to keep contact with the natives to an absolute minimum.' He clicked his tongue against his teeth in resignation. 'All right, off you go, Sampler. You can have dinner on me tonight if you can make head or tail of what the blighters say. Damn Welsh they will insist on speaking. That is –' he added as an afterthought, 'that is, if they do anything as civilised as dinner in Carmarthen, which I rather doubt.'

Samuel and Owen Pugh were screaming and chasing one another round the garden, firing imaginary guns into the air. Mrs Pugh was boiling her baby's nappies in a great pan on the fire and Meredith was sitting in the corner of the kitchen with the baby in question sat upon her lap. The curdy, milky sick upon her shoulder was only now beginning to dry into a crust and she held the child as far away from her as she dared. The little thing was noisy and slippery and she viewed it with profound misgivings and once again thanked heaven that her Isaac was so careful.

'We can't afford a baby just yet, *cariad*,' he'd say to her sorrowfully, rolling from her at the last moment in the bed upstairs.

'You thank the Good Lord for a sensible husband,' her mam had said, and as the baby Pugh wriggled and butted liquidly on her lap she thanked the Lord with fervour.

'You all right there, lovie? He's a bit of a handful, that one.' Mrs Pugh wiped her hands on her apron and began cutting up potatoes. There was a rap on the door. 'That'll be trouble,' she said, and wiped her hands again. As she opened the door, Captain Sampler took off his helmet and ducked his head in a bow specially modified for the natives. There was something in what the Major said, after all.

'Lord preserve us, trouble it is,' said Mrs Pugh without a backward glance. 'Yes? Can I help you?' Crisply she put her hands upon her hips.

'We seem to have lost our way. I wonder if you can tell us how to get to Carmarthen?'

Mrs Pugh looked over his shoulder. The 'we' consisted of rank upon rank of shining, polished soldiers. She pursed her lips. Meredith jumped to her feet with her mouth open and alarm in every gesture. Mrs Pugh half turned towards her. 'Thank you, Meredith dear. If you'll just mind the baby I'll see what I can do to help these gentlemen. We must all do our bit, mustn't we?' and she smiled her fullest smile as she brushed past the Captain. Meredith moved to the threshold and watched her, stupefied, as her arms weaved through the air, pointing and gesticulating, making the directions to Pontarddulais as complicated as she knew how. When, at length, she came back into the kitchen, she avoided her neighbour's eye.

'My Mr Pugh will have more than his supper to thank me for when he gets home tonight,' she said briefly, and went on cutting up potatoes.

By the time the marching men had reached Carmarthen it was no longer hymns that they were singing. Each little village that they had passed through had dutifully given up their able-bodied men for the day, but as they reached the slums which clogged the outskirts of the town, those that joined the slow procession were the poorest and most degenerate of men: miners who had not seen a coalface for twenty years and during that time had lived on nothing but bitterness and beer; those who had spurned the Workhouse gruel because they did not see why they should work for it; the disenchanted, the drunk, the dispossessed. And so the hymn-singing stopped. A rowdy clique at the front of the crowd shouted the farmers down and began their own filthy refrain and a coarse, squat man with a spirit bottle in his hand made much of farting in time to the tune.

In the middle of the crowd Jac looked grim. 'Some people just never grow up, do they? Idiots like that really are a splendid advertisement for our cause. Let's hope we lose them soon.'

'They'll be legless by the time we get to the Town

Hall, I shouldn't wonder.' William sounded doubtful.

The big man at the front farted like a trumpet, drained his bottle and sent it flying through the air. It cracked against a window pane and as the glass clinked and chinked to the ground the faces of the crowd slowly inflamed with intent. Other bottles appeared, drawn from pockets and jerkins, and were passed from mouth to mouth. The empty ones were smashed against the walls of houses or thrown into shop windows; one hit a dog that was scuttling to find shelter. William's heart was beating in his throat; everybody round him had linked arms and body pressed against body, constricted by the narrowness of the streets. Jac was struggling to keep his placard upright in the crush, his pale face red with anger.

'We'd better get our petition delivered soon or the lid's going to blow right off this lot.'

The crowd sucked back and then pitched forward. Somebody stood on William's heel and took his shoe clean off. He struggled to turn round, to burrow down and retrieve it but the crowd flung him forward again with a force that he could not resist. God help the man who trips up now. He'd be trampled to death, he thought, as he strove to keep his balance, his naked foot tender amongst its booted brothers.

'Damn that woman. Damn the whole lot of them. Blasted Welsh.' Major Parlby called the Fourth Light Dragoons to a halt once more. 'I don't want any more of your bright ideas, Sampler, I just want to know where we are now.'

'Er, I think it's called Cross Hands, sir.'

'Well, it certainly isn't Carmarthen, is it?' The Major's tones were acid.

'No, sir. I'm sorry, sir.'

The Major picked up the map as if it were infected and was once again scanning the horizon when his gaze was arrested for a moment. 'That chap's not wasting any time, is he?'

Cresting the hill at thunderous speed a horseman came riding towards them, waving one hand vigorously above his head. He was shouting something and his words were fluted and uneven in the wind. 'Major Parlby and the Fourth Light Dragoons?'

The Major's spine snapped immediately into position. 'Yes. I am he. What do you want?'

Breathlessly the man reined in his horse. 'Thank God. There have been messengers looking all over for you.'

'I'm afraid we were misdirected.' The Major dwelt on the word and Sampler shifted uncomfortably in his saddle.

'Never mind that now, sir. The rebels have surrounded the Guildhall. It's pretty desperate. Anything could happen.'

Briskly, the Major gathered up his reins. 'If you would be good enough to take the lead . . .' and at his command the Fourth Light Dragoons began a gallop which was to cause two horses to drop dead with exhaustion before they reached Carmarthen.

The petition was never delivered. As they neared the Guildhall the fat man at the front massed his cronies together and they turned and addressed the crowd.

'Me and me mates reckon, and I think you'll agree with us, that we haven't got this far to waste our time talking to a bunch of farts –' he demonstrated amply ' – like the ones in the Guildhall there.'

There were shouts of approval from near the front. The Rees brothers in their petticoats looked redundantly at one another and shrugged their shoulders helplessly. The day was no longer theirs. The fat man continued his burbling oration.

'Me and me mates reckon that our place is with our own kind. Don't you think, me lads –' he flung his arms wide and rocked slightly as he shouted, the veins in his neck straining purple ' – don't you think we'd be better off going to where we know that we'll be welcome? Let's get off to the Workhouse and have no messing here.'

To block dissent, his mates started singing and stamping their feet.

Around William people were arguing the point, weighing up the odds – the bloke was right, they'd got this far, why not press on? William took advantage of the moment of stillness to bind up his foot with a strip torn from the end of his smock. Somebody's clog had scraped the skin right off his toes and as he wound the material round the glazed redness, Mary's neat hemming was a reproach to him. Before he could finish, the spreading, angry column of men was on the move again and it was all he could do to hop and jump and still keep Jac's placard in sight.

They reached the Workhouse in no time and somebody threw a brick at the gates by way of knocking. It was as if a giant stone had been snatched away: the insect matron scuttled out, her eyes popping and her hair in corkscrews on her head. She threw up her hands in horror and scuttled back to fetch her husband. The crowd roared at the Punch and Judy display as the couple reappeared, moving in double time, and the Master unlocked the gates. He did not have to fling them open. The rabble did that for him and swarmed like worker bees into the hive. To the inmates the taste of liberation was not exactly honey-sweet. The rioters were wild now, and the alcohol upon their breath was like petrol, as flammable and as dangerous.

Mrs Parry stood in the entrance to the dining room. She had seen the other women make for the schoolroom, but she was unable to reach them and spun slightly, and staggered, as man after man thrust and pushed further into the building. A massive, black-bearded figure with the blood up in his face slammed the dining-room door back on its hinges and caught her a glancing blow which sent her dented body rattling to the floor. She lay still, her big bony hands covering her head like the skeleton of a leaf, and prayed that it would end.

The men locked in their sheds at the back threw down their mallets and beat on the doors, shouting to be let out. In the schoolroom, pressed together at one end, the women screamed at their would-be rescuers. 'For the love of God, go home. Leave us be. Go to your homes and leave us to ours. This is where we live. This is our home. Call your men off and get out,' and Harry Howell felt ashamed of his mother. His black bullet head shone fiercely at her elbow; he wanted to be out there with the rebels, climbing the stairs with a knife between his teeth.

Nobody saw the Mayor arrive and afterwards nobody could explain how suddenly, as if from nowhere, he appeared on the sill of a first-floor window. Inside, the drunks and the mob from the slums had found the larder and the Master's private apartments and were making themselves at home in both, so as he raised his arms and shouted for silence, it was to the true children of Rebecca that the Councillor spoke. Now that they had actually broken into the Workhouse most of them were not quite sure what to do – you couldn't pillage those who were worse off than yourself, and besides, hadn't they set out that day to talk to the Mayor, and if the Mayor wanted to talk to them, well the least they could do was to let the man have his say.

Major Parlby and his glinting gold dragoons clattered into the town at breakneck speed. A local constable, dithering and panicky, lurched his horse into a canter to meet them and the sweat streamed down the Major's face as he listened to the news. He took a dim view of the Welsh at the best of times, and this man was no better than the rest of them; the blighter was practically incoherent. It was not as if he had just galloped twenty miles without a break and lost two horses into the bargain. The chap was jabbering away and the Major wiped his upper lip and tried to grasp just what was going on.

'Workhouse sacked. Mayor's trying to hold the rabble. Rest of the police gone into hiding. Whole situation out of hand. Do whatever you have to.'

Without waiting for the end of the tale, Parlby

ordered his men to draw their swords and, with barely a pause, they streaked into the town. The constable brought up the rear still spluttering and anxious. 'Situation very tight. Glad relief's at hand. I can give you full authorisation. Do whatever's necessary. Slash the bastards if you have to.'

When the Mayor shouted for silence he was astonished to see the men below him shuffle, come to a halt and then turn their hot and shiny faces up to his. The last thing he had expected was to be given a hearing and for a second he was too surprised to speak. There was a small surge of movement near the door below and this jolted him into action.

'Gentlemen.' A kind of silence fell over the yard. The expectant faces waited in their thousands, oblivious to the crashing and the smashing and the breaking that was going on inside. They were waiting for the Mayor to play his card and he led with the only one he had.

'Gentlemen. Most of you here today are farmers. You are men of the earth and are as strong and as stout and as sensible as the earth itself. Whether you are children of Rebecca,' nobody breathed, 'or simply children of toil, I appeal to you. Whatever your grievances, and some of them may well be just, don't throw away the little that you have. My hands are tied. If you continue with your conduct now, you will oblige me to read out the Riot Act. As you know, once that is done I cannot be answerable for your lives. The police force is at hand – and once the Act is read they will do whatever is necessary, and I must stress that, *whatever* they feel is appropriate, to put the riot down. Think of your wives and families. Be sensible. Go home to them in peace and all of this will be forgotten.'

Rebecca's children looked about them. Read the Riot Act and they were caught like rats in a trap. William could just make out Jac's banner on the far side of the crowd. Justice. He supposed there was a kind of Justice in what the Mayor said; a half-baked effort to be fair. He shook his head, miserable. The whole day had gone disastrously, irretrievably, horribly wrong. What of the petition now? Things were much better as they used to be. A short sharp raid which made the point and left nobody with any lasting harm. Why were people so desperate for a change in tactics? Look what it brought them. His fair hair drooped on his brow and disconsolately he pushed it back off his face. Slowly, reluctantly, men who knew they had no choice were trickling towards the gate, and whispers of 'But what else can we do?' marked their passing. He put his foot to the ground and it hurt like hell. The makeshift bandage was long gone and the flesh was so raw and bruised he could hardly walk.

William was almost through the Workhouse gates when the soldiers came into sight. He leant his weight on the cool wrought iron and watched uncomprehendingly. Justice? What kind of Justice was this? He winced as the first man fell, trampled under the hooves of the horse at the front. This was a trick. This was the Council's doing. The horses pounded closer. Justice? Justice demanded that the Act be read. Justice demanded that the troops fire over the heads of the crowd. It didn't look as if they

201

were going to stop for that. The charge was at full
pelt now, the hooves slicing at the street. Men were
screaming, reeling like swatted flies.

William felt bleary inside; he moved his head
leadenly, uncertain, disbelieving. He was pushed up
hard against the gate and the wrought iron against
his back was sane and cold. Everything else was heat
and shouts and noise and fearful screams. Justice?
The soldiers had their bayonets fixed. William
crouched and held onto the gate, the only solid thing
in his world, and watched the passage of one man.
He thought he knew him. It might be Isaac Hughes
who ducked and rolled and fought his way out of the
yard. There was blood all over Isaac's face.
Somebody had caught a blow across the eye.
Sickened, William looked at the ground. There was
blood there, too. His own blood. Lots of it, by the
look of things. The nail had been torn right off his
toe and it was bleeding and bleeding. It was the sight
of his own blood that brought William to. He jerked
upright and started to fight and push as well. He
spilled out of the yard as the first of the Dragoons
won through. A soldier near him, right up close, gave
the order to bar the gates, to take as many prisoners
as possible. William swerved to the left. People were
running in all directions and the Dragoons were
riding in circles rounding them up, their swords
flailing through the air making arcs as silver as
angels' wings. His lame foot was slowing him down;
he rounded a corner and flung himself into a
doorway.

'That one's mine!' The words detached themselves
from the noise and the din and the shouting and hung

isolated in the air. William heard them quite clearly but never dreamt that they were meant for him. He was in the doorway, standing on one leg, balancing his foot upon his knee and the blood from it ran down his shin. He tore a strip of cotton from his smock at the exact moment that the bayonet ripped into his back. The sound of each was equally precise, defined and lengthy. William did not feel the cut; what he felt was loss of feeling. He fell sideways awkwardly and hit his cheek upon the door jamb. That hurt him. That was all he remembered: falling, hitting his face, being hurt.

7

They were the first strawberries of the year and Mary sat with a bowl in her lap picking them over, admiring their polished summer dimples and the smell of them . . . so sweet, and full of rosy promise. She glanced out of the window; it was nearly nine o'clock and yet the shadows were only now beginning to crumple softly at the edges of the garden. If William didn't hurry home for his supper she wasn't sure how long she would be able to resist. She knew all about that meeting. You would have to be blind, deaf and dumb not to know that half the county was meeting outside the Plough and Harrow that morning, while the other half, the female half, was shut away at home waiting and wondering. She shivered lightly; it was always chilly in the kitchen at this time of day, in spite of the summer weather. She wondered whether to pop upstairs and fetch her shawl, but paused for a moment to savour the anthem of evening quiet and then decided not to bother. She was twirling the hull of a strawberry – it looked like a tiny green carousel between her fingers – and she watched it intently as it spun, lost in concentration, so that when she heard the rap on the door she almost leapt out of her skin. Smiling at her own alarm she gathered up the bowl and lifted up the latch, wondering what William was up to, for it must be him, after all.

At first Mary did not see her brother; all she saw was Jac Tŷ Isha. She opened the door with a good-natured rebuke on her lips and saw Jac Tŷ Isha covered in William's blood. It was matted and caked down one side of his body but still glistened wetly at his neck. The bowl of strawberries fell from her hand.

'Oh my God,' was all she could say and she felt her strength drain out of her, flowing out of her like blood. Not thinking, she half stooped to pick up the broken pieces of the bowl. Jac staggered slightly and it was then that she saw her brother. He was slumped almost diagonally across Jac's back, his head lolling and his face blue in the blue shadows of the night.

'He's drunk.' The words were whispered in disbelief. 'He's drunk. How could he –'

Jac spoke at the same time.

'I'm sorry, Mary. I'm terribly sorry. I think it might be too late but I had to bring him home to you. I didn't know what else to do. Can you help me? Take him from me.'

Mary took her brother's awkward body into her arms and held him close. His head was unaware against her shoulder and she felt that he had gone from her, that he was lost and far away, quite out of reach, and she held him close.

'Oh no, oh please God, no. Let it not be. Please God,' she whispered. Jac eased the body out of her arms.

'Come along. We must lie him on his front. It's his back that's hurt.' Together they laid him on the table, the same table that had held the dead weight of his father only four years before. One arm was tied with a piece of cloth to his side, the other dangled loosely to the floor. Mary shook her head; she couldn't help thinking that he looked uncomfortable, although she knew the thought was inconsequential. She gathered the trailing limb back into place, struggling to think what best to do. 'We must get a doctor. He needs a doctor. I can't –'

'I thought about that in Carmarthen, but they were arresting everybody in sight. I thought it was too much of a risk, and he would certainly die if they took him into prison. I thought they'd be checking all the doctors in the town. I'm so sorry. I didn't know what to do. It's probably me that's killed him.'

Mary was at her brother's head. His thick fair hair had the same bluish tinge as his face. All the colour had gone out of it, the blood had washed the colour all away. She felt for the pulse in his neck. His neck was faintly warm.

'You haven't killed him. He's not dead yet and he won't die. It just – well, it's not possible, that's all.' She looked up and the shock was clear in her face, 'But Jac, how did it ever happen? He's still a boy, who could have . . .?'

'I didn't see anything, I don't know. The whole yard was in such chaos, the soldiers came charging down the street and it was just – well, everyone for himself, I suppose. I ran into the Workhouse and out the other side over the wall at the back. It seemed the best bet, there was no chance of getting through the gates. I ran into Isaac Hughes. He's another one.' Jac's mouth wrinkled up as he saw Isaac's face in his mind. 'He couldn't see where he was going, his eye was half out on his cheek, but he told me he'd heard one of the soldiers shouting and riding down on William and that he thought he might be hurt. I didn't know what was best, whether to run or wait or somehow take advantage of the confusion. In the end I waited a bit and then thought I'd circle round from the side, out of the way. I practically walked straight into him. He was in a doorway. They'd just left him where he fell. Maybe they thought they had killed him and it was best to leave well alone, not be responsible. Anyway, it was prisoners they were after. I didn't know how to move him, how to get away, anything. I bound his wound up as well as I could and went to look for help. I thought they wouldn't touch him. I was dead right, they didn't.' His pale face was grim. 'In the end I took the hand cart from the bakehouse yard. There was so much running about and shouting, nobody knew what was happening. Anyway, nobody bothered with me. I brought him here in the cart – it's in the stable. I suppose you'd better burn it later.'

Mary was only half listening. 'Do you know Thomas Lewis: Dr Lewis? He used to live in Llanboidy. Can you do one more thing for us? You've done so much already. Can you go to Thomas Lewis, tell him that you've come from me, that William is . . .' her voice shook. 'Can you tell him that William is badly hurt and that we need him. Take Jonah, and hurry, don't be long.'

Alone in the kitchen Mary touched William's body

gently, remembering how many mornings she had gone in to wake him and done just that, a little gentle tap on his shoulder. Only this time he didn't roll over, didn't mumble, didn't promise crossly to be downstairs in five minutes. He didn't move. He was hardly breathing. She touched him tentatively again. His body felt cooler now. She ran upstairs and fetched a blanket and a cushion. There. He looked more comfortable but it wasn't long before a scarlet chrysanthemum of blood seeped into the creamy blanket. She thought quickly. Better to take his clothes right off and to clean him up before Thomas came. One of his shoes had gone. The foot was mauve and swollen and there was blood on that as well. She winced when she saw the missing nail and the blackened crust which had formed in its place. Poor William. Poor damaged boy.

She filled all the pans that she could find with water and put them on the fire to heat and then went upstairs to her mother's black oak chest and took out the clove-scented sheets that were waiting there, put by for Mary's wedding day. In the kitchen she tore the sheeting into strips, ten broad strips for the ten long years that she had not been married. She folded the glistening blanket back so that only William's legs were covered and then with her sewing scissors, snipped at the cloth which bound his right arm to his chest. The cloth was soaked in blood; it made her hand wet. She swallowed, her face screwed up with fear at what she was going to find. She threw the cloth into the flames, where it gave off a slow sticky hiss. Then, biting her lips ferociously, she cut her brother's smock from hem to neck. The left half slid loosely away at the touch of the scissor blades, the rest of it stuck like red raw skin to his back. Mary could hear the sound of her own breathing as she peeled the bloodied cotton away bit by bit. The wound was surprisingly small considering all the blood, about five inches long at the most. She peeled the smock back further and cut along the length of the sleeve. Holding her breath she looked at the gash again. It was very deep indeed, right under the shoulder. She could see some of the bone pushing through. It looked so white and polished and well kept. Poor timid William, such a long way out of his depth. Mary's eyes prickled; she sniffed and set to work.

Thomas Lewis's gingery forehead was beaded with sweat. He arrived in some distress and followed Jac into the silent and waiting kitchen at Dolwilym.

'Thank you for coming, Thomas.' Mary barely looked up from her sponging. She had cleaned and washed her brother's body and was dabbing cautiously at the lips of the gash itself.

Thomas came anxiously forward, clutching his bag in agitation, 'I heard about this dreadful business at the Workhouse, but I had no idea that William had got himself involved. What was he thinking of? Did you know what was going on?' Incredulously he looked at the girl he might have married. 'People are saying the most frightening things; sixty men taken prisoner, nobody knows how many wounded. Katherine wasn't at all keen for me to come out, you know.' He handed his bag to Jac, who opened it and laid the instruments on the dresser. 'She sends you her best wishes by the way.' His square pink hands were busy about the motionless body. He peered at the oozing wound.

'Mmmm. Probably a knife or a bayonet. Seems to have missed the lung, which is a mercy.' He tilted the body slightly. 'That's interesting . . . the blade must have sliced right under the shoulder. Quite a clean cut really; it's done a fair bit of damage though. He's jolly lucky it wasn't a gun-shot wound; it's no fun poking about trying to retrieve a bullet, I can tell you. How long has he been unconscious?'

Mary looked to Jac.

'Hard to tell, really. He was out cold when I found him, but he came to a few times in the cart. Didn't seem to know what had happened . . .'

Thomas sucked his lips. 'Mmmm. He's lost a lot of blood by the looks of things. He must be very weak by now.' He looked thoughtfully at the fire. 'We could try to cauterise the wound, I've brought some pitch with me, but I'm inclined not to use it. The shock would be colossal, there's no possibility that he would remain unconscious and at least he's not feeling the pain as he is.' He looked at the gash again, pressing the edges of it together. 'I'm rather in favour of a bit of stitching and a bandage. Once the wound has dried out you can put some lotion on it. Either St John's wort or comfrey. If I were you I'd steep some valerian as well – that might help him with the pain when he comes round. It's just a question of watching and waiting. He's going to need a lot of nursing . . .'

Mary nodded without taking her eyes off William's face. 'That's all right. I'll do anything, whatever's necessary, as long as – '

'Right. If you could go to his head, Mary . . . He might need something to bite on if he comes round, so if you can have something ready . . .'

The morning light was smoky on the hills when Thomas Lewis finished his work and finally rode away. They had bandaged William and carried him carefully up the stairs to his bed. Every time she looked at him, Mary thought he had grown smaller and more frail, all in the space of one short black night. She worried that lying on his front would obstruct his breathing, but made him as comfortable as she could, smoothing the gossamer baby hair that spilt across his forehead. As the doctor cleared away his things away, Mary looked at Jac, tired and drawn, the chill light of the morning making him paler than ever, and she smiled wanly.

'You must be longing for your bed as well. Poor Jac.'

'Now remember what I said.' Thomas Lewis was on the threshold. 'I'll look in first thing tomorrow. And please –' he looked sheepish, 'don't mention this to anybody.'

'That goes without saying,' Mary replied quietly. 'And Thomas, thank you for all you have done. If we can ever pay you back . . .'

'The best payment will be when William himself is able to buy me a drink, but perhaps not at the Plough and Harrow.' Thomas was almost cheerful, so relieved was he to get away. 'Till tomorrow.' He touched his hat in salute to Mary. 'Goodbye, Mr, er . . .?'

'Jac Tŷ Isha.'

'Goodbye, then.' With a crisp tug Thomas Lewis closed the door behind him.

'Oh Jac, what a night this has been,' breathed Mary, resting her forehead on the beam above the fire. Some of the pans were still simmering, forgotten, and clouds of blood eddied in the clear bubbling water. 'What a night.' Her back was aching from bending so much, she could even taste the tiredness in her mouth. Jac had fetched some water and was scrubbing at his jacket, trying to sponge away William's blood.

'Oh dear, your clothes. They're ruined, I'm afraid. I'll get you some fresh ones, that's the least I can do.' Mary moved towards the door.

'Don't worry, they'll be all right. Nothing a good soaking can't shift. Me mam will see to that.'

'Well let me get you a jacket at least. Yours is all torn and there's one of my father's –'

'No, Mary. You're very kind but no. It will come out, don't you worry.'

She moved beside him to the sink.

'Here. I'll do this, then. You don't want to be troubling your mam . . .'

The water was so slippery with William's blood they couldn't help the touching of their fingers.

'You sit down,' whispered Mary to hide her embarrassment. He was as close to her as pain; like pain he made her breathing difficult. He did not move away from her, he took his hands out of the water, dried them, then slowly rolled the sleeve up Mary's arm.

'You don't want to get it mucky now, do you?'

Mary didn't stop pounding the jacket and the blood

213

and the water, but her neck was hot and her mouth was dry. Jac folded the cloth of her other sleeve back upon itself, then ran a finger over her bare wet wrist.

'Mary Jenkins . . .'

She paused. 'Say my name again.'

'Mary . . .' The breath from his whisper slipped between her collar and her skin. She could feel it running down her back like sand; she could feel it resting warm in the hollow of her spine. He breathed on her skin again before he kissed her, and then he touched her hair and held her close.

'What a night this has been, Mary Jenkins.'

He kissed her twice, then dried her hands on a towel and held each finger to his mouth in turn.

'They're cold. Poor Mary. What cold fingers.'

His breath again, on her fingertips, on her palms. She wanted to curl her hands together and hold it there.

'Do you mind?' He smoothed her hair back from her face and his arm rested gently on her shoulder. She could only watch his mouth; she could barely shake her head in answer to his question.

'How could I mind? Oh Jac—'

Their lips touched again, and Mary's twenty-six unkissed years seemed to wheel about her head. Time was dislodged, adrift; she was in the arms of Jac Tŷ Isha.

He took her to her chair and sat her down, then knelt beside her, watching her all the time. He told her she looked like a little bird, all folded up.

'Won't she mind?' Mary could not stop the question. 'Your girl. Won't she mind?'

'I was wondering when you were going to ask that

214

one.' Jac's gaze lay on her face like sunlight. He never took his eyes off her. 'It doesn't matter if she minds or not. It was all over the night of the fair in any case. That's why I ever gave you –'

'Oh your present, I know, Jac. It's gone, I lost it on the way –'

'Will I have to give you my heart once again then, Mary Jenkins?' It was only half a question, and his face was strained and pale as he spoke.

Mary leaned towards him and, taking that thin grave face between her hands, she kissed his forehead, then the corner of his mouth.

'There,' she said. It was a promise.

'I ought to squeeze my jacket out and get home really,' he said reluctantly.

Mary was staring at her boots, difficult phrases forming themselves inside her head. 'I don't quite know what will happen to us after tonight,' she began, 'but whatever does, you've been a good friend to William and me and neither of us will ever, ever forget it. There's nothing I wouldn't do for you . . . but you know that.' There was a long pause, the words lingering between them. 'You're probably wondering what on earth I'm going on about, and I'm not sure that I know myself, really.' By now her eyes were riveted to the toes of her boots. She felt deeply embarrassed. 'If ever you find yourself in a position of need, no matter what it is or where you are, you must send us word and we will help. Whatever it is, regardless of what happens to you and me. That's all.'

The air in the kitchen began to circulate again. Jac pulled on his sodden jacket.

'Will I pass?' he asked, holding his arms out wide. Mary could have stood in his embrace till long after dawn had broken, but she kissed him hard and quickly, then sent him on his way.

'See you soon,' she said.

When he had gone she stood looking at the floor in immense, unreasonable distress. She felt an overwhelming need to cry, as if the world were going to end, but at the same time she was glad that salt water could not wash away all that had happened that night. And so she went upstairs to William.

For the first time ever, Hugh Williams rode down the winding track that led to Dolwilym. All around him the wood was busy with secrets, with chattering and scuttling that was suspended from time to time in uncoordinated silence. Beneath his horse's hooves the loam was soft and acceptant, the trees arched and rippled in the sunlight, and there was a loose seduction even in the movement of a leaf. As he clattered into the yard, the pony that he had often seen William riding whickered dejectedly, its long grey face hanging low over the stable door. Hugh tied his own horse close by and knocked on the door at the side of the house. There was no reply. He removed his hat and smoothed his hair back across his head, an unnecessary gesture, fingered his cravat for a moment, then licked his lips and cautiously opened the door.

The kitchen was empty. A damp and herby smell came from a pan warming over the fire; to him the room felt neat but very cold. In the hall beyond, the shaft of the stairs rose darkly upwards. He mounted slowly, looking uncertainly over his shoulder and listening intently. The only sound was the accommodating creak of the treads beneath his feet. At either end of the landing was a black oak door. Hugh eyed them both and the quietness enclosed him completely. He felt that he should call out her name, announce himself, but the desire beating inside him to catch her unawares, unguarded, kept him silent. He opened the nearest door. The room was empty.

Mary's bedroom. He stepped inside and breathed deeply. The bed was stripped of its clothes, abandoned, and he sat gently on it and, with his finger, traced the hollow where her body lay at night. The eaves closed round the room like wings around a bird, there was such softness in its smells and contours. He inhaled and closed his eyes for a moment, unaware of his trespass, aware only of experiencing a kind of intercourse with her, aware only of his wanting . . .

A tiny sprig of creeper scratched at the window and Hugh was immediately alert. He smoothed his hair again and stood up reluctantly. She must be in the other room. So. This was the moment that he had ridden from Carmarthen for. He half opened the second door. The room was slightly larger; it must have belonged to Mary's parents once. A dark wooden bed lay along one wall, rumpled with faded patchwork, and a makeshift bed had been made up on the floor opposite. It was stiflingly hot, in contrast to the rest of the house, and a fire roared in the cramped grate. William was lying on his front in the bed, his head uncomfortably to one side. He looked awkward, trussed, and his jaw was set with pain;

tears rolled silently down his cheeks which were flushed and shiny. The scene had a static, long-established feel which Hugh's interruption did not at once disturb. He stared at Mary kneeling by the bed, her hand on her brother's head and her face turned in close to his, and for a moment he felt an awful guilt inside. I wanted William to bring you close to me, that's what I used him for, that's why I encouraged him to get involved. I didn't think that it would come to this. There was no sound in the room at first. It was as if there were nothing adequate that could be said.

At the click of the opening door Mary turned and Hugh felt the lines of his face stretch as the puppet strings of convention pulled them taut.

'I only heard last night. I was wondering where you had got to. I'm so sorry, Mary.' He slid the brim of his hat easily through his fingers, but inside his mind was reeling. Her face. Her pretty, ravaged face, so grey, so thin, and those leafy eyes blackened with shadows. Her dress was open at the neck and the sight of her skin glistening made him almost giddy in the heat of the room.

'Hugh.' Her lips parted but there was no animation in her face. It was as if she were trying to recall something from a long time ago. She turned back to her brother.

'Look, William, you've got a visitor. Hugh's come to see you.' Her breath was gentle in the boy's ear. He turned his neck a little, struggling to see the new arrival, but the movement was ineffectual and the tears still flowed down his cheeks. Hugh stepped into his line of vision.

218

'Hello, William. Old Ashe at the office told me what happened. Where he gets his information from I just don't know.' Hugh laughed lightly, weakly.

William glanced at him as if to place him in his mind and then looked away. 'I'm hot. I'm hot.' The words were between a choke and a whimper. 'It's so uncomfortable. Can't you take a blanket off at least? Why does it have to be so hot . . .?' he tailed off. Around his mouth and eyes the pillow was sodden. 'Mary, please . . .' It was a wail which lined the walls of the room, filling every corner.

'Shh. Shh.' With a wad of material soaked in something sweet Mary wiped his face and the back of his neck. Hugh watched each movement minutely.

'Shh, my pet. Shh. You know that Thomas said we had to keep you warm. We're doing all we can to make you well, my darling. Quiet now. There. Shh.' Hugh felt each caress on his own skin and his mouth was dry. She turned her face towards him; her dark woody hair was tied at her neck and hung loosely down her back. He had only ever seen it strictly dressed before and now it entranced him; he wanted to bury his face in it and wind its silk around his throat.

'We're not really up to receiving visitors at the moment.' Mary was distracted, formal. 'The doctor comes every day, and Jac said he would try to call.' Did her voice soften? Hugh could not bear to think that it did. 'It's very kind of you to come, though. I wish we could be more welcoming.' She turned back to William, privately tender.

'I don't wish to intrude.' Hugh matched her formality coolly, but the vulnerability of her shoulders, curved and protective above her brother, made him helpless. 'I hoped there might be something I could do.'

Mary hesitated; she could not afford the luxury of politeness and good form. She looked at Hugh, surprised that he had come at all. It was so much trouble.

'Well, there is something . . .'

Hugh's spirits lifted; he had won her face again. 'Yes?'

'Well, it will be time for me to change the dressing soon. The doctor has shown me how. There's some valerian boiling over the fire. I wonder . . .' She was tentative. 'I wonder if you would be good enough to strain the liquid off and bring it up. It does seem to help ease the pain for him a bit.'

He was disappointed, but as he took off his jacket he felt he had a stake in the situation at least. Rolling up his sleeves, he went down to the kitchen and strained the hot and greenish water into a basin, unsure if the boy was to drink it or be bathed with it. He was back on the landing when he heard the first scream.

'Mary, don't. No, please! Please don't. Don't hurt me. Please. It hurts me so much. Leave me alone!'

The sounds pinked the air and Hugh stood outside the door, looking at his boots, knowing that this time he had no place inside. He listened for the murmuring of Mary's voice. He could not make out what she was saying; all he could hear was anguish. The basin was burning his fingers but he stood debarred, alone on the landing. He stood like that for five minutes, maybe more, before he dared go in.

The bedclothes had been kicked to the floor and William lay on his front naked, curled like a shrimp in the big black bed. Hugh cleared his throat.

'Put it over there, will you?' She did not even look at him. 'Thank you.'

Adrift, he hovered behind her and watched her thin hands at work. A crusting black line formed a ridge along the bruising on the boy's shoulder. It was shiny, malicious, almost like the blade of a knife itself, and Mary's fingers so gentle round it . . . She dabbed some lotion on it, crooning and explaining all the time. William's face was stifled in the pillow but occasionally his body jerked like a whiplash.

'There. Isn't that better now? It does help, you see. Poor William. There. Shh now.' She put a clean piece of cloth on the hardened wound and began winding the bandage back into place. 'There. Drink some of this now.' She reached for the valerian. 'And then try to sleep.'

'Don't go. Don't leave me. Stay with me here.'

Hugh could see that the hot choking of the boy's voice tore her apart. Her hands dangled by her sides and she spoke with restraint, as to a child. 'I'm only going to the kitchen, William. I've some more lotion to prepare and there's your lunch to think about. Don't fret now. You can call down if you want me.'

William's face creased tearfully and she turned her head deliberately away.

'You'll stay for lunch, Hugh?' He could see that she was tired and the invitation was given only out of courtesy.

'I'd like to very much, but there's nobody in the office. It's all right – ' seeing her worried face he could not speak quickly enough ' – we can manage until you come back. You will come back, won't you, Mary?'

She ushered him out of the bedroom with a last, anxious look back at her brother. Down in the kitchen Hugh watched her carefully, her gait was leaden and unfamiliar; she hit her hip on the dresser and her movements were slow and ill-judged. The crisp, contained woman who absorbed him so was somehow lost. He laid his hat upon the table.

'I don't want to press you at all. About coming back to work, I mean. I wouldn't dream of it. But we've come to depend upon an extra pair of hands about the office, and I know that my wife enjoys the time that you are able to spend with her.' He had a flash of inspiration. 'She asked me to give you this.' He dug into his pocket and pulled out a sovereign remembering as he did Anne's reaction to the news.

'People ask for what they get, don't they?' Acidly she had smacked her mouth shut; otherwise her spreading body remained unmoving in the pine-green parlour.

His neck twitched slightly and he laid the coin on the table with embarrassment. 'She was most concerned for you both.'

Warily Mary put her hand to her forehead and closed her eyes to think. A sovereign was a lot of money; would it be right to accept? How could she turn it down? Hugh's arms closed around her in a pretence of sympathy. He chewed at the inside of his mouth, disliking his own opportunism, but still he held her body close. Mary hardly moved, remembering Jac's embraces on that heady, grieving night when he brought her brother home to her. She hadn't seen him since then. Steadily, she detached herself and moved away. Hugh waited, every muscle inside him waited. Nothing. No rebuke, not a word, no response at all. He saw that she was looking at the money on the table. She nodded quietly to herself and stretched her hand towards it.

'Thank you, Hugh. I don't know what to say . . . but thank you, you're very kind . . .'

He watched the coin slip out of sight into some secret fold in her skirt. She looked him in the eye for almost a second.

'I must fetch some water in. Excuse me, won't you?'

He could hear her movements in the yard and the rhythmic pulse of the water hitting the bucket, a pulse that was slower and colder than his own. Christ! He must be fifteen, twenty years older than she, but what did those spare years of sophistication, knowledge, experience, add up to? Precisely nothing. He looked about the room and saw her presence printed on the fire, on the table, on the dresser, on the flagstones. She was everywhere. Oh, the stealth, the insinuation of unattended desire. He had wanted her the first day that he saw her, wanted her when he gave her employment, and looking back, he had wanted her every day since then. Four years. He smoothed his hair back across his head. He had waited. He had been happy to wait; it was logical. They came in the end, they always did; even Bethan, the maid, had come to him in the end. What was it with Mary? What was it that disconnected her from her feelings, from her flesh, and therefore from his own? Had she no sex at all? The pumping in the yard ceased and he could hear a few drips sprinkling the surface of the water, but his own pulse continued to beat until he thought it would bruise him inside.

Mary returned in a different frame of mind. She poured the water into a pan and floated some leaves on it. 'Thank goodness for this stuff. I don't know how we would manage without it. Thomas suggested it. Valerian, comfrey, wound-wort. It really seems to soothe him, you know.' She paused. 'Oh Hugh, I'm so frightened for him. I'm so afraid.' She halted again and he could see that she was crying. This time he didn't touch her. He didn't dare. He pulled a handkerchief from his pocket and handed it to her mutely.

'Oh, I know he's better now – thank you . . .' for a moment she lost her face inside the handkerchief. 'I know he's better than he was and I know it's only early days, but still I'm frightened he can't move his arm at all. Not even his fingers. Not even a little twitch. He can't even feel it when I touch his hand.' Hugh watched her, aghast; her eyes and mouth were creased up into weeping seams in her face. 'Oh, Hugh. What am I going to do? He screams when I change his dressing and do you know I'm almost glad to hear him. Glad that he can at least feel something.' Her sobs came quicker now. 'But all the way down his arm is all dead. He can't move it. He just can't feel.' She wiped her wet and puckered face. 'There is no life for a cripple in the country. What kind of a farmer can he ever be now?' She bit her lip and sniffed and then was still. Hugh watched the feeling drain slowly away from her.

'I'm sorry,' was all he could find to say.

'Oh yes. Everybody is sorry.' She was brief and composed now, and she gave a final sigh. 'Everybody is sorry.'

'Right.' Colonel Love rose to his feet on the platform at the end of the schoolroom. 'I'm making my headquarters here for obvious reasons . . .'

Oh yes, obvious to whom? Timothy Powell sniffed dubiously. Seemed damned insensitive to him to set up in the Workhouse. Nothing short of provocation.

'Does this fellah know what he's doing?' he hissed to his neighbour, Major Parlby. Now the Major was definitely a good sort. He'd got them out of a tight corner, he and his Dragoons. He was a man whose opinion could be trusted. Parlby looked at the vast red-faced man to his left and was heartily glad not to have regular dealings with him. He wasn't sure about the locals: competence did not seem to be one of their strongest suits. The Mayor had done his best in the heat of the moment, of course, but Captain Davies seemed to be a bit of a lost cause – and as for Powell . . .

'I think you will find that the chaps in the Home Office know their business. Colonel Love here served with Wellington in Spain, you know.'

'Well, Spain ain't South Wales, with all due respect.'

Major Parlby rubbed his chin patiently. 'I believe he helped with the troubles in Merthyr a few years back and again at the Newport rising in '39. Pretty good credentials, wouldn't you say?'

'We'll see.' Timothy Powell belched comfortably. 'Soon enough.'

Studiously Major Parlby re-directed his gaze towards the Colonel. Here was a man whose reputation travelled before him. He had a melancholy face, like mauve gauze. His lips were thin and determined and a little blue at the edges and his hair had yellowed on his scalp. He had a pendulous, ponderous air, but he was said to be a man of some fire in the field. He should give the Welsh peasants a good run for their money.

'Now I like to work in consultation wherever possible and there are one or two things you should know.' His delivery was confident and fluid. 'Our weakest area would seem to be Intelligence and on that score certain investigations have been set in motion. We feel that Mr Edward Lloyd Hall merits particular observation in light of the meeting he had with representatives of the rioters shortly before last Monday's outrage.'

Edward Lloyd Hall! Timothy Powell spluttered none too quietly to himself and the cane chair creaked unhappily as his weight shifted. Well. They were barking up the wrong tree from the start. Lloyd Hall. Effete kind of a radical, he was. No spine. Not for this kind of work at any rate. He began to fiddle with his watch chain and then his pipe. If this was the best that Colonel Love could come up with, then they could all spend their time more profitably elsewhere. He'd heard rumours of a dog fight at the Travellers Rest . . . Mmmm . . . Might just make it . . .

'On a more practical level, I am sure you will be greatly cheered to hear of the deployments we have in hand. I have asked the War Office to send us two field pieces and I expect to take delivery of them within a matter of days. As far as manpower is concerned, we hope that Major Parlby will keep up the good work in Carmarthen –'

A few polite 'Hear, hear's' rustled round the room.

' – And he will receive additional support from my own regiment, the Seventy-Third Foot. I'm sending a troop of the Castlemartin Yeomanry to Newcastle Emlyn, one to St Clears, and the third will be held in reserve at Pembroke. That seems to me to cover the significant trouble spots. We are also expecting one hundred and twenty Marines to arrive in the region by ship, so all in all I anticipate having about nine hundred men at my disposal. I think that you good gentlemen will be able to sleep undisturbed from now on. Any questions?'

'Is it over? Can we go?' Timothy Powell's bleating was lost in the hum of approval which filled the room.

'Thank you, gentlemen.'

'You look fagged out, Mary. There's nothing to you. You want to watch yourself, girl.' Mike Bowen planted a fat kiss on her cheek; she ducked too late to avoid it and laughed shyly. Behind him, Jac's slight figure lingered in the doorway. He kept his cap on and touched it briefly when she caught his eye. Mary felt hot all over her body, even the nape of her neck felt hot. He's not coming in. He won't stay. He wants to get away. He's changed his mind. That was all she could think of.

Mike Bowen's hands were on her shoulders, feeling, teasing. 'You're skin and bones, Mary. You should take more care of yourself. Never mind that no-good brother of yours.'

As she wriggled from his grasp he turned to Jac with a broad grin on his face. 'Any excuse, eh?'

Mary felt even hotter than before; hot, awkward and embarrassed. Floundering, she saw Jac lean loosely against the doorpost with his hands shoved into his pockets and his smile, when he turned it on her, was tense and guarded.

Mike Bowen looked from one to the other and clicked his tongue speculatively in his mouth, 'Ah well,' he shrugged slightly. 'Now, speaking of young William, as we were . . .' and he was back in his stride again. 'How's the patient doing? Behaving himself, I hope. Receiving visitors, is he?'

As a means of establishing order in herself once more, Mary met him full on.

'You know, Mike Bowen, I never thought the day would come when I would actually be pleased to see you in my kitchen.'

He hung his head in mock injury and gave her a wounded, piteous look.

'But today I am. I'm really pleased to see you. Both of you.' She did not trust herself to look at Jac, nor did she realise how apparent her vulnerability was. 'I'm very glad you came. The last few days haven't been that easy and he could do with cheering up. The wound itself seems better, thank God.' Even Mike could see that there were deeper lines around her eyes.

'There's been no infection and it seems to be healing well and I do thank the Lord for that. . . not much improvement in his arm though . . . but I'm sure it's early days . . .' and she gave them both a bright, untruthful smile. 'It'll do him a power of good to see you and catch up with all the news . . .'

'Aha! Rebecca strikes back, and all that,' Mike trumpeted as splendidly as ever.

'Oh, does she? I mean, has she?'

'You haven't heard the half of it, my dear. Have *I* got a tale to tell you.'

'Let's save it till we get upstairs. Are you coming, Jac?' Mary hardly dared to say it.

'I'll pop in. Can't stay long.'

'What do you mean you can't stay long? You know what happened better than I do.' Mike was insistent and Mary could only be pleased.

'Well, shall we say that you tell it better then?' There was wryness in Jac's face as he moved towards the stairs.

Mary bustled into the bedroom, a different person from the tentative, nervous girl who had met them below. She was fuller and more robust, strident almost, as she rallied the prone figure in the bed.

'Here you are, my pet. More people to see you. I bet you never dreamed you were so popular, eh? We had him sitting up yesterday. Bit of a struggle but we made it in the end. More comfy on your tummy today though, aren't you?'

William's face remained turned away from them.

'I'm not comfortable whichever way I am, so it doesn't really matter, does it?'

'William.' There was a hint of remonstrance in her voice. 'Jac and Mike have come all this way to see you. Don't be tetchy now.'

'Bringing you news from the big wide world!'

Mike's gaiety was also a little strident, a little forced. 'Listen, boyo,' he planted himself determinedly on the bed, 'we've got loads of things to tell you. Like, number one, your honour's been avenged.'

'How do you mean?' Stiffly William turned his head around.

'When I say "your", of course, I mean it in the collective sense of the word. For "your", read: "all the good children of Rebecca who suffered or fell on the glorious twenty-first of June," or words to that effect.'

'I don't want to hear about Rebecca. That's the last thing I want. Haven't you heard of rubbing salt in the wounds?'

'Don't take on so.' Mike was not to be deterred. 'I thought you'd be pleased to hear we'd cocked a snook at the soldiers and the magistrates. Thought you'd be glad to hear it.'

'Well, you were wrong.'

'I'm going to tell you all the same, though. Do you good. And I don't want any lip from you while I'm telling it, right?' Steering well clear of the bandages, Mike jabbed him in the ribs.

'Get off. That hurts.' William's face was implacably hidden in the pillows.

'Liar. Now listen to this. They've got this new chap down here. Colonel Love. He's supposed to put Rebecca firmly in her place. Well, that remains to be seen. For weeks now he's been marching his troops round in circles trying to find us, and we've brought down seven gates in four nights. Never say die, and all that.'

Mary looked at Mike Bowen gratefully. She could

see how hard he was working, though his smile was sunny and his energy simply bubbled out of him so that it did not seem like work at all. Even Jac's thin white face had relaxed in amusement.

'That isn't the good bit, though. I've been saving this one up for you, William my boy. This is a tale of bloodshed, of revenge, of love that is unrequited –'

'Come on. Get on with it.' Jac moved to the window, and she feared his irritation. Mike was in full flood now.

'Picture, if you will, three people: Daniel, John and Elizabeth. Now Daniel and John both vie with each other for the hand of the fair Elizabeth and it is Daniel who wins her. One night he tells her that he has been chosen for the highest honour in the land. He has been chosen as Rebecca. Our hero acquits himself bravely and the dastardly John, eaten with jealousy, takes himself off to the magistrate and blows the gaff to him. Whew!' Mike reverted to his usual manner and gave William another prod. 'Go on, Jenkins, give us a smile then.' And William's face emerged grudgingly from the pillow.

'Anyway, old John thinks he may as well do a thorough job of it and so not only does he point the finger at Daniel, but he nails some others who were out that night as well: Matthew and Henry Morgan and their old Dada Morgan Morgan too. Not what I'd call fair play, really. But the plot thickens.'

'Help me up, Mary. It hurts me like this.'

Swiftly, before he could change his mind, Mary helped her brother into a sitting position. Mike looked extremely pleased with himself and fulsomely mouthed a kiss in her direction.

'Early on Sunday morning, the Chief Constable, the Inspector and two policemen turn up at Cwm Cile with warrants in their hands and seize young Matthew Morgan a few yards from his own front door. The two bobbies stand guard on him while the Chief and the Inspector fling open the door of the cottage.

' "This is the Sabbath. This is the Lord's Day. You must leave us in peace to worship," squawks Mother Morgan, while son Henry dashes up the stairs saying he's come over a bit queer, like. The Chief tries to block his path. Oh fatal move. Oh ill-judged moment. The second his back is turned, Dada Morgan goes for him with his stick, old mother takes a poker out of the fire and does her bit, while sister Margaret comes from nowhere with a pan of boiling water and slings it right over him and the Inspector. They bundle the Chief out of the house and sister Margaret sees fit to do his head in with a reaping hook. He goes for his gun, they try to stop him, and he shoots another little Morgan, John by name, in the stomach. Back comes Henry with a hatchet, another brother joins in with a hammer and all hell's let loose. The two bobbies hear the gunshot and come trotting up and, with that, the family scatters. The upshot is that our brave boys in blue return to Carmarthen with Matthew and John, stomach wound and all, under arrest. But the best of it is, they send the whole of the Seventy-Third Foot to round up the two women, Mother Morgan and her daughter. Proves we've got 'em rattled, see?'

'What happened to Daniel and Elizabeth, after all that?' Mary was grinning as widely as Mike himself.

'Oh, he's in Swansea gaol with the rest of the crew and she visits him every day. Touching, really. But when all is said and done, the moral victory definitely belongs to Rebecca. We'll get the boys out of the clink one way or another and who's going to take the authorities seriously after that, I ask you?'

'The trial should come up within the next three months which will give us time enough to spread the word about what verdict we expect. We certainly have our work cut out for us, and I shouldn't be wasting time chattering away to you, invalid or not.' Jac was making his way to the door and Mary half rose as he passed her.

'Can I see you for a moment?' he said under his breath. 'That's why I came, really.'

Mary's face was crumpled up with worry. What has he come to say? That he's had second thoughts? That his girl wants him back? Feeling suddenly unassembled she turned to face the others.

'I'll just see Jac on his way,' she swallowed. Mike and William exchanged a look. 'I – I won't be a minute. Go on with . . .' and she was out of the door with a scarlet face and a heart as big as a Bible box.

'Well, well, well,' Mike Bowen whistled. 'I could see that coming a mile off. Couldn't you?'

'What? You mean Mary and Jac? You must be joking.'

'You think so? Your sister's like that normally, is she? All pink and jumpy? They're up to something, if you ask me.'

'Oh.' William felt crestfallen, let down. He couldn't

find it in his heart to be glad. Not now. 'I'm not so
sure. Mary doesn't really go in for that kind of thing.
Well, she never has up till now.'

'It'll do Jac good.' Mike's assessment was casual.
He scratched his back as he spoke. 'Get him away
from that black-haired madam he used to be sweet
on. She was trouble, if ever I saw it. Might stop him
getting quite so het up about Rebecca too. He can't
think straight at the moment. Do you know what he
was doing when I went to call for him today? He had
his poor old mam hanging on to the reins of his horse,
while he sat in the saddle firing his gun into the air.
Didn't half look embarrassed when he saw me. Said
it was to get the nag used to the noise in case he gets
his turn to be Rebecca. He's cracked in the head, that
boy. He needs someone sensible like your sister.'

Mary wasn't feeling sensible as she raced through
the kitchen after Jac. How much more of a stranger
you become to somebody once there has been
intimacy between you. She felt that very strongly as
she caught up with him in the yard. His eyes were
shaded by the peak of his cap and this took him
further from her.

'Yes?' Her face was flushed and tremulous. 'Yes?
What is it? What–?'

'I just wanted to say that I'm sorry about the other
night.'

Mary's heart shrivelled. She was glad his eyes were
shaded from her; she wished she had the same dark
refuge. Instead she felt lime-bright in the sunny yard.
How could she have hoped? How could she have
misunderstood so much?

'You must think very badly of me,' Jac went on.

'I've been blaming myself ever since it happened. I don't know what came over me. Well, I do, but I should never have let it.'

'What do you mean? What are you saying?'

'I took advantage of you. I behaved like a pig. You were upset and I thought nothing of it, I just went barging in. You're a good girl, Mary Jenkins, anyone can see that. And I shouldn't have done what I did. So I came round to apologise and to ask you to forget it ever happened.'

'Oh, Jac, I can't do that. How could I do that?' Mary was flooded with an overwhelming, all-or-nothing feeling. She held her hands towards him. 'Don't think badly,' she stammered. 'I don't.' She studied the colours in the gravel at her feet. 'I'm glad. I've been glad ever since . . . it's the only good thing . . . please don't feel bad.'

Jac was looking at her outstretched hands. Awkwardly she dropped them to her sides.

'You're not angry with me, then?' His voice was doubting, cautious.

'Why? Why would I be angry?'

'I thought you would be. I don't hold you cheap, Mary Jenkins, don't think that.'

'Oh, Jac.'

'Will you walk up to the road with me?' he asked uncertainly. 'I've got a meeting to go to, otherwise –'

'I'll get my hat.' Her face was warm and soft and smiling.

'No, don't get your hat. You look lovely as you are.' A smile was seeping round his mouth as well.

When they paused for breath at the first steep bend of the track, Jac linked his fingers into hers.

At the second bend he kissed her cheek, at the third her mouth, and by the time they passed the little chapel he had his arm around her waist.

'Pinch me.' Mary said the words with her lips against his throat. 'Pinch me. Tell me this is really happening.'

'Only if I can kiss you after.'

'Pinch me,' said Mary once again.

Under the archway to Dolwilym they leaned in one another's arms lopsidedly, like drinkers.

'Oh Jac, *'nghariad gwyn i.*' She touched his cheekbone, then let her finger wander down his jaw. 'My white love,' she whispered.

He caught her hand and held it to him.

'It's going to be hard, you know, to start with. I can't turn my back on Rebecca. There's so much to be done, especially now. And I can't always tell you where I am or what I'm doing. It's asking an awful lot of you, I know. I'm just asking you to understand. It means too much, it's too important.'

'I'll try. I promise you I'll try. I'm not much good at that kind of thing but—'

'And you'll be my girl, Mary Jenkins?'

'Will I ever,' she answered shyly.

'I'll see you soon.' He kissed the smile between her lips. 'I've got to dash. I'm sorry. I'll see you soon.'

Mary watched him till he was out of sight, then watched the air where he had been. Light as thistledown she floated back along the track, and the only thing which made her feel substantial was the way her heart was beating out the words.

'It's going to be all right. It's going to be all right. Everything will be all right.'

* * *

'You should be getting some sleep, William. You're not used to all this excitement, are you?' Mary could have danced around the bedroom. 'Mike, you don't mind, do you? He's tired now. It's been a long day for him.'

She held the door for Mike Bowen to pass through and then stood in the kitchen and watched him stride across the yard, turn, wave, and then vanish into the trees. For a long time after that she sat with her head in her hands, trembling with the memory of Jac Tŷ Isha.

At teatime Mary tiptoed into William's room with a bowl of mushroom soup in her hands. He was half-sitting, half-slumped, with his head rolled forward and his eyes closed. Dead tired. Poor child. He seemed like a child to her now, a frail, broken thing. She stroked at his unfeeling fingers and he did not stir. Sitting on his bed, the bowl of soup growing cold on her knees, Mary sank into thought. She tried not to think about her brother, of what the future might hold for him . . . Instead she thought of Jac and Mike, and the others of Becca's children, and of her promise to try to understand. They were brave, there was no doubt about that: brave to go in the face of all the soldiers ranged against them, brave to go on when their own kind were being hurt or imprisoned. She thought about Elizabeth visiting her Daniel every day in Swansea gaol. The bowl was cold between her knees now. There was a skin forming over the creamy surface of the soup. What a waste.

William tipped forward slightly and then opened his eyes.

'What are you doing?'

Mary roused herself with a sigh. 'Oh, I was just thinking . . .'

'Is that my supper?'

'You were asleep. It's gone cold now. I can heat it up.'

'What were you thinking about?'

'I was thinking it might be a nice idea to take a parcel of food to that poor man in Swansea gaol.' She smiled gently at her brother. 'After all, we're both finding out what it's like to suffer because of the soldiers and the magistrates, aren't we?'

There was a catch in William's voice and his eyes shone rather too brightly. 'But it will go away, won't it, Mary? It won't go on like this forever?'

She patted the hand that still had feeling. 'Of course it will, my pet. Now, I'm going to heat up your soup.'

8

Thomas Campbell Foster pulled out his fob watch and flipped it open; on the inside of the lid his own reflection stared back at him, silvered and cold. No wonder the locals are wary of talking to me, he thought, and then smiled encouragingly at the tiny face and watched the effect carefully. The pale grey of his eyes was hardened into steel by the watch lid and even in miniature his cheeks still looked fleshy. His hair crinkled round the rim of the metal and he looked at it critically. He never could get the parting straight. He ran his finger round the edge of his collar, exhaled, and listened in dismay to the squeaking in his breath. His chest had been tight ever since he got to Carmarthen. It slowed him down rather, which was a nuisance – there was more than enough for him to do.

In London they were saying that the Rebecca Riots, as they were being called, were the most significant civil disturbance since the Great Rebellion in 1688. That was quite a claim to make. Foster looked thoughtfully at the wall opposite him; there were shadows on the violet flock paper. Damp. He had thought as much. Well, that would account for his wheezing . . . 'The Ivy Bush', the editor had said as he shook his hand in confirmation of the assignment. 'I'm told they have the best rooms in Carmarthen. It wouldn't be right for a man from *The Times* to be seen in second-rate digs. The good name of the newspaper and all that . . . And, Foster,' the editor had looked at him meaningfully, 'cover this well and it could be the making of you.'

More than two weeks had passed since that interview in the London Office and now, as he looked around the musty parlour, Foster considered the editor's words again. Best digs in Carmarthen? Phtt. He hoped the man was not as out of touch in more important matters. There was certainly a story down here, there was no doubt about that. The difficulty was in getting at it.

What was at the root of the trouble then? He paused in his writing and searched the undulations in the violet walls for an answer. The animosity against the toll-gates provided part of the picture, but there was more to it than that. In the grudging and evasive replies that the locals gave him, one theme was constantly repeated: Justice. They said that the system as it stood was corrupt and undemocratic, and the words were alien and peculiar in their mouths but the feeling with which they were said convinced him that this grievance was at the heart of the unrest. Thomas was sure of it.

Thomas gave a squeaky sigh and sucked at his pen. The prospect was gloomy and things could only get worse. At the moment, in the eyes of the Law the action of gate-breaking was merely a misdemeanour, punishable by a fine, but he had heard that there were moves afoot to make it into a felony, which would mean transportation to Devil's Island for those convicted. There was bound to be a backlash if this amendment were introduced. As it was, the tension in the streets was so acute you could almost reach out and touch it. In the last few days a rash of posters had appeared on the walls of inns and shops, even on the toll-houses themselves, offering rewards of up to fifty pounds for information. That was twenty-five years' wages for a labourer. What poor sod was going to turn that down? Everywhere he looked there was suspicion, avarice, fear.

He sealed up his report and briefly consulted his pocket book. On the first page was a list that was starting to haunt him. It was the names of all the people he hoped to interview and he was not yet in a position to cross off even one name. He frowned slightly and scanned the page: Colonel Love, Major Parlby, a magistrate. Foster's frown deepened. Somebody had suggested Timothy Powell because he was influential and indiscreet and therefore could be useful. The list went on: the radical lawyers, Lloyd Hall or Hugh Williams, and in large letters right at the bottom, REBECCA. Fat chance of that. He shrugged despondently. What he needed was an ally, a guarantor, somebody to vouch for his neutrality – and unless he found one he could achieve nothing, that was becoming abundantly clear. If someone would take him into their confidence even a little that would be a beginning, something to be getting on with. But such disclosures were difficult to come by, they could not even be bought; he had tried that and the money had been wistfully, fearfully returned.

Foster rested his forehead against the chilly glass of the window and watched the secretive Welsh go about their business. For a moment his eyes idly followed a woman as she walked down the street. Slim, with something woody and russet about her. She was like an apple freshly arrived at market. When her face came into view he was surprised at how grave she looked. A grave and open face . . . his eyes narrowed and he ceased to notice her as the thought slowly hatched in his mind . . . The men kept their mouths shut, he knew that to his cost, but he had never known a woman refuse to talk. He grabbed the dispatch from his desk and, moving as quickly as his miserable chest would allow, was out in the street in seconds pursuing the lady in the green dress.

'Excuse me, miss?' He was panting slightly. 'Miss? Excuse me!' She slowed down and Foster was able to catch his breath. 'A moment please.'

'Do you mean me?' The young woman turned in surprise. He nodded, his shoulders ached with the effort of breathing. 'Can I help you, sir?'

For a second Foster wavered. Close to, the woman's face was sweet, but in an irretrievably sad way that he found disconcerting. She looked so drawn, as if her substance had been washed away leaving only shadows and angles.

With an habitual glance up and down the street, Foster collected himself. 'I'm a stranger in the town. I need to find the evening mail coach. Must get this off to London.' He waved the dispatch vaguely in the air and the movement made him cough. He listened attentively as Mary began to give directions which he already knew by heart and he became so lost in his performance that when she broke off he was almost startled.

'I'm going that way myself; it's probably easier if I show you. That is, if you don't mind.'

Foster beamed and clicked his heels together in a bow of assent. Excellent. He'd hit the mark right away. It couldn't be better.

'Will you be in Carmarthen long, sir?'

'Depends on my business. Difficult to say.' The woman was walking quickly; at this rate he would not have enough time really to get down to the nub of the matter. Foster staged a spectacular coughing fit which had the desired effect for his companion slowed down considerably. He wheezed some more for good measure. 'I do beg your pardon. I think it's the change of air. I'm a city man myself.'

She looked at him rather sharply, he thought, and he continued more smoothly, 'I must say, I seem to have landed myself in the thick of it coming down here, don't I?'

'How do you mean?' He must tread carefully. He sensed the woman's guard go up.

'Aren't you a bit scared yourself, a young lady like you, out and about with all these Rebecca-ites on the loose? I know I would be.'

Mary bit her lip and remembered the night of the fair at Narberth and in her mind she felt the hand across her mouth again, and tasted blood . . .

'Oh, they're not bothered with people like me. It's just the gates they're after, not people. It's only the gates.' And she thought of William propped in bed at home and how plaintive he had been when she set out.

Foster felt the first stirrings of hope. If he could play upon a need for reassurance . . . something might come of it . . .

'To a stranger like me it's extremely unsettling, I can tell you. They are talking of nothing else in Lon – ' he felt the speculation in her look ' – at home. I don't suppose you have any recent news . . .?'

'I don't live in Carmarthen, sir, so I am rather out of touch.' Mary spoke thoughtfully, unsure of her audience. Instinctively she felt cautious, for although she told herself she had nothing to give away, always in the back of her mind was William. William's wound. That must remain secret at all costs. She speeded up. What a terrible chest he had, the man beside her. She stole a glance at him. He seemed nonchalant enough, probably meant no harm . . . He was waiting expectantly and she cast around for something to say.

'I believe our MP is down from London,' she began. That seemed safe enough. 'George Rice Trevor. They say he had a meeting with the Turnpike Trust at Newcastle Emlyn and there has been some progress. I expect you've heard that though?'

'No. No, no. I've heard nothing,' Foster lied eagerly.

'Well, the riots are all on account of the toll-gates, see. And it seems the Trust has agreed to put prices back to what they were in 1837, and they've promised to move some of the most troublesome gates and they're not going to put back all of the ones that Rebecca has taken down. So, all in all, everybody is pretty optimistic that there is going to be a peaceful settlement.' Now it was Mary's turn to lie enthusiastically. Even she felt that there were scores to be settled now. Too much blood had been spilt, and too many people hurt.

The unforgivable tattoo of horses' hooves thundering through the Workhouse gates still beat in her brother's head at night and disturbed his sleep. These days the peace had gone from Dolwilym and in its place was fear of betrayal, fear of loss, fear of further pain. Mary was only making the journey into town that day so that she could show her face in Hugh's office. People had been asking where she was. Far too many questions were asked, one way and another. She looked again at the man beside her, a longer look this time. She watched as another inquiry was framed upon his lips.

'I don't believe I caught your name?' She interrupted quickly, keeping her voice even. The man's Adam's apple dropped out of sight beneath his collar.

Blast, he thought, and said out loud, 'Foster.'

Well, well, well. Mary turned the corner into Hugh's street. Thomas Campbell Foster, the London reporter. That would certainly account for his interest. Biting her lip, she tried to remember all that she had said.

'I work for *The Times* in London.' Best to make a clean breast of it. Maybe an outright appeal would serve his purposes more.

'I know you do. Even out where I live people are talking about you.'

'I wasn't trying to trip you up or trap you.' The woman raised her eyebrows. Serves me right, thought Thomas and decided to be more frank. 'My job isn't being made terribly easy for me, you know.'

His eyes were the colour of Welsh slate, an inappropriate grey, and they were fixed upon her, expectant even now.

'Are you surprised, with the town full of soldiers and policemen – and reporters? So many strangers, how can we possibly know – ?' she broke off. Pasted on to the wall quite close to Hugh's office was another of those posters. Fifty pounds offered for information leading to the arrest of anyone actively involved with Rebecca. How many people had seen William lying wounded in the street? How many men would be tempted by a notice like that? How many tongues would be seduced into talking?

'Posters like that don't exactly inspire confidence about the questions of strangers. So you see, Mr Foster . . .' she tailed off, still trying to calculate the risk.

'I'm not in the business of collecting rewards, Miss.' Thomas spoke self-righteously because he was irritated. The same brick-wall response all over again. 'My dearest ambition at the moment is to convince one of you that all I want is to make a fair and just representation of the facts. I've visited the Workhouse, I've counted the toll-gates and I think I know suffering when I see it. It's time the people in London, in the government, were made to see it too and then maybe your blessed Rebecca would really begin to get somewhere. But people won't listen and people won't talk and so no progress is made. I won't presume upon you any further. Good day to you.' Thomas had lost his temper, something he tried never to do, and he felt mortified. He turned on his heel, intending to stamp away with as much dignity as possible, but his throat was beginning to fasten itself closed and he couldn't stop himself coughing furiously.

Mary felt as if his attack had been directed personally at her, and the feeling hurt. 'There is usually a good reason, sir, for not talking, and you should respect that. I'm sure you are here with the best of intentions, but it's life and death for some of us. I suppose that is what sells newspapers, though.' She looked at the journalist with the beginnings of concern; he was propping himself against the wall and wiping his lips with a handkerchief. 'You should get that cough seen to,' she said more gently.

'I'm fine at home. I think it's the damp down here, or the dust, or something.'

Mary stood for a moment irresolutely. Looking up, she caught sight of Mr Ashe's beady face in the widow of Hugh's office. Ashe was a man who knew about everything. She did not like the fact that he had seen her with the reporter. The poor man was still wheezing. 'Did you mean it? What you said about a fair and just representation?'

'I've got no axe to grind. I'm just here to hold the mirror up, as it were . . .'

Mary could feel Mr Ashe's eyes riveted to her and she was suddenly aware of pressure. She panicked slightly, and suspending all judgement she said, 'I believe there's to be a meeting next week at Cwm Ifor. You should get yourself into that. Ask at the Stag and Pheasant. Say that – no, don't say anything –' She gave the reporter a final look and prayed that he could be trusted, then she sped off down the street, already regretting what she had done. As she got closer to the office, Mr Ashe's gaze flicked back to his work. In her mind she saw the huge, reproachful eyes of Jac Tŷ Isha and guiltily she shook her head.

Thomas rested his back against the bricks and breathed more easily. He allowed himself a little sigh of pleasure. A meeting at Cwm Ifor. And what else had she said? Ask at the Stag and Pheasant. He straightened himself and as he did so, spotted the Notice of Reward pasted to the wall. She had been rattled by that. He paused in his stride for a moment, hoping that the girl in the green dress had not taken any risks, and he blessed her quietly as he walked on to catch the mail.

The mid-morning brandy was still warming Timothy Powell's belly and he laid his tight-sleeved arms across his waistcoat as if to remind himself of the taste of it. Time for another soon. He salivated loosely at the thought. As soon as this blasted meeting was over, at any rate. He looked about him, sick of the sight of the Mayor's office. Colonel Love was rambling on about the placement of troops in the area.

Major Parlby shifted in his chair. His moment of glory at the Workhouse gates was already beginning to feel uncomfortably far away. The last few days had seen to that. He smoothed the edges of his moustache and then leaned towards the Colonel.

'Colonel Love, sir. In spite of what you and I talked about earlier, I think it might be advisable to put the gentlemen of the Council more fully in the picture. Don't you think?'

Colonel Love looked piqued. He rose to his feet to emphasise his authority.

'Gentlemen. There has been an incident at Porth-y-Rhyd. You're bound to hear of it sooner or later, and it may as well be from the horse's mouth. Parlby's right to bring it up.' Here he threw a tight-lipped look in the Major's direction. 'It does highlight some of the problems we are having at the moment. Information, mis-information, troop mobility, that kind of thing. We were given a warning from what we took to be an unimpeachable source that Rebecca was planning an attack on the gate at Porth-y-Rhyd on July the twenty-first.

'We set off to the north of the village, having detailed a second detachment to cover the southern approaches. Needless to say, not so much as a rabbit stirred in Porth-y-Rhyd that night and our time was wasted. However, we conducted a certain amount of surveillance in the region and had the galling experience,' the blue-tinged lips were tighter now, 'of hearing Rebecca using gunfire to signal our every move to the wretched "Daughters" she had posted in the area. To cap it all, less than an hour after we had passed through the village of Tumble, one of the gates there was taken down.'

Timothy Powell snorted with amusement and all eyes swung in his direction.

'Yes?' The Colonel's mouth was a mere pencil-tracing in his face.

'Damned flies, they get everywhere,' the magistrate exclaimed, feebly swatting at the air. As a matter of fact, only minutes ago he had squashed one on the back of his hand, leaving a brown and matted stain amongst the hairs.

Colonel Love continued sharply, 'It gives me very little pleasure to see my soldiers ridiculed in the way they were that night and it seems to be a common feature of Rebecca's campaign. We have the disadvantage of not knowing the countryside and of being at the mercy of the whims of informers whose truthfulness is at best doubtful.' The lips slacked off into a sigh. 'Even when we know that they are genuine they often recant at the last moment for fear of reprisals. It's a bit of an uphill battle. More like playing cat and mouse than any military strategy I've ever been involved in.' He shut the folder in front of him and prepared to call the meeting to a close, when the Mayor mouthed a single word to him.

'Ah yes, one last thing and then we can leave for today, you'll be glad to hear.

'We have reason to believe that the gate at Tumble was destroyed by a bunch of colliers. Now, you don't need me to tell you that until now, as far as we can reliably assess, the culprits in this bout of gate-breaking have been farmers or agricultural labourers, so this definitely constitutes a significant development. For one thing, the nearest mines are towards Swansea which indicates the unrest is spreading to the east, but more importantly, we can expect to find that as the nature of the men involved changes, so the type of trouble that they cause may also change. At the moment the best that we can hope for is to protect the towns and villages in the area, and possibly potential trouble spots such as workhouses, but to imagine we can extend beyond that is unrealistic. All things point towards more frequent and, I'm afraid to say, increasingly violent outbreaks of the disturbances. Thank you, gentlemen.'

The chambermaid popped her head round Thomas Campbell Foster's door.

'There's a lad to see you. Says you're expecting him. Not the kind the manager would normally admit, so I thought I'd best make sure . . .'

Thomas was ready. A woollen scarf to protect his chest, the stoutest shoes he owned, his pocket book and several sharpened pencils . . .

The maid looked taken aback. Everyone said that the London reporter had peculiar ways, but he couldn't surely be going out on a night like this, not with a chest like his and all.

'It's a mucky night, sir.' She thought she had better mention it.

Thomas peered at her distractedly; in his mind he was already on the way. 'Yes, so I believe . . . I think perhaps a bottle in my bed tonight . . . Could that be arranged?' He patted his pockets. Everything in order. Time to go. He was shouldering his way into his overcoat when he first saw the lad they had sent; a sullen, lard-faced youth. Thomas wondered drily if it was their way of trying to put him off.

'Me name's Dafydd. They said you're to come with me. I suppose you still want to.' The boy tossed his hair back and shifted his weight from one hip to the other. The whole business was clearly an immense and insupportable burden to him. Thomas assumed a look of steely joviality. Nothing, but nothing could deter him now, although he noticed that the boy's sweat smelled badly of burned toast. It filled the lounge of the Ivy Bush. He could see that the maid had smelt it too.

'Right. Let's get saddled up and be off.'

'No horses.' The boy eyed him coolly and gave a defiant sniff.

'Really? Can I ask – '

'Too noisy. It's not far. Six miles or thereabouts. We're all on foot tonight. You coming?'

Thomas was happy to escape from the hotel and the curious gaze of the maid. Dafydd was wearing rough clogs, yet he could hardly hear him on the road as he sped along in a strange trotting gait. He had to run to keep up. From time to time the boy would dart behind a hedge or into a ditch, always the wettest he could find, and squat down, listening, glaring as Thomas panted. He suspected that this exercise was not because of some perceived threat but to make his own life as uncomfortable as possible. Every time he coughed he bit his lip, angry to be fuelling the boy's sense of irritation so obligingly.

The countryside was hilly now; the hills were interlaced with small fields that made up the tiny farms on which these angry farmers lived. The gradients seemed to get steeper as they travelled and Thomas felt as if his lungs were plugged up with Welsh clay.

'Where's the meeting to be held?' he rasped, during one of the intervals in a ditch, breaks in the journey that he was increasingly grateful for.

'Cwm Ifor.'

Thomas refused to be withered. 'I'm aware of that. I wondered whereabouts in Cwm Ifor.'

'You'll see soon enough.'

It was not long before Foster began to notice figures on the road ahead of him, shadows of men that seemed to glide from the solid ranks of trees and vanish into the blackness, who slid in and out of the hedgerows just as he and Dafydd had been doing for what now felt like hours and hours. One of these shadows came up to them and fell into step behind the lad. Immediately Dafydd's peculiar trotting quickened, leaving Thomas barely within earshot. The shadow spoke,

'Yer Da not out tonight then, Dafydd.'

The lard-faced youth shook his head onerously. 'No, he's harvesting. He's up to his neck in it at the moment. Sent me instead.' Thomas noted with satisfaction that the sense of encumbrance was not reserved exclusively for him.

'Sent yer friend too, did he then?' said the shadow with a backward jerk of his head. For a moment Dafydd allowed himself to puff up a little before remarking with studied dismissiveness:

'Oh no. He's the reporter down from London. Can't put me finger on his name just now.'

'You've got to be joking, mate.' The shadow stopped in his tracks and was staring at Thomas as if he could not believe his eyes.

Dafydd shrugged. 'Lads at the Stag and Pheasant said he could come, so here he is.'

'I've often wondered if those boys know what they're doing, now I –'

'Hush your mouth or we'll never get there.'

For the rest of the journey the shadow kept looking at Thomas as if he wanted to reach out and touch him to make sure he was real. And then without warning Dafydd suddenly swung off the road to the right, squeezed his way with impatience through a kissing gate and, as he followed through, Thomas found himself at the edge of a crowd of almost three hundred men. He was astonished by how little noise they made. He looked round for Dafydd, but the lad had detached himself and was talking with now familiar truculence to four men at the centre of the gathering. They were staring at Thomas in consternation. Well. There was nothing else for it. He flipped open his pocket book and began to scribble.

'You writing your report, then?' the shadow said with awe in his voice.

'That's right. Perhaps you can tell me exactly where we are?'

'Will it be in the London papers, then?' the shadow asked with round eyes.

'That's right.' Thomas said again with practised patience.

'Don't know as I should, then.' The shadow was doubtful.

'What if I promise not to mention you by name?' It was like talking to a young child.

'Well if you're sure then . . .' The shadow moved his layers of clothes right up close to Thomas. 'It's the burial ground of the Baptist Chapel and over there—'

'All right, my sisters.' A Welsh voice carried quietly from the group of men around Dafydd.

'Can you tell me what he's saying?' Thomas licked

his lips, his pencil poised. The shadow shifted uncomfortably.

'Don't know as I should. He's talking about you, see.'

'Please.' Thomas could not keep the entreaty out of his voice.

The shadow fixed him with a stare and dubiously began to translate. 'First of all I should tell you we have an unexpected guest. We have the reporter down from London here tonight.'

Already three hundred faces were looking at him, for the shadow's commentary was several beats behind. Thomas was prepared. He pulled out the cutting from his pocket. It had worked before.

'They say that anybody could have cut that out of the paper,' the shadow pointed out a minute later. Foster paused, frowning, and then went through all his pockets. Out came several visiting cards, a handkerchief, receipts, some of his own scribblings, and, the Lord be praised, last of all a code of practice issued by the editor to all of the staff reporters. Thomas had been insulted when he was given it. Now he could have kissed the wrinkled piece of paper. Duly it was passed round until at least twenty men had looked it over. There was much nodding and shaking of heads, and dialogue that the shadow tactfully declined to translate. Finally, rubbing his ear, he turned to Thomas.

'They say that you can stay. No names, mind.'

'No, I promise on my honour. No names.'

'There's a schoolroom above the Chapel stable. Looks like we're going in there. You'd better follow me.'

And so, aware that hundreds of pairs of eyes were staring at him just as the shadow had first done, the reporter down from London followed his interpreter further into the Chapel grounds. He paused by the iron-bound door, taking advantage of the faint light from the stars to rummage again for his pocket book and pencil. A man was standing by. Thomas thought he looked rather like an attendant at the theatre.

'You won't be needing those,' he said grimly, snatching the tools of his trade from the reporter's hands. 'This is secret, see?'

Thomas was still working when the maid came in to clean the grate at six o'clock the following morning. He had his overcoat wrapped about him and his scarf wound round his neck. The meeting had lasted several hours and Dafydd had left him to find his own way home . . . He was still cold, and very, very tired. He scarcely turned his head when the maid came in so he did not see the look of perplexity on her face.

'You all right, sir?' She cocked her head to one side.

His tongue tasted like metal in his mouth and his fingers were clenched up with cramp.

'I'm sorry? What did you say?' He blinked a little, but kept his eyes fixed on the end of his pen.

'Can I get you something, Mr Foster?' she began again.

Painfully, Thomas straightened his back.

'I can't stop just yet. Have to get this finished. I simply cannot miss the morning mail.' He turned stiffly to look at the girl. She was so new and fresh and there was kindness somewhere in the confusion in her face.

'Perhaps a pot of tea, sir?' Her voice was eager and he nodded wearily, feeling he could not refuse.

'That would be very kind.'

While she was gone he read his article again, checking carefully in the knowledge that, God willing, soon it would be triumphant on the front page of *The Times*. An exclusive. Even now, worn out as he was, Thomas Campbell Foster held his breath at the thought. He smiled a pleased and private smile, savouring the sweetness of childhood dreams and youthful expectations made real, black on white, on the page in front of him. 'Cover this well,' the editor had said, 'and it could be the making of you.' He read the pages through again.

The little maid returned with a pot of tea which she poured solicitously for him. He dismissed her with a distracted 'Thank you,' and lapsed deeply into thought. His report was sealed up and ready on the desk in front of him. He looked at it abstractedly, thinking, weighing the matter up. No names, they had said, and he had promised . . . no names . . . His brain was busy and his eyes quite vacant as the tea went cold in its cup. No names. Very well. He pulled a fresh sheet of paper towards him and wrote out a second, identical account of the night's events. He was frowning when he wrote out the address – Timothy Powell – but as he rested the second letter on top of the first he comforted himself with the thought that if the JP wanted to pass it on to the Home Office, as he undoubtedly would, then that was his affair. His own duty was done. In any case the whole country would be reading about it in a few days' time. The pen slid out of his fingers. He was fast asleep in his chair when the maid came back to collect the untouched tray.

Meredith lay in the double bed with her nightdress up around her neck and her eyes shut as her Isaac pushed inside her. She kept her lips tightly closed as well and strained her head back against the pillows. Sometimes he pushed so hard she couldn't stop the sounds coming out of her mouth, and when that happened she wondered if Mrs-Pugh-Next-Door could hear what he was doing to her. He was moving quicker now, his exacting body butting in to her again and again. It was like fielding blows. Surely it couldn't go on much longer. She opened her eyes and all she could see was a great gaping mouth hanging over her.

'*N . . . o . . . w.*' The single word was stretched until it was a minute long and her Isaac tore himself out of her to finish the business off in the darkness at the far side of the bed. She waited until he was quiet and motionless, and then she smoothed her nightdress back around her body. At least he was still careful. That hadn't changed. No baby yet, thank the Lord. She turned onto her side away from him.

'*Cariad.*' His hands groped heavily for her across the mattress. 'Don't take on now. One day, my pet, when I'm better and we've got a bit of money. Then we will. I promise you that. We just have to wait a little bit longer.'

Meredith did not move as he arranged the wetness of his body round her; he liked her to sleep right in the crook of it. 'When I'm better.' She curled her lip at the thought. It had been bad enough before.

Before he came home on that terrible day. That day he had helped to sack the Workhouse in Carmarthen. He had stood at the foot of the bed crying out her name until she woke and saw that this face around his eye had been cut to pieces. The eye was still in its socket but only just. A dragoon, he had said, as he begged and pleaded with her to put him right. 'It's got to be stitched, *cariad*. You're good with your hands. You've got to do it for me.' She had gone into the garden to be sick and then she had thought of Mrs Pugh. Meredith had sat in the next-door kitchen with the baby on her lap and listened to the screams coming through the wall as Mrs Pugh had stitched the torn strips of her Isaac's face back together. Oh it was bad enough before, but now she couldn't bear it, couldn't bear for him to touch her, to fix her with that mobile, damaged eye, to enter her. She shuddered slightly and gave a little sigh.

'Sleep well, my pet,' her Isaac whispered in her hair. But her body remained on the defensive, pulled tight against the invader and she could not sleep. Fifty rigid minutes ticked by before she heard the first tap on the door. There was a pause. Meredith had barely raised her head when the tap came again. She slipped out of her Isaac's lumbering embrace and stood at the top of the stairs listening, tense.

'Wakey, wakey.' The voice was slurred and heavy and a sharper tap accompanied it. Meredith padded down to the kitchen, feeling frightened and bewildered. She thought of calling up to Isaac; she almost did, but then she stopped herself. What if he wanted to start all that again when they got back into bed? She slid the bolt back and, shielding herself behind the door, opened it slowly. Eight or nine men had thrust their way through the garden gate and were crowded onto her doorstep.

'Evening, Miss. Or is it Mrs?' The speaker's lips were black against his blackened face. He had thick black forearms folded over his chest and a black cap pushed to the back of his head. The faces behind him remained a jumble in the dark.

'It's Mrs, actually. My husband is upstairs. He's asleep.' There was a slight gust of wind and her nightdress licked at the kitchen door. She knew that the man had seen it, for his mouth opened in a slow smile.

'Husband, eh? Well, isn't that a pity?'

Meredith pulled the door closer to her. 'I'm sorry. I don't think I know you.'

The man's red mouth began to move again. 'No, I don't think you do. I come from Swansea way so the chances are we haven't met before.' He spoke with a drawl. Meredith noticed that his foot was lodged in the doorway and she swallowed.

'What do you want with us?' She swallowed again, for her mouth felt dry.

'Well, what I want with your husband and what I'd want with you are two very different things.' He gave a lazy laugh which the rest of the group took up.

'But I told you, he's asleep.'

'Best wake him up, then.'

There were calls of 'Wakey, wakey' from the back. They're drunk. The thought flashed through Meredith's mind and for the first time in ages she wanted her Isaac, wanted him badly. She turned and called his name, keeping hold of the door all the time.

'Matter of business,' the man slurred softly at her. 'I'm in business myself. In the mining trade. That's not the kind of business we're on here tonight though, eh lads?'

The arrival of Isaac stumbling into the kitchen interrupted the chorus of agreement that was sloshing round the group. The man at the front had his whole body in the doorway now. Meredith backed off towards her husband, clutching at his hand.

'You're a lucky man, Mr – ?' The man's eyes were fixed on her nightdress as he spoke.

'What do you want?' Isaac pushed his wife into the corner and planted himself in the middle of the room. The man's mouth closed in a whistle and his body looked at home and relaxed leaning against the door jamb.

'Keep yer hair on, mate. Only paying you a friendly call, like. Wondered if you were coming out with us tonight?'

Isaac's huge face creased into a frown. There wasn't a single man that he knew out there. You couldn't be too careful these days, what with rewards and informers and all.

'Where are you from?'

'From the mines down Swansea way. Heard there was fun to be had in this neck of the woods of an evening, like. Hate to miss out on a bit of fun, don't we, lads?'

The chorus behind him was obliging with its support.

'So we popped into the Stag and Pheasant for a bit of a bevy there. Lads put us in the picture and here we are. Are you coming or not?'

Isaac put his hands upon his hips and took his time in sizing up the situation. 'I don't think I am. I don't know you from Adam. You can quote the Stag and Pheasant lot until you're blue in the face but I don't hold with some of the new lads there and it won't wash with me. That clear?'

The reply came right from the back of the crowd, from somewhere amongst the garden shadows.

'Coward.'

Meredith, shivering with the cold, watched as her Isaac seemed to swell right up. He waded his way through the men until he found the one that he thought had spoken and fed him with a cold, immobile stare.

'See that?' He pointed to his eye. 'That's what Rebecca's done for me, right? I done my bit same as everyone else and that's the thanks I got for my pains. I was one of the first men into the Carmarthen Workhouse, so don't talk to me about coward, lad.' He grabbed the man by the collar of his shirt, shook him once, hard, and then let him go. The man who led the group was still leaning easily in the doorway.

'You won't change yer mind?'

Isaac, moving back into the kitchen, spoke gruffly.

'You're bloody right, I won't.'

'It'll cost you.' The man looked at Isaac levelly. 'It's common practice now – you don't come, you pay for the privilege of a night in bed. Worth it in your case, I should say. Anyway. Those of us who do turn out have to cover our expenses, see?'

'Bugger off, mate.' Isaac didn't even turn round. The man wasn't lounging any more, he was upright, taut.

'You know the form, mister. We're not going out on a picnic. We've got guns, you know.'

'Isaac.' There was a tremor in Meredith's voice.

'We've got guns and you've got a very pretty wife.'

Isaac turned round deliberately, but Meredith was already at the dresser, rummaging through the little pot which held her few pence of housekeeping. Her fingers were cold and stiff and they shook. So did her voice when she spoke.

'My Isaac's a sick man. It's out of the question for him to go out with you tonight. Like he said, he's done his bit. Here.' She touched the man's hand briefly as she gave him the money. 'Take this. It's all I can find.'

The collier jingled the coins in his hand and looked speculatively from them to her, before closing them into his fist.

'Right-o. Since you put it so nicely.' He turned with a swagger, 'Come on, lads.' He looked at Isaac. 'Some of us have work to do tonight.'

Husband and wife stood in the kitchen in silence, looking at one another. Meredith felt the full weight of her tiredness and she hung her head, shivering and lonely.

'You shouldn't have done that,' said her Isaac as he turned heavily. 'You shouldn't have done that at all.' And he walked upstairs to bed, leaving her on her own in the cold.

First thing on the following morning Meredith padded round to Mrs-Pugh-Next-Door. She did not speak to her Isaac at all; she just got up, dressed herself and padded round to her neighbour.

'Look at me! Right behind myself I am this morning.

Only half the children fed – Owen, hold the baby will you?' Mrs Pugh was speeding her way around the crowded kitchen, children and objects flying in all directions as she passed. 'I'm halfway through a hundred different things and not one of them finished yet. Now Frances,' she spoke fondly to her eldest, 'time you were at the fields, my pet. Don't follow your mother's example. You get along now like a good girl . . .'

Meredith was used to the scrum. She sat herself down, made herself quite comfortable and with wide, indignant eyes she told her tale. Mrs Pugh did not appear to listen, but at the end she turned, her face soft, and with pity in her look that the young girl did not see, she said, 'Never mind what your Isaac said, you did the right thing, my pet.' She hoisted an infant off the ground and on to the rangy comfort of her hip. 'They came here too. We didn't have the price of a loaf of bread in the house so my Mr Pugh had to go along. It's just as well your Isaac wasn't there.' Her large, cracked hand smoothed at her baby's hair.

'What do you mean?' Meredith was disgruntled; she didn't like to have her story capped. Two of the boys were playing dragoons down the hallway but Mrs Pugh's eyes were remote and far away.

'They took down the Tŷ Coch gate. It's managed by an old woman, she must be seventy at least. She came running out of the toll-house screaming for help and one of Becca's children set about her with an iron bar, broke her arm, called her an old hag of Satan. An old woman like that.' The baby put its tiny fingers on her cheek. 'My Mr Pugh did nothing about it. He just came home and went to bed. And so, my pet, I think it's

264

just as well your Isaac wasn't there.' Mrs-Pugh-Next-Door placed her toddler carefully on the floor, gave him a spoon to play with and then went on with her washing. Meredith sat in silence for a time.

'My Isaac will be waiting for his breakfast,' she said at last.

'There's some Welsh cakes cooling over there.' Mrs Pugh nodded. 'You take him some of those and tell him from me that he's better off at home in bed with his wife at night than breaking gates for Rebecca. Tell him there's work to be done there as well.' She looked significantly at the girl's flat tummy. Meredith smiled weakly and with the warm Welsh cakes held in her apron she padded back home to make her husband's breakfast.

William was slumped in Mary's chair in the kitchen. The cushion felt lumpy in the small of his back but he could not reach it; he had tried but it was just no good. He hunched his shoulders as best he could and leaned his head back in an awkward, sulky gesture. Mary had bullied him into coming downstairs. Nagged at him until he was fed up with the sight of her. And when he had given in and agreed, what had she done but swan off to Carmarthen leaving him all by himself?

'I'm spending the morning at the office and I promised I'd look in on Mrs Williams on my way home. Hugh says she has had a cold and is feeling a bit out of sorts. It won't take me long. Is there anything you want me to bring back?'

It was all very well for her. He thought that she avoided his eye as she tucked the blanket round his

265

legs and fussed over him. Deep down inside he felt that part of her wanted to get away. He heard her singing to herself as she saddled up Jonah. She popped her head round the door.

'I'm off now. You'll be all right, won't you? Oh, I almost forgot. I brought you a copy of *The Carmarthen Journal* last night and then I never gave it to you. It's over there on the dresser. You have a little look at that while I'm away. Have you got everything you want now?'

She was just salving her conscience, fussing over him, pretending she was concerned. He felt that she couldn't get away fast enough. Oh yes. It was all very well for her. William's head rolled loosely on his shoulders, his good arm felt leaden and his bad arm felt non-existent. It was all so hopeless really.

When Mary had gone he fetched the newspaper. It was a difficult operation like everything else these days: heaving himself out of the chair, dropping the blanket, picking it up again . . . He had got into the habit of carrying his bad hand in his good because he could not bear the way it swung about on its own, heedless of the rest of him. He preferred to carry it neatly against his body as if to remind himself that it was still a part of the whole. It made carrying anything else rather complicated, so fetching the newspaper was a long and difficult operation and there was bitterness in his face by the time he dropped back into the chair again.

The newspaper sat on his knee. Turning the pages was a two-handed occupation that was not easy to adapt. He opened the front page and the entire middle section slithered down his legs and onto the floor. Tears of frustration filled his eyes and he wiped them away with his good hand and then gave the pages on the floor a futile, angry kick. He could do that at least. For twenty minutes he sat with his face puckered, rocking himself gently. And then he sighed. A deep, unhappy sigh. Well. Just have to make do with page one, that's all. How else was he to pass the long, resentful morning?

Looking down, he almost changed his mind. The whole of the front page was crammed with a story about Rebecca. He didn't really want to know, didn't want to hear about the triumphs and the setbacks, the ins and outs of it all. Didn't he know enough already? For a while he sat with his eyes averted, just thinking and remembering. He remembered how passionately he had felt. He shook his head at the thought. If only he had known then . . . Memory was nothing but punishment and derision. Eventually his eyes dropped to the *Journal* again, grudging the interest which lingered after all these weeks. Well, there was nothing else to do . . . half-reluctantly he began to read.

The story that it told was not a pretty one and as he read, William bit his lip and his face wrinkled up with disbelief and horror and regret at the misery of it all. Rebecca and her daughters, fresh from the mines, went to New Inn on the way to Cardigan and tore the solid, five-bar gate to pieces. They made so much noise that the toll-collector's wife looked out of the bedroom window to see what was going on. It was the last thing that she did see. One of the rioters took his gun and fired at her at point-blank range. The gun was only filled with powder, not with shot, but still the man took it and fired it right into her face. Into her eyes. The other men got the scent of blood then. One of them took aim at what he thought was the toll-collector himself, but it turned out to be his coat hanging inside the house instead. The next morning thirty slugs of shot were found embedded in that coat. The woman groaned, for the pain was beginning to register, and someone asked the toll-collector if he was hurt. He told Becca's children that they had murdered his wife.

'What a pity!' the leader said, and ordered the collector to come out of his house. They left the woman groaning in a pool of her own blood by the window she had so rashly opened and made her husband ride with them to Chapel. They banged on the door of the minister's house until the old man woke up, and, holding him at gun-point, demanded a bottle of his best Communion wine. Rebecca took the bottle and thrust it into the toll-collector's arms.

'There,' she said, 'take that back to cure your wife with,' and then she and her daughters rode off home to their dusty, coal-black beds. But the toll-collector's wife could not be cured, for Rebecca's visit had made her blind for life.

William read the article, cradling his deadened hand against his chest. He couldn't feel the tear which fell upon his palm and for a moment did not realise that he was weeping. He sat in his sister's chair, surrounded by the lost sheets of the paper and his body was helpless under the blanket as he wept. He wept for the toll-collector's wife, he even wept for the poor old coat, but most of all he wept for himself and found that he could not stop.

9

Jac came for her at nine o'clock that evening. A fluting whistle in the yard, the same that had signalled to her brother in times gone by, now brought Mary to a halt in the kitchen and turned her skin from pink to white to pinker still, while the blood sang around her heart.

William heard, but said nothing. 'That's it. I'd better go,' said Mary, flooded with guilt and excitement all at once.

'You've changed your tune rather,' remarked her brother. He'd been cajoled into slicing up fruit, ready to be bottled for the winter. Pears and apples skidded between the sleeve of his dead arm and the chopping board. Mary thought he made the job more difficult than he need, then reproached herself for her unkindness.

'Oh, you know what Jac's like,' she said lightly. 'He can talk a person into anything.'

'Evidently.' William sat with his back to her. A piece of apple bucked its way along the table out of reach. 'Oh for God's sake!' In bitterness and anger the words were almost shouted.

'You're doing fine.' Mary was tentative, expecting

269

him to snap at her. William banged the knife down on the table and buried his head in his good arm. She rested her hand on his hair for a moment and then picked the knife up.

'You've got to learn new ways, you know. I can't do everything on my own,' she coaxed him softly. 'Come along. You were doing so well, don't be cross now.'

But his face was still surly when he took the knife back from her. 'It's all very well for you.'

It was a surliness she understood.

'Jac's waiting. I won't be long. There now.'

Jac's face was pale and shy and his face knocked awkwardly against hers as he kissed her cheek. Mary had noticed this, that it always took them a few minutes to grow into one another once again. He stooped, more to hide his face than to tie his bootlace, although that was what he did.

'I've missed you, Mary Jenkins.' His voice was gruff. He straightened up and dared a glance at her.

There was something piercing, almost painful, about Mary's face: eyes too brimming, lips too lightly parted to be bearable. Her feelings were writ too plainly; she looked altogether breakable.

'Oh, Jac, I've missed you too. It's seemed like ages.'

'Moon's up. We'd best be getting along.' He looped his arm through hers. 'You don't have to do this, you know,' he went on. 'Whether you do or not won't make any difference to what's between you and me. They're separate things.'

'I know.'

'It's just that you haven't always seen eye to eye

with Rebecca. I don't want you to be pressured into something because, well, because . . .'

'I don't feel pressured. Don't worry about that. I'm here because I want to be. Because of what's happened to William as much as anything else. Anyway, that's beside the point really. You'd better tell me what – '

And then he kissed her. The sweetest, gentlest pressure. They looked at one another breathlessly.

'You'd better tell me . . .'

'I think I'm falling in love with you, Mary Jenkins,' he said, then he pulled her by the hand and began running. 'Come on,' he called. 'We won't get there at all at this rate.'

'But what – ?'

Half an hour later Jac put his hands to her waist and jumped her down from a stile. He pulled her onto the grass beside him.

'Are you cold?'

'No.' She shook her head, tucking herself more closely into the crook of his shoulder.

'Right. This is the situation. It's a chap called Mostyn tonight. At the meeting we held to arrange everything, he made it quite clear that if he was going to be Rebecca he couldn't manage the baby on his own. There was a lot of talk and argument, people saying that women should never be involved, but he put his foot down, said that on no account would he be shut up in a carriage with a puking baby and no one to give him any help. In the end he won the day. The others agreed that if a reliable, discreet girl could be found, that in this case, just for once, it might be allowed.' He paused for a moment. 'The baby's mother would be missed at the Workhouse, otherwise she'd be the obvious choice.'

Mary had her eyes closed, remembering the details of his profile.

'I see,' she said.

'There is an element of risk, you know. It would be wrong to say there wasn't.'

'It's all right. I understand.'

'You're a good girl.' He looked at her fondly.

'Hadn't we better be going on . . .?'

He helped her to her feet.

'I'll come and collect you after.'

Mary sat in the corner of the carriage with the baby screaming on her lap and a loaded gun touching her left knee. The gun alarmed her rather; it belonged to the man who was bunched into the carriage with her, taking up the whole of the opposite seat. In spite of the distraction of the wrestling, fighting baby, she could not tear her eyes from him, but kept darting him glances of hypnotised amazement. He was wearing a horsehair wig which had slipped off-centre, giving his ruddy face a strangely scalloped fringe. Brass curtain rings hung in his ears and he was continually patting them into place with an affectation which Mary found bizarre. He wore a high-waisted dress of saffron muslin, its wrinkled bodice tied at the back with frayed strips of cotton. Metal-rimmed boots peeped out from under his petticoats and he had a pipe in his mouth. He ran a finger between the neckline of the dress and his own smock which he had on underneath.

'Dreadful hot, it is,' he remarked. The child

screamed in reply before Mary could stop it and with a hand that shook she offered it a butter biscuit. She had come prepared for this, at least. Anxiously she watched the baby as it pushed the biscuit into its mouth, sucked it for a bit, pulled it out to examine it, dropped it onto the floor and then screamed again.

'I'm sorry. I'm not doing very well, am I?' she said nervously.

The figure opposite took the pipe from his mouth and with a hand the size of a meat pie brushed the soggy crumbs off his knuckly yellow knees. 'Frock belonged to my great aunt. They say she got it in Cardiff.' This was not an invitation to talk, for the pipe went straight back in his mouth and he folded his arms across his chest with sturdy emphasis. 'Any chance of it going to sleep, do you think?' he asked five minutes later, watching the writhing and grizzling of the infant rather doubtfully. 'I've got a tot of brandy somewhere, if I can just get to it,' and he began hoisting at his skirt as Mary said, with a doubt that matched his own, 'It'll tire itself out soon. You'll see. I don't think brandy is a very good idea . . .'

'That's good. More for me,' he said, and yanked a small flask out of the side of his boot. He rinsed the brandy through his teeth and swallowed, looking at the child more benignly.

'Poor mite. Not his fault. Hasn't been brought up proper. Still, we'll soon put that right . . .' He tailed off and brought the brandy bottle into play again. In fact, the child was quieter in Mary's arms now, and she made much of wrapping her cloak round it and rocking it and whispering a song in its ear. The eyes flickered closed and for a while she held her breath, looking intently at the little snippet of a face. It was a perfect copy of its mother, a tiny version of the anguished woman who met them in the broken shadows of the Workhouse gates. The girl had tears streaming down her face and she kissed the child ferociously. 'You be good now, and your Dada will love you and give you a good life, better than your Mam ever could. And remember, your Mam loves you very much.' Another kiss. Mary turned her head away as the woman hugged her baby one last time.

'You'd better take him now.'

The grey, protesting bundle was pushed through a gap in the bars left by the Dragoons on the day they saved the Workhouse. That same grey bundle was now fast asleep on her knee, Rebecca was smoking a pipe opposite her and Mary didn't know whether to laugh or cry herself . . .

Mostyn leaned out of the window, holding his wig on with one hand. His pipe was tucked into the front of his dress and he was talking to the coach driver. After a few precarious lurchings he dropped back into his seat.

'Right, now listen. Here's what we're going to do. It's best that nobody knows you've been along, so you're to sit tidy in the carriage, keep the blinds down and don't say anything. When I ask for the baby, just hand it through the door and then back out of sight with you. There shouldn't be any rough business but if it does happen we don't want any screaming or fainting fits or anything like that, see? And if it all goes well, your reward will be in heaven. Right. Here we go.'

The carriage bounced off the road and hurtled

down a rough farm track, gathering speed as it went. In her arms the child stirred, and Mary watched as its thumb disappeared into its mouth and it pressed closer to her under the cloak. She peered past the edge of the drawn blind into the blackness and saw an unlit building loom into view; the coachman's whip was cracking and slicing the air and the eyes of Mostyn-Rebecca were glittering with the waiting.

The horses clattered to a halt and the coachman's voice rang round the farmyard.

'Hello there?'

A barn door slapped back on its hinges and through her slit at the window's edge Mary thought she saw a light wink in one of the upstairs windows. It bobbed and weaved behind the panes and she watched its inquisitive progress until the window was thrown open and a man in a nightcap leaned out. This was the coachman's cue. He jumped down from his box and as he lowered the carriage steps Mary had to smile. She had her first proper view of him and saw that he was little more than a boy really. He was done up like a negro servant, the sort that you saw in picture books. Like his mistress he was blessed with a fine horsehair wig, gathered neatly into a pigtail at the nape of his neck. He had a shiny black face – boot polish most probably, Mary thought – a brocade waistcoat with breeches to match and white stockings without a single hole in them. She looked at those with envy. The lad opened the carriage door, made an odd little bow which he had obviously given a lot of practice, and handed his mistress down from the coach.

'Wish me luck, then,' said Mostyn-Rebecca as he went.

The carriage door was left open and Mary pressed herself and the child back against the seat so as not to be seen. She had a good view all the same.

Mostyn strode forward till the light from the farmer's lantern shone fully on his face and with an instinctive pat at his earrings he began. 'Mr Llewellyn?'

'Yes. What do you want?' the farmer stammered.

'Rebecca here.' Mostyn watched the impact of his words with evident pleasure. 'I've popped by on a family matter you might say. Wondered if I might have a word?'

The farmer looked over his shoulder into the room and then back at the figure who glowed golden in the light of his lamp.

'What do you want?' he said again.

'I don't think the farmyard is a tidy place to receive a lady, is it?' Mostyn picked at an imaginary speck of dust on his sleeve and waited.

'You got any of your — what d'you call them — your children, with you?' The farmer searched at the darkness of his backyard.

'I'm waiting,' Mostyn said, the heavy boot tapping.

'All right. I'll come down. I'll come down.' The farmer disappeared from sight, the bedroom settled into blackness again and soon they could hear the bolts on the door flung back.

'Let's be having the poor little mite, then,' Mostyn said cheerfully to Mary and the child made soft sucking noises as it was passed over. 'You sit tight now,' he said over his shoulder as Llewellyn appeared on the doorstep in his nightshirt, his eyes still scouring the hidden corners and shadows of the yard.

'Say hello to your Dada then,' crooned Mostyn to the baby, and a speechless Llewellyn stood aside and let them into his house.

They reappeared about twenty minutes later. Mostyn's face was full of smiles and the arms of the farmer were full of his sleeping child. Mostyn clapped him on the back and then, remembering himself, dropped a low curtsey.

'Let's hope we never have occasion to meet again. Not being unfriendly, like, but you know what I mean.' This last was said rather darkly. 'Take care of the little one now and we'll say no more about it.' He clapped his hands to the coachman and shouted out, 'Right, boy, I'm ready,' before clambering up the hem of his dress and into the carriage.

The wig came off and the bottle came out and Mostyn spread himself across the narrow seat.

'Well, that took some doing, I must say,' he said, with a brandy sigh. 'Just hope he's to be trusted, that's all. Our friend Mr Llewellyn is not quite the honourable family man that he might seem to his friends and neighbours. He got one of the servant girls into trouble a couple of years back, and when she told him she was expecting, like, what does he do but give her the sack and turn her out. Poor girl has no choice, she has to go to the Workhouse to have the child. We get to hear about her sorry state and – in the spirit of setting things to rights, no matter what the wrong has been – here we are tonight. You can fill in the rest for yourself.'

He offered her the brandy bottle as an afterthought. Mary shook her head.

'I told him, I made it plain –' his big fist was clenched around the flask '– I said we'd be keeping an eye on him to make sure he did all that a good Dada should, and that if we found him wanting in any way then he could look forward to a second visit.' He lifted the blind and stared out into the night. 'I hope he's to be trusted. You never can tell, can you?'

Mary shook her head. 'No.' She hesitated. 'Do you think I might have a sip of the brandy after all? It's turned quite cold,' she said timidly and settled down for the rest of the journey back.

Jac was waiting at the crossroads just as he had promised, hunkered down against a gate, his face tense with listening. As the carriage rolled into view, he scrambled to his feet.

'Everything all right?' He stuck his head through the small half-window, addressing only Mostyn. His voice was businesslike.

'No trouble, mate. Want some?' Mostyn proffered the dregs of the brandy, but the neck of the bottle was back in his mouth before Jac had a chance to accept.

'I'd best get the girl home,' he said. 'I promised I would.' He opened the door and pulled a face as light from within spilled tellingly over the grass verge. 'See you Friday, is it?'

'Maybe.' Mostyn would not be drawn. 'Might send me brother-in-law. I'll see.'

'Right. Many thanks for tonight.'

This was said over Mary's head as he helped her

down the steps. She looked timidly into his face, tasting the inimitable estrangement of lovers and wondering what could possibly have effected such a mood change in him.

But as soon as the carriage had gone again Jac put both arms around her. 'Well, that's that. Business is business and pleasure is – ' his mouth smiled against her mouth, his lips touching her lips ' – pleasure,' he sighed. Later he asked her questions. His arm was curved around her shoulders, his cheek lay against her hair and the breath from his asking warmed the dark of her neck.

'How was it? Were you frightened? Do you love me? Did the child behave? Were you seen by anybody? Do you love me? Say yes, just say yes.'

'Yes, of course I do, silly. How could I not?'

They walked for ages, their feet heavy and slow with love. Lane twined into lane as the dawn thickened the sky.

'Are you tired, sweetheart? You must be. It's not far now. Shall we sit for a bit?' Enough tenderness to make a woman weep.

They sat under a hedge. The morning leaves were wet and cold. She shivered slightly, then gritted her teeth, unwilling to show weakness.

'Here,' Jac took off his jacket and wrapped it round her. Mary examined the material for traces of her brother's blood.

'It's all gone. I told you it would.'

She blushed. 'Sorry. William says I'm much too tidy always.'

'I don't think you're much too anything.'

His aching, familiar lips . . . Mary wanted to learn

them off by rote. She pulled him close to her, opening
the jacket to warm them both.

'Do you want to . . . I mean, it's all right . . . if you
do . . .' She hesitated. 'I don't mind, if that's what
you . . .'

Jac kissed the words away. 'Not now. You're kind
and wonderful and I love you, but not now, not yet.
It wouldn't be right. You're a good girl, Mary Jenkins,
you remember that.'

'Kiss me again then. Kiss away the hours of
sadness.'

'There isn't any sadness to kiss away, is there?'

'Oh, there's always sadness, Jac. It's always there
somewhere.' Mary twisted a curl of his hair around
her finger, feeling deflated, inopportune, passed
over. Jac leaned away from her. For a moment there
was loss between them.

'Home?' he whispered.

Mary nodded. 'Yes, I think so.'

Dawn lay like sediment across the sky, real and
grey. They walked towards Dolwilym with the sense
of having squandered something. There was regret
in their silence, and Mary's heart felt unappeased.

Colonel Love pressed his palms together. The pads
of his fingers were the same undernourished blue as
his cheeks and his lips were the thinnest part of his
cold and bony face.

Timothy Powell looked at him apprehensively. All
these meetings, and none of the news ever any good.
At least the Home Office had got a move on and sent
down two field pieces. For a moment Powell almost
wished he were a military man himself. A couple of

big blasts from one of those and they would soon have Rebecca lifting up her skirts and running for the trees.

'Do you mind if I smoke?' Major Parlby smoothed at his moustache with a gesture which betrayed his tension.

A good fat cigar. Thank God somebody was showing a bit of sense at last. Timothy Powell reached for one with alacrity while the going was good and wondered if he dared suggest a glass of brandy all round. He looked at the assembled faces, drawn with worry, and reluctantly bit his tongue. Timothy Powell settled his chins more comfortably on his chest and angled his chair so it was out of the direct line of fire. Forty winks and then it would soon be time to go over to the Travellers' Rest, see if Alwyn meant what she had said the night before . . .

Colonel Love ran his hand through his thin yellow hair.

'I expect you've all heard about Rebecca and the Llewellyn child. It was all over *The Carmarthen Journal* so you can't really have missed it. Well, we have reason to believe that the same person was responsible for a visit to a farm near Haverfordwest. The farmer had put a bit of corn by, waiting for the prices to rise before he sold it, which he had a perfect right to do. Rebecca turns up in some kind of a ballgown, fine carriage, string of servants – the hallmarks are all the same. She ordered him to thresh the corn and bring it to market the following Saturday so that the poor people could buy it at a reasonable price. She threatened him with arson, so the unfortunate man had no option but to kiss goodbye to all his profits and do exactly as he was told.'

'What you say is very worrying. It really is most alarming,' the Mayor piped up, his chain of office tinkling with agitation. 'You know what it means, all of you. It means that a person of some standing in the county, dare I say it, somebody from our own class, is involving himself in these ventures. Where else could Rebecca obtain all her paraphernalia – the coaches, the dresses, the jewels? All I can hope is that every man here is square with his own conscience.'

'I don't think there is any doubt of that, sir.' Major Parlby straightened up considerably. 'In fact, I rather resent that implication, if I may say.'

'It's all right, Major, there is no need for you to take it personally,' Colonel Love interrupted wearily. 'And the Mayor is quite right: none of us should consider ourselves to be above suspicion.'

'Do you know it's almost funny really,' Captain Davies said mildly, his elbows on the table. 'I mean, you have to admire her nerve. A chap I met the other day told me a story about the vicar of Bangor Teify. He and his wife have lived apart for twenty years, all very amicably, it's just what suited them best. Well. In the middle of the night Rebecca arrives at the woman's house, gets her up, takes her to the neighbouring parish where her husband lives, gets him out of bed and gives them both a lecture about upholding public morals. Says she wants them to live together and cherish one another properly from now on or they will incur her severe displeasure. They had to agree, didn't they? No use trying to cross her once her blood is up. It made me laugh when I heard it though.' He ended lamely and an unamused silence fell over the Council Chamber. Timothy Powell purred gently in his sleep.

'Rebecca will soon be telling us what we may or may not have for breakfast,' said Colonel Love acidly. Each of these incidents was an affront to him, a humiliation. They called his honour and ability, everything that he cared about, into question.

The mention of breakfast woke Timothy Powell as if by magic. He sniffed the air hopefully.

'I'm glad you find the antics of Rebecca so amusing, Captain Davies.' The Mayor's agitation was turning into petulance. 'I woke up this morning to find that somebody had dug a grave in the middle of my lawn. Rebecca had thoughtfully left a letter explaining that it was for me and that I could expect to find myself in it within the week. You can imagine how I fell about, I absolutely died laughing.' He leaned forward. 'However, I did not ask Colonel Love to call this meeting in order to tell you that. I felt I should inform you that the Home Secretary has appointed a Special Commission to inquire into the Rebecca Riots. He's convinced that there is serious subversion at the root of it. So let's hope that we begin to achieve some results. In the meantime, Captain Davies, if you hear any other good jokes I hope you will be kind enough to share them with the rest of us. Good day to you.' He slid his chair back and the meeting came to a close. The Captain looked utterly crushed and for a moment Timothy Powell almost asked him if he wanted to come along. Then he thought better of it. After all, it was most important to get Alwyn on her own . . .

* * *

'Rees Goring Thomas will just have to collect his own tithes for a little while longer,'said Elizabeth Edwards as she pushed her husband back against the pillows. 'You can "if" and "but" all you like, John, but you'll only get yourself into a moither and nothing's going to make me change my mind, see? Hannah will back me up on this–' She looked over to her daughter for support. Her head was bent over a book and one hand was propping her spectacles onto the bridge of her nose, for the fire in the sickroom made her hot and they had a habit of slipping down.

'Hannah, I'm right, aren't I ?'

'Sorry, mother?' The girl looked up, her face damp and her fingers twisting in her hair the way they always did.

'I said I'm right about your father. He's in no fit state to be up and about yet, with the fever still on him.'

'Oh no, mother, certainly not.'

Elizabeth looked at her daughter's shiny face. 'Yes mother, no, mother', her nose always in a book. There was no life in the girl. Twenty-three and no sign of a husband, which was hardly surprising when you thought what a bookworm she was. There wasn't a decent man in the district who would want a blue stocking for a bride. Hmmph. She turned to her husband in the bed.

'Is that understood now, John?'

The dull and listless shape sighed and turned his head on the pillow. 'I suppose so, dear.'

'Hannah, will you perhaps be kind enough to read

to your father for a while. It does no good to anybody
if you sit in the corner on your own all day and I
haven't got the time myself. There's his broth to be
made and a house this size doesn't run itself, you
know.' She stayed to watch Hannah move her chair
up to the bed, then she nodded gruffly and went
downstairs. I'm becoming a sour old woman, she
thought, standing alone in the kitchen, but what with
this chest complaint dragging on and on, and Hannah
moping, and all the troubles in the county at the
moment . . . Elizabeth exhaled dejectedly and pulled
the recipe book towards her. Four sheep's trotters
simmered in nutmeg and milk. If that didn't put John
back on his feet she'd have to have the doctor out
again, nothing else for it. She set to work.

At midnight the only light in the house at
Gelliwernen came from a furtive candle in Hannah's
bedroom. Her dark head was bent heedlessly low
over the tiny flame. She just wanted to read to the
end of the chapter . . . and then another . . . and
then the church clock struck one . . . and still she
read. Occasionally a sound made her pause and flick
her eyes towards the window; gunshot puncturing
the darkness again – it happened almost every night
now, somewhere or other along the valley. Tonight
it came from the direction of Morlais Bridge. Quite
close. Hannah pulled her shawl around her. She
almost liked the noise; it made the house feel safe
and warm. There was a scattering of light thrown like
loose change over the horizon. She crossed to the
window and pulled the curtains tighter, shutting out
all possible distraction, and then she found her place
again and continued to read.

Five hundred men were gathered on Morlais
Bridge, waiting. As many again were expected to join
them once the meeting at Llanedy was over. Five
hundred men with blackened faces waited for
Rebecca to give them their command. Knives were
unsheathed, guns were loaded and rockets were
ready for firing as soon as the first horn sounded,
and the whole valley hummed as men and horses
filed along the lanes which converged on
Gelliwernen.

A rocket exploded at the end of the garden just
above the greenhouses, and for the first time Hannah
really jumped. She was about to pick up her book
from where it had fallen when a rat-a-tat-tat of
gunfire clipped the air like terrible applause and she
froze where she stood.

'Hannah.' The fear in her mother's voice filled the
corridor although she was only speaking in a
whisper. 'Hannah, you're to come to our room. Keep
your head down and don't make any noise. We don't
know how many there are yet.'

She tucked her book under her arm and crept along
the corridor. Outside, eight hundred flares filled the
air with the burning reds and golds of autumn; the
torches looked like leaves flaming in the hands of
men as black and angry as winter trees. She stood,
staring. She had never seen anything so beautiful.

'Hannah. Are you all right?' Her mother crouched
in the doorway beckoning fiercely. 'Quickly.' The
same orange light lapped and flickered round the
sickroom and her father looked as if he were toasting
fretfully in his bed.

'He'll be no use to us,' her mother hissed. More

286

gunfire, closer. There was a blast from a hunting horn and the mob began to stamp and shout and scream.

'Come out, John Edwards, or we'll come in to get you.' Hannah looked at her mother and saw that she was trembling.

'John Edwards. John Edwards. John Edwards.' They were beating out his name on the gate to the kitchen garden. 'John Edwards. John Edwards –'

'I'll have to speak to them.' Her mother's eyes were glazed. 'He can't even get out of bed.' She moved to the window, ready to lift the sash. She need not have bothered. A whole pane of glass smashed onto the floor as the back wall and door were sprayed with shot and the force of the blast sent her reeling against the chest of drawers.

'Mother –' Hannah reached out a hand towards her, but already her mother had steadied herself.

'I'll have to speak to them,' she said again, and sliding her hands along the wall, she moved back towards the window.

The same.

Her mother stood in the corner of the room, sobbing, out of control. The back wall was blistered with shot; there was even some lodged in the headboard of the bed. Her father was struggling against his pillows, hauling himself upright.

'It's me they want –' he began. Another pane of glass went crashing to the floor. Hannah could feel herself sweating: it was running down her scalp, her neck was wet. A brick came thudding through the window, splintering the floorboards where it landed.

'Keep down,' she said to her father, 'just – keep

down.' Her legs seemed to bowl her along the corridor of their own free will. She ran down the stairs, half tumbling, holding on to the bannisters. Giant shadows doubled the height of the hall and her fear made her sticky all over. She pushed her spectacles up her nose and her hand slid on the doorknob. There was a reflex of silence as she stood alone in the porch, a slight, sallow figure, with her novel forgotten in her hand. And then a cracking and a splintering as the first stone cut through the glass roof. Another followed it, and then another. Hannah stood bemused, sheltering her head in her arms as the shards of glass danced around her.

'Stop. Hold on.' A man's voice. About twenty paces away. 'Wait. It isn't Edwards. It's the girl – '

There was a surge in the barracking at this. Men threw their bonnets in the air, stamping and cat-calling and clapping their hands. Five or six of them came lumbering towards the porch.

'Rank has its privilege, eh lads?' burped a ginger-haired man at the front. He was four, maybe five paces from her and his sticky eyes gloated on her nightdress. He put his hand to his flies and his little coterie shouted their approval.

'Me first, I think,' leered the carrot-head. Like white spiders, his fingers unfastened the buttons of his trousers.

Hannah closed her eyes. 'No, no, please, no. Please don't. Please.' Nobody heard her moaning.

There was a light drilling sound and then a roar of laughter. She forced herself to turn and look, to prepare herself. The redhead was urinating on the broken glass of the porch, his belly splayed, his trousers sliding further down his legs. He was pissing and laughing, pissing so hard that the beery drops danced on the glass and splashed her nightgown. The man next to him began to follow suit; soon there were three of them standing in a row, expending themselves.

'John Edwards. John Edwards. John Edwards.'

Then breaking through the never-ending chant, she heard the voice of the man who had first called attention to her. 'Give it a break. You're bloody animals, the lot of you, just pack it in.'

The man on the end of the line insolently flicked the last few drops in the speaker's direction, but he and his mates hauled their trousers back into place and ambled to one side, waiting for developments.

The speaker looked embarrassed. He leaned towards her in a fumbling, placatory manner and when Hannah flinched, he said, 'Your mother and you have nothing to fear, but I wouldn't set a greater value on your father's life than a feather thrown before the wind. We must have our tithes lowered – and we will.'

'John Edwards. John Edwards. John Edwards.'

Hannah's hands dropped to her sides; her muscles felt pulsating and weak. She took a deep breath. 'My father is sick in bed. He's had a fever in the lungs for days now. He cannot possibly come down to you.' Her voice was fluttering in her throat, but some of the men were listening. It was a start. 'That only leaves my mother and me. We have no chance against you and there's nothing we can do to help you in your fight against the tithes. In the name of decency and humanity, and please, in the name of

God, don't do us any harm. Leave us to look after my father and sleep in peace.'

A different voice, sullen and thick, spoke. 'I don't know about the rest of you, but I'm not here to fight with women and girls. You can count me and my lot out if you want to carry on.'

'Please. Go home now. Leave us be.' Hannah was feeling giddy.

Another man spoke. 'I haven't walked seven miles for a cosy chat, like. It's a very touching scene, I'm sure, but I came here to fight for a cause and I mean to see it through.'

A voice sounded from further back in the crowd. 'Hang on a moment. I'm with Ianto, I'm afraid. We can't fight women. We'll have ourselves a bit of fun another time. Let's be off home now.'

'Well, at least he's had a warning . . .' and so it went on.

Hannah stood braced in the broken porch, feeling as if her knees were going to buckle at any moment. As the crowd argued and debated, the heat seemed to go out of them. A few moved off. There was a crash of glass in the distance. The greenhouses. The men nearest her seemed cheered by this, as if there was still some purpose in the outing. They began to peel away from the house and their resentment at having to do so was vented on everything that they passed. Rose bushes were tugged out of the ground, shrubs flattened and she watched motionless as the fig tree trained against the garden wall was methodically hacked to pieces. As the mob's spirits revived, the gunfire started up again and Becca's children, freshly jubilant, began to scramble back the way that they had come, plundering and despoiling as they went. Hannah never forgot their laughter, their songs and the sounds of their blades biting.

She stood in the porch, rigid, until the last few stragglers had left the grounds. When they had gone she started to shake, violent, jerky shaking, and her body folded in upon itself. She stared at the rubble and splintered glass all around her. Desolation. And then, under a fractured window pane, she saw her book. She felt like giving a wild shout of laughter, it looked so solid and domestic, so out of place. Instead, she leant over to slide it carefully out from all the jagged edges. There. Gently does it. She hugged it to her and the cover and pages were stained and splashed all over with her blood.

Mike Bowen looked round the bar of the Stag and Pheasant. It was a quiet night there – only a few drinkers, who sat silently with their pints. The landlord, William Walters, was giving a rare polish to the pint pots hung round the bar. Things must be bad for him to be driven to that. Mike swung disconsolately on his chair, swilling the cider round his glass and watching its despondent spiral. Opposite him, a man was staring glumly at the floor, tracing patterns in the sawdust with his boot. Mike frowned, trying to place him. A huge, black-haired man with a scar running close to his eye. Isaac Hughes, that was it. Hurt the day the Workhouse was sacked. Of course. The man looked up, aware of Mike's stare, and they exchanged deficient smiles.

'Bad night the other night, I hear,' Mike said, by way of conversation.

'Gelliwernen?' said Isaac, shaking his head. 'Pointless exercise really, wasn't it?'

'I heard the girl was cut badly. Flying glass. Someone said she went to Llanelli for stitches.'

'It's probably not the fashion to say so just now, but it makes me sick. All this terrorising of women. Blinding the toll-collector's wife at New Inn, beating up the old lady at Tŷ Coch. I only just got out of that, you know. Bunch of colliers called round looking for volunteers and my missis gave them money to go away. I was mad at the time, but now I'm glad she did. I'm fed up with the whole business, to tell you the truth. It's not what Rebecca is all about, it's not why we started.' Isaac glanced round the bar and then looked out of the window, as if to disassociate himself from his own statement.

'I was Rebecca once.' Mike could not quite keep the boast out of his voice. 'Yes. Really.' He nodded ruminatively. 'We put the screws on Henry Thomas at the Water Street gate in Carmarthen.'

'Ohh.' Isaac gave a connoisseur's sigh.

'Maybe I'm biased,' Mike was leaning chattily on the table now, 'but in those days I think it was all different.' How glamorous and remote Water Street already seemed. 'I mean, it was all a bit of a lark then; a friendly warning, like. We didn't mean any serious harm. I gave my children – ' he threw the line away as casually as he could – 'I gave them specific instructions not to damage the room the family was in. Well, you wouldn't see anything like that now, would you?'

Isaac shook his head and took a long swig from his glass. 'It's the colliers,' he said in a low voice.

'They say there's a strike on at the copper mine Swansea way, so all the miners there will be out and about and looking for trouble. Going out with Rebecca is a tidy way to earn a few bob when there aren't any wages coming in, and there's many farmers who are happy to pay to have the dirty work done for them now that it's time to gather the harvest. I know I would be. I've paid and I'll gladly pay again if it gets me out of roughing up women and children.'

This time Isaac looked with some defiance round the bar. There was a lull in the conversation. A man sitting on the far side of the room struck a chord on the harp in his lap and began to whistle softly in accompaniment.

'Now there's a tune, Dai,' said the man with him, a corpulent, red-headed figure, who looked as if his muscles had been stuffed into his skin, but only just. 'Louder, Dai, sing up now. Drown out the poppycock they're talking over there.' Flexing his shoulders, he rose to his feet and swaggered slowly to the table in the window. He was chewing a piece of tobacco which he spat on the floor near Isaac's boot as he sat down to join them.

'Talking about the miners you were, weren't you?' His right arm, weighted with tattoos, leaned on the table like a challenge. 'Good lads, good lads all of them. Won't hear a word said against them.' He looked at Isaac Hughes; it was a long, conjectural stare. Then, as if to give him the benefit of the doubt, he said, 'Mine's a pint of beer, man.'

Isaac rose to his feet, tight-lipped but determined to keep the peace.

'That'll be one for my friend as well. Dai, come over here.'

The harpist stopped playing and languorously stood up. His russet whiskers were out of keeping with the spiky shock of black hair on his head. 'Don't mind if I do,' he said, sitting down beside Mike.

'I'm a mining man myself,' said the red-haired man with menace in his voice. 'That, amongst other things: spot of labouring, spot of prize-fighting; even served Her Majesty in the Ninety-Eighth Foot.' Isaac returned with the drinks and the man swallowed half of his in one go, wiping his mouth on his jerkin. 'So I reckon I know what I'm talking about and when I say I won't hear a word against the miners, that's exactly what I mean, see?' He looked belligerently from Isaac to Mike. 'Is that understood?' He leaned back in his chair. The movement revealed a knife-handle stuck into his belt. He downed the second half of his pint.

'Mind you, I'm not saying you were wrong about Gelliwernen – got any tobacco? – there was a disaster all right. Bloody mess, it was. If I was in charge, as I shortly intend to be, I'd have had Edwards out of his bed and slit from arse to chin.' One by one he cracked the bones in his fingers studiously. 'As easy as kiss yer hand. And then the mother. And then the girl. What d'you say, Dai me boy?' He embraced his friend clumsily across the table. 'Gentlemen, may I present Dai 'r Cantwr, honoured at the Eisteddfod, poet of the hedgerows, once a preacher, now the only friend of Shoni Sguborfwr.' He pinched his cheeks sentimentally. 'A round of applause for my friend Dai the Singer.' He clapped three or four times and there was silence. Dai let another chord fall from the harp strings, while Shoni watched with moistened eyes. 'Dai 'r Cantwr.' He mouthed the words under his breath.

Mike Bowen stood up and shot Isaac an apologetic glance. 'I have to go.' Shoni raised his head. 'You can't go now, man, not when my friend Dai is going to sing for you. You can't just get up and leave.' His voice rose to a shout.

'I'm sorry but I have to go.' Mike's voice was calm, quiet, decided.

'Buy us a drink, then. A pint for Shoni and a pint for Dai and then we'll let you go.'

Mike threw a few pence onto the table.

'Get it yourself. I'm going. Are you coming, Isaac Hughes?'

Isaac rose thankfully to his feet and followed Mike outside. The evening sickened him; even the sweet, outdoor air made him sick. He leaned for a moment against the wall of the Stag and Pheasant; the stones were cool against the back of his head.

'I know I shouldn't take the name of the Lord in vain, but honestly, Sweet Jesus, am I glad to get away from those two.'

Mike grunted; he wasn't really listening. A handbill was glistening on the wall near Isaac's head. The paste was still wet and the whole thing came away quite easily. He wiped it dry and put it in his pocket.

'I'd best be off home. Got a wife waiting for me, I have.' Isaac was always hopeful – after all, she might have missed him, she might be wondering where he was. She was probably looking forward to his coming home, she just didn't always show it that clearly. How could you make out what women felt anyway? He shrugged his shoulders. 'Be seeing you then.' With his head hanging low he walked off in the direction of home, and Meredith.

Back in the house at Tre-lech Mike Bowen smoothed the handbill on the table and read it through carefully.

'Behold! Disastrous days have come; yea, days are these when men are traitors, hot-blooded and bombastic, loving to commit outrages during the dark hours of the night. Hardly a night passes without hearing of the destruction of toll-gates here, possessions fired there, and – what is much worse – treacherous attacks on the lives of those who venture a word of protest against the Rebecca movement. Among others who have been the object of sinful attacks by the thieving workmen of the night, I have become at last an object of visitation.

'Between one and two o'clock on the morning of the twenty-fifth of August the destructive goblins descended on the toll-gate of Glangwilli and in a short time they completely destroyed everything; they stole from my house nine pounds nineteen shillings and fivepence, they burnt many of my valuable books in order to have light with which to carry out their thieving actions. Not only that, but when I escaped from their clutches, one shouted, Shoot him! Shoot him! and another attempted to strike me with an axe. Yours, rendered a pauper because of the above circumstances, D.W.J. Glangwilli.'

Mike Bowen shook his head. Poor bugger, he thought. I know how you feel, mate. I know just how you feel.

*   *   *

Mr Ashe looked acerbically across the room. The Jenkins girl was sitting at her desk, her head bowed, but he could see that she was not writing. She was miles away. He rapped a ruler on the arm of his chair to see if she jumped. Only slightly. He had been doubtful about her from the start. One of Mr Williams' charity cases. Sometimes he behaved in the most unconventional way. To begin with she had worked hard, but just lately . . . well. She arrived in a rush, occasionally she was even late, and you could see that she was dreaming half the time. He shook his head. No use saying anything to Mr Williams, though. A waste of words in that quarter. The man was making a fool of himself, mooning over her like a silly boy, and he with a wife at home . . . Mr Ashe pursed his lips. He was not one to sit in judgement, but all the same . . .

The door from the street opened and Mr Williams himself came in. Ashe seized a pen, propped his head in his hands and gave the sigh of a man who just will not be defeated no matter how much effort is involved. This study of diligence was entirely wasted, for Hugh threw his umbrella into the stand, walked straight past him, said curtly to Mary, 'I'd like to see you in my office in ten minutes,' and disappeared into the inner room.

At least Mary Jenkins looked taken aback; Mr Ashe felt pleased. You could see that she felt uneasy, watching the door that Hugh had slammed behind him. Good. Maybe this signalled the end of favouritism in the practice. Ashe allowed himself a small, dry cough of satisfaction.

Mary put down what she had been doing.

'I suppose I had better go in to him, then,' she said out loud, stalling for time. Why was Hugh so angry? She had never seen him so white-hot before. Certainly never had the heat of his anger been directed at her. Quite the reverse. She hesitated a moment longer. Perhaps he had heard . . .? No. He couldn't possibly – only Jac and Mostyn knew that she had been out that night and she didn't think that Mostyn even knew her name. Better that way, he had said. So what was it?

'Best not to keep him waiting when he's in one of his moods,' said Mr Ashe maliciously, without looking up, but Mary hardly heard him. Her hand was raised, ready to knock on Hugh's door and she was lost in thought.

'Come in.'

He was writing when she entered, his hand racing across the paper as if he wanted to carve it into little pieces. He jabbed a venomous full-stop, flung his pen into the writing tray and sat biting his lips, staring at the desk.

'I'm sorry,' he said. There was a momentous pause between them. Mary stood awkwardly by the door waiting for the blow to fall.

'I'm sorry,' he said again. 'I should never take my anger out on you. You're the last person . . .' He looked up and into her face. 'Oh, Mary,' he sighed, both soothed and troubled by what he saw, 'come here, sit down.' She sat, and he looked some more, his eyes on her neck and shoulders, not meeting her eyes. Then abruptly he stood up, as if her closeness was too much. He picked up a bundle of letters and tossed them in her direction. 'Look at those.'

'What do you mean?' On the wrong tack, Mary felt quite blank.

'Look at them. Carefully. What do you see?' There were half-a-dozen letters in the bundle, all of them addressed to him. Mary turned them over one by one.

'Nothing. They're just letters.' What was Hugh getting at? She felt baffled, unsure of her ground.

His anger flared again. 'Can't you see that they've been opened?'

'Well of course they have –' she began, but he cut in without listening.

'I mean that they were opened before they reached me. Look at the seals.'

Mary examined the wax carefully, looking at both sides, at the broken edges, at the fragmented imprint on each one.

Impatiently Hugh came across to her. 'Look,' he said, pointing. Squinting closely under the light she could see that the top surface was in fact an added layer, delicately, expertly imposed over the original. He took the bundle back from her and threw it onto the desk.

'The Home Office is reading my mail.'

'What?'

'My mail. My letters. They are being read by the Home Office.'

'I don't understand what –'

'I'm a subversive. An inciter to rebellion. I mean, you can tell, can't you?' His sarcasm was painful to hear. 'Just because I stand on a few London

Committees which support the Chartists, because I say what I think, and because I have taken on a few cases which nobody else would touch, suddenly I'm a revolutionary, a betrayer of my country, somebody to be watched, to be spied upon. The whole thing's ridiculous.' He flung himself into his chair and drummed on the desk with his fingers.

'They started with Edward Lloyd Hall. He was hot favourite to begin with, because the farmers consulted him after a meeting at Cynwyl Elfed. But try as they might, and they can try very hard when they've a mind to, the Home Office just couldn't dredge up anything against him. So now it's my turn. Apparently people are saying that I am responsible for orchestrating the entire Rebecca movement. In the Name of God! If it wasn't so serious I'd be laughing. I really would.'

'But Hugh, are you sure? How do you know?'

Hugh looked at her more soberly. 'I was told. Tipped off. An old client who had got it into his head that he was in my debt. It seems that Sir James Graham has read some of my writings –'

'Writings? What do you mean? These letters?'

'No.' Hugh looked almost embarrassed. 'A collection of poems actually, and a few pamphlets. That sort of thing. Anyway, the Home Secretary has got his hands on them and has announced that he finds them "very mischievous and exciting". What a splendid turn of phrase he has. Obviously he thinks them sufficiently mischievous and exciting to justify this kind of surveillance over me.' He flicked the letters again and said nothing for a moment, lost in his own anger. 'So. I thought I would spice up his spying for him. I've written this.' He handed her the sheet of paper he had been working on when she came in. 'Go on. Read it. I'd like your opinion.'

Hugh's story sounded so unbelievable that Mary could hardly take it in. This was the nineteenth century, Queen Victoria was on the throne: things like this simply did not happen. Not in Wales. Not in Carmarthen. She took the letter and read it through. It was to the point. There was no signature at the bottom.

'The people, the masses to a man throughout the three counties of Carmarthen, Cardiganshire and Pembroke, are with me. Oh yes, they are all my children. When I meet the lime-men on the road, covered with sweat and dust, I know they are Rebecca-ites. When I see the coalmen coming to town clothed in rags, hard worked and hard fed, I know they are mine, these are Rebecca's children. When I see the farmers' wives carrying loaded baskets to market, bending under the weight, I know well that these are my daughters. If I turn into a farmer's house and see them eating barley bread and drinking whey, surely, say I, these are members of my family, these are the oppressed sons and daughters of Rebecca.'

'It's very strongly put.' Mary bit her lip and wondered why she could never think of anything intelligent to say. 'Who are you going to send it to?'

'I'm not.'

'What do you mean?'

'I'm going to leave it in the offices of *The Welshman*. They'll publish it. It will give Sir James Graham something to chew on, at any rate. If he's going to intrude on my privacy like this, I'll make sure he has plenty of cause. And then he and the whole wretched government can go hang.' He looked her fully in the face, searchingly. 'I'm right about this, aren't I? Tell me that I am right.'

Mary returned his gaze and her voice was unsure and hesitating. 'Yes, Hugh. I think you are.'

He gave a wan smile. 'Good. That was what I wanted. Now, I'm going to seal this carefully and ask Mr Ashe to drop it into *The Welshman* for me. And, Mary,' his heart was in his mouth as he spoke, 'thank you.'

But Mary was already halfway to the door, carried by a flood of relief. Was that all? Was that all that the fuss was about? It meant she and Jac were in the clear, that everything was still all right. Silly Hugh, for frightening her so. She paused, as if only now remembering him.

'Will that be all then?' she said and then turned and rushed away, leaving Hugh stricken by her brief, distracted smile.

10

Hannah Edwards sat in the window fiddling with the frayed edge of the bandage round her wrist, watching. For a couple of minutes now, the man had stood at the end of the devastated garden looking at the house. He walked a few paces along the smashed boundary fence and glanced uncertainly at the hills and woods around him. Finally he made up his mind; she frowned slightly as he began picking his way up the garden, watching him with a soft-edged malice as he paused by the dismembered branches of the fig tree. They were scattered in his path and he seemed unsure whether to climb over them or go round some other way. He put a tentative boot in the flower-bed and looked up anxiously at the house.

Hannah pushed her glasses up her nose and peered at him hard. A squat man, dark complexioned. She ran through the faces in her head but could not find a place for his. He was almost directly beneath her now with his hand raised to knock at the door of the boarded porch and she screwed up her eyes and tried to remember again. She was fairly certain that it was the farmer from Cefnybryn. Davies. That was his name. She put her hand against her forehead as if to press at her memory. Had he been there? It was so difficult to tell. He was not amongst the three who had – who had been nearest the house but he could have been further back. Just thinking about it made her agitated, it troubled her breathing, made her feel on edge. Once again she twisted at the bandage round her wrist.

'I'll go.' Her mother's voice sounded in the hall. 'Yes?' The door was opened, the question curt. Hannah crept along the corridor, drawn reluctantly. The man was speaking, testing out the ground and she stood in the white plaster elbow of the stairway, hidden from sight, listening.

'I didn't ought to be here really, Mrs Edwards, but I heard what happened to you and your family, see, how brave your daughter was turning away all those men. So in the light of that, and knowing Mr Edwards' reputation in the county, I thought you might be interested . . .'

His voice was soft and rich with malice too, and standing with her head tilted back against the wall, Hannah rejoiced. A score to settle. Oh yes, he certainly had a score to settle, though she doubted if he had as much at stake as she. Her face was shiny in the gloom of the stairs. She smiled, and the man continued to talk.

'. . . It's going to be tonight, that's for sure. Pontarddulais. They might try Hendy as well if they have the time. I've got names too, Mrs Edwards, everything you need to know. Jac Tŷ Isha is going to be Rebecca, David Jones will be with him and John Hugh as well. I could mention others. About one hundred and fifty expected in all. Usual time. So there you have it, Mrs Edwards. All the information that you need. What you and your husband do with it is up to you; at least I know I have done my bit now. After all, we can't go on living like this, can we?'

Hannah had heard enough. She glided downstairs, past her mother who was busy ushering the farmer on his way, and into her father's office. She sat at his desk and took out a piece of paper, dipped her pen in the ink and wrote down verbatim what she had overheard. She faltered for a moment, wondering whom to address her letter to. What she wanted was a local man who knew the area well. She did not want a single one of Rebecca's children to slip away this time. That left her with only one choice: William Chambers – he was the magistrate at Llanelli. He was unlikely to be infected by his colleagues' sense of failure at Carmarthen. He could be counted upon, she felt sure. She finished her letter and sealed it hurriedly. The riot was planned for that night; it meant there was practically no time at all.

'I'm going to find someone to deliver a letter,' she called to her mother and banged the porch door behind her. A sliver of glass chinked to the ground. In the kitchen, Elizabeth Edwards watched her daughter running down the path. At least the girl was going out. It was the first time since . . . well . . . she was going out again, that was what mattered. Hannah ran on and on, weaving in and out of sight along the lane, while her mother stood rooted in the kitchen with only one thought on her mind: if I pass what I've been told, who's to say Rebecca won't come back to Gelliwernen and punish us again? She shook her head and wished from the bottom of her heart that Davies the Farm had never thought to come bothering them with his secrets. Lost for a moment, Elizabeth wiped her hands, rubbing at the lines on her palm, rubbing at each finger separately and then at the spaces in between until they were all quite, quite dry. Then she went upstairs to ask her husband what to do.

Within half an hour of being summoned, the Chief Constable of Glamorgan, Captain Frederick Napier, was sitting with limited patience in the office of William Chambers, JP, listening to him talk. Hannah's letter lay open on the table between them.

'Pontarddulais.' The magistrate was speaking in sharp excited tones. He could barely sit still but was forever crossing and uncrossing his legs, leaning in close to talk to Napier, swinging back on his chair, rereading and then discarding the note. 'Well, it does make sense, doesn't it? I've never thought of it before but it's an obvious target. Any farmer wanting to take his goods from Carmarthen to the markets in Glamorgan is going to have to pass through the gate at Pontarddulais. I'm only surprised they haven't attacked it before.'

'You're absolutely sure about the letter, then?' Napier was more cautious. He liked to be sure of his facts and he had heard too many tales of the Carmarthen police being set up by Rebecca and then humiliated for him to risk his own neck easily.

'I think we can trust the Edwards girl. After all, her father is on our side in all of this, and if it's true that she gave Rebecca's Children a piece of her mind when they came knocking on her door the other week, then I see no reason to doubt her now.'

'Well, if you're convinced . . .' Napier raised an eyebrow with a superciliousness which angered Chambers. What more did the man want, for goodness' sake? Impatiently he leaned forward again and his jaw was tight as he spoke. 'With all due respect, I do not think that the authenticity of our information is at issue here.'

'No?'

'Absolutely not.' Chambers caught himself grinding his teeth, a habit of his since childhood.

'As you wish.' Napier was still and contained in the depths of his chair. He seemed to be waiting. Chambers rested his chin on his hands and took a couple of deep breaths.

'Now, as well as inviting assistance from your good self I have sent messengers to Major Parlby and the Fourth Light Dragoons in Carmarthen and to the Seventy-Sixth Foot who are stationed here in Llanelli. I think we will benefit from having both cavalry and infantry at our disposal. I can't speak in terms of numbers yet, but of course I will assign a detachment of each to you to hold your position in Pontarddulais.'

Captain Napier appeared to be engrossed in the business of the street outside.

'No thank you,' was all he said.

The magistrate wrinkled up his face, wondering if he had heard correctly. 'I beg your pardon?'

'I intend to use only my own men.'

'Captain Napier, have you considered – ?'

'Naturally you are free to take with you as many soldiers as you wish, Mr Chambers. That is your prerogative. However, I believe there is a lesson to be learnt from the way in which Colonel Love and his trusty Major have been blundering around the countryside while Rebecca and her Children run rings around them. It would certainly make me think twice before including them in a venture of my own.'

'Captain, is this quite necessary?'

Napier barely acknowledged the interruption but continued smoothly, 'I believe I have some small reputation as a strategist and it is my contention that stealth and mobility are our greatest weapons here. I do not see how one could use those to best advantage with both infantry and cavalry at one's back. I shall take ten men with me. That should be sufficient. That way we shall be able to capitalise properly on the element of surprise and that is where our strength lies.'

'You'll need a magistrate with you to read the Riot Act. You can't fire a single shot unless that's done.' Chambers felt a momentary shame at the spite in his voice. Napier gave him the coolest smile.

'How kind of you to point that out. I will most certainly take a magistrate with me. I shall take two if it makes you happy. The rest of the party will be drawn from my own police constables. I have every confidence in them.'

A silence followed in which Chambers glared at the blotter on his desk and tried not to grind his teeth. 'All right, Captain. Ten men, you say. On your own head be it. But I have to say this, sir, I only hope your bravado doesn't prove to be our undoing.'

It took Napier three clenched and quiet seconds to rein in his temper. Not even an eyelash moved.

'I think perhaps you might be glad of what you call my bravado before the day is through. Now. I need to brief my men in some considerable detail before we set out, so if you'll excuse me I will take my leave.'

The air in the office hummed with constraint. Chambers folded his lips over his own feelings and rose to his feet.

'Until tonight then, Captain.'

At the door Napier turned and held out his hand. He was not relenting, it wasn't that, but he believed in never allowing personal feelings to get the better of him, especially not before an important assignment. It clouded the mind so. He clasped Chambers' hand without any warmth and said grimly, 'I'll catch Rebecca for you, and what is more, I will catch her red-handed. That is a promise.'

It was not a statement of intent, it was a statement of fact.

Over the farm the silence sighed as the clock struck nine. William had gone over to spend the evening with the Bowens. Mary sat with Jac Tŷ Isha in the kitchen. The candle had long guttered out and now only the light from the fire shone in their quiet, nervous faces. At one end of the table was a neat pile of clothes – a white underskirt, white nightdress and a straw bonnet which had been the envy of every girl in the neighbourhood in the twenties. They'd gone unworn since her Mam died; Mary had never had the heart to put them on herself. But she wanted it to be special for Jac tonight. She found she could deny him nothing. She looked at him now, his pale face sharp in the embery light of the fire. This was what he wanted. This is what her Jac had longed for ever since Rebecca had first swished a petticoat through the

counties of South Wales in 1839. *My white love.* She
put a hand on his sleeve and let it lie for a moment.
The firelight made the gesture look untender,
implausible, as if it were a stranger's hand resting on
his arm. She shuddered. He put his hand over hers
and stroked her reddened fingers.

'You have such honest hands,' he whispered.

He laid her palm against his cheek and held it there.
The clock ticked. Jac sighed and then sighed again.
He could feel his pulse beating, not in his heart, not
in the place where it should be, but beating in the pit
of his stomach. Every other part of his body was still.
The clock struck half past nine and he turned Mary's
hand over and gently placed four kisses in her palm.

'There, my darling. One for every year that Rebecca
has kept me waiting,' and he closed her fingers over
where the kisses lay. Her eyes glistened in the half-
light and she brushed her cheeks in answer to his
brief, questioning smile.

'It's nothing. A bit of dust that's all.' But in spite of
what she said the glistening grew brighter. 'I'm the
proudest woman in the whole of Wales tonight.' She
stood up and turned away, her hand groping in her
apron pockets. 'You'd better get ready.' There was
only the hint of a sniff.

Jac pushed his chair back and began undoing the
buttons of his shirt.

'No.' Mary stayed his fingers. 'Don't. It'll be cold out
tonight. I don't want you to catch your death . . .' She
kissed a fingertip, his chin, the corner of his mouth.
'I wish you weren't . . . I'm sorry. Here –' She shook
out the underskirt and held it for him to step into.
'You'll need this and more, I shouldn't wonder.'

'You got your finery out for me then, Mary?' Jac smiled as she tied the ribbons of her mother's Sunday petticoat round his middle.

'It's nothing more than you deserve. Hold up your arms.' She dropped the nightdress over his head. 'Go on now. Shake out your skirts so they fall properly. There. Lovely as a bride.' Her laughter was young and barely formed. It caught in her throat. 'Time for the bonnet. Oh Jac, you should have seen it when it was new. I can just remember my father giving it to my Mam. It was the most beautiful thing she'd ever owned. It was so fancy. My Dada took it out of the box and showed her how to put it on, how to tie the bow. He said she looked so pretty she could charm away the devil.' And Mary tied the ribbons under the young man's chin and prayed that the devil would be busy elsewhere that night, too busy to bother with her Jac.

'Come now,' she whispered, and she wrapped her shawl around her shoulders, lit the oil lamp with a taper from the fire and led him into the yard. The springy grey gelding was hitched to a ring in the stable wall. He had been groomed until he shimmered under the moon; there were ribbons of red satin in his mane and tail.

'Oh, Mary. Oh, my darling Mary.' Jac held her close. 'Wish me luck tonight,' he whispered into the wooded darkness of her hair. 'Wish me luck, won't you?'

She said nothing, lost because he held her. She watched him mount his horse and he sat in the saddle with his legs dangling free of the stirrups and for a long and silent moment he regretted the night which lay ahead. He coiled and uncoiled the reins between

311

his fingers until Mary put her hand up and touched him.

'You'll be late.' She saw the veins were thudding violet under his pale skin.

Jac looked beyond her to some point in the darkness.

'Do you remember when we first . . .?'

'I remember.'

'It seems so long ago.' He bit his lip.

Mary looked at the white lace falling over the flank of the horse, and then looked into Jac's white face. There was a trace of pink along his cheek, more colour than she had ever seen there before.

'Oh Jac, I wish –'

He leaned down to kiss her mouth, filling her briefly with his colour.

'I love you. I love you so.' She felt she must insist.

'Goodnight, Mary Jenkins wish me luck.' And he wheeled his horse around and clattered away from her, while Mary groped in her apron pockets for a handkerchief, her eyes glistening under the moon.

'Hssht.' William Chambers snapped his head round; two of the soldiers were whispering further along the line and it grated with him. He was crouched down, resting his back against the wall of Hendy Bridge, trying to keep his nerves intact. It had been a difficult journey; the night was translucent with silver light shining into every hollow and shade along the march from Llanelli. The road might have been lit with torches, it gleamed so tauntingly in the darkness. They had been forced to abandon it and march through the fields instead and all the while the men of the Seventy-Sixth Foot appeared to think they were going to a tea-party.

Chambers was almost spitting – not that he was afraid, it was the waiting; he hadn't bargained on the waiting. Thank goodness the Seventy-Sixth Foot had turned up promptly; these forty, whispering men had been on time, at least. Not like the Fourth Light. Major Parlby had given every assurance that his men would be there with all speed. Chambers flicked open his watch. Twenty to one and not a sign of them. Perhaps Captain Napier had been right about Carmarthen after all . . .

There had been abundant signs of Rebecca though. Chambers had been crouching low for almost an hour, his back damp against the lichen of the wall. During that time flashes sprayed across the sky – Rebecca's distant Children were firing their rockets and in the juddering light, trees and hills and houses seemed to move like horrible clockwork. He felt everything distort around him: horns brayed but he couldn't tell where, the whispering of the soldiers sounded like screams under the arches of the bridge and the wings of the night owl shredded up the sky. He looked at his watch again. A quarter to one and still no sign of the Dragoons. What game was Parlby playing? Along the line a soldier laughed and Chambers ground his teeth and tried to stop himself from shouting out. He reached for his watch again but then thought better of it. Instead he prayed to God that Napier was in position. A small half mile divided them, that was all, yet the Captain and his men might have been on Devil's Island for all the comfort they afforded William Chambers at that moment. He couldn't bear to be so still. He had cramp in his knee and longed to straighten it but it was too risky to stand up, you never knew who might be lurking. Another explosion pocked the sky. If only he knew what was going on. That was the worst of all. Not knowing.

Napier marched along the border of the field accompanied by not one, but two magistrates. It was a gesture of insolence towards Chambers which he was beginning to regret for it had left him with only seven other places in his party, and one of the Constables had already done himself a mischief. Napier had insisted that they cover the last part of the journey on foot, so they had left the horses tethered some way back and Constable William Williams had stabbed himself in his leg with his own cutlass as he dismounted, an incident which did more injury to the Captain's feelings than it did to the Constable's thigh.

The two magistrates were brothers, John and Lewis Llewellyn. Lewis took out his pocket watch.

'A quarter to one. How much longer d'you think, Captain?'

Napier signalled to his men to stop. 'We're close. About five or ten minutes off, I should think. Listen, can you hear?' The little party was barely breathing, they kept so still. Sure enough in the distance came the sound of hammering, of metal on wood, slow, premeditated, full of intent. The Captain nodded slightly, marking the rhythm of the blows. Rebecca's Children were busy at their work, cracking open the kernel of the night.

'We'd better move quickly or they will have the job finished before we get there,' he said crisply. 'A final reminder of your orders. On arriving at the gate you are to form a line across the road and await further instructions. Any man who fires a gun or takes any kind of unauthorised action does so at his own peril. Is that absolutely clear? Right. On the double. Quick march.'

Jac Tŷ Isha flung back his head and laughed out loud for sheer pleasure. Solomon reared up, snorting; the sweat had dried to a white scum on his neck and Jac's petticoat stuck to his rump. In spite of his training, the sound of gunfire made him dance across the road, his hooves slippery and scared. The sound of gunfire made Jac's heart dance inside his chest. It was a feeling better than drink, this, better than anything he had ever known.

This was it. He could have crowed. He had ridden for three hours round the district collecting excuses, money and men. A hundred and fifty of Rebecca's Children, with their faces blackened and their white petticoats ragged in the wind, had galloped behind him up the last hundred yards of the road to Pontarddulais. He thought the small town would burst with them. There stood the gate, its five stout bars as complacent as folded arms.

'Come!' Jac shouted, and it was like a release. The wind snatched the word from his mouth, multiplied it and scattered it along the length of the street. 'Come! Come! Come!'

His two lieutenants, David Jones and John Hugh, fired their guns into the air and, taking their cue, the Children nearest the front pitted the gate with shot. Riders galloped up, swung hatchet, axe or crowbar

315

into the wood and then arced away into the darkness in a dance which swirled with violence and revenge. One man struck for justice, another for an end to the tolls, a third for something better than barley bread to put in his children's mouths. Some of them struck for cash: half a crown sent their axes splitting into the wood that night. Blow after blow. The horses looped round in vicious, easy circles. Jac galloped with them, riding low over Solomon's neck so that the ribbons tied in ruby knots flushed scarlet in his face. He was shouting he didn't know what, calling out, exhorting, crying. Three of the bars were down now, and one of the standing posts. The gate was nearly low enough to jump. He wheeled his horse around and rode head on towards it, ribbons and lace streaming in the wind. Solomon's body gathered itself in tight and ready, but he did not jump, he reared wildly over the broken spars and it was in that plunging second that Jac first saw them.

Half a dozen figures, blue and glossy in the flame-light, were lined across the road like soldiers made of lead. They were hardly real and he thought that if he rolled a wooden ball towards them they would probably topple over. Smoke from his Children's torches bleared the air, filling it with uncertain shadows. Jac rocked as Solomon rose and fell, his hooves slicing the road. The dream began and ended in a moment. He raised his gun, pointed it –

'Stop!' cried Captain Napier.

Jac fired.

He blinked and opened his eyes. The toy policeman had not toppled, instead he was shouting, 'Mark that man!' shouting and raising his gun. He pulled the trigger and Jac felt the bullet burst in Solomon's stomach. The horse leapt and spun, dancing and spiralling and spurting blood.

'Fire!' shouted Captain Napier to his men and, obediently, the shiny lead figures pumped shot from their guns. Round after round stung the air. Solomon gave a moan and fell to the ground, the red ribbons dripping blood across his punctured side. Jac kicked himself free of the dead weight. Lead was spitting down the street. He put his head down and began to run.

Jac Tŷ Isha was brought to the ground by a flying tackle of which Captain Napier remained modestly proud until the end of his days. Jac had two skirts to contend with as well as the wiry Captain and it was all he could do to prevent him from snatching his short sword out of its sheath and putting it to use. Jac wished he could burst the seams of Mary's nightdress as he strained beneath the Captain's persistent and savage embrace. They rolled and grunted together, neither giving way until suddenly, without warning, the veins that were bulging in his opponent's neck went slack, his grip loosened and Jac began to scramble away as Napier's body rolled over in the road. One of Rebecca's stoutest Children gave Jac a thumbs-up sign, waved an iron bar in the air and scythed his way back into the heart of the crowd. Jac did his best to remember his face for he wanted to buy him a drink for that tidy bit of work – it was a thought that he remembered later and found absurd.

Free of the Captain, he hopped from one foot to another, trying to release himself from the clutches of his costume as well. Mary's beautifully tied bows were knotted and obdurate now and he stopped, ready to tear the cloth if necessary. Losing his balance slightly he wrenched at the hem, and then wrenched again at the exact moment that a bullet seared into his elbow, went skidding along the bone and buried itself somewhere near his armpit. It was a perfectly timed sequence. The material ripped and his arm was raised ready, lifted as if in greeting, to receive the shot. The pain was livid, but it wasn't the pain which threw him to the ground, it was the shock of the blow as much as anything. With one arm he pulled himself along in the grit and the dust, while his elbow flamed and stabbed out in the darkness on its own. He had only covered a few feet and he felt exhausted, reeling. There were blows and shots raining in all directions. People were running and people were falling, everywhere there was noise, terrible and unrelenting. Jac lay still for a moment and then, wearily and ineptly, he tried to pick himself up off the ground. He managed a stooping, stumbling run for a few paces, bowling along like an animal. When a policeman stepped into his path and levelled a gun at him, he was glad of a reason to stop. He screamed when they touched his arm, but otherwise told them his name and where he came from, let them bandage up his wrists with heavy chain and lead him like a hurt dog along the road that led to Swansea. He was dazed, fumbling and obedient. The dream began and ended in a moment.

11

'There's no excuse. It just won't do any more.' Mary was shaking, not with anger, but with the hurt and the fear and the worry that was driving her to say these things to William, poor sickened William, broken William, who lay shrunken in his bed, his mouth sulky and his eyes filled with tears of self-pity. To stop her trembling she planted both fists on the bed and leaned in close.

'Do you think this farm runs itself? Do you? Do you ever stop to think what keeps Dolwilym going? It doesn't happen on its own, you know. It's because of me. It's because I go into Carmarthen twice a week to work in Hugh's office, and when I'm not doing that I'm labouring across to Kidwelly, looking after his wife. That's what brings us in our money. And in the meantime who is attending to all the work that needs to be done around here? Well, it's not really a question, is it, because we both know the answer – it's me, it's all *me*!'

William moved his head closer into the pillow. He remained remote and out of reach.

'I'm sorry for what has happened to you. Please believe me, I'm sorry from the bottom of my heart.

But being sorry doesn't change things, it doesn't make them any better. I just hope you understand that. I know . . . I know it's difficult, but there are things that you can do with your good hand . . . anyway, that's almost beside the point. If you would just show willing, just show a bit of interest even. At least that would be something. But all you can do is sit at home all day, moping, feeling sorry for yourself . . .'

'Oh for God's sake, Mary.' His words made private grief public, they were etiolated and uncomfortable and Mary did not know how to answer them.

'Blaspheming won't help,' she snapped, and then, 'I'm sorry. I'm sorry, I didn't mean that.'

'You'll never understand.' William was looking away from her, staring at the wall. 'If you're lucky, if you are very lucky, you will never know what it's like.' He rolled over, his right arm as white and crumpled as the sheets. 'You are absolutely right. Everything you say is right. I sit around at home, sometimes I read if you've remembered to bring in the newspaper. Most of the time I stare at the wall or at the floor, or I wear myself out counting the squares in the blanket or the cracks in the beams, or I listen out for the weather. Counting and listening and staring. It's all exciting stuff. You've no idea what you're missing out on, Mary.'

She turned to go. She could not face him any more.

'Do you know why I do it?' He wanted her back now. 'Do you know why? It is because I haven't any choice. None. Not like you. I'm a cripple. How far can I get with that?' He picked up his withered arm and shook it violently in her face. The grey and stressless fingers jigged obligingly and then he let them fall.

'Try Carmarthen.' Mary's voice was low and bitten-back, filled up with feeling. 'We can take the cart. I'll get Jonah ready. We should leave in about half an hour. It would be nice if you would come.'

Brother and sister exchanged a helpless, naked look before Mary closed the door behind her and went downstairs. Her eyes and nose were streaming and she had no handkerchief. Why do I always make it worse? I want so much to help him, yet all I can do is hurt him even more. Dear God, please tell me why.

Half an hour later and with considerable difficulty William closed the kitchen door behind him. His clothes were far too big for him now and it made his fumbling worse. He looked lost inside them. Climbing into the cart was a painstaking business which he undertook silently. He jerked Mary away when she tried to help him up. The journey to Carmarthen was also silent. William looked at his boots most of the way. Mary saw that he had not been able to tie his laces. She wanted to reach out and touch him when she noticed but he held well back, making it quite clear that he was only there under sufferance. He did not even make a comment when dusty, dirty Henry Thomas greased his way out of the toll-house in Water Street and took their fourpence from them.

He was thinking of the argument that he and Mike Bowen had had with him after auctioning the animals, trying to remember how long ago . . . it seemed like . . . well, never mind. Rebecca had changed all that, she had touched every corner of their lives. Nothing was the same any more.

Carmarthen was seething that day. People were talking and buying, talking and selling, talking and going about their business, but always talking. There was news in the air. Mary shot a sidelong glance at her brother – William was oblivious to the bustle, too busy remembering.

The knots of people grew more dense as they neared the centre, the chattering was louder and the consternation more apparent. People were shaking their heads with worry or nodding them with the satisfaction of having been right all along. Something had happened, Mary felt sure. She slowed the cart down, intending to stop someone and ask. They drew level with a rotund figure in formal dress who was leaning against a shop wall, coughing and coughing and coughing, mopping his brow and trying to catch his breath. The London reporter. Mr . . . Foster something. Campbell Foster, that was it. Mary smiled: there would be a certain aptness in asking him. She waited for him to collect himself and just as he was about to hurry on his way, she called out, 'Mr Foster. Mr Foster, sir, excuse me.'

His crinkly grey head swivelled round, trying to locate her voice, and having done that, she could see the wheels of recollection spinning behind his reporter's eyes, trying to place her, trying to work out who she was. William was busy pulling his jacket sleeve low so it hid his withered hand when Thomas approached the cart.

'Good day to you, my dear young lady.'

'William, this is Mr Foster down from London. He's the reporter for *The Times*. My brother William, sir.'

Foster held out his hand with an occupied,

important smile. William ducked his head and then looked away, his right hand lifeless on his knee.

'So what is the news, Mr Foster? Are you having better luck these days?'

At last Thomas remembered her. Of course. The girl in the green dress who had told him to try the Stag and Pheasant. That was the time his fortunes had really begun to look up. Yes. The girl in green who had such troubled eyes. She was wearing sky blue today and it suited her. He smiled enthusiastically.

'Dear me, yes. I seem to be getting along famously at the moment. Still troubled by the damp. My chest, you know. But otherwise I can't complain. In fact you find me on my way to post a rather important dispatch. There has been a most exciting development.'

'I thought so. There is such a hum in the town this morning.'

'The police have arrested Rebecca. They caught him red-handed destroying the gate at Pontarddulais and now he is safely locked up in Swansea gaol. In the Infirmary, I believe. Shot in the arm whilst trying to run away. It is a terrific coup for the local Force.'

Mary frowned and pressed her hand to her chest. Her heart was beginning to tick fast. William remained expressionless beside her.

'What happened?'

'Needless to say, you will be able to read the full account in my paper shortly, but I might just spare you a few details now.' Thomas rested his elbow conspiratorial on the wheel of the cart.

'It was the Glamorgan police. They arrested three

men altogether: Rebecca and two of her lieutenants – David Jones, who had three sword wounds to his head, and John Hugh, who just had minor cuts and bruises. Rebecca is the catch though. They caught him with two letters on him, both signed in Becca's name. He was carrying money extorted from farmers who must have lost their taste for gate-breaking, and he was armed to the teeth – powder, shot, you name it. The evidence is pretty conclusive. I should think the trial will be just a formality.'

Mary's mind went spinning off on its own. She swallowed and spoke carefully.

'And Rebecca? You didn't say who he was.

'Didn't I ? Dear me, and that's the heart of the matter. His name is Jac Tŷ Isha. Now I must hurry or I will miss the mail coach. Good day to you.' And as he sputtered his way out of sight, the blood drained right away from Mary's heart.

Jac in prison, hurt, locked away in Swansea gaol. Mary never knew how she managed to reach Hugh's office. Jonah picked his way through the streets of Carmarthen without any guidance from her. *Jac in prison.* The words tolled inside her head so that she hardly heard William, now roused from his own thoughts while she was lost in hers.

'Old Jac in prison. Well, I never,' he whistled. 'He's the last person I would expect to get nabbed by the police. If it had been Mike, now that would have been a different matter, but Jac – he's so restrained, so careful, not the type to get himself into trouble at all. I shouldn't like to be in his shoes today, all boxed up like that in Swansea clink. No thank you.'

The old grey horse ambled on peaceably, delighted

to be setting the pace himself for once. In the cart, brother and sister lapsed into silence for a few moments before William began again.

'It makes you think, doesn't it? Jac was one of the best. He really believed in what we were all fighting for, not like some of the others. Not like me, I suppose. But if they've got him now what hope for the rest?' His childlike face creased up, sad for someone else, for a moment. 'I don't see the point of it, I really don't. Not any more. The government and the magistrates and the Turnpike Trust are bound to win in the end, so why go on? It's such a waste.'

Dumbly Mary looked down at her hands. They were shaking. It was hard for her to grip the reins. *Jac in prison.* He might be there for months. How could she bear it? It was unthinkable. It couldn't happen, not this. Mechanically she looked down the street, at the untouched, ordinary faces of the passers-by. They were smiling, chatting, taken up with their affairs. Not locked away. Not shut away in Swansea gaol. Jac. Jac Tŷ Isha. She might have said his name, she wasn't sure.

William nudged her side. 'Show him the whip. He's practically at a standstill.' Jonah stretched out his neck and blew comfortably through his nostrils.

'Leave him be. We're nearly there.' Again, she hardly knew if she had spoken. She closed her eyes and struggled to see Jac's slight, pale face in the bruised, bereaved darkness beneath her eyelids.

'Mary! Look where you're going, he's all over the place.'

Although her hands were trembling still, she tightened the reins and chirruped at Jonah who broke into a trot, realising that his luck was up. She knew that the pain was not going to leave her for a long time yet, that somehow she must learn to live with the tenant despair. Somehow. Even as she thought it she felt sickened at herself, sickened by her expediency, sick with the whole world. She had had enough.

'Well, well, well. There is Mr Ashe, as beady-eyed as ever.' With his good hand William pointed at the doorway of Hugh's office in a gesture that turned into a wave as Ashe caught his eye. Twittering, the little man abandoned his look-out post and came up to greet them.

'What a treat it is to see Mr Jenkins again. It has been such a long time since we've had the pleasure. There has been no misfortune, I trust?' Speculatively he noted William's thinness. 'We could certainly use an extra pair of hands in the office today, the place is in an uproar. I've been instructed to keep an eye out for Mr Williams' carriage, hence the absence from my desk. You'd best hurry along inside. I suppose I can tether the horse for you.' He took Jonah's reins gingerly for he was a town man through and through. 'Our four-legged friends, eh?' He laughed uneasily. 'Well, go on then. Mr Williams will be waiting.'

With her head bowed Mary waited on the pavement while William climbed his way down from the cart. He took a moment to work out how to lever himself off the seat and control the swinging of his arm at the same time. Mary was aware only of the stillness in her own heart, for Jac was in prison. She felt as if she too were locked away, out of bounds in her own desolation. Mr Ashe watched William's efforts with narrow-eyed interest. What was the boy doing? What had he been up to? No sign of him for nearly three months and then suddenly he shows up two stone lighter and something wrong with his arm by the looks of things.

'You having a bit of trouble there, Mr Jenkins?' He gave a fat-lipped, unpleasant smile. Disorientated, Mary raised her head, trying to remember something important. What was it that mattered so? What could it – ? Of course. Nobody knew. That desperate, long-ago worry to keep William's injury a secret . . . Nobody knew what had happened to him. That was it.

'My brother had an accident on the farm. Nothing serious. Just a bit sore still, aren't you, William?' She moved round the back of the cart. 'Can you tuck your arm inside your jacket? Or in your pocket? I don't mean to be tactless, but Ashe doesn't know. Nobody does, I thought it would be best. We don't want people asking questions, especially not now.'

Mr Ashe smelt a rat. He peered over Jonah's neck and tried to make out what they were saying. Looked like the boy had hurt himself somehow; he was very awkward in his movements, anyway. He sniffed. What kind of farming accident could that be? Bitten by a sheep, was he? Not likely. Instinct told that there was more to this than met the eye. He rolled his tongue around his mouth and watched as brother and sister disappeared inside the office.

Hugh went bright scarlet as Mary came into the room. He hadn't seen her for four days. He stood up from his desk and smoothed his hair back from his forehead watching her body all the time. He would save up the pleasure of looking into her eyes for a few seconds longer. He remembered to notice William who was standing, his face as bleached as milk, in the doorway. He hadn't seen the boy for weeks, not since that day at Dolwilym, when he had stood in the kitchen and held Mary in his arms for a moment. Hugh looked into her face at last and was shocked by what he saw. She had the glazed, suspended vacancy of one who is feeling pain deep down inside. Her voice, when she spoke, was higher than usual, like a thread stretched tight.

'Hugh, they've arrested Jac Tŷ Isha.'

'I know. That's what all the uproar in the office is about.'

'He is a friend of ours, both of ours. William's and mine.' She was staring right past him. Hugh drew a long, slow breath. No. It could not possibly be – he looked into her face again. Her cheek looked so soft that all he could think of was resting his own against it. How soft she must feel underneath her dress. Jac Tŷ Isha with soft-skinned Mary Jenkins? It was out of the question.

'I'm sorry he's a friend of yours,' he spoke shortly. 'He's in very serious trouble.'

Mary found her way to a chair and sat down. William remained near the door, uncertain of whether to move or not.

'Why? What do you think will happen?' The same strained voice. Hugh feared the sound of it. It was like her and yet unlike. It made him feel he had no access to her.

'It's hard to say. I'm going over to Swansea straight

away to see what sort of case we can make for him. I want to get Edward Lloyd Hall on to it as well. Your friend,' he stressed the word, he couldn't help himself, 'your friend is going to need all the help he can get.'

'Why? Gate-breaking is only a misdemeanour. I thought that meant a fine, a suspended sentence, something like that.'

'The charge isn't just gate-breaking. He'll be tried for Riot as well.'

'What does that mean?'

'Transportation. Could be a life sentence. Twenty years, if he's lucky.'

'Transportation?'

Hugh watched her little head go down, her lip tremble and then lie still. It made his own heart jangle painfully. Her hands lay curled up in her lap and she studied them attentively, as if an answer might be written in the lines of her palm.

'What can we do to help him?' That voice again, high and light and unfamiliar.

'To be honest with you, Mary, not a lot. He is not allowed to speak in his own defence. What he is allowed is to call witnesses either to the facts of the case or as character references. The only people able to give testimony to the facts would need to have been in Pontarddulais in person, so they would automatically incriminate themselves if they gave evidence. Therefore, the only line which we can usefully pursue is that of his good character. Does he have one? I don't know.'

His question was brutal and Mary did not answer.

'We shall have to choose a pretty good barrister.

He will find himself up against the Attorney General himself, I shouldn't wonder. They are bound to want to make a big showpiece out of this one.'

Mr Ashe popped his head rather too quickly round the door. 'Mr Williams, your carriage –'

'Thank you.' Hugh swept up a bundle of documents from his desk. 'I'm going to conduct a few preliminary interviews, see what we can make of it all. I hope to be back in the office by tomorrow afternoon.'

Mary raised her eyes and fed them on the silk of his waistcoat. 'May I come with you?' Hugh clenched his lips. She can't even look me in the face to ask, was all he thought. 'No.' He wanted to blunt his anger somehow. 'There's plenty for you to do here. Nice to see you again, William,' and he hurried from the room.

William looked at his retreating back and thought what an unaccountably moody man he was. Turning round he saw Mary crouched over the desk, her head resting on a stack of paper files, weeping silently as if her heart were broken. He put a cautious hand upon her hair. It was hot and damp, and matted along the margin of her face.

'Mary?' It was the softest whisper. He could not bear to see her cry. If Mary cried, things must be irretrievably wrong. 'Mary.' He stooped over her, wanting to put his good arm round her, to cradle her to him and stop the recurring clatter of her sobs. 'Shh. Shh.' As he leaned towards her, his withered hand slid from where he had tucked it in his jacket and dangled down hopelessly. Blindly she turned and held him, the sobs racking out of her, and soon the hand that had no substance to it was wet all over with her tears.

The shutters were closed at the Stag and Pheasant but some light spilled furtively through the gaps in the rickety windows. The door was locked. Inside, the wheezing of the fire went unnoticed, pint pots were left half-empty on the sticky tables and a dispute over a game of shove-ha'penny had long since petered out. Rebecca's Children were crammed into every possible corner of the room. One collier had even sat himself on the bar but William Walters, the landlord, gave him short shrift over that. There was a small margin of space around the table nearest the hearth, enough for the cat to thread her way through from time to time in search of scraps, otherwise the place was packed with faces: anxious, thoughtful, bullish. A few notes trailed from the strings of a harp and were lost under the tables, amongst the boots, along the skirting of the room.

At the table near the fire Shoni sat hunched over his muscles, his face slung low with his bottom lip inches above his half-filled mug. The red hairs on his arms moved softly as he spoke. His thick beery words were addressed to Dai the Singer, who played his harp with a liquored grace, but every man in the pub was listening, as Shoni intended that they should.

'William Chambers is our man.'

'I thought it was Captain Napier as was in charge?' Dai hicked gently.

'No. You're wrong there, mate. Chambers. It was him got the letter, he set the whole thing up. And he may not have got to Pontarddulais until the end but I know for a fact he was seen bending over one of our wounded sisters ready to finish him off.'

William Walters had a plate of gravy hidden under the bar and he was mopping it up with a piece of black bread.

'I thought he was giving the man a drink. That's what I heard.' He licked his fingers.

'Balls,' said Shoni, without looking up. 'No. Chambers is our man. Stands to reason. The responsibility rests with him fair and square.'

'What about John Edwards and his daughter? What about them, then?' said a miner who was squatting near the door.

Shoni swilled his beer.

'Small fry. Waste of time. It's got to be Chambers. He's got farms at Maensant, Tynywern and Gelligylwnog. I want them all done over good and proper. You could drop in at his pottery at Llanelli while you're at it. We've got to put him straight, see? A man can't go round behaving like that now, can he? I tell you what though,' his eyes followed the movement of Dai's fingers on the harp strings and in a moment of benevolent concession he said, 'I tell you what. We'll have a crack at the gate at Hendy, seeing as the lads never got as far as that the other night.' He pinched Dai's cheek and then slapped him on the back. 'Yes. We'll have a go at the gate at Hendy. There now, that's a promise.'

In the days following the news of Jac's arrest Mary spent as much time as she could with Hugh. He was her only link, however tenuous, with Jac, and the hours that they spent working together, or simply talking, allowed her to feel that she was contributing to Jac's case in some way, however obscure it was. She sought Hugh out as she had never done before but for him it was a pleasureless experience, filling him with anger and suspicion and an utter loss of hope.

One afternoon Mary was sitting at her desk making a laborious copy of a speech that he intended to give at a political meeting. She had to steel herself to do it as it left her mind uncomfortably free to wander . . . She tried to remember that at least it left Hugh able to use his time where it was most needed. When the doorbell jangled and a couple walked in she hardly glanced up, for Mr Ashe regarded any visitors as being entirely within his particular province.

'Is Mr Williams in?' said the woman.

Mr Ashe put down his pen, folded up his fingers and leaned forward unctuously. 'Perhaps I may be of help?' The fat-lipped smile spread itself across his face.

'Well, I particularly wanted to speak to Mr Williams himself.'

Mr Ashe pulled the office diary towards him and made a great to-do of scanning the pages. He shook his head regretfully. 'Most unlikely, I'm afraid. He's working on an exceedingly important case at the moment. Unless, of course, you have an appointment?'

The woman bowed her head helplessly. 'I had no idea an appointment would be necessary.' She gave a look of studied winsomeness at her companion and sighed expressively. 'What are we to do? And we've come all the way from Tumble, too. All the way from

Tŷ Isha farm for nothing.' She looked at the floor, waiting to see the effect of her words.

Mary's head was resting in her hand as she wrote. Her pen stopped at the end of the line and she hardly moved. All she had to do was to lift her eyes and see the woman who had once been Jac's girl in all her full-blown, dark-haired splendour, but she couldn't bear to. She couldn't bear to look at the cat-green eyes that he had looked into, to see the softness of the red mouth which he had kissed, to watch the woman that he once had loved . . . She rested her head in her hands, closed her eyes and saw the face and hair and figure of the woman printed large inside her head in any case.

'You see, I believe Mr Williams is acting on behalf of somebody I know. He was arrested the other day at Pontarddulais. So unfair, it was.'

Mr Ashe's nose was up. 'From Tŷ Isha, did you say?'

'That's right. I wanted to be certain that people were doing everything possible for poor Jac.' She unfolded a tiny white handkerchief and dabbed her eye. The man who was with her was the true beneficiary of her performance and he put his arm round her shoulders in acknowledgement of the fact. She looked at him gratefully. Across the room Mary was burning inside.

'Would you see what you can do?' Jac's girl gave a brave little smile.

Mr Ashe was on his feet already, shooting his cuffs and preparing to do his utmost. 'Most certainly. Of course. I'm sure Mr Williams will – would you like to follow me?'

334

As they disappeared into Hugh's office Mary let the breath go from her body. Why? was all she could think. Why? A tear rolled down the end of her nose and splashed over Hugh's fine argument. She wiped her eyes with the backs of her hands and then thumped the table hard, angry with herself and angry with Jac's girl. She was cashing in on the situation, that was plain to see. But what if Jac — what if he . . . She shook her head, her face squashed and futile. In front of her the words of the speech were distorted and magnified by inky tears. The whole page was spoiled.

Before long, Mr Ashe was shepherding the dark-haired girl and her gentleman friend out of the office.

'. . . No, no, no, my pleasure, absolutely. And please, do feel that you can call in at any time you wish.' He rubbed his hands together. 'And rest assured — we are doing everything . . .'

The bell twanged as he closed the door behind them. He straightened himself up, brushed at his shoulders and crossed back to his seat, humming a tune as he went.

Hugh spent some time alone in his office putting two and two together and reaching conclusions which he found painful even to think about. The seed of jealousy, as light as pollen, settled in his airways, spread through his veins like an irritation and torched his blood, giving him a swollen gut-full of emotion which made him choke. Mary's grief at Jac Tŷ Isha's capture and her continuing concern for him was all that he could think about. He dared not shut his eyes, afraid of uninvited images. Instead he sat staring at nothing, with his elbows on the desk and his hands covering his ears. Something must be blotted out – why not the whisperings of her love for someone else? But the sibilants of passion were under his fingers, in his ears, inside his head. He took his hands away and stared at them.

The solution, when it came to him at last, had such simplicity, such desperation to it. He would infect her with his own infection, make her jealous of Jac Tỹ Isha. The tool for doing so had only just left his office. It would be so easy, it was so, absolutely, necessary.

'Mary?'

Hugh was standing at her desk. She swung round – she hadn't even noticed him. His eyes were fixed upon the spattered page in front of her and his face was wintry.

'I'd like a word with you. Can you come through?'

She followed him into his room and closed the door behind her, pausing for a moment with her hand still touching the handle.

Hugh crossed to her and stood close, looking down intently at her face. 'I wanted to cheer you up,' he said shortly. 'You've been so down in the mouth lately. I suppose you must be worried about your –' He flicked his eyes away from her. He felt appalled at himself. He felt driven. ' – about your friend. I thought you'd be pleased to hear how firm support is for him, how many people are working on his behalf. I've just had his young lady in here.' He was half turned away from her, jabbering, almost. 'She seems to be a splendid woman. She said she'd do anything she could to help him. And every little bit counts.'

Mary leaned back against the door, her palms pressed against it as if it were a talisman she touched for luck or for salvation. The look of incomprehension on her face was total.

Hugh was breathing heavily. 'Difficult for her when they had made so many plans. But still, the fight goes on,' he said.

'I've made rather a mess of writing up your speech. I think I'd better—' Mary felt treacherously light-headed. She felt bemused by what she thought it was that Hugh was trying to say. It had no reality, such reality could not be possible, therefore there was no need to feel — anything. There was no need to feel anything at all. 'I think I'd better—' she said again.

'Mary.' Hugh turned her face towards him, as a friend would, with concern. 'You really don't see, do you?'

She dropped her eyes. 'I don't know what you mean.' Her voice was low, reluctant.

'You love him, don't you?' Hugh was almost spent.

'Oh, Hugh, I don't know what I —'

'There's no future in it. You must see that.'

'I don't know what to think. I just — I . . .' Once again the tears splashed down her face. Hugh took his opportunity gratefully, putting his arms around her and letting his chin brush against her hair. She rested against him with the obliging affection of a doll, watching with watery eyes as the pulse hammered in his neck.

'You'll never have him, Mary,' he said sadly, 'even if he isn't transported. She will have him before you ever do. Isn't it better to give up now, forget . . .' He moved his lips along her hairline, barely kissing it, trying to believe that winning her by default would be better than not winning her at all.

Mary's breath came in short, sobbing bursts. She didn't see Hugh's hair, or his neck, or the curve of his shoulder; she saw the black and green wetness of early morning leaves decking the hedgerow, some smiling foreign girl who was not quite Mary draped in a jacket, holding a pale-skinned man in her arms. Dimly she heard the words, '*Not now. You're kind and wonderful and I love you, but not now, not yet . . .*'

The sound of weeping chased the words away.

Doubt. How could she doubt? How could she not? Jac's girl had been there that morning, had said she'd come from Tŷ Isha farm, the farm which Mary had never seen herself. How could she not doubt? Hugh said . . . Hugh said – Hugh. She could feel his pulse tapping insistently at her face as he pressed her cheek under the curve of his chin. Her own heart felt as if it were hardly beating at all, and she hung in his arms desolated, comfortless.

'It's such a waste when you're so beautiful.' With a sickly feeling she closed her eyes, but Jac's thin face was in the darkness there.

'*You're a good girl, Mary Jenkins, you remember that . . .*' *The green leaves wet against her face like tears.*

'No,' she whispered, shaking. 'No.'

She looked out beyond the embrace into the room, seeking corroboration, but seeing only the blackness of Hugh's hair, his shoulder, and with this searching, shifting movement, unintentionally she lifted her face up to be kissed.

* * *

That afternoon in the office loomed too large for either of them to ignore and yet Mary continued to seek Hugh out. She felt secure when he held her and so from time to time she allowed him to come close. He was her only contact with Jac. There could be no treachery in consolation, surely? And besides, it made Hugh happy, he said so, and then he smiled and laughed and touched her cheek or waist. And Mary liked to see smiles and laughter; she fed on them with the detachment of someone who eats, not because they are hungry, but because they know they must be fed. In her heart she felt nothing but loss, as if her inside had been laid to waste, and it was the shell that was left of Mary which went on her daily rounds.

Accordingly she went with Hugh when he addressed the meeting at Mynydd Sylen, and again at Bryn Cwmllynfell. Together they went to the demonstration at Alt Cunedda and at Pencrwcybalog, at Cefn Coed, Penrhiw-fawr and Llechryd. He never invited her on his trips to Swansea gaol to visit Jac Tŷ Isha, and she never again asked if she could go, unable to bear the thought of seeing Jac without the blessing of privacy.

There were meetings all the time now. Rebecca went about her business almost every night and in the daylight hours the people of South Wales met on the mountainsides and in the valleys to talk and argue and express their anxiety and expectations. Mary was there when Hugh spoke before the meeting at Llyn Lech Owen. Three thousand men trudged through the drizzle to the high ground on Mynydd

Mawr to listen to the speech which she had written out for him. She found herself a space not too far back but close to the edge of the crowd. She felt more comfortable there. Even with her cloak pulled tight around her and her shawl wound round her head, she still attracted curious looks. Not many women braved the weather on the mountains for the pleasure of listening to their men talk politics. Although she knew that she was out of place, Mary felt a sense of complicity. Hugh stood on an outcrop of rock. His hair, usually so carefully swept back, stood bolt upright in the wind, and she relished the secret involvement of knowing what he was going to say next. He had drawn up a petition to the Queen. Already the men from six neighbouring parishes had agreed to sign it, and the farmers here and now were raising their hands in support of the demands which Hugh was proposing. Mary could have recited them in her sleep: reassessment of the tolls, the tithes, high rents, the poor law, the role of the Magistrates. He was carried away at the end. With his arms stretched out so that he looked like a branch of knotted gorse, he told the men who were clumped about the mountain in wet grey groups that Parliament, as it was, would never answer their needs because it was unwilling and unable to. Mary tried not to think how the juices of the men at the Home Office would flow when they heard about this, and Rebecca's Children were smiling as they thrashed their way home through the rain.

12

Cardiff Gaol. The window was small and set high in the wall; way, way out of reach. Huddled in his corner, Jac realised that he had not even got to his feet since the warders had shoved him into the cell and slammed the door behind him. It had been different in Swansea. He had been kept in the infirmary there, on account of the wound to his arm. He still wore the sling they had given him that first night. He peeled it back with apprehension – the cross-grain of the material was dark and stiff with blood that was old now. He looked at his elbow ten, fifteen, maybe twenty times a day, always anxious, watching for signs of blackness. It had already been infected twice and he could still smell the pus and the fever on himself, in his clothes, his hands, his hair. There had been talk of gangrene then, that second time – gangrene and a poisoning of his blood. The surgeon had left the room to discuss the possibility of amputation, but Jac knew what he was saying all the same. Not that, please dear Lord, not that. Punishment, yes, that he could bear, but not . . . He thought of William Jenkins, flushed and weeping in the oak bed at Dolwilym, and shook his

341

head. He would not weep for William, nor for himself, nor for David Jones, even though he screamed so pitifully in the gaol at Swansea every time they changed the bandage on his head. One of the gaolers said he had seen his brain coming through where the sword cut was. Jac laid the cloth of the sling back in its place. No weeping, none. Silence then.

Silence indeed. There was no talking at all in the gaol at Cardiff. Not permitted, anywhere. Twenty scant minutes allowed each day for exercise, but even that was to be taken in utter quietness. Jac liked the crunch of the gravel under his boots; it made him feel like a rebel still, like the faint recollection he had of the Jac Tŷ Isha who charged the gate at Pontarddulais. He gave a dry laugh that made no sound at all.

'And they blessed Rebecca and said unto her, "Thou art our sister, be thou the mother of thousands of millions and let thy seed possess the gates of those which hate them." '

The tarnished litany ran inside his head. Best not to think at all, for what kind of blessing could there possibly be in a cell in Cardiff Gaol? Best not to think. Silence then, and quiet.

Sarah Williams sat by the stove in the toll-house at Hendy with her hands folded on a pile of letters in her lap. The heat fanned a wisp of hair on her chin and her mouth was sucked close, with gum resting on empty gum inside. Her eyes were wide open though, wide and dry like berries in the late summer, their gaze unblinking, looking at the door. She wished she had a gun. Even with the shutters barred, the door double-locked and a chair propped under the handle, she wished she had a gun. An attack of nerves and her fingers swelled, they always did, something about the sweat and the fear . . . anyway. It made her clumsy as she leafed through the collection of letters once again. Sheets and sheets of red on white, letters from Rebecca, written in blood. They came almost every day now. And all because she had raised the toll the week before. Why shouldn't she? Why not? She had a living to make, same as the rest of them. She had her rights.

She rose to her feet and swallowed a toothless yawn. Some nice hot milk, that might do the trick. Back to the stove with a saucepan of milk; put it on to warm. There. While it was heating she brushed the cat hairs off her black cloth skirt. She found them everywhere, even though it was ten days ago at least since the thin mottled body had been dumped, dead, on her doorstep. She shook her head, sucking in her mouth even further. She poured the milk into a thick clay cup and watched a skin form as it cooled. It was very quiet indeed that night; nobody on the road, it seemed. When her drink was finished she paced over to the door and listened. Nothing. Like a grave out there. She did not hear a sound.

They travelled on foot again that night. On foot and in silence in spite of the drink. Show the amateurs who had buggered up the night at Pontarddulais exactly how a gate should be dealt with. That was the plan. Teach the bitch at the toll-house a lesson too, while they were at it.

They shot the lock off and set about the hinges

with an iron bar. That was the first sound that she heard, and the milk still creamy warm inside her mouth. Only one man forced his way through the door to begin with and she hid behind the settle knowing that he knew that she was there. With massive, red-haired hands he rummaged through her things and found the cash box right away, as if by instinct. He pocketed the money and then crouched down by the stove. He took one of the letters from her pile, grinned and lit it carefully; then, shielding the flame, he crossed over to the bed and set fire to the hangings one by one. With a freshly burning letter, he set fire to her blanket on the settle and then to the rag rug on the floor. She could hear the ringing of axes raining down on the gate outside. The man stood in the middle of the room and covered his face with his hands.

'I'm going to hide my eyes and count to ten and then I'm going to come and get you.' He made a noise halfway between a giggle and a belch.

'One.'

Behind the settle Sarah shivered and pressed her thickened hands up to her mouth to stop the nausea there.

'Two.'

It was no good. He knew where she was anyway. There was nothing for it, she would have to make a dash –

'Three.'

He swung round as she brushed past him, with her head down and her skirts hitched up, lurching for the door. His arm was heavy and indulgent as he waved to the men outside to let her through. There would be time enough for her later on . . . and then, hiccoughing comfortably, he went to finish off the looting before everything was burned.

Once she was out of the building and safely past the gate-breakers, Sarah Williams started to scream. She spun round in the road and watched as the shutters of the little house first scorched and then kindled. The man with hair like flame and arms as big as timbers stood in the doorway lobbing the best of her possessions into the street. She spun in the road again, uncertain of where to go, and as she reeled and turned, knives and forks and spoons sprayed onto the pavement. That was too much. That was too much to bear. She gathered up her skirts with thick unbiddable hands and moved in, crouching low, planning to retrieve all that she could. The iron saucepan, grey with the scum from her milk, bounced in the road and caught her a blow on the shin. She looked up. The man with red hair was lumbering towards her.

'Here, kitty kitty kitty; here, kitty kitty.'

There was a smile on his face.

She broke into a hobbling run, forgetting the silverware he had scattered, forgetting the cottage he had burned about her ears, intent only on getting away from him. As she ran her chest worked tightly and reluctantly; it was as if her old body just wasn't interested any more. She reached the nearest house scarcely able to breathe, for the smoke had crept the whole length of the street and even now the sparks were trailing and entreating in the air. She hammered on the door.

The curtains upstairs twitched instantly and she

guessed that they had been watching all the time. Two faces were sheltering behind them. John and Margaret Thomas. He was a carpenter. She remembered that he had fixed a window for her once. The woman shook her head, her eyes quite glazed with fear, and let the curtain fall back into place. Sarah Williams screamed on the doorstep, howled to be allowed inside, but the curtain did not move again. Her rickety body moved away of its own accord, drawn back towards the fire, towards her home, hopeless with inappropriate habit. The red man laughed when he saw her, laughed and bent low, rubbing thumb and forefinger together.

'Kitty kitty kitty.'

She moved uncertainly, but at every point in her stumbling circle he came between her and the house.

'Meeow. Meeow.'

All at once he seemed to tire of his game. He stood upright and came striding over to her, reaching with his hand behind his back. Even his eyes looked red, and those were all she saw: his red eyes, and perhaps her cottage burning in the background. When he pulled out his gun from behind his back and fired, only a few feet from her, her body emptied and dropped with a feeling of relief.

Margaret Thomas found her in the road the following day, as a quiet dawn broke. Rebecca's Children did their duty at the inquest, where it was decided that '. . . the deceased died from the infusion of blood into the chest, which occasioned suffocation, but from what cause is to this jury unknown.' Nobody mourned her passing, and the word 'murder' was not mentioned once.

*   *   *

At first Timothy Powell refused to attend the meeting called by Colonel Love. He had a fine morning's shooting lined up and didn't see why he should heave himself all the way to Carmarthen to be bored and depressed by one of the Colonel's dreary reports. He sat over his breakfast chewing a piece of bacon into a fine pulp and then washing it down with some porter. As he chewed he thought, and as he thought he undid the top button of his trousers and gave a gassy sigh. That was better. More bacon then. If he kept company with those blighters, the other magistrates and the soldiers, well, Rebecca was bound to include him as a potential target. But there again if he held back (and had a good day's shooting into the bargain) he might lose the advantage of safety in numbers.

For the life of him he couldn't work out the best thing to do. It seemed to him that he stood to lose out either way; in which case, why miss out on the shooting? But there again . . . He threw down his fork and shouted for the housekeeper: 'Mrs er, Mrs –' and then stomped over and pulled the bell rope. 'I want the carriage. I'm going out,' he barked at her without turning round, and then stood in the window with his eyes small and disconsolate, searching for rabbits on the hillside.

When they told Colonel Love that they were sending down a superior officer to take over from him in South Wales, he had argued, disputed and fought for all he was worth with no success.

Now he sat in the council meeting, the last that he

would preside over, and his face was grey under its lattice work of broken veins.

'Gentlemen. It is with reluctance that I must inform you that my work here is almost done. My role is to be supplemented by Sir George Brown, whom I am sure is well known to you all. He will be responsible for co-ordinating strategy to put down the rebellion and I wish him . . . I'm sure we all do . . . yes, well, thank you.'

He looked at the unhelpful faces around him. The Mayor was lost in calculation, Major Parlby looked plain worried and the beatific face of Timothy Powell was a complete blank.

'There are one or two matters I would like to clear up before I go. I think we may have got our hands on a reliable informer at last. He's called David Lewis and he has been able to tell us a good deal about last week's attack on the ironworks at Gwendraeth. Of course, we have yet to process the information and corroborate it, but I am cautiously optimistic that we will soon be in a position to issue some warrants of arrest. Sir George will, er, well, he will be attending to that.'

There was genuine sadness in the Colonel's voice as he called the meeting to a close. He was conscious of it himself but hoped that none of the magistrates had noticed. Dejectedly he pressed a yellow strand of hair back into position on his scalp and then gathered up his papers. He was right. None of the magistrates had noticed.

The Stag and Pheasant was deserted when Mike Bowen arrived. Even William Walters, the landlord, was elsewhere, leaving his wife dithering alone behind the greasy bar. As Mike sat reading at the table in the hearth, her little head bobbed anxiously round the bottles and barrels and clutter, shooting him fretful, suspicious glances. The fire was unlit and the grate cloudy with ash and everywhere there were dirty glasses standing where they had been left, in sticky, blistered rings.

'Quiet tonight, eh?' Mike did not look up from his paper.

'I'm sorry?' Her creased face appeared where he least expected it. 'Did you say something?'

'Only that it's quiet.'

'Oh yes. Quiet.' She bobbed out of sight, leaving the impression of her frown opaquely amongst the bottles.

'Mr Walters not here, then, and all the others?'

'Mr Walters – !' She came scurrying right into the centre of the room at this. 'What do you want with him?'

'Nothing.' Mike looked up for the first time and saw that the woman's hands were shaking under her apron. 'Nothing,' he said again.

'Well, that's all right, then,' and she was gone, but as he sat and read, he could feel her eyes upon him as she fluttered about the bar. She was not tidying anything up, but he could tell by the small distracted sounds she made that she was constantly on the move. After a time it began to get on his nerves.

Since their chance meeting with one another in the Stag and Pheasant, it had become a habit for Mike to spend the occasional evening with gentle, ugly Isaac Hughes. The man rarely talked of his home life, though he seemed glad of a chance to get away from it. He liked to speak in vague resentful terms of women's shortcomings, and once he arrived at the pub smarting and sore, having hit his wife and then walked out.

'She asked for it, see? She's been riding for a fall, that one. I didn't mean to hurt her. Far as I can see she don't have any feelings anyway.'

He spoke of her even less after that. Mike looked through a gap in the shutters. It was dark outside and Isaac was late. He ordered another beer and the woman was slow and nervous about bringing it. She spilt some as she put it down and didn't stay to apologise. Mike buried himself in his newspaper and waited.

Rebecca was everywhere you looked, it seemed to him. In prison, on the rampage, under investigation, under threat, awaiting trial. The papers were full of her exploits these days, full of reports that told tales, but said nothing really. Nothing about the brutality of her lost idealism, her viciousness, her vanity, the mindlessness of the rioting on these unrepentant nights. He sipped his beer and idled his way through one of the stories anyway. He had time to kill.

The door of the pub slammed open. Somewhere behind the bar the wispy woman knocked a bottle over in her fright but she still remained hidden from view. Mike could hear her scrabbling about amongst the bits of broken glass. Isaac Hughes stood on the threshold. His blinded eye had a shocked, forlorn expression all of its own, while the rest of his face expanded with a massive grin.

'They've got 'em.'

'Oh, my God.' It was barely a whisper from somewhere in the shadows but Mike's ears, well-attuned now, heard it clearly. He folded up his paper as Isaac strode over to the bar and banged tuppence down on the counter.

'Hello?' he called. 'I'm not surprised the place is like a grave, considering all that's been going on. Anybody home?'

The landlady came quivering out of a corner and mutely served him his drink.

'Got who?' she whispered, but Isaac didn't hear. He knocked back half the glass in one go and then sauntered over, redolent with news, to where Mike sat.

'Well?' said Mike.

'Well, indeed,' said Isaac. 'The game is up, as far as I can see.'

'What do you mean?'

'They've got Shoni and Dai. Arrested them this morning. They're all tucked up safe and sound in Carmarthen gaol.'

'What did they get them on? The Hendy case?'

'Funnily enough, no.' Isaac pulled a face. 'It's strange what a mixed bag Justice can be. No. They didn't get them for the old woman, although I shouldn't think there is any doubt that they were there. What they nailed them for is something really quite insignificant. But there you go . . .'

Isaac was enjoying spinning out his tale.

'Well, go on then –'

'Give us a chance, give us a chance.' Isaac took several long swallows of his beer and put his glass down with a pointed twinkle in his eye.

'Oh, all right then.' The pint-pot was refilled as swiftly as the poor landlady could manage, Isaac was slow and fulsome in his thanks and with his vast elbows propped on the table, at length he began his story.

'As I said, it was nothing to do with the Sarah Williams case. But it seems that sometime last week Shoni and Dai and the rest of the gang from here – '

Mike could hear the listening pause behind the bar.

' – got it into their heads to have a go at the iron-works at Gwendraeth. They are owned by a fellow called Newman, but he wasn't there that night, lucky for him. It was his manager, an Englishman called Slocombe, who got the brunt of it, or rather his wife did. Shoni, Dai and the rest of the lads turned up at the dead of night. Usual stuff. Loads of guns going off, rockets and things, shouting, cheering. Well, you know, don't you. Shoni bangs on the door while the faithful Dai marshalls the rest of them and gets them to surround the house. No sign of Slocombe. Then his wife, who must be a pretty brave woman – I don't know that I'd have done the same – throws open the bedroom window and starts shouting down at Shoni: "Who are you? What do you want with my husband?" etc., etc., etc.

'Well, Shoni announces that he is, in fact, Rebecca, and again demands to see her husband. She refuses him. Maybe there is something to be said for the English after all. He starts calling her all sorts of names, hammers on the door and asks to be let inside. Still she says no. Finally Shoni calls up, "Mr Newman has behaved well and we will not hurt him, but if Mr Slocombe is not out of the country within a week we will make him a head shorter, for no Englishman shall manage in Wales any more.'' Mrs Slocombe, bless her, was about to protest some more when Shoni pulls out his gun, fires up at the window and then aborts the whole mission. Doesn't want to lose face in front of the others, I suppose. The night ended with the good woman's courage being rewarded and Rebecca and her Children getting mighty drunk in here, I would imagine.'

'That doesn't explain how they got done, though.'

'Hold on, mate, give a man a chance now.' Isaac took an amiable swig from his glass. 'Right. One of the Children – David Lewis, skinny little man, I'm sure I've seen him round here cadging drinks – well, for a few days he feasts his eyes on the reward posters up in Carmarthen, does his calculations, works out the risks involved and decides that, for the sake of fifty quid, it's worth a go. He hotfoots it round to the police and spills the beans. They hum and haw a bit, not certain what to do, then they cart him off to a magistrate and make him tell the whole story again under oath. The magistrate consults with another, who checks with a third, who refers the matter to Colonel Love, and then a whole lot more checking and corroborating goes on before finally, with fingers crossed and much holding of breath, they issue an arrest warrant. Shoni and Dai are hauled out of their beds and taken off to prison, which is no more than they deserve, in my opinion.'

'What about all the others?' Mike asked the question not for himself, but for the woman who wavered unhappily behind the bar.

'What? This lot? The Stag and Pheasant gang?'

Isaac put back his head and laughed. 'They're all falling over themselves to become informers too. They just can't dish the dirt quick enough. There seems to be a feeling in the air that the way to save your own skin is to point the finger at your best friend. They're queuing ten deep at police headquarters. Shoni and Dai began the trend, as you might have guessed. As soon as they were safe inside the gaol they started naming names – times, dates, places, whatever the authorities wanted to hear, they were more than happy to supply. Like I said, the game is well and truly over now. The police files are bulging with useful tip-offs, the cells are respectably full, and Rebecca's day is done. A man would be mad to think that it wasn't. Can I get you another?'

Mike shook his head. He felt inexplicably sad. He folded up his paper and put it in the pocket of his coat. He wanted to go home now, on his own. He felt that strange, sleepless limbo between the ending of a party and the beginning of a headache. Part of him needed to grieve alone, that part which had crowed irrepressibly the night he helped to burn the gate in Water Street. He was also one of Rebecca's Children, one of the lost and disenchanted ones, and he wanted time to salute her passing. He shook his head again.

'I don't think I will, mate. Thanks all the same. Best be off home now. Thank you, though.' He walked towards the door feeling sullen and empty. Isaac's bad eye was mournful in its socket; with his good one he watched his friend slowly fade out into the darkness, then he sighed and finished the dregs in his glass. For a time he sat with his palms stretched flat on the sticky table, absorbing the dullness in the air. All the excitement and the passion was suddenly snuffed out, Rebecca was a spent force, and Mike Bowen had gone home in a mood. Home. Isaac felt cold inside when he thought of it. What a loveless, silent place that had become. Meredith . . . His big hands curled into fists that were injured and confused. What was the point? She made him sleep downstairs in a chair by the fire now. Said it upset her so. Upset her? She didn't know the half of it. He raised his head sorrowfully and saw the little landlady gazing at him in helpless, mesmerised alarm. He returned her look with kindness for a moment but she didn't seem to notice.

'Goodnight, love,' he said, and buttoned his jacket right up to the neck. There was no reply and so he trudged off down the road that led him home to his wife.

Meredith lay curled up in bed with her knees bunched in close. For a time she lay on one side, then on the other. She didn't lie on her back. She felt restless, tense with the listening. A hundred times she thought she heard his boots coming up the path. All this because she had stopped letting him. The first time she said no, she had a headache, he had been gentle and tried to hold her in his arms. That made her uncomfortable. You never knew what he was going to try next. Another night he shouted at her, 'You're always having bloody headaches,' and that bad eye of his was out on a stalk with anger. Then one evening he hit her. Hard. On the face. Said she didn't have any feelings so it didn't matter; then he slammed out of the house, and came back drunk and slept by the fire. That was nothing, though.

Meredith pulled the bedclothes safely under her ears. That was nothing. It made her tremble to think. She had told Mrs-Pugh-Next-Door afterwards, well, half told her. And Mrs Pugh had said it wasn't their fault, men had to do it, they couldn't help themselves. But not like that. Dear God, not like that. He came up the stairs and burst the lock to get the door open. He stood in the light with his face all wet and then came over to the bed, pushed her down hard against it and made her do it. He made her. 'How else can I show you that I love you?' he shouted above her screams, and then he made her do it again. Next morning she tried to mend the lock herself but the wood was all splintered round it. So every night now she wedged a chair underneath the door handle, listened to his heavy feet on the stairs, watched the door handle spin angrily in its socket and the chair rock, then listened again as he went away, and kept on listening until everything was quiet. One night she thought she heard him crying. Well, it wasn't her fault. She wasn't to blame. But he was later than usual tonight. She turned over in the bed and lay with her chin on her arms watching the night sky. Always, underneath it all, was the thought in the back of her mind – whatever shall I do if he's given me a baby?

Isaac didn't go directly home. He couldn't face it. With his hands shoved deep into his pockets, he strolled up and down the black Welsh lanes for an hour or more, alternately thinking and trying not to think. The perished smells of autumn filled the air: woodsmoke, rotting leaves, and the sour and salty scent of the earth laid bare for winter. He could almost feel the land degenerating round him and his own sap seemed to drop away inside him as if in sympathy. He kicked at a stone and heard the gentle bumping sound as it rolled down the camber and into the grass. The same bumping rhythm was taken up three, four, maybe five fields away. His feet stopped their crunching on the road and he stood still for a moment, struggling to hear. There it was again, the familiar, abusive sound of a rocket going off.

Rebecca.

It couldn't be anything else. Without quite knowing why, Isaac broke into a run, his great lumbering strides eating up the road. His breath hung in a cloud of steam above his head as he pounded along, faster and faster. They were further away than he first thought, and not many of them from the noise they made. It sounded like furtive work, a kind of hurried afterthought.

Isaac went bowling down a slight hill, his huge momentum carrying him along. At the bottom, the few raw, exposed cottages of a tiny village came into view. He hadn't a clue where he was. For a moment he stood bent over with his hands on his knees, catching his breath, and heard only the loud workings of his body. As soon as he could, he moved off again, his one careful eye searching the road ahead. Nothing. Not the glimmer of a torch, nor the scrap of a petticoat, not even the startled striking of hooves leaving the valley. All quiet. He wiped the sweat from his face. Maybe he was mistaken after all.

He paused, then shrugged his shoulders and was about to head for home when he thought he saw a lone silhouette just at the limit of his vision. He walked a few steps uncertainly and then his face broke into a smile. Of course. There had never been any doubt really. It was a gatepost, stricken and disfigured but a gatepost all the same. On the other side of the road its partner stood unharmed in the shadows. Isaac bent low to inspect the damage. It was sliced up and down with axe-cuts but the structure was sound enough. Perhaps he had scared them off with the business still unfinished. He scratched about in the road. None of the usual shards or the scattered planking that Rebecca normally left in disarray behind her. Just one ravaged post and the other untouched. He ran his fingers through his hair and peered in the darkness round him.

There. He looked more closely. Caught in some incongruous cartwheel, up on its end in crazy abandon with its nose buried deep in the ditch, was the gate itself. They must have carried it bodily for thirty yards before dumping it. He tested his weight against it, trying to lever it back to the horizontal, but it was sucked more deeply into the mud than he had realised. The older timbers were clogged with water, heavy with it, and for five minutes he strained and shoved and pulled before it showed any sign of shifting. At last, with sucking, salivating sounds, the mud gave way. He turned the gate up on its end so that it dwarfed him in the awkward, walking dance to get it back down the road and level with its posts.

After that, turning it back on its side and slotting

its iron rings into position on the prongs in the gateposts was as easy as pie. He wiped the moss and rust from his hands onto his trouser leg when he had finished. Then he closed the gate, opened it and closed it once again. Just to make sure. He had a bursting feeling of satisfaction inside him, and stood for a long time leaning on it, with its wet, familiar roughness pressed against his chest and under his arms. '*Cyfiawnder*.' He whispered the word softly into the timber. '*Cyfiawnder*.' It was Rebecca's password. Justice. If you wanted justice to be done these days you had to see to it yourself. That's how it seemed to him at any rate.

13

Colonel Love heard it lying on his back in his billet at the Blue Boar. He was awake as usual, his eyes tracing the shapes of the plaster flakes on the ceiling while his mind was bitter and busy. He listened all the way through, reached out into the cold air to look at his watch and then allowed himself to lie undisturbed in the warmth of the blankets. It was no longer his concern.

In the family bed in Water Street, Henry Thomas listened with one ear. Life at the toll-house was like that now: listening out, expecting and fearing. His wife nestled deeper into the mattress, willing the noise to go away and take the day with it too. Between them, their daughter Minty made drowsy little eating sounds with her tongue and teeth. She didn't hear it at all.

Thomas Campbell Foster had already been up an hour. He did his best work in the morning, still in his dressing-gown when the light was keen and clear. No need to worry about eyestrain then. As soon as the bell began to ring he hopped up from his desk, threw open the sash window and leant out.

'Hear Ye! Hear Ye!'

It must be important for the Crier to be up and about broadcasting at such an early hour. Thomas craned his neck as far out of the window as he dared and tried to make out what the man was saying. The constant ringing of the handbell did not make it easy for him.

'By the Queen. A Proclamation. Whereas in certain districts of South Wales . . . tumultuous assemblages of people, disguised and armed with guns . . .'

A Royal Proclamation. Thomas fetched his notebook, wedged it onto his lap and, grasping the window frame with his free hand, endeavoured to listen and write and balance all in one go. The Town Crier had his back to him now.

'. . . have violently entered and destroyed tollhouses . . . We, therefore, have thought fit . . . to issue this, our Royal Proclamation . . . to repress all tumults, riots, outrages and breaches of the peace . . .'

A carriage passed. Thomas was close to blaspheming.

'. . . We do hereby promise and declare, that any person or persons who shall discover and apprehend . . . the authors, abetters and perpetrators shall be entitled to the Sum of *Five Hundred Pounds*.'

Thomas whistled in spite of himself.

'. . . and shall receive our most gracious pardon for the said offence, in case the person making such discovery as aforesaid shall be liable to be prosecuted for the same . . .'

This was important. Thomas swung himself back into the room and looked at his nightshirt in dismay. He wanted to go racing out and speak to the Crier now, get all the details. It would never do to throw an overcoat over his dressing gown, but if he stopped to change the fellow would be halfway across the town and it would be impossible to catch up with him. He sped back to the window. The red-coated figure was just rounding the corner at the far end of the street.

'. . . given at our Court at Windsor, this second day of October in the year of our Lord 1843 and in the seventh year of our reign. *God save the Queen.*' Soon all that was left of him was the jangling of his bell.

Thomas dressed anyway, and as he put his clothes on he gave the matter serious thought. Five hundred pounds for information leading to a conviction, and a free pardon into the bargain. That was laying it on a bit thick. The government must be more rattled than he had imagined. One could almost accuse them of taking a sledgehammer to crack a nut, and certainly of closing the stable door after the horse had bolted. Since Shoni and Dai had been taken in, the authorities were practically turning informers away, they were so inundated with them. He fingered the buttons on his waistcoat thoughtfully. The men of South Wales were already doing of their own accord what the government was now trying to compel them to. It was superfluous, provocative, and could undermine the progress which was now in such a delicate state of emergence. He gave a doubtful sigh and reached for his pen.

Thomas did not immediately start work on his article. Instead he sat at his desk and thought long and hard about the position of the Rebecca-ites. It wasn't just the proclamation. The Special

363

Commission was due to open in a couple of weeks too. The Home Secretary had promised it as long ago as July and it had taken him three long, incendiary months to set the Inquiry up. It meant people would have a legal channel to express their grievances through. They wouldn't need to go out burning gates. What with that, and all these promises of rewards and pardons, he couldn't really see a place for Rebecca any more. No. None at all.

Mary did not discuss with Hugh whether she should accompany him to the trial in Cardiff. She arrived at the office with a little leather bag her father had used to store documents, neatly packed with a change of clothes. All afternoon it sat by her desk, a doughty statement of intent. Hugh saw it at once, but gave no indication that he had; no sign of the pique, the pleasure and the jealousy it made him feel. At four o'clock he came out of his room and told her loudly and formally, so that Mr Ashe could hear, that the carriage would be collecting them in half an hour, just as if the arrangement had been made weeks ago. Mary thanked him with a coolness that she did not feel. The thought of going so far away unnerved her. And, if she was honest with herself, she was a little frightened of going all that way with Hugh. Alone. She bit her lip at the thought, and then felt ashamed at what she was thinking. He must know the situation. They hadn't discussed Jac since the day his former girl called in, and Mary had lost track of, or tried to forget, the vague kisses they had exchanged since then. But all the same he must know. The limits of their relationship were clear to her; they must be equally clear to him too. It was as simple as that. Nevertheless, he made her nervous.

And Jac? The thought of seeing him again? She hardly dared to allow herself to feel. Certainly she was prepared for it to be painful, remote even, and impersonal, but she didn't know how she could prepare herself to contain the soaring in her heart when the moment came. Just to see him, no matter how far away he was. And that was what she was thinking about when Hugh handed her into the carriage.

'Have you found yourself a room?'

Mary blinked and smiled from miles away. 'I'm sorry?'

'A room. Have you found somewhere to stay?' Hugh was looking at her outline in the half-light of the carriage.

'I've got an address to try . . .' Mary began looking in her bag.

'I shouldn't bother. I'll ask my hotel to sort you something out. I wouldn't like to think of you on your own in a strange place. Particularly with the trial on. There will be all kinds of people in the city for the next few days and in a way you are my responsibility.' His hands were immobile in his lap. His body seemed very immediate to Mary in the smallness of the carriage. She was aware of his size, of his stillness, of the slow movement of his gaze about her.

'Thank you, Hugh.'

It wasn't what she wanted at all. She wanted privacy and time alone to think. She didn't want to dine with Hugh, talk with Hugh, or be with Hugh.

All of which he would expect. She wanted time inside her head for her and Jac. It was all that she could hope for.

'Thank you, Hugh. You're very kind.'

There could have been seven hundred people outside the courthouse; Mary wasn't sure. She didn't really care, she wasn't counting. She was hardly looking at them and she barely saw the buildings or the colour, the smoke and the bustle of Cardiff, or noticed its size. Hugh had gone into the building more than an hour ago and was with Jac even now. With him, and John Hugh, and David Jones, and the barrister Matthew Davenport Hill. Edward Crompton Lloyd Hall was in there too, acting as Hugh's assistant, all of them talking together, discussing strategy, what the prosecution might come up with, where their own strengths lay. And Mary was on her own on the pavement outside, waiting to be let into the public gallery with all the rest. Hugh had explained quite firmly that he could not find a place for her on the benches; it was out of the question. Women weren't allowed and she would have to fend for herself. Mary had nodded and said very little.

A string of carriages was coming into view. They had a sleek, judicial sheen in the sunlight and looked like the huge shiny links on some splendid municipal chain. They travelled at an exact distance from one another and the redcoats of the military escort provided a kind of jewelled setting for them. The soldiers of the Seventy-Third Foot presented arms while the judges' trumpeters gave a fanfare. One of the first coaches released a swarm of footmen who buzzed to the carriages behind and fussed around, helping the two judges themselves safely onto the pavement. Mary pushed her way nearer to the front. She didn't mind being ruthless, not now. She wanted to see exactly what these men were like, to see close-to the faces who would sit in judgement over Jac.

First up the steps was the High Sheriff, sword in hand. He didn't matter: he was just more of the ceremonial, he had no say . . . The judges took their time, aware of how impressive they needed to appear. The word of the law made flesh in front of the Welsh peasants' eyes. They wanted to ensure that the subversives were suitably dazzled. Mary looked at them closely. One was older than the other, although they were both so old anyway it hardly made a difference. He must be Baron Gurney. Hugh said he was the one to watch, known to be harsh; a stickler, a reactionary. And between the blood-red robe and the furling wig she saw a face of benign cruelty, that looked straight ahead and was impossible to deflect. Discouraged, she dropped her eyes for a moment. That was when she noticed his hands. They were discreetly clasped, as smooth and as reasonable as prejudice can be and they were carrying a folded black hat. Mary's heart was pumping like a piston inside her as she looked at the second man, searching for something a little more like kindness. Sir Cresswell Cresswell. Their only source of hope. His face was closed and vain, his expression torn between self-love and self-righteousness. It gave nothing away except, perhaps, enjoyment.

Jac had marched for justice once. Mary felt as if she had seen too much already.

* * *

All she wanted was a clear view of the dock. The public gallery was steeply banked and cavernous under the arches of the ceiling. Nevertheless the tide of bobbing heads rose swiftly as the crowd streamed into place and within two minutes there was not a seat to be had.

'Mary Jenkins! Mary Jenkins! Over here –'

She swung her head round. Right at the back and quite high up was the reedy, waving figure of Caleb Morris, once their minister, now resident near Cardiff. He was signing and beckoning vigorously, so that his sleeves caught the faces of the people next to him.

Half-heartedly, Mary made her way towards him. More than anything she wanted to be on her own.

'Look, there's a seat beside me here,' he began. 'I was saving it for my sister, but I shouldn't think she'll be here now. Go on. You sit down.'

Mary looked down to the dock. The passage between her and where Jac would be standing was clear and unobstructed: it was as good a place as any.

'Thank you,' she answered dimly, 'but what about your sister . . .?'

Caleb settled them both down. Already the courtroom was hot; four or five people sitting where only three should, strange bones and angles rammed uncomfortably together.

'Well, this is an unexpected pleasure. I haven't seen you and your brother for quite some time.'

'William hasn't been very well. I've been looking after him.'

'I'm sorry to hear that. I hope he's on the mend now. Nothing serious, was it?'

'Oh, he's much better, thank you . . .'

Silence.

The minister engaged himself in the difficult business of trying to polish his steel spectacles with his arms pinioned to his sides. Suddenly he doubled himself up and Mary saw he was trying to breathe on the lenses to give them a better shine. 'There we are.' He ducked his head down and hooked the wire frames over his ears. 'That's better.' He juggled his handkerchief back into his pocket as best he could.

'I don't know what your Dada would make of all of this,' he said thoughtfully. 'He was a great one for the politics, Morgan Jenkins was. I expect you get your interest in it from him.'

Mary knew that he was probing gently. 'Oh, I – I – I'm not interested,' she replied quickly, crossing her fingers for lying to a minister. 'Not at all. I'm only here because of, er, because of Mr Williams, you see. I help out in the office . . .'

If Caleb knew that she was lying he was kind enough to disregard it.

'I'm not generally a political man myself. It's difficult when you're – ' fleetingly his hand gestured at his habit. 'But I've been following this matter in *The Times* and it's rather caught my interest. The way people are talking you would think we were on the brink of civil war. Anyway,' he was settling comfortably into his conversation, 'I was owed a few days' holiday and I thought now would be a good chance to come over to Cardiff. I've a sister here you see, so I thought I could stay with her – she's a widow – and use the opportunity to keep abreast of all of this. I must say – '

Mary was smiling and nodding, but she couldn't take her eyes away from the dock, for Jac himself might walk into the court at any moment.

A door at the back of the courtroom opened and the lawyers began to file in and take their places. Busy black figures bartering points of law with one another right up to the moment that the judges made their entrance. Mary watched the preoccupied nodding of Hugh's head with an ache inside her as she rose to her feet with the rest of the public.

'Oyez. Oyez.'

'That must be the clerk,' Caleb Morris whispered beside her. She smiled and nodded again.

'All persons having business before my Lords the Queen's Justices draw near and give your attendance.'

Judges, attorneys, clerks, and even the Sheriff exchanged a succession of bows before rustling into their seats. Then came the cry that Mary had been waiting for weeks to hear.

'Put up Jac Tŷ Isha.' The clerk's voice sounded through the court like the dropping of a stone into water.

He was still in the jacket he had worn on the night he had brought William home to her, the jacket he had once covered her with. That was the first thing Mary noticed. Her head shook slightly as she looked into his face, but that was the only sign of her distress. He was so pale, sheet-white and thin, so terribly thin, and his poor arm in a sling after all this time, like the snapped wing of a bird. His chains clinked lightly as he waited and the sound was all wrong, it was a smug and indolent sound, like money, as if he were bound up with ropes of sovereigns, and not with leg irons. Oh Jac *bach*, oh, Jac *nghariad gwyn i*. She dreaded her eyes filling up with tears and looked high up into the ceiling, willing them away.

The clerk cleared his throat. 'Jac Tŷ Isha, you are charged in this indictment on the first count that you, on the seventh day of September, in the County of Glamorgan, did unlawfully, riotously and tumultuously assemble together with divers others, to the disturbance of the peace. How say you, Jac Tŷ Isha? Are you guilty or not guilty?'

Jac looked directly at Baron Gurney when he answered, and his voice was clear and cool. 'Not guilty, my lord.'

All that Mary could think of was that the mouth which spoke those words had rested in her hair once, and kissed her mouth, and then had gone away.

'And on the second count you are charged for that you on that day and in that place did feloniously, unlawfully and with force begin to demolish and pull down the dwelling house of one William Lewis. How say you? Are you guilty or not guilty?'

'Hugh didn't tell me about this one.' Mary's face swung round, her eyes aghast. 'He didn't say, he didn't tell me.'

'Not guilty.'

The minister took her hand in his and patted it. He had the delicacy to say nothing. Then he put her hand carefully onto her knee, but kept on watching her out of the corner of his eye.

'And on the third count you are charged for that you on that day and in that place did shoot at one

Charles Frederick Napier with intent feloniously and with malice aforethought to kill and murder him. How say you? Are you guilty or not guilty?'

'Not guilty.'

'You may sit,' said the judge, and with a soft tinkle like money Jac sat down in the dock of Cardiff Crown Court.

A large part of the morning was taken up with swearing in the jury, a procedure which Mary found frustratingly slow until she saw the point of what was going on. The men assembled by the Sheriff for selection were gentlemen and tradesmen from Merthyr and Cardiff; there wasn't a single member of the agricultural community, nor anyone from West Glamorgan. Mr Hill, speaking on Jac's behalf, rose to his feet and challenged the Sheriff's indifference and impartiality in choosing these men. Gurney asked if he had any evidence to support his accusation, but after a whispered consultation with Hugh and Lloyd Hall, Hill was obliged to lower his head and admit that he could produce nothing concrete. The Attorney General, speaking for the prosecution, was pleased to point out that farmers had indeed been approached over the matter of jury service in this case, but they had all, to a man, claimed exemption or paid fines rather than appear, such were the threats and pressure they had been subject to. There was an uneasy silence in the public gallery at this, as Rebecca's tactics rebounded with such a whiplash effect. How alone Jac looked, straight and silent and white in the dock, as the three gentlemen and nine tradesmen of whom the jury was eventually composed ranged themselves in two rows opposite him.

Captain Napier thought he gave his evidence impeccably. He was determined not to show the smiling that he felt inside, but standing in the witness box gave him the same steady pleasure he had felt in organising the operation at Pontarddulais and in carrying it out. He regretted that William Chambers was not there to hear the tale told again, but that was his only regret; the rest was sheer delight. It seemed to him that the whole courtroom sang with his evidence, as rack upon rack of rapt faces listened, waiting to hear all the details of how the thin cold man in chains before them had refused the command to stop his passage of destruction, but had wheeled his horse around and shot at the policeman instead.

Mary couldn't believe it. She could not believe that Mr Hill could bluster on about why the police were armed. It seemed such a pointless technicality to her. She wanted to block her ears as the minutes ticked by and all he could talk about was the exact moment that Napier gave the order to fire. What did it matter? How could it help? She was trying to absorb Jac with her eyes but he never once looked up at her, he seemed to disregard the public gallery altogether and remained solitary and remote in his despair.

Mr Hill was now wading through the vague supposition that Rebecca's Children were not carrying guns themselves with the intention of shooting at anybody, that they carried them to create an effect. Caleb Morris watched quietly as the girl beside him bitterly shook her head. The Attorney General continued to press his case home, delivering swiping blows to Hill at every possible opportunity. When he had done he took his seat again and his black gown closed about him like a beetle's wings. In the public gallery people let out their breath, and shifted their position where they could. Now. It was the turn of Jac's defence.

First of all, Mr Hill tried to attack the wording of the indictment and have the case dismissed that way. The attempt failed. To Mary it seemed as if judges took pleasure in ruling against him. He began calling witnesses to Jac's good character. Two farmers ambled on to the stand one after another, and were followed rather sheepishly by the innkeeper from Tumble, near his home. I would have spoken for you. I would have stood up in front of everybody here and said what a strong and honest and gentle man I knew Jac Tŷ Isha to be. The words, the tears, the regrets and the appalling sense of doom were all one inside Mary's broken little heart. Caleb Morris could feel the warmth of her breath as she sighed in the crush beside him, and he wished he could take her hand again, and give her comfort.

Mr Hill's summarising speech in Jac's defence was rousing, Mary couldn't deny him that, but it had little effect. As Hill sat down, Baron Gurney began to address the jury, telling them that there could surely be no doubt that Jac was at Pontarddulais on the night in question. He told them it was their duty to weigh up the facts of the case and then decide if the prisoner was guilty of the crimes with which he was charged. With a dark look he dismissed them from the court.

They only took half an hour to make up their minds. Afterwards, Mary could hardly believe that it could take so little time to condemn a man. Thirty short minutes. The minister stayed beside her during that time, chattering, and watching her. Other people went to stretch their legs and talk to friends, but Caleb Morris continued to sit beside her. She thought that perhaps he was talking about the justice of Rebecca's cause and the beneficial effects it would have on the county, but she wasn't really listening, for she was all consumed inside.

Their brief consideration over, the members of the jury were led back to their seats by the court usher. The judges returned to the bench and with a mournful clinking of his chains Jac once again took his place in the dock. The clerk cleared his throat and silence fell.

'Have you elected a foreman to speak for you?' he asked. One of the tradesmen stood up and glanced nervously up at the gallery, wondering how many of Rebecca's Children were up there, ready to mark him down. The clerk continued speaking.

'Just answer yes or no. Are you agreed upon a verdict on the charges against the prisoner at the bar?'

'Yes.'

'How say you on the charge against Jac Tŷ Isha of riot? Do you find him guilty or not guilty?'

'Guilty.'

Nobody breathed in the courtroom.

'And do you find Jac Tŷ Isha guilty or not guilty of beginning to demolish and pull down the dwelling-house of William Lewis?'

'Guilty.'

Again.

'And do you find Jac Tŷ Isha guilty or not guilty

of shooting at Charles Frederick Napier with intent to murder him?'

'Guilty.'

'And that is the verdict of you all?'

'It is.'

The faintest murmur ran round the gallery. It was like a roar in the ears of the foreman of the jury. He glanced again at those he thought were his accusers.

'But we recommend the prisoner to mercy on account of his previous good character,' he said, and then sat down very quickly, and never once raised his eyes from the floor.

The two judges consulted one another briefly and then Baron Gurney spoke. 'Take him below.' He gave a cold nod in Jac's direction. 'The court will adjourn until tomorrow.'

Around her people began to elbow themselves to their feet, adjusting hats, buttoning coats and talking. The 'did you evers', and 'I never thoughts', and the 'fancy thats', bayed and yapped right round the gallery and Mary felt abandoned amongst the predators. The noise was deafening. She sat in the pool of her own thoughts, her coat undone and spilled around her, and her hands powerless to move, dropped open in her lap. She found it difficult to think at all. It was like watching herself bleed to death and doing nothing about it, except, maybe, remarking on the rich red colour of the blood. She couldn't even find the strength to lift her eyes from their hanging stare into nothingness. It didn't matter if she sat in the courtroom and stared like that all night. At least then she would be close. A hundred feet below her Jac was sitting in his chains inside a prison cell. A convicted felon. And he would stay in his chains for the rest of the time they kept him in Cardiff, and then on to the prison at Millbank, and he would remain chained up for all those weeks at sea, going – she didn't know where. Australia? Tasmania? And for how long? Five years? Ten at the most, surely. The jury had asked for mercy, after all. What was all this for, this suffering? For what? For Rebecca. Exacting, devouring Rebecca. Is this what she wanted for her Children, for Jac, the most devout and dedicated of them all? It was impossible to assemble any understanding.

'Which way are you going?' Caleb Morris was still beside her, patient and kind. Mary peered at him as if the light was suddenly very bad. Oh yes. The minister. Yes.

'I wondered if I may walk you home. Which way are you going?'

Mary struggled for a moment but couldn't think of anything to say.

'I . . . I don't know. The hotel. I hadn't thought . . .'

'Come along. I'll take you home. Wherever it is you're going.'

'The hotel. I've got the card somewhere. Stupid. I can't think of the name.' Still she sat. Her fingers and hands looked unfamiliar to her and she turned one of them over, looking for marks of identification.

Caleb Morris helped her gently to her feet.

'Fasten your coat. It will be cold outside. There.'
She did as she was told.

'This is awful. I'm so sorry.'
The wire spectacles smiled back at her. When the

light caught them she couldn't see his eyes. 'You said you had the hotel's card?'

'Oh dear, yes.' Mary felt in all her pockets, these strange hands of hers strangely obedient. 'I can't think where I put it. It must be in my bag.'

'Shall I look for you?'

She smiled and nodded and wondered what he had said. It was her first taste of the desolating kindness of the uninvolved. Caleb Morris helped her out of the courtroom, tucked her hand, which didn't seem strange to him at all, into the crook of his arm and walked with her through the alien streets of Cardiff. He took her into the entrance hall of the hotel and spoke to the proprietor.

'This young lady isn't well. I'd like to see her to her room. Would you be kind enough to arrange for some hot soup to be sent up to her in about an hour's time?'

He led her up to her room, helped her off with her coat and sat her in the chair next to the empty grate.

'Oh, look at that. No fire. I'll see that somebody attends to that on my way out.' The wire spectacles beamed again at Mary. 'Now. Is there anything else I can do for you?'

She shook her head. 'Thank you. You've been most kind.'

'You're not thinking of going back to court tomorrow, are you? I don't think it would be wise.'

'I must. I have to hear them pass sentence.'

'I'm sure you'll be able to read about it in the papers, and then you could save yourself the –'

'Thank you. But I have to be there.'

'Well, it's none of my business, of course.' As Caleb

Morris bowed his head Mary had a brief glimpse of the kindness in the eyes behind the glasses. 'I shall look out for you tomorrow,' he went on, 'and perhaps we may have the pleasure of sitting together again. Well, I must be going now. Goodnight, Mary.'

With the click of the door behind him he left her to silence, and the dying light. She sat in the chair with her hands, palms together, between her knees, and her eyes unmoving, not really thinking, simply absorbed in the state of being. That, and the feeling of loss. It unfurled inside her as the light went: her stillborn hopes, the condition of unloving, of trying to unlearn love. What a labour there would be to lose all this from inside her. Nobody came to light the fire. One star prickled the evening sky, and still she sat, and thought, and felt, and wished the day undone. There was a knock at the door. A girl came in with a bowl of soup on a tray and put it down for her.

'Oh dear. The fire. I'll send somebody up.'

But nobody came. Cardiff closed its blinds and settled in for the night. Oh, Jac *bach*. Oh, Jac *nghariad gwyn i*. My white love. Jac. Mary pressed her cheek into the wing of her chair and hoped that the night would drown her in its darkness.

There was a tap at the door.

'Mary? Are you asleep?'

Another tap.

'May I come in for a moment?'

She had known this would happen; it was almost as if she had been sitting in her chair and waiting.

The handle turned.

'May I come in?'

379

Hugh.

He stood in the doorway and didn't look her in the eye, and it occurred to Mary that he was nervous. He looked enormous in the tiny room and yet in that moment she knew that he was scared. He closed the door, wincing at the noise it made, and then licked his lips.

'What a day. Have you eaten? Oh yes, I see. I'm sorry I couldn't get to you at the end, but there were so many other things to do. I had to see David Jones and John Hugh, and talk to them. With a verdict like that, there was absolutely no point in the two of them coming on to the stand tomorrow and pleading not guilty. No point at all. Much better for them to change their plea and hope to mitigate the sentence. That's what I had to explain to them. I had to make it clear, you see. The sentence is almost an irrelevance anyway. I shall be amazed if David Jones survives the voyage – those head wounds. I don't know.' He couldn't speak quickly enough. Something – nerves, guilt perhaps – was driving him on. 'May I sit down? Thank you. Anyway, at last they agreed, so that was that. Then I had to have a conference with Hill and Lloyd Hall. By the way, I thought Hill did a jolly good job. In fact, at the end of his big speech the Attorney General passed him over a note of congratulations. "Very well done in the circumstances." That kind of thing. It's not often the opposition makes a gesture like that. It hasn't been an easy day.'

Mary was looking out into the darkness, divining.

'I'm terribly sorry, Mary. This must be hard for you. I don't know what there is between you, and

I don't quite understand, but that's what I came to say really, that I'm sorry.'

One tear slid down her cheek. She couldn't move. 'It is hard. You're right. It's hard and it hurts. Oh, Hugh, help me, help me, please . . .'

He was on his knees on the rug next to her chair, his hair falling forward into his eyes. It was the first time she had ever seen it out of place.

'Oh, Mary, I love you. I know it's not what you want, but there's nothing I can do about that except to keep wanting you, and I do. I want you in every way, everywhere and in every minute of the day. Such a kind of wanting. I want you now. I want to hold you and love you and make you smile and cry out and forget. Don't make me ask, please don't make me have to ask –'

She put her hand on his hair and smoothed it back into place. He used the gesture, the slight opening up of her body, to lift her to her feet. She felt his hands in her hair, pulling out the pins. Every part of his body was touching her and his mouth was touching her in every part. Her own mouth was quite dry, and her heart was still. Except perhaps for the merest, slightest fear. There was only one thought, flickering somewhere in her head. Perhaps this was the way. This was the way to exile Jac from inside her. The way to banish him. Let Hugh banish him for her, let the act of dispossession be his and not hers. Maybe that was possible. If Hugh could tear Jac out of her with his bare hands, his bare body, then it would be over and done. Finished. Peace.

'Let me,' she said, so quietly she hardly heard herself. She moved away from his arms and unfastened her dress. No urgency, no fumblings. The room was dark and she didn't mind; she thought that he could hardly see her. She slid into the bed. *My white love*.Hugh was pulling at his necktie, his face straining with intent. She didn't know what to do. What do people do? She didn't know. She thought of the animals in Dolwilym, Phoebe the mare when she was young. As Hugh climbed into bed beside her she knelt on her knees and elbows, passive under the arced sheeting, waiting for it to be done.

'Oh, Mary. Oh my sweetheart.'

She didn't smile, and she didn't cry out; and she did not forget.

Hugh was gone when she awoke, Mary having hardly slept at all, except for the moment of his leaving. He had been ardent and tender and he had broken her heart. All night long he had held her to him, nursing her and loving her. She hadn't expected that, she hadn't expected him to love her, just to do the act and then leave her. He had spoken once, lying on his back in the darkness with his arms around her.

'It's a bit like catching thistledown, isn't it? You clap your hands together, an expression of delight almost, and then you open them and there is nothing there.'

Is hurt contagious? Mary wasn't sure, but it seemed that it was that night.

'I'm sorry, Hugh.' Silence. The silence of the separateness of lovers. 'I thought it was what you wanted.'

'It was.'

'I'm sorry.' And when she woke up he was gone.

* * *

Caleb Morris was on the courtroom steps looking out for her. He waved when he saw her, asked her if she had spent a good night and began to polish away the smudges from his glasses. He saw how grey she looked at the edges and shook his head. Poor girl. What a pity.

They found two seats together in almost exactly the same place. The court was fuller than it had been the day before, if that was possible, packed to the rafters with the carrion public. Mary sat quietly waiting, staring at Hugh sitting on the benches way below. She found it hard to imagine that she had had any intimacy with that body, that person, now formally parcelled into black robes, light-years away from her. The professional at work.

The prisoners were led up from their cells, all three of them; this time David Jones and John Hugh too. Individually regarded, you could tell that they were people with families and jobs and their own private pasts; collectively, they looked like dishevelled *sans culottes* who had lost their way. They looked like felons, they looked the part.

Jac. Jac was in the middle. Mary gave him a naked and confessing look. There was no shelter in her gaze. It was a silent, staring admission of love and disloyalty. She could still feel the stickiness of Hugh's seed, although she had washed and washed and washed. She had tried to wash the whole night away, but the stickiness was there still, between her legs, gumming up the strings of her heart.

'The court will rise.'

The two judges filed in, studiously grave. Mr Hill

rose to his feet, took a deep and thoughtful breath, and then began to speak.

'When prisoners think it right to submit themselves to the law without trial perhaps it will not be considered presumptuous in me in venturing to call your Lordships' attention to this fact as showing their contrite spirit and doing all that lies in their power to atone for the offence of which they have been guilty.

'They all belong to respectable families. A few months ago they might have held up their heads with the proudest in the land, because they were innocent; because they were men acting according to what was right, and walking within the bounds of the law. From that state your Lordships see into what an abyss they have fallen.'

David Jones still had bandages round his head and he was swaying slightly in a rhythm of unreality. John Hugh looked at the ground, his face crimson and repressed. Between them stood Jac with his face level, pale and unmoved. Mary felt as if he were somehow absent and that all that was left of him was a kind of haunting.

Mr Hill was pointing out that two of his clients had already received some punishment in the form of gunshot wounds, and that if the judges were to show mercy in their sentencing it would amplify the positive and constructive feelings which were now growing in the region as a result of the Queen's Commission of Inquiry.

Baron Gurney gave a curt 'thank you', and leant forward in his chair.

'Jac Tŷ Isha, David Jones and John Hugh. You

stand convicted of a felony, and a felony of a very aggravated description. The jury, after a long and patient hearing, have found you, Jac Tŷ Isha, guilty; and you, David Jones and John Hugh, have pleaded guilty to an indictment of a similar description, and your learned counsel in his address to the court has very properly impressed upon us the contrition which you have both manifested.

'The circumstance is not forgotten, but still an example is necessary. You, from the respectability which you formerly maintained and occupied, are persons of whom it is particularly necessary that an example shall be made, to deter others from a repetition of your crime. You are all liable to be transported beyond the seas for the term of your lives but, considering all that has been stated in respect of you, David Jones and John Hugh, the court is of the opinion that it is impossible to pass a lesser sentence than that which I am about to pronounce, which is that each of you shall be transported for the term of seven years.'

'Your lad now,' said Caleb Morris, touching Mary's clenched fist only briefly.

'With respect to you, Jac Tŷ Isha, the court cannot entertain the same view of your case. You appear to be one in a station far above the rest – one not likely to be misled by others – and yet, upon the evidence, you proved to be a leader, if not *the* leader, of this lawless multitude.

'You have been recommended by the jury to the mercy of this court. The court finds extreme difficulty to lessen in any degree the punishment which the law awards to your offence. The law says you are liable to transportation for life and, giving all consideration to the recommendation of the jury and to all the circumstances which have been so ably stated by your learned counsel, the court is of the opinion that you be transported beyond the seas for a term of twenty years.'

Mary thanked Caleb Morris for his kindness, but said she would prefer to walk home on her own.

'Perhaps I might give you my card?' He produced a small leather case from the breast pocket of his coat, and took a card from it. 'Here, let me write down the name of my relatives in Cardiff, just in case.' He printed an address on the reverse. It was the only response he could think of. The girl was muted, silent almost, but the feeling of loss, of need, which seemed to pour out of her in spite of her silence, was overwhelming. He peered at her above his spectacles, making sure that she tucked his card away somewhere safe.

'Thank you.' So brief, so preoccupied. He watched her careful passage along the street, his own face condolatory and a little sad. Ah well, he'd done what he could. Life goes on. That much was certain. He buttoned his coat and turned into the wind: home to visit his sister.

Mary felt curiously dead inside, not even in limbo, just dead. In a way the anticipation had been far worse than the actuality, and the conviction worse than the sentence. Sometimes it is more comfortable to live without hope. She did not go up to her room; it was too full of the alien intimacy of the night before. For a while she sat in the hotel sitting-room and read, but she found it hard to concentrate; she was distracted by her own calmness. She had some supper alone. Steamed fish – it was like eating nothing. After that she hovered, moving uneasily from dining room to sitting-room to hall and back. Deep down inside her was a feeling of expectation. Hugh did not come in until after ten. She was sitting in a chair which gave a view of the front steps, not reading a copy of *The London Illustrated News*. He went up to his room first, and she wondered if he had passed her door, and tapped, and waited for an answer . . . It was half an hour before he found her, and there was a dreariness in his expression which took her by surprise. He sat down on the arm of a chair; he almost slumped.

'I hate to lose a case. I hate it. Each time it's as if it were the first time. It leaves such a horrid taste. What a mess. I know we did our best, and I know the odds were stacked against us, but all the same . . . The rigging of the jury didn't help.'

Mary was trying to put the day at a safe distance from her. She turned the pages of the journal and looked at him occasionally.

'What about you? Are you all right?' Hugh's questions were almost brusque. He slid down into the seat of his chair, clasping a paper file in his folded arms.

What about her? What about last night? Why this manner, this abruptness? Mary kept staring at the pictures in front of her.

'I'm all right.'

There was silence between them.

He came and stood beside her chair watching her

387

read, his hands nearly touching her and his face pent up with a wanting that was almost spiteful.

'I must go up. I've got a letter to write. I want the tradesmen on that jury to feel the consequences of their actions. There's a Chartist in the town, Francis August. He'll take care of it.' The quietness unwound itself about them. 'Goodnight then.' He turned to go.

'Hugh —'

He drove the silence relentlessly on before he answered, returning the hurt her lack of caring for him made him feel in equal measure. 'Yes?'

'Nothing. I thought . . .'

He wasn't looking at her. 'What did you think?'

'Well . . . I thought that . . . maybe . . .'

'You have changed your tune, haven't you?'

That was cruel; it made Mary flinch.

'I'll say goodnight, then.' She brushed past him towards the door and he caught her arm.

'It's no good, you know. It's no good if just one of us wants it. You've got to want it too.'

She could feel the restraint in his hand.

'Oh, Hugh, I don't know what I want. I want someone to hold me. That's what I want. That's all.'

'And I'm the lucky man, am I? Well, I'm sorry, but no thank you.'

She listened to his footsteps going down the hall. Then very slowly she climbed the stairs herself. She undressed and got into bed and lay on her back. One by one the tears streaked down her temples and into her ears, into the hollow in her neck, over her collarbones. Half an hour later there was a tap on her door.

14

Jac sat in the straw on the floor of his cell, his bad arm resting sorely against his knees. The tendons felt charred by the pain which had burnt so persistently into his elbow all these weeks now. Since the trial they had taken his sling away – one of the warders had pointed out that he might use it to hang himself, although looking round the cramped pit they had put him in he couldn't see from what, really. The bars of the window perhaps? Well, it would be one way of getting a glimpse of the sky. Without the sling his whole body felt on edge; he was afraid to move in case he triggered off the searing, tender pain. They had left him unprotected.

Even as he had trudged from Pontarddulais to Swansea Gaol, he had known his time was up, that at twenty-six he was beginning the epilogue of his life. That was what it felt like, some strange shadow play tagged on after the main action was over for somebody else's amusement. There was no plot, no hero, no reason for the curtain not to fall, yet the obligation was there, to go through the motions somehow. He was beginning to like the silence. After weeks of fermentation it had a special potency now, it allowed him to be his own man, gave him privacy, dignity. He liked the half-life, the dreaming and the thinking and the drifting; it made it easier to shut the world away. He would never see Mary again. He was finished with Rebecca. What was there left that was real? The pain, and the solitude, and the tricks they both played. He was absorbed by the notion of self, insubstantial, silent, mystic, and by the possibilities of becoming, quite literally, lost in thought.

One by one the bolts on the door slid back, the key turned in the lock, and a man stood before him. Jac tried to focus his eyes. It was the warder, no food with him, seemingly about to speak. What a strange distortion of the daily pattern.

'On yer feet.'

The focusing was incomplete. A kick followed.

'I said, on yer feet.'

Jac clambered up and stood leaning against the wall. Moving made him giddy and his arm was flaming. With huge concentration he straightened himself up.

'Follow me.'

It was very soon. He didn't expect to be on his way this soon. December, somebody had said. Could it be that already? He didn't believe in chipping calendars into the walls and marking off the days, it tied you down too much. But he didn't think it could come this quickly. Tricks again; his own or someone else's. He wasn't sure.

The corridors were endless, winding round and round themselves. Clever, that. The warder stopped in front of a door.

'Governor wants to see you.'

He knocked.

Jac walked into the room. He had the sensation of walking into bright light, although it wasn't bright really, it was more the effect of walking into a room with people in it. Unexpected. The Governor was there, sitting at his desk. David Jones was supported by two guards, slumped between them. They hadn't taken his bandages away from him, Jac noticed. John Hugh stood on his own. Jac peered at him. Do I look as haggard as he does? Probably. He touched his cheek. It was hard to tell.

'Good morning Jac Tŷ Isha.'

'Good morning, sir.' Good. It was easy so far.

'You can read, can't you, Jac?'

'Yes, sir.'

'Good. Well, read that.'

The Governor slid a sheet of paper across his desk. Jac picked it up and his hand shook. Funny. He hadn't noticed that inside his cell.

'Read.'

'Yes, sir.'

It was a letter he had written, though he hadn't written it at all. More tricks.

'To the Public generally, and to our neighbours in particular.

'We Jac Tŷ Isha, David Jones and John Hugh, now lying in Cardiff gaol, convicted of the attack on Pontarddulais turnpike gate – and the police stationed there to protect it – being now sentenced to transportation, beg, and earnestly call on others to take warning by our fate, and to stop in their mad course, before they fall into our condemnation.

'We are guilty, and doomed to suffer, while hundreds have escaped. Let them, and every one, take care not to be deluded again to attack public or private property, and resist the power of the law, for it will overtake them with vengeance, and bring them down to destruction.

'We are only in prison now, but in a week or two shall be banished as rogues – to be slaves to strangers, in a strange land. We must go, in the prime of life, from our dear homes, to live and labour with the worst of villains – looked upon as thieves.

'Friends – neighbours – all – but especially young men – keep from night meetings! Fear to do wrong, and dread the terror of the judge.

'Think of what we must, and you may suffer, before you dare to do as we have done.

'If you will be peaceable, and live again like honest men, by the blessing of God, you may expect to prosper; and we, poor outcast wretches, may have to thank you for the mercy of the Crown – for on no other terms than your good conduct will any pity be shown to us, or others, who may fall into our almost hopeless situation.'

Jac looked the Governor in the eye.

'Very good, sir. A very good letter.'

'Yes, well . . .' The Governor fiddled briefly with a pen. 'If you'll just sign it where the other two have, then I can act as witness, and everything will be in order.'

'No, sir.'

'I beg your pardon?'

'I can't sign this, sir. Not this letter.'

The warder took a step towards him, close to his elbow.

'I'm sorry, sir.'

'Jac.' The Governor strung the name out into several syllables. 'It is an order, you know.'

'Yes, sir.'

'Well, then.'

Jac looked at the page. David Jones had managed to write his name, but only just. He wondered if his hand had been held steady. John Hugh had simply put a cross.

'We can quite easily put a mark beside your name, you know. People would be none the wiser.'

'Yes, sir, you could do that.' Jac put the paper carefully on the Governor's desk.

'We have had the best intentions in drawing this up, you know.'

'I'm sure you have, sir.'

'I see.'

There was a silence. The Governor made strange sucking movements with his mouth as he considered the matter. He folded his hands and leaned on the desk. 'Have you no thoughts of trying to reduce your sentence? You make it very difficult for us to help you. Twenty years is an awfully long time, you know.'

'I aware of that, sir.'

'If you co-operate with us –'

'Shall we be frank with one another, sir? You know as well as I do that I won't be coming back. So let's –'

'That is an unfortunate attitude.'

'I can't help that, sir.'

'Of course, it's your parents I feel sorry for.'

Jac looked at the floor.

'You're probably not aware.'

'Sir?'

'Well, your father got up a deputation, three hundred men in all, I believe. They had a meeting with William Chambers, the magistrate, your father acting as spokesman. He said that they were wanting a restoration of peace and quiet in the neighbourhood and to that end had come to offer their services as Special Constables. Quite a turn-up, you must agree. However, there was a sting in the tail – they asked for the commutation of your sentence in return.'

Oh Father, Father, what have you done? Jac remembered his angry face as he flung out of the house on the night of Pontarddulais, washing his hands of the whole affair. What have you done now, Father?

'It would be nice to think they would be warmed by a gesture like this from you Jac.'

Jac looked at a point beyond the Governor, remembering. He wondered what the police had done with Mary's mother's petticoats and the bonnet that she loved. He remembered the kisses he had folded in her hand. Four. One for every year that he'd been waiting. There should be twenty more to add to those by rights. Not that they would let him see her. That was out of the question. His gaze returned to the room.

'I don't really have a choice in this, do I?' he said quietly.

With studied absorption the Governor was clipping the end off a cigar that he had taken from a fine wooden box on his desk.

'Not really, no.' He smelt the cigar appreciatively. 'You see, if you refuse, it only means we'll have to fake it for you. Think of the bother you'd be saving us.'

'All I can think of is that the pack of you stink.'

He heard the warder's tread behind him. The pain in his arm lasted for days and days and days after that.

It was New Year's Eve, early in the morning, the last dawn of the year and the day was young and rosy. The window was wet and it squeaked as William rubbed a little hole to look out of. Outside, the mist was light and graceful over the garden and the whole of the valley was cupped full of yellows and pinks. William smiled back at the filtering sun as if to acknowledge its promises. He dressed as quickly as he could, which by now was pretty fast; in fact, he was fairly confident that it wouldn't be long before he was downstairs before Mary. If he laid his clothes out properly the previous night, with the buttons undone and the legs of his trousers rolled so that he could step into them easily . . . It was just a question of working it out in advance. The only things that could floor him now were the ones that he hadn't accounted for.

Mostly he had his little ways. He could saddle Jonah, although he needed Mary to help him with the bridle; he could harness him to the cart; he had even managed a little driving. On Christmas Eve he had driven over to Mrs Lewis in Llanboidy all on his own, for their annual exchange of chickens. They couldn't bear to kill their own and then tuck in at dinner on Christmas Day. The arrangement suited both families and they had done it for years. It had never meant anything to William until he made the journey alone. He had even caught Sly, the cockerel, without too much assistance – just in the tying of his feet. And returning that night with the other bird, Mrs Lewis' hostage to Christmas, backing the cart into its place and settling Jonah down for the night had meant more to him than – he didn't know what. Things could be done, see?

He clumped down the corridor to Mary's room, his loose boot-laces chattering on the floorboards. That was one of the things he couldn't manage – that, and tying the tapes on his jacket. Mary had sewn them to the sleeve of his bad arm so that it could be tied around his waist out of harm's way. Otherwise it had a disconcerting habit of swinging about of its own free will and getting bumped or battered. A couple of times he had come into the kitchen streaming with blood from a cut he didn't know was there, and if he tucked his dead hand into a pocket or the front of his smock it used to roll out at the most awkward moments. He used to wonder, if he stuck it into the fire, how far up the flesh would burn before it started to hurt. Anyway, the tapes were a good idea, they solved several problems, and strapped across his front his arm made a useful ledge for balancing things on – and the Lord only knew what he had stuffed away in the crook of it by the end of a working day.

William didn't bother to knock on Mary's door; she was only his sister, after all. He felt pleased with himself as he breezed in and took it for granted that she would be pleased as well. All along, his recovery had been a kind of conspiracy between them both.

'Will you do me up?' He drew the curtains as he spoke. Mary looked startled; she was wiping her mouth. The room smelt of other people's sleep, and something else, something sour and milky.

'It's a lovely day outside. Look what you're missing.' He perched easily against the window ledge. 'Boots first, or jacket?'

Mary scrabbled out of the bed with a cornered look in her eyes. She stood with her back to him, holding her forehead in her hands.

'Just a moment.'

William picked at a bit of food which was embedded in the smocking across his chest, and felt a quick flush of shame. Eating was still incredibly difficult, not something he would ever do in front of anyone except his sister. That was a promise he had made himself. One supper time he had asked her not to help him with the cutting up, and since then she never watched him, looked anywhere but in his direction, yet still he felt embarrassed.

'Right, I'll do you now.' There was a wan smile on Mary's face. She looked pasty. 'Boots first. Stand up straight. Go on.' She tied his laces rather slowly. 'Now your jacket. There. You go on down. I won't be long.'

Mary sighed as William clumped back down the corridor. He wasn't a big man, but he took up so much space, even now, when – She turned back the bedclothes; there was a stream of watery sick just where the pillow met the sheet. She could have wept.

Breakfast was easy. The milk was still warm from Bron's inside, but William put it over the fire to heat, just the same. While that was doing he crumbled yesterday's bread into his bowl – part of his mother's marriage set – then a dollop of honey on top of that, pour the milk over and leave it to soak for five minutes in the warm by the grate. He lumbered into the yard, drew some water and went to collect the eggs from under the dusty chickens. He could line three eggs at a time along the shelf of his arm, which meant he didn't have to make so many journeys back to the basket in the middle of the hut. Mary was fond of boiled eggs. She always had them, although she was picking at her food a bit of late. He frowned for a moment. Come to that, it wasn't like her to be still in her bed when it was gone seven o'clock. William balanced the last egg in the basket. It looked bland against the straw and for a few moments he squatted down tracing the curves from egg to egg. Poor Mary. She had taken Jac's trial hard – at least, she'd been pretty grim since then, so he supposed it must be that. She was usually such a sensible girl, not given to mooning about, but she looked quite peaky sometimes now. She must have got it badly. Poor girl. A couple of times she had skipped going to work, said she didn't feel up to coping with Hugh and the office and everything. Not like her at all. And considering the interest she had shown in Jac's trial, she hadn't taken a blind bit of notice of the latest round. Shoni, Dai, all that lot . . .

He rocked gently on his heels. Rebecca. What a lot of fuss. Well, it was over now, all of it, really. The Special Commission had shut down, no doubt the three blokes who ran it were busy scribbling away frantically somewhere, writing up their report. Nobody talked about Rebecca much now. Not the ordinary people, anyway. Not any more. Bit like a dream in the end, if it wasn't for – He ran his finger along his bad arm; he often did it, just to see. Well. William straightened up, dusted his knees and picked up the basket of eggs. The bread and milk would be just about right by now. Suddenly he was starving.

Halfway through breakfast Mary pushed her plate away sharply, ran to the door and was sick all over the back step. It sounded endless to William, a great noisy tide wrestling to get out of her. She had almost finished by the time he reached her, and was panting slightly. The hem of her dress skimmed the mess and the smell was the same as the one in her room.

'I'm sorry.' She gulped and coughed. 'I'm sorry. I'll clear it up. I'm sorry.'

William put his good arm around her and drew her back into the warm.

'Shall I get you some water? Would you like some water?' He didn't think she was listening even though she nodded in reply. He came back from the pump with a jug of water and wiped her mouth for her, and her chin, and smoothed back the hair from her face. Then he wiped her hands, which were hot and sticky.

'Poor old thing.'

She was staring into the fire.

'Better now? Drink some of this.'

Obediently she drank.

'Probably too much good food over Christmas. It can quite easily upset your stomach when you're not used to it.' William still retained the invalid's medical expertise. Mary was back to staring at the fire.

'It's not that.'

'Must be something you picked up in the town, then.'

'No, William, it's not. I'm going to have a baby.'

There was a long silence, in which all the promises of the early morning were broken.

'Oh . . . right . . . I see.' William sat down with a bump. The chair seemed to arrive more quickly than he expected. 'Well.' He did his best to keep a grip on the silence which followed. She couldn't be serious. She couldn't be.

They both spoke at once.

'Are you sure?'

'I've known for about three weeks now. Well, that's how long I've been certain.'

William shook his head. He must have got the whole thing wrong.

'Does Jac know?'

'Jac? Oh don't be so stupid, William.' Mary laughed and the loudness of it surprised them both. 'It isn't his – how could it be his? Use your head. He's been in prison since September.' She took a sip from the cup of water.

'How long? . . .' He spoke timidly. He didn't want her to laugh again.

'I don't know much about these things. Two and a half months, I think. Something like that. I don't know how you tell exactly.'

William felt as if something important was eluding him; it was all rather a struggle. 'You mean it happened more than once? I'm sorry, I don't mean to –'

'It's all right, you're not prying, if that's what you mean. Yes. It happened more than once. It happened lots of times.' That was what hurt her most, that was what she found impossible to forgive herself for and her voice was brittle with unpardoned pain. 'Lots of times. Last week, even.'

'Who?' He couldn't think why he was whispering. The occasion seemed to demand it. The world had gone mad, in any case. Mary was having a baby.

'Hugh.' There, it was said. Would confession lead to absolution? She didn't think so.

'Jesus!'

'William, please.' Old habits die hard.

'Hugh? Jesus, Mary. I thought you were going to say – well, I don't know, Mike Bowen or somebody, I don't know. But not Hugh. I mean, he's married, he's –'

'You don't have to remind me.'

William stared at his sister throughout another long pause. 'Are you sure?' he asked. 'Not about Hugh,' he added hurriedly, 'about – it.'

She nodded.

'Well.' The bread and milk was solid in his bowl, and no longer very warm. 'Well.'

'I'd better wash the step down.' Mary did not move.

'Have you thought what you will do?'

'No, William. I can't find any answers at the moment. I don't know what to do. I'll think of something, I suppose.'

'Does Hugh know?' Hugh, the lover of his sister,

Hugh with Mary. William couldn't make the picture fit at all, he couldn't even begin to try. 'Have you told him?'

'No.'

'Will you?'

'I don't know. Ask me just about anything and that's the answer. I simply don't know.'

He had a surreptitious glance at her stomach and she caught his gaze with a rueful smile.

'Not yet.'

He looked away, embarrassed, and she came and stood beside him.

'You'll have to help me, William.'

'Yes. Of course.'

'I'm sorry. I'm so –'

'Don't. It'll be all right. You'll see.' He shoved his chair back. 'I'd better get started. The morning's half gone – all this talk.'

William clumped out into the yard. The morning was unaltered by the news. The mist was still rolling gold along the valley floor and now the sun had elbowed its way up above the rim of the hills. Even the blanched slopes and the fields rattled their winter bones with expectation. William sniffed. There was a definite hum in the air, a stirring. He thought how unreluctantly the land lets each old year fall away, without any sentiment at all. That was probably the best thing to do. Yes. He wouldn't be sad to see the back of 1843 himself.

15

Mary pulled her cloak more closely round her. Underneath it she had on an old jerkin of her father's which William sometimes wore, and she had bound her hands with rags under her mittens, but still the cold bit right into her bones. There was ice on the steps of the mailcoach – she had slipped and almost fallen as she climbed down. Now she banged her hands together and breathed hot wet air into her gloves for a few moments of relief. It didn't last longer than that. Further along the quay some dockers were clustered round a brazier, waiting for their next load to come into port. From a chilly, wistful distance Mary watched as the flames licked themselves warm. She dared not go any closer. One of the men had already invited her over in rough, unfamiliar, city Welsh. She shook her head and began to walk in tiny circles to keep warm, marking time.

She had done a lot of that lately; marking time. Waiting to be sure about the baby, being sure. Waiting for a decision to become clear, deciding. And now, waiting in the cold in Cardiff once again. In all her life Mary had never been more than twenty miles away from home, and now within the space of three short months, she had been to Cardiff not once but twice. She stamped her feet on the icy cobbles. Twenty-six patient and unchanging years, a rhythm of receding seasons, of coming and going, of growth, of peace, of repetition. Now all of that was changed. A year ago she had felt that life could offer no surprises for her; now she had seen so many they no longer took her by surprise. To be in Cardiff again, in Cardiff docks, was nothing but a hiccough in an ordinary week now. She had never seen a ship until today, but after an hour of waiting in the cold they provided only incidental interest, a sideshow to the main event.

Hugh told her. It was one of the embittered acts of kindness which he occasionally gave way to. Sometimes his ambivalence towards her made her feel uneasy. She knew that he resented her, resented her empty heart, yet at the same time she thought that it scorched him just to be in the room alone with her. They were extremes she couldn't understand. She knew that he punished himself, both for his kindness to her, and for his cruelty. He could be very cruel. One day she sat reading to his wife, Thursday afternoon as usual. She had her chair positioned near the open door; it was the only way she could stand the heat which raged from the fire in the dark green parlour. Thursday afternoon as usual; Anne was fast asleep on her chins but Mary kept on reading, knowing the old lady would wake up if she stopped. Bulwer Lytton's *Last Days of Pompeii* – they had been reading it for weeks now. Glancing up from the book on her lap, Mary saw Hugh standing at the far end of the passage, talking to Bethan. They were deep in conversation. The next time Mary looked, he was kissing her, a studied and malicious kiss, his body pressing hers against the wall. It formed a picture which she never forgot, a shadow cameo of unkindness – not just to her, to Bethan too. The sight made her pause halfway through a sentence. Anne's head rolled loosely and she gave a short, disturbed grunt. Mary continued to read, but the pain inside her was real and acute. Hugh should be pleased at that, she thought.

And then his kindnesses. This last, in particular. Mr Ashe was out of the office working on a case, and Mary was sitting at her desk busy with the accounts. She put her pen down when Hugh came into the room. He had his hands in his pockets and his head down, and he said nothing. For a few minutes he paced the length of the rug under the window, and then he gave some time to lining up the tassels on the end with the toe of his boot. Mary went back to her figures and almost forgot that he was there. Now he stood in the middle of the rug and looked out of the window.

'Jac Ty Isha is being shipped out next week. He's going by boat to Bristol, then by train to the Millbank Penitentiary. He'll wait there until the *London* is ready to sail. Tasmania, I believe. I thought I ought to tell you.'

Mary's pen hung in the air.

'Thank you.'

For weeks and weeks she had been trying so hard not to think about him, to be busy, to be bright.

'Thank you, Hugh.'

There was so much now to think about in any case. The baby. Her love for Jac had become a kind of imagined happiness, lost in the time before Rebecca had cut a swathe across their lives. Maybe it had been all in her mind in the first place. She felt that she could no longer judge such things.

Hugh moved over to her desk and with a colourless smile placed a sovereign on the blotter. 'There. That ought to get you to Cardiff and back. I think he should have someone on the quayside to wave goodbye, don't you?'

With that he went back to his room, his head still bent low and a hard expression on his face. His punishment of himself was sometimes savage to see. The act of love was a kind of punishment to him too, a grief. And standing on the quay of Cardiff docks a few days later, Mary still felt the guilt of it.

The packet to Bristol was ready to leave. Most of the passengers had disappeared into the warm and only a small bunch of sailors was left on deck, leaning on the rail, talking, waiting for the convicts to arrive. They always left it till the last minute. The prison governor said it was a matter of security but the sailors found it a pain in the neck. Mary edged closer to the boat. She felt conspicuous, as if every eye in the port were fed upon her. One of the dockers passed too close to her.

'How much, love?'

He had a huge load on his back and he whistled as he went. She looked out at the sludgy sea and tried to batten down her feelings. She knew why she had come that day, and the reason was a good one, the best. It didn't matter what anybody else thought.

There were weeds, and bits of rope, and rotting food floating on the surface of the water, gently buffing the ship's bows. Mary shifted her weight from one foot to the other and breathed into her gloves again.

The carriage arrived from the prison late, like a doubtful bride. It was black and windowless except for a small pair of shutters behind the coachman's seat and even these were tightly closed. It rattled grumpily along the quayside, as if objecting right up to the last moment, and ground to a halt only feet away from the bottom of the gangplank. The coachman held the horses while one of the guards began undoing all the bolts on the thick black door. Mary stood as close as she dared, about twenty feet away, watching and waiting.

A warder jumped down first, breathing hard as if he had been running, and mopping at his face. He reached behind him into the darkness of the interior and yanked out a skinny man with gingery whiskers. Dai 'r Cantwr, the street singer. Mary had heard him talked about years before he hitched his waggon to Rebecca's star. A shambling dreamer, people said, who seemed to have a talent for drinking in eight different inns all at the same time. He used to boast that he had once won a prize at the Eisteddfod, although nobody knew if that were true. And then he fell in with Shoni, and here he was today . . . As soon as his feet touched the ground, one of the waiting sailors grabbed at the loop of chain which dangled between his wrists and hauled him up the gangplank. Dai loped obligingly out of sight with a shuffling run that was born of fear. He would be running like that for the rest of his life.

John Hugh came next. He stopped for a moment to gawp at the boat in front of him, his round farmer's face registering slow amazement. He even had the temerity to sniff the air; then one of the warders punched him in the kidneys and he broke into the same eager and appeasing run, the irons on his legs shrilling out 'I'm sorry, I'm sorry, I'm sorry' as he went.

And then came Jac Tŷ Isha. His hair was longer than it used to be, and his face was a little thinner, and paler than frost. He was dressed like the others in grimy canvas with black arrowheads branded everywhere across it, and only the raw redness of his hands to show how cold he was. He didn't turn his head or look about; he didn't pause, but there was still the look of the valleys in his eyes as he walked onto the ship and away from Wales.

'Jac –' The impulse was unstoppable; it came unchecked, directly from her heart. And then he turned, and looked.

'Mary Jenkins.'

He raised his hand, making the chains tinkle like laughter.

'Goodbye.' A dark smile of love to end it all.

'Goodbye, Jac.'

One of the warders struck him across the face, leaving it stinging red, humiliated.

'Get along now, Miss. This is no place for you here.'

Mary could not move. Jac had reached the top of the gangplank and for a moment his profile was set like jet against the white winter sky. She raised her hand, numb with the cold, to wave. He disappeared. A dark smile, a blow, and he had gone.

Goodbye.

She stood briefly staring at where he had been, at the empty sky. They were dragging David Jones up the gangplank. He couldn't walk alone, so two warders had strung him out between them and were trawling him onto the ship. Mary turned away, flexing her hands, which were now so cold, without thinking. Something flexed itself against her stomach wall as well, a gentle, unacknowledged butting. Hugh's baby was unfurling like a flower inside her, but Mary hardly noticed; her mind was on other things. She walked a few paces and then reached into her bag, her fingers slow and unelastic. Inside was a letter from Caleb Morris. She had written to him: in the back of her mind was the promise that he had made long ago to her Dada, that if she learned the reading and the writing, then one day he might be able to find her a post as a governess. On the steps of the courtroom he had asked if there was anything he could do. *Help me now*.

Mary took a gulp of air. She had explained she wanted to move out of the area, and his letter suggested they meet at his sister's house in Cardiff as he could combine the trip with some business. They would expect her at two o'clock. Half an hour to get there. The docker whistled as she passed the brazier. *Help me now*.

Thomas Campbell Foster puffed as the porter helped him with his bags. He was astonished that he had collected so much stuff. A lot of extra woollens, of course – he had arrived in South Wales equipped as if he were going to the colonies. It made him smile to think about it now. Then there were his notes – reams and reams of them, endless interviews, statements, memos, copies of all his articles, copies of *The Carmarthen Journal* and *The Welshman*, not to mention the report of the Special Commission. In spite of his reservations, Thomas felt the three commissioners had done the job reasonably well and drawn some fairly sound conclusions. They suggested that the multiplicity of turnpike trusts should be honed down within each county and that the roads themselves should be managed by special boards. They acknowledged that tithes had gone up by seven per cent and suggested that, as they were basically a tax on land, the landlords should make redress for this to their tenants. They also admitted the inadequacies of the judicial system which allowed magistrates to be ignorant of Welsh and frequently absent from petty sessions. Locally it was fervently hoped that the recommended reforms would be made law one day and Lord Cawdor had promised to do his best to have the matter raised in Parliament. Rebecca's Children would have to be patient, and wait and see.

'Careful with that!'

The porter threw a small leather box into the corner of the luggage van.

'Careful, please. In fact, I think I'll take it in the carriage with me. Would you mind, er . . .'

With a sullen face, the porter climbed up into the van and pulled the small box out.

'There you go, mister. Will that be all?'

'Let me see. Two trunks, yes. Two boxes, yes. I've got this,' Thomas had the small box in his hand now, 'and you say you've put my bag into the compartment already?'

'Yes, mister.' The porter was looking over Thomas' shoulder, down the platform at something which he found more interesting than the journalist's luggage.

'Excellent, right, well. Um. Oh yes.' Thomas fished in his pocket and brought out a silver three ha'pence. 'There we are. Thank you.'

'Thank you, mister, sir.' The porter stowed the coin away without appearing to do so. 'Thank you kindly.' He wasn't looking at him.

Thomas climbed the steps into his compartment, brushed the seat by the window carefully, flicked out the tails of his coat and sat, hugging the little box on his knees. He had never been on a train before, and he took it as a mark of extreme favour on the editor's part to allow him to do so. The letter recalling him to London had thanked him for his industry and ordered him to take the train from Bristol to London. 'I expect you are sick of the sight of toll-gates and such like. Why don't you come up to London by train?' That's what the note had said and Thomas was only too happy to oblige. He thought he might do a piece about it. He had been especially careful when packing to make sure that his pocket book was easily to hand, just in case. The engine whistled and screamed like a banshee and Thomas' heart began to bump rather. They said the locomotive could do speeds of up to thirty miles an hour. He was longing to stand up and stick his head out of the window and watch as they pulled out of the station, but he was worried about all that smoke and steam and coaldust. It couldn't possibly be good for the chest. So he sat tight and pressed his face against the window, his breath cloudy against the glass.

The effort it cost the train to leave the platform was roughly equal to that required to get Thomas out of a nice hot bath. The same straining, the same feeling of weight, the same final push. At first he felt slightly queasy as houses and then trees and fields ripped past, and he discovered that he was gripping the armrests rather tightly, but the sound of the great iron wheels was insistently soothing and before long he began to loosen his hold. His gaze moved away from the streaking view outside and settled on the shiny leather box in his lap. It was a presentation case. He ran his hand over its sleekness and let his fingers rest on the clasp. Just one more look. He hadn't really had a chance since it was given to him, what with the packing and all the preparations. The clasp snapped back. There was blue watered silk lining the inside. He felt that too, and eased the lid further open. Inside was a silver goblet and salver, a gift from the people of Carmarthen – well, from some of them. Others had been noticeably absent from the little ceremony held at his hotel. Those who did attend, and there were several faces that he did not even know amongst the group, had thanked him for drawing the attention of the whole nation to their troubles and for helping to shed light on them. There had been polite applause and then a toast was drunk. His face went pink as he remembered. Reluctantly he shut the lid and refastened the clasp, recalling as he did how closed those same people and their town had been to him when he had first arrived. That was, until he had his lucky break, the day he met the girl in the dark green dress.

'Working late again, Miss Jenkins?' Mr Ashe was taking the devil of a time to leave the office himself. At least he had his greatcoat on now, and he was standing by his desk regarding his reflection in the windowpane. Furtively he brushed at his shoulders when he thought that Mary wasn't looking.

'Er, yes. There's a lot to do at the moment, isn't there?' Mary continued to write, keeping up the pretence that she was busy.

'Seems rather quiet to me,' said Mr Ashe, fastidiously drawing up the rank of pens next to his writing pad. 'But then, I wouldn't know. Nobody tells me anything these days.'

'Hmmm.' The abstraction came easily to Mary. She risked a glance at him. He was sitting down again, scratching at his chin.

'Mr Williams working late too, is he?' He paused in his scratching.

'I don't know. You'd better ask him.'

Mary kept writing, and Mr Ashe kept on sitting at his desk. He ran his finger along its bevelled edge, watching the tide of dust and making tutting sounds. Then he sat back and rocked slightly, appearing to be deeply preoccupied with listening to the creak of the chair. Mary shielded her forehead with her hand. He'll start to whistle in a minute and then I will have to say something, she thought. The minutes ticked by. Mr Ashe whistled a scrap of an undistinguished tune.

'You'll be late for your supper at this rate,' said Mary through lightly gritted teeth. She did not look up from her page.

He stopped rocking abruptly, sucked at his lips noisily for a moment and then stood up.

'Yes. I suppose you're right.' He lifted his hat from the hat stand and then spent a long minute putting it on and adjusting it and adjusting it again, all the while admiring his reflection in the window. Another quick brush of the shoulder.

'Right, I'd best be getting along, then.' He hesitated for a second with his hand on the doorknob, and cast a final conjectural glance at Hugh's office. 'Goodnight then.'

'Goodnight, Mr Ashe,' said Mary firmly.

As soon as he was gone she went to the door, watching him until he was safely round the corner of the street. She pulled the blinds down; her palms were sweating slightly and she wiped them against her skirt. Then she went and knocked on Hugh's door.

He stood up as soon as she went in.

'Has he gone? At last!' His tone was light and laughing. He kissed her on the mouth. 'Here, I've got something to show you. Come over here.' He sat at his desk and pulled her on to his knee. She felt foolish sitting there, self-conscious. She wondered if he noticed how heavy she was becoming. He gave her another feasting kiss, holding her close to him by the nape of her neck.

'Oh, Mary.' He lost her name somewhere in the hollow of her shoulder.

Mary swallowed. 'What did you want to show me?'

Hugh searched at her face, uncertain for a moment. 'Here, it's this. You'll probably think it's very silly. Just something I scribbled down. But I wanted you to see it.' He pulled a sheet of paper towards her. She said something about the light being bad and took the opportunity to move away from him, sitting nearer the lamp.

On the piece of paper were a few verses, untitled and with several crossings-out. She looked at him doubtfully, thinking that this wasn't what she had come for at all.

'Go on, read it.' Hugh moved over to her, although he did not try to touch her. Instead he ran his fingers through his hair.

Mary read.

> O deign, dearest maiden,
>   My suit to receive –
> I'd not for existence
>   Thy true love deceive..
> I heed not for station,
>   Nor riches in store –
> 'Tis thy grace I value,
>   Thy virtues adore.
>
> I'll not leave thee, thou lone one,
>   To droop in the dell,
> Since the lovely are mated,
>   Come mate thou as well;
> For kindly I'll treat thee,
>   And cherish thy home –
> Not far from thy presence
>   Will I ever roam.

And soon will I follow,
  When thou shalt decay,
And from love's gentle circle
  The charm glides away.
When fond hearts lie wither'd
  And chaste ones are gone,
Oh, who would inhabit
  This bleak world alone!

Mary gave a wan smile and let the poem fall into her lap.

'It's very nice,' she said awkwardly.

'Yes, well . . .'

'Hugh, we've got to talk. There's something I've got to tell you.'

'Yes?'

He wasn't making it easy for her. Maybe she had upset him over the poem. She wasn't sure.

'I've been thinking a great deal lately. About everything that's happened – Rebecca, William, and Jac too, I suppose. And I've been thinking . . .' She tailed off. Now that the moment had come she didn't know how to frame the lie; it was not something she was used to doing. All that she knew was that she didn't want him to know about the baby, she couldn't cope with that as well. It would be better, tidier that way.

'Yes?' There was neither warmth nor encouragement in his voice any more.

'Well, I've been thinking about us as well.'

He had his back to her.

'And what have you thought about us?'

'We've got to stop, Hugh.' She blurted it out.

416

'They gave your precious Jac a last-minute reprieve, did they? Or did he jump ship and nobly strike for shore, back to the arms of the woman who loves him?' he added, after a pause which was stitched through with malice.

'No, it's not that at all.' Mary felt almost relieved. She could deal with his anger; it was the misery and the sadness that she had been dreading.

'What is it, then?' His back was still towards her and there was vindictiveness even in that.

'Well, Hugh, you're married, you've got a wife, a home, a life of your own that I can have no part in –'

'I don't recall that bothering you three months ago.' He threw the remark over his shoulder. The poem had dropped to the ground and Mary stooped to pick it up.

'It's not just that, although that's partly it.'

'Oh, so it's not just moral concerns. How progressive you are, Mary, what a liberal. I didn't think you had it in you.'

Mary was beginning to smart all over. She felt very hot. There was a tiny eddy in the pit of her stomach. This time she felt it. The baby. The reason for it all. She sighed and put the poem on his desk with distracted neatness.

'I'm going away, Hugh. I won't be able to see you. I'm going to Cardiff.'

He turned around this time and there was a look of disbelief on his face. 'You're what?'

'I'm going to work in Cardiff.'

'But you work here. You work for me.'

'I know, I know. You've been very good to me. But just lately –' she sped on, beginning to see a way through ' – just lately I've felt that my position here is rather ill-defined. I'm not sure where I fit. I don't feel comfortable any more. I don't know where I belong – I teach a bit, I help out here, I sit with your wife although I know she doesn't like me. It's too much, too many things. I want to do one thing and do it well.' All this was partly true; it made it easier.

'And you have to go to Cardiff to do this, do you?'

'Well, I was talking to our old minister – '

'Oh yes.' Hugh's tone was biting once again.

'Yes. I've known him all my life. He sort of kept an eye on us when my Dada . . . He's the one who taught me – Anyway, I, I mentioned to him that I was looking for some kind of fresh start and he said he knew of a position which might suit me and he made a few inquiries and the upshot is that I've taken it.'

'And what is this position that he's found?'

'I'm going to be a housekeeper for his sister.'

'How stimulating. How life-enhancing.'

'Please don't be angry, Hugh.'

He shrugged his shoulders. 'I'm not.'

'I don't want to upset you. I think it's for the best, that's all.'

'I'm sure you're right.'

There was a brittle silence. Mary was beginning to feel quite wobbly inside.

'I'm sorry, Hugh.'

'What about your brother? What about Dolwilym? I thought it meant so much to you.'

William. The thought of telling him haunted her more than anything. She had put it off and put it off.

'I don't know. He's going to have to learn to

manage on his own one day. It might even be the making of him.'

'You're very optimistic. I think it doubtful that a cripple could run a farm all on his own. Even a small farm.'

Mary winced inside.

'I know. I'm going to arrange for one of the local lads to help him out. He'll get by.' She could hardly bear to think of William struggling to cope, struggling to keep going, struggling. Again and again she pushed the picture from her mind.

Hugh took a step towards her; he stood quite close, looking and looking at her as if trying to fathom her out. She could see the battle being waged inside him: to touch, or not to touch. In the end he leaned towards her and brushed a loose strand of hair from her shoulder. All his sadness was in that gesture.

'Why have you got so hard, Mary? What's made you hard like this?'

She hung her head.

'I don't feel hard inside. Not at all. Oh, Hugh.'

He looked down at her, noticing how glossy her hair was, how her cheek curved. He did not comprehend at all.

'I'm sorry. This is awful. I'd better go.' She wiped her eyes, although at that moment they were dry. She was starting to feel very shaky indeed.

'Will I see you again?' Hugh had never asked that of anyone before. It cost dearly.

'I think it's better not, don't you?'

He shrugged his shoulders. 'It's up to you.'

'Better not, then. I've got such a lot to do. So many things to sort out . . . William . . .'

'When do you leave?'

'A couple of weeks. Not long, really.'

'No. Not long.' They both stood mutely for a moment, and their silence was full of reaching out, and reasoning, and rejecting.

'Well,' Mary breathed out, then swallowed. 'Well. I'd better go.' She moved to the door.

'Mary –'

She turned for a second and looked at him, and shook her head, then closed the door behind her.

Hugh sat down heavily at his desk, staring at nothing for several minutes. The poem which he had written for her lay where she had left it. He drew it towards him and glanced it over with bitterness in his face. Neatly he folded it in half, and then in half again, and again and again, until the rebuff it represented was a bunched-up nubble of paper which could be held in the palm of the hand. He wanted it to be contained as easily as that. Then with careful calculation he threw it so that it arced across the office and dropped into the wastepaper basket. That was that, or so it would seem. The oil lamp burned with great forbearance while Hugh sat and sat and never moved. He made the whole room sullen, hunched forward with his hands dangling between his knees, brooding and unforgiving. Let her go then. Who did she think she was, anyway? She flattered herself to think that he cared for her. 'I don't want to upset you.' Simpering, wretched, insincere. But he *did* care. It was the caring that he was trying to blot out most of all as he sat there keening in his anger. He cared, he cared, he loved her. Stupid, foolish – What had got into her to make her go? What notion, what idiotic whim? She was just like all the rest of them, there was no knowing, no telling, ever. Nothing to be done.

He looked at the clock. Anne would be waiting for him, that vast expectant bulk, his wife. 'But, Hugh, you're married, you've got a wife, a home, a life of your own –' Was Mary sneering when she said that? She would be right to sneer. His marriage, yes, well. He almost laughed. The clock struck eight. It was time for him to go. He found it ironic that tonight there would be nothing to explain away, no excuses would be necessary. He was stiff when he stood up, and felt much older than his years, though not as old as Anne, of course. Nobody could ever be as old as she. He put on his coat, turned out the lamp and locked the office door. He locked up all his feelings at the same time.

She was in bed when he got home. He managed three paces down the hall before the bleating began.

'Hugh? Is that you, Hugh? Are you back?'

He did not move. Let her call, was all that he thought. Bethan came down the passage from the kitchen, her apron straining amiably.

'Evening, Mr Williams. Shall I take your coat? Mrs Williams has turned in early; she's had one of her bad days. She said you were to go up when you got in. I've saved some dinner in the oven for you, nice and warm. Everything all right in the office, then?'

'I've got some paperwork to do. Would you bring my supper to me in the sitting-room in half an hour?'

'Hugh. Hugh.'

The call dropped like a stone down the well of the

staircase. It made his insides turn to lead. Bethan
stood behind him to help him off with his coat. He
thought he felt her body brush against him, he wasn't
sure. He wasn't particularly interested either. Not
this time.

'Half an hour then, Mr Williams.' Her skin shone.
She was slippery all over, that one.

'Hugh? Are you coming up? Hugh?'

He walked into the sitting-room and closed the
door on his wife's cry. He wanted some peace, he
wanted to get away.

He read for an hour and ate the food which Bethan
brought for him. At eleven o'clock, when there was
an odds-on chance that Anne would be asleep, he
steeled himself to say goodnight to her. He crept into
the bedroom, the lamp was still lit and she lay like
a swelling in the marital bed. He hadn't slept in it
for years. He looked at her; she was bloated and she
smelt and she was seventy-two years old, but for all
that, his greatest sense of revulsion he reserved for
himself. That was how she made him feel: appalled
at himself. He had married her because she had
money, and everything came back to that. You
couldn't get into politics without any money, and
therefore he couldn't get into politics without Anne.
It had been a high price, one that he had to keep on
paying. Extortion was one of her indulgences . . .

'Where have you been? I wanted you to –'

'I had some work to do.' He stood at the end of the
bed, out of reach of the lamplight.

'I'm on my own all the time and you can't even –'

'You've had Bethan to look after you.'

'Huh.'

'Look, Anne, I'm sorry. It's been a long day. We're very busy at the moment. I'm tired. I just want to go to bed. I'm very tired. Let's talk at breakfast. We'll have it in your room together. I'd like that, it would be nice. You go to sleep now. All right? Have you taken your tonic? Good. I'll see you in the morning. Sleep well.'

He left quickly before she could haul herself into a position more suitable for arguing. He had got away with the minimum and it made him feel unkind. His feelings were meagre and unhappy – so what did a bit of unkindness matter too? He headed off down the corridor to his own room. There was a glimmer of light licking its way slyly under Bethan's door, enough to make him pause. He looked at it and deliberated for a moment. It would be very easy. She wouldn't mind. It might provide some sort of comfort, it might bring some relief. Hugh nodded to himself and granted dispensation. He scratched softly on the door.

'Come in.'

He let himself into her room. It was heavy with her scent and she was naked under the blankets. She is as cynical as I am, he thought. Those knowing eyes, that round, shiny face. She was smiling as he peeled his clothes off, and she rolled over in the bed to make some space for him.

'You're a good girl, Bethan.'

'Thank you, sir.'

He thought of nothing as he pushed himself inside her, and afterwards he thought of nothing until he fell asleep.

*   *   *

Under the eaves at Dolwilym, Mary's room was stripped quite bare. The curtains stirred and waved from time to time, but everything else had been rolled up, folded and boxed away. The little drawing of the bottom field which her father had done was carefully wrapped in newspaper; even the rag rug which her mother had made when she was a girl, before she was married, had been tied up with string, ready to go. Mary wanted to take everything with her, everything that spoke of Dolwilym, of the farm – everything that smelt of home. She had gone to her mother's black oak chest and taken out the robe in which she and William had been christened, and as she held it up to the light to examine it for moth the situation suddenly felt very real to her. This is for my child. In four months' time the baby that's inside me now will be wearing this. My baby. She rubbed it against her cheek, imagining, but she found it hard to connect the dim notion of what lay ahead with now, with today. Most of the time she lived in a kind of mechanical dream, ticking the milestones off one by one: Jac going, telling Hugh, telling William. There was only the leaving to do now; she had kept the worst till last.

Telling William. Sitting on her bed in the empty room, his anguish, and his face, were clear in her mind. She wondered if they would stay that clear during all the months and maybe years that she would spend in Cardiff. How can you tell the effect that absence will have when you have never been away? How can you best prepare? She only knew that no amount of rehearsal inside her head had made it any easier to tell William her decision, and that she could never forget his hurt and his anger and the white glassiness of his look.

'Why?'

She could not answer straight away, but made a lame and speechless gesture.

'I don't understand why. Why do you have to go? What's the point? What's it going to solve?'

'It will solve a lot of things, a lot of very basic problems.'

'Like what?'

'Like, William, who am I going to say is the father of this child? When Mrs Lewis asks me, or Mr Ashe, or anybody, who am I going to say? How am I going to explain it away?'

'Well, I don't see how going to Cardiff will help.'

'Of course it will. Don't you see? It means I can come back in a couple of years with a baby and some mythical dead father, it gives me a chance to create a past for myself which will account for me having a child. No one is going to go checking up on me, and it means that we will be able to settle back into some kind of a life here without people asking questions. It will make what has actually happened seem possible and be acceptable. I don't see any alternative, to be honest. I can't produce the child like a rabbit out of a hat and say I don't know how it got there, can I?'

'I'm not suggesting that.'

'Well what do you suggest then? Have you got any better ideas, because if you have I'd love to hear them.'

'I don't see why you can't just stay here. We're cut off, we can live quite privately—'

'Yes, but on what? It's because I go out to work that we can manage at all, and I can't very well turn up at Hugh's office with an infant wailing on my hip. He would be bound to start putting two and two together.'

'I don't see why you don't tell him anyway.'

'I can't.'

'Why not?'

'I just can't, that's all.'

'But why? He might be able to help us out.'

'I don't want that. I don't want him to be so much a part of me, to have a hold over me, to be able to make claims. It's just a feeling that I have. I can't explain it.'

They were facing each other head on, glaring. The embers in the grate winked and blinked as if in alarm.

'You'd rather go to Cardiff instead?'

'Yes.' Mary shouted it out as if she really meant it, when deep down inside her she felt as if she had no choice.

William turned away from her slowly, thinking. At last he said, 'What about me?'

It made Mary bereft to hear him. His tight and injured sadness robbed her of any adequate response. She stayed silent, empty.

'What about me? Have you stopped to think – I mean, have you had any bright ideas about how I'm going to cope? You're looking at a man who can't even tie up his boot-laces on his own.'

'I know.'

'You know, but you just don't care, is that it? As long as you're all right, that's the main thing.'

426

'That's not fair.'

'I think it's perfectly fair. You got us into all of this, after all.'

'Don't, William. Please don't.' She moved over to him, needing to touch, to reconcile, but he brushed her hand away.

'How am I going to manage, Mary? Stop and think for a moment. Think what it means to be like this.' He gestured at his arm. It became more and more emaciated every day now. There couldn't be a more eloquent accusation than its grey, wrinkled deadness.

'I'll send my wages back from Cardiff. One of the boys from Bachsylw will come over every day. I've arranged it all with Mrs Prŷs and she has agreed to bake for you once a week. My pay should cover that. I know how hard it's going to be, believe me, I do. But it won't be for ever, and for now it really is the best that I can think of. I can't stay here, it's as simple as that. I can't have the baby and work for Hugh as well, and if I don't work, where will we be? We could lose the farm and end up in the Workhouse. I don't know about you, but it's not a risk that I'm prepared to take.'

Now it was William's turn to say nothing.

'Please believe me, poppet. I'm not trying to hurt you. I want to do the best for us both. But I need you to help me, to be on my side. Please, William.'

Please, William . . . he had stayed silent for a long time after that, for days. He stopped coming in to her room for help with his clothes in the morning; he wouldn't accept any assistance from her at all and it upset her to see how awry he sometimes looked.

But if that was how he wanted it to be, what could she do? She shivered, for the room felt chilly. Without her bits and pieces it looked unfamiliar and cold. But nowhere as unfamiliar as the room she would be sleeping in that night.

Caleb Morris had been as kind as she hoped that he would be. He had ushered her into his sister's parlour – mustard-yellow brocade and thrusting plants were all she could remember. He had taken her freezing, mittened hand and led her to a chair near the fire. Then he had poured her a cup of tea. It was luxury that Mary wasn't used to at all. He let her take a few sips before he spoke.

'My sister will be with us presently, but in the meantime why don't you tell me all about it.'

And out it all came tumbling. No, not all of it, not quite. She did nothing to correct his vague, ill-thought-out assumption that the child was Jac's; it seemed simpler not to. The minister listened without interrupting and his spectacles were shiny and benign, so that if he had any thoughts about the evils resulting from fornication, they remained well-hidden. When Mary had finished talking, he took his glasses off and polished them, while he framed what he would say.

'How difficult, my dear. I see your problem.' He paused. 'What you want is to disappear somewhere, I suppose.'

Mary nodded dumbly and fiddled with her glove.

'Cardiff is the furthest I've ever been, sir,' she said in an undertone.

He nodded and his glasses slipped a little on his nose. 'Mmmm. Cardiff. Yes. Well, it's just possible.'

He stood up and began pacing round the room.

Mary noticed he was wearing slippers, faded tapestry ones. She found it oddly touching.

He stopped abruptly. 'I suggested we meet here because I thought my sister might be able to help us. It's rather a long shot, but it might be worth a try. Will you excuse me for a moment? I shan't be a second. Do help yourself to more tea.'

He was away for fifteen minutes, and Mary sat in an anxious thaw beside the fire. When he returned he was not alone.

'I'd like you to meet my sister.'

Mary shook the woman's hand. She was wearing black lace gloves, her dress was black and her hair was gun-metal grey, although she couldn't have been more than forty. There was loss and sadness in her face. She made Mary feel like a country girl.

'I hope you don't mind.' Caleb hovered while his sister sat down. 'I've explained evening to Alice, and she was most concerned to hear your story.'

The woman smiled and looked at her brother. Mary was only partly reassured. She wondered if it had been right to come. Suddenly she felt like public property.

'I'm a widow, you can see – ' the lady indicated her dress. 'I was married very late and very happily. We had a child, a boy; he's four now. But then my husband got consumption. He died ten months ago.'

'I'm sorry.' Mary mouthed the words, but the woman went on.

'The house is large enough and Caleb thought, well, he suggested that I might, well, that it would be good to have some company. Good for little Glanmor, and for me too. I could offer you a room and a salary of sorts. And in return you could help me with the housekeeping and maybe give some lessons to my son when he's old enough. Caleb says that you can teach.'

'But what about my baby?' Mary found it hard to speak above a whisper.

'I'm sure we shall all rub along together. It's good for a house to have children in it. I know that Glanmor would benefit from some company. He gets very lonely . . .'

'What do you think, Miss Jenkins? Would it suit, do you think?'

Mary felt pink in the cheeks, pink from the fire, pink because she felt like a charity case. She *was* a charity case. She felt she had ceased to be a person and had become simply an opportunity for this woman to do good.

'You don't have to make up your mind just yet,' Caleb hovered anxiously.

Mary looked at the woman's face and once again she saw the loss there. Maybe she does know what it is like. The gun-metal hair, the mourning. Maybe she knows.

'Oh, no, no. You're very kind. I don't know what to say. I would be terribly grateful.' Really she had no choice.

'Well, that's settled, then.' Caleb rubbed at his forehead in considerable relief and his sister smiled with folded lips. Mary looked round the room which could never be a home.

'I'd like it very much, if that's all right. Thank you.'

'More tea?'

* * *

William came into her room.

'It's ready.'

The lad from Bachsylw had come over for the first time that morning, to help with the loading and get to know the farm.

'Are you coming?' Monosyllables were the best that William could manage with her, but nevertheless he had offered to drive her in the cart all the way to Cardiff. She had suggested that she should go by mailcoach but he shook his head.

'No. It's family,' was all that he had said. He stood in the doorway now, reluctant to come into her room.

'I'll be down in a minute.'

'Well, don't be long. Jonah's all hitched up, waiting. You know what he gets like.' He turned on his heel and went.

Mary shut her eyes and sat still for a moment, letting the angles of the eaves close about her as they had done every night for years and years and years. It was dark inside her head, dark like the past, like the future. She sighed, stood up and walked down the stairs without looking back. It seemed dark in the kitchen too, full of so many shadows. She shook herself slightly, almost resolutely, took a deep breath and then stepped out into the yard, blinking at the light.

Epilogue

The woods around Dolwilym sighed because the night was overdue and it was time for the farm to settle down and sleep. In the old kitchen the fire was almost out; the flames were tiny blue surrenders in the bottom of the grate, but Mary did not get up to tend it. Now that the story was told she sat unmoving. Eleanor was on her knees beside the chair, her face lost in her mother's lap and her arms spread round her. Neither of them spoke any more. They had been like that for hours.

At length Eleanor lifted up her head. Her face was crumpled like an empty glove, with the lines made by Mary's dress etched across it. She ran a hand back through her hair, her father's gesture, and gave a half sigh.

'I suppose I'd better go and wash,' was all she said.

'Are you all right, my pet?' Mary hung back, letting her go out into the yard alone. When she returned the spray from the pump was still splashed across her cheeks. She pressed them, wet and cold, against her mother's. It was a brief embrace.

'Are you all right?'

'Yes. Yes, I'm all right.' With her finger Eleanor

was smoothing a drop of water across the back of her hand, spreading out its area until it almost disappeared. She was lost in the tiny movement. All that Mary could do was look at her.

'I shouldn't have told you,' she said at last.

'No, Mam, don't say that. I'm glad you did. It's such a lot to take in, though, to try and understand. You can't imagine what's it's like, to have everything you thought was – well . . .' she tailed off.

Mary looked dumbly at her daughter. I can't apologise for giving you life, she thought, and yet every other apology should stem from that. And so I can't apologise at all.

'. . . I'll get used to it, of course I will. I just need a little bit of time.' Eleanor's hands dropped to her sides. She looked wan and tired and very young. 'Can we talk some more tomorrow? There's a lot I'd like to know, now. All those stories about our time in Cardiff, when I was small. I don't know what is me and what is not, any more. Oh, Mam, I just don't know –'

Mary put her arms around her and held her close.

'It's not all bad, you know, my poppet,' she whispered into her daughter's hair. 'It's not all bad. Think of all the times we've had together here. You and me and William. It's not all bad, you see. You'll understand one day, I promise you. And till then I'll do everything I can, I'll explain everything, we'll talk, and then perhaps you'll see.' She stopped. Eleanor's lashes brushed against her neck as she closed her eyes. 'Come on, my darling, I'll take you up to bed. You'll feel better after a good sleep. Things are always worse in the night. Oh, my poppet, I love you so.' She led her to the door, and up the stairs and into the room under the eaves which Mary had slept in before her child was born. 'There now.' She turned the bedclothes down, patting the bolster superfluously. 'Would you like me to fill you a bottle?'

Eleanor shook her head. 'No, Mam. I'll be all right. You go now. I'll be all right.'

Mary hesitated for a moment by the door.

'Please?' Eleanor looked away from her, so that she felt she couldn't stay.

Before she went downstairs Mary opened her mother's black oak chest and rummaged around inside it. Right at the bottom, under Eleanor's cast-off clothes and the linen which was neatly prepared for when she married, was a bundle of papers and cuttings. She took them back to the kitchen, stoked up the remains of the fire and sank into her chair beside it. She tucked her feet in close to the ashes to keep them warm and loosened the packet so that its contents were scattered across her knees.

All kinds of things she hadn't seen for years. The curl of wool Mike Bowen had cut from one of the sheep that day he drove them to the market to be sold; the newspaper report about Rebecca's attack after the fair at Narberth; one of Hugh's poems; *The Horn of Liberty*; Mr Evelyn's vile lease upon Dolwilym; Eleanor's birth certificate with Hugh's name upon it as her father; the ticket to Cardiff when she had gone to see Jac's boat set sail; the map of Tasmania she had copied from a book to see where he would be. Little pieces of wreckage in her lap.

She sifted through them slowly, remembering.

Each snippet had a sadness of its own and was part of a grief in the lives for which she was, in one way or another, liable. All those years she had spent shielding Eleanor, and loving her, and rearing her. For what? It seemed inevitable to her that now the years ahead would be spent in expiation, earning absolution for something over which she had had no choice, earning Eleanor's forgiveness. As the darkness shrivelled into dawn, sitting on her own in the kitchen just like she always used to do, all that Mary could feel was sadness and a terrible responsibility.

She turned the papers over one by one, looking for justification, for some scrap that she could show her daughter which would perhaps explain, or mitigate, or offer hope. In her hand was a page of close and sloping writing. Caleb Morris. Dear Caleb, who had done his best for them in those dreadful early days. She leaned closer to the fire so that she could read by its scanty light. It was a short paragraph, a part of his journal which he had once read out to her when she was feeling very low. Later on, timidly, tentatively, she had asked if he would write it out for her, so that she would always remember . . . She read it through again, seeing him as clearly as if he were across the table from her, his spectacles shiny on his nose.

'The mental and moral activity of the Welsh people is in advance of their material condition. Their spiritual happiness is greater than their temporal comforts. Becca-ism, bad though it may be, is an expression of inward development. It is a sign that the reign of immobility is passing away. Numbness and inactivity in civil matters is gone. Becca-ism has made people of all classes think of their individual social interest and a new era has begun. There is a power at work. May it be wisely guided and decided to noble ends. There is great need for reform. Let us work and pray for our fatherland.'

Dear Caleb, kind and wise and understanding. When Rebecca was at her bloodiest he was able to see the possibility of inward growth and change, and to look for new beginnings. She put his little cutting to one side. That was what she would show her daughter. If Caleb could believe that in those darkened, troubled years there was a power at work, then maybe Eleanor would see as well, and be lighter in her judgement. For Mary, the dawn was slow in coming, but when it came she felt a little hope.

Hugh lay in the massive bed at home for the last time. It had been built on a scale to support his wife – his first wife; he made the correction carefully. He lay in the hollow that her rolling, grunting weight had left behind, on his back, his eyes open, wondering if he could free his arm without disturbing Elizabeth. She was aloof in sleep, her head cradled on his shoulder, her eyes moving gently under lids that were violet in the half-light. He felt skinny and inappropriate beside her, his ripe and drowsy bride. She turned her face a little, as if coming up for air, and he was obliged to gather her more closely to him, further into his sparse embrace. Her shoulder pressed against his, the lines of her thigh and knee followed his own and her stomach was rounded against his hip. He cupped his palm around it one more time, feeling the slightness of the curve, only the length of a hand span.

Will you give me a daughter, my Elizabeth? Old men should have daughters, daughters with black hair and woody lights to their eyes, shy with wet lips, daughters like mine and Mary's . . . He smoothed the nightdress over Elizabeth's skin. Sleepless nights watching while the child inside her grew; measuring, possessing. He wanted to watch this child most particularly.

The Bible promised that you would reap what you sowed, but with Mary and her daughter he had never had the chance. Now there was this late harvest in his life, Elizabeth. Tomorrow they would move to Ferryside, and forget, and leave the rest behind them.